Traffic

Dan Cotton

Traffic

First Published in 2024
Copyright © Philip Mayne

Published by R.Ohm Estate
PO Box 115 Wooroloo
Western Australia 6558
dan_cotton2@outlook.com

Cover design by Philip Mayne
Cover photo – Wallace Chuck - Pexels.

Our Border Collies Echo and Tika
2010 - 2023

Chapter 1

As Rebecca emerged from her classroom, a man followed her to her car, taking care no one had seen him. But someone had. Tom Gregory. At just turned 18, and 6 foot 4 inches in the old money, Tom was a tall boy by any standards, and he was the captain of the school's basketball team. He'd recently received an offer of a sports scholarship at an American university, but it came with the proviso that his academic achievements reached *their* minimum requirement.

Not the sharpest tool in the shed. Tom needed all the help he could get, and Rebecca had been coaching him for several weeks. Only recently, she'd given up her Thursday lunch hour to help him polish his examination technique.

Rebecca was an attractive young woman and only a few years older than Tom. They knew the implications, though erroneous, were obvious, and they were both aware of the school's objections to extramural activities and the risks if someone complained.

Tom would normally keep his head down and wait until she started her car. He would then race her through the back streets, on his bike, to be waiting when she arrived at her unit. Today was Friday, and he'd noticed her boyfriend hanging around the school, watching for her. He was an older man, and Tom suspected something other than tuition might be going on between them.

He'd become convinced of this when the home security cameras his dad had installed had recorded a car, parking opposite, on the nights she came to his house. Shortly afterwards, the same car began arriving outside of her unit just as he was completing his ride. He began watching for it and noticed it would always park up the street a little, but its driver would never get out.

Rebecca knew Tom's parents well. She was the daughter of a long-term friend of the family, and they thought of her as a competent professional concerned only with the future education of their son. If the pair worked late, Tom's mother would insist she stayed the night and make the spare room available to her.

So far, it had proved to be a good system and Tom's progress had benefited greatly from the additional tuition. Until the last time she had stayed with them, and she didn't turn up at school the following morning. The following day, she arrived wearing dark glasses, her lips looking swollen and sore, and she was uncharacteristically nervous.

After this occurrence, Tom Gregory spoke quietly to his teammates and advised them of his suspicions. They agreed to take it in turns to watch her back and it wasn't long before one of them reported Rebecca's harassment by a man fitting the boyfriend's description.

The man Tom had recognised walking away from the school that morning was the same man he'd seen in the car.

He wasn't receiving tuition on this day, so he watched while the man met her at her car. There was a short discussion before they kissed, more like old friends than lovers, and she handed him her keys before taking her seat on the passenger's side. Soon afterwards, the car started and negotiated its way from the carpark.

Tom followed at a distance. Providing they stayed on the city roads, he would have no problem keeping up, but the car deviated onto the freeway and headed north. He knew he had no hope of catching them then, but he had an idea. He sent her a text:

> I thought we had a session today, Miss, have you
> forgotten?

He noticed the three dots appear to indicate she was responding, and then they disappeared. He texted again:

> Miss?

This time, the dots didn't appear. He entered her number and pressed Call. The phone went to the message bank. They couldn't be out of range, not yet. Tom's normally cool demeanour was fragmenting. He asked himself, *does this make me a stalker?* He sent another text message:

> It's okay, miss. I'll call you later.

He put his phone back in his pocket. There was nothing else to do but return to school and cop the flak for being late back from lunch.

As he rode into the school precinct, he noticed her car was in its usual place in the carpark. Tom apologised for being late and joined his class.

The rest of the afternoon was pretty much a waste of time, and her car was still there when he left for home. When he arrived, he texted her again:

Are we still on for tomorrow, miss?

There was no response. He dialled her number and got the message bank. She never had her phone off. Her car was in the carpark so she must be around somewhere. Now, anything he did or said might risk compromising her to her colleagues. There had been so much bad press lately, about inappropriate teacher-student relationships, and Tom thought about his parents. How would they react to his suspicions? He'd followed her while she was going about her, apparently, private business. He'd sent her several texts, he'd called her, and even he was beginning to have doubts about his reasons.

It was still early, and he decided to ride back to the school to see if her car was still there. It was. He checked the school buildings, found all the doors locked, and the place deserted. *She won't be missed until Monday.* He returned to her car and tucked his hand into his sleeve. He knew enough from TV crime shows to take care as he checked the door handles. It was unlocked, and then he saw the keys on the floor of the driver's side.

***

'When did you last see your teacher, Mr Gregory?' The detective asked.

'Lunchtime, sir. I saw her go off with a man who, I believe, was her boyfriend. I followed them for as far as I could, but when they reached the freeway, I gave up. When I arrived back at school, her car was there, but she wasn't.'

'Did she drive?'

'No, sir, he did.'

'You liked your teacher a lot, Mr Gregory?'

'Yes, Miss was coaching me for my finals. I have to reach a certain score to qualify for my scholarship.'

'You call her Miss?'

'We call all the teachers Sir or Miss, the school insists, and it's easier.'

'You spent a lot of time with her, then?'

'A couple of evenings a week, Thursday lunchtime, occasionally Tuesday's.'

'It's Friday today, so you were with her at lunchtime yesterday?'

'Yes sir.'

'Why were you following her?'

Tom shrugged.

'I asked you a question. I need the answer.'

'I was worried about her.' He shrugged again.

'Your phone shows a number of text messages and a couple of calls to her phone today.'

'Yes.'

'If we talk to your other teachers, will they confirm you were in class for the entire afternoon?'

'I-I don't know. I was a little late back from lunch. Like I said, I was following them.'

'Your texts seemed to be inferring you had a session with her today, but you have no reason to be seeing her until at least Tuesday of next week.'

The line of questioning was beginning to worry Tom. 'I need to go home now. It's getting late. My parents will be worried,' he said.

'Sorry, son, that's not going to be possible. You see, we've found a body. Its owner is still to be formally identified, but the age and description approximates that of your teacher. The time of death of the victim ties in with your story, and it seems you were the last person to see her alive.' The detective signalled to a uniformed officer, who stepped forward and placed handcuffs on Tom's wrists. 'He's over 18, so you can caution him as an adult and then arrest him on suspicion of murder.'

Just then, a car drew up and a man in an overcoat alighted. He pulled back his sleeve and exposed a rather unusual watch. 'The time has come,' the man smirked. 'Let's get on with it.'

'That's him. That's the man I followed,' Tom called out as they bundled him into the back of the police car.

The detective laughed. 'Good try sonny, that's my boss, DCI Peter Clitherow. He's in charge of this investigation.'

Chapter 2

Tom Gregory was Angela Carter's last appointment of the day and as she walked to her car, she felt something bugging her. It had all been too easy, too cut and dried, and her client was little more than a kid, albeit a big kid. She'd sat with him longer than normal, trying to wheedle out of him what would make him kill someone who was in effect his best friend. The poor kid was traumatised, and worse, his parents seemed to have spontaneously disowned him.

She decided to take a different route home and, on the way, stopped at an industrial estate that was effectively a group of large fenced off sheds.

Angela Carter had never been inside the building she was about to enter, and she wasn't sure what to expect. She could hear the muted sound of rock music, feminine squeals, and masculine guffaws, as she steeled herself to open the heavy steel door.

After the bright West Australian sun, she needed to squint to see in the darkness. A loud screech made her jump, and she looked around, wondering what would happen next.

The music increased massively in volume as an internal door swung open, and as her eyes adjusted to the new light, a heavily built and tattooed man confronted her.

The door behind him closed, and before she had the time to speak, he said, 'Fuck off,' and pushed her back towards the entrance.

Before the door had completely shut, she saw a naked girl slither down a shiny pole to spread eagle herself on the floor before her baying audience. Angela shuddered. *What's this you've got yourself into, Jim?* Angela eyeballed the tattooed man and said, 'I'm looking for Jake Chandler.' She lowered her eyes and rubbed her belly.

The man laughed, opened the door, and shouted, 'Jake! You have a visitor—or two.' All eyes were locked on the pole dancer, and none seemed to have noticed the interruption. Then she saw the man she was seeking work his way around the bar until…

'Shit!' He flinched as he entered the foyer. It was as though someone had stuck a knife in his neck. He grabbed her roughly by the arm, as though intending to drag her from the building. 'What in Christ's name are you doing here?'

'Sorry. I need to talk to you. It's urgent or I would have done things differently.'

'Where's your transport?'

Angela nodded to the car park.

'Get in it. Lock your doors and don't move again until I join you. I won't be long.' He hauled her by the arm to a fire exit and shoved her out into the sun.

The sudden brightness blinded her, and she shielded her eyes until she could orient herself sufficiently to find her car. It was scalding hot inside, so she started the engine to enable the air-conditioning and locked her doors to wait.

He said he wouldn't be long. She looked at her watch. Half an hour had passed and there was still no sign of him. *Fuck you, Jim,* she thought, and was about to head for home when he banged on her passenger window. She lowered it.

He reached in, unlocked the door, and flopped onto the seat. 'Move it and don't stop until I tell you.'

Angela drove toward her home without speaking. As she was about to turn into her drive, he said, 'Keep going. I'll tell you when you can stop.'

'You know I live there?'

'I know where you live. Just keep moving.' He adjusted the wing mirror on his side and concentrated. After several kilometres from the city, he pointed and said, 'Pull over and stop there.'

Angela slipped into a dirt-based truck bay and stopped.

The stoney faced man she had shared her ride with then turned and smiled. 'How are you, sis?'

Angela glowered.

'Nothing changes then?'

'I don't need you in my life, Jim, but I need your help now. You promised once, remember?'

He smiled. The almost artificial whiteness of his teeth sparkling behind a two-day-old stubble that was glistening with sweat. 'You haven't changed much. Since you became a lawyer.'

Angela nodded. 'Trying to be, Jim, or should I be calling you Jake? That's why I'm here.'

'Oh?'

'There's a kid. He's being held on suspicion of murdering his teacher.'

Jim Carter's smile changed to a laugh. He nodded. 'There, but for the grace of god…'

'I don't think he did it.'

'So?'

'I'm convinced he's being set up.'

'Ah, so what the fuck do you think I can do?' He turned towards the woman he'd always regarded as his baby sister and saw the look in her eyes. He stared long and hard and Angela matched his stare with a glare. 'I can't, you know I can't, and you've already compromised me. I hope it's still only at the potential stage.'

'Okay, forget it. I'll drop you back.'

'Wait.' Jim sat for a lengthy pause without speaking. 'A kid, you say?'

'18 years old, living the dream and working towards a basketball contract in the USA. His teacher was helping him boost his academic results. Without them, he was a goner.'

'Shit, Ange. If I help you…'

'I know… I just thought, I don't know, hoped, I guess… I remember your ambitions.'

'Look where they got me.'

'Slippery Clitheroe is the Senior Investigation Officer. I just need something that proves they are trying to screw the kid. That's all.'

'Shit, Ange.'

'Whatever you think of me, I'll understand if you can't help.'

'You won't ever come into that place again, announced or otherwise?'

'Promise.'

Jim reached into his pocket and pulled out a smart phone. 'Burner. You know what a burner is?'

Angela nodded.

'There is a preset number in it. It's a similar phone but switched to silent, so I might not answer immediately.'

'Can I call you later?'

'No. Don't ever call me, not even if it's a life-or-death situation. I'll call *you* when I'm free to talk. I use the name Jake Chandler for a reason, and you obviously know that which is a worry.' Jim leaned over and kissed his sister on the cheek. He pulled back and grinned. 'So good to see you again, Ange. I have a lift organised. Take care.'

With that, he dropped from the car and slammed the door shut before she had a chance to protest. A second or two later, a Land Cruiser stopped to pick him up, before following Angela's car down the road to her home. It stopped for a while before roaring off at speed.

She used the remote to open her garage door and immediately began having second thoughts about approaching her brother. Their estrangement began when she completed her law degree and began working with a company of lawyers with a reputation for successfully defending corporate criminals. He'd begun to distance himself from her as soon as he got the word.

Chapter 3

He watched his sister's vehicle disappear into her garage. Then James Carter made a call on a different phone.

His driver didn't speak and when they arrived back at the industrial area, he was unceremoniously dumped from the car.

'Fuck you, pig bastards,' he shouted as the unmarked police vehicle raced off into the fading light.

He made his way back to the fortified shed that was the headquarters of The Ferals MCC and pushed in through the inner door. Nothing much had changed since he left.

Except that a new girl was gradually disrobing while sliding up and down the shiny smeared pole and there were a few more empty cans of premix cluttering the tables. He shook his head and made his way to the side of the room where he was when Angela arrived.

'Where have you fucken been?'

'None of your fucken business, Jesse.'

'Good looking chick, Jake. Auditioning?'

James rankled. 'Maybe.'

The man who had spoken thrust a can of bourbon and coke into his hand. 'Mind you, from what I gather, the pole will be out of the question in a few months.' He threw his head back and laughed heartily. 'Me fucken next. Hey, big daddy?'

James sucked a mouthful from the can before glancing at his watch. 'Gotta go, Jess. Need to see the quack.'

'Fuck, Jake… you haven't…?' Jesse laughed even harder than before. 'Gone the whole hog, eh?'

'No, I fucken haven't, Jesse but. I'll be away for a few days. Might take that long to fix it.'

'Okay… Take it easy, bro.'

'I will.' James sidled out of the building, threw his leg over his Harley, and headed for the hills. He saw no one in his rear views, but he knew that would be unlikely. No one trusted anyone these days, and they were all tracking each other with electronics. As soon as he had the chance, he stopped to run his handheld detector over his bike. He smirked as he flicked the magnetic device off with the blade of his pocketknife and slapped it on the tank of the Hyundai Getz he'd parked behind.

Another check satisfied him he was in the clear. He'd spent months wrangling the trust of the Ferals, even to the point of a short term of imprisonment. He was now so close to the end of his run that he could not afford to let his guard down for a single minute.

Tonight would be special, though. He breathed in a lungful of fresh air, gunned his motor, and made a U-turn.

It was a pure fluke that Angie had turned up to drag him from the club. She couldn't have known that it was his wedding anniversary and that he'd promised his wife he would get there over hell or high water.

Detective Sergeant James Carter felt a shimmer of goose pimples as he parked the Harley in a lock-up garage, not too far from his home. He stripped off his Ferals leathers and replaced them with clean jeans, a fresh t-shirt, and a clean shave, before shrugging on a high-end denim jacket and mounting his BMW R1250.

Having shed his undercover image, he shoved his head into a full-face helmet and eased the purring machine, almost silently, to the road, before opening the throttle to a powerful grumble.

The Harley, noisy and crude by comparison, would stay in the lock up until he was ready to return to the club. Right now, he was free of the constant scrutiny that his undercover work insisted upon.

He rode into the drive of an ordinary suburban home, flicked the motor off, and kicked down the stand. He hadn't spoken to, nor contacted his wife, for almost six months. The neighbours all believed he was away on business and the secrecy of his work had always kept him incommunicado. Like every other time, he wasn't sure how she'd react.

He saw the fuzzy outline of Stacey's figure moving through the crinkled glass as she approached the door. The lock turned. The door opened and her face brightened.

'You remembered?'

James slid inside and pulled the door shut behind him. He pulled her close and whispered, 'I've told them I have to be away for a few days. How about…?' He felt her hand wrap around his as she drew him to the kitchen. 'Something smells good.'

'I always live in hope Jim, and it is your favourite.'

'Not much longer, Stace. I might be compromised.'

'What does that mean?'

James kissed her on the lips and said, 'It means someone other than me and my handler knows about my work. I've told *them* I'll be away for a time, medical stuff. Before this happened, I was going to say, how about heading away for a few days?' He reached into his pocket and pulled out two flight tickets.

'Where?'

He handed her the tickets.

'Bali?' she said, nodding to the child in a basinet. 'Andria's just gone off and Oli's in bed. We'll need to hurry if we're going to catch that one.' She pointed to the flight time.

'Oh…?'

'No. It's fine. How long?'

'Back in 5 days. I know, it's short notice, but something's about to happen that might throw a bit of a spanner in the works.'

'Oh…kay.'

James Carter pointed at the headline on a newspaper lying on the table. 'I think that kid is being framed.'

'How do you know?'

'Angela.'

'Shit! You haven't spoken to *her* in years.'

Jim nodded. 'Conflicts of interest. But…'

'But?'

'She tracked me down. She's always putting herself forward for pro bono stuff and the cops have saddled her with his defence. I think, because it's in line her corporate principles, but the evidence is overwhelming, and the Senior Investigating Officer is, you know who.'

'Slippery Clitherow?'

James nodded. 'The "evidence" smacks of his involvement, and you really don't want to know what *I've* been doing for the last twelve months.'

Stacey rolled her eyes. 'Never again, Jim, or we're done.'

'After this, I reckon I'll be back at traffic and home for dinner every night.'

Stacey laughed, 'Yeah right.' She plated his meal and set it before him on the table. Then she opened a bottle of Shiraz, kissed him on the top of his head, and filled his glass.

'I'm dinkum, Stace. I've had enough.'

'What about the project?'

'I'm almost ready to pull the pin on my target and Clitherow is right in the centre of the shit that will hit the fan when that happens.'

'Corruption?'

'Everything. Perverting the course of justice, money laundering, people trafficking, drugs. Should I go on?'

'No. Eat. We'll have an early night if we're to catch that plane to Bali. While you eat, I'll start packing.'

***

Angela Carter returned to her apartment, poured herself an SSB, sat in her favourite chair and contemplated her actions. *Did I do the right thing?* She and her brother had never been close, but the distance grew when she became a lawyer. She always knew he was engaged in some kind of undercover work, and she felt guilty that she might have breached his confidentiality to the point of compromising him.

Oddly, his undercover work seemed to be a known fact among her professional colleagues. A shiver ran down her spine. 'If I know… if they know? Who else knows?' She found the burner and texted him:

I think I've compromised you, Jim. Sorry.

He'd know who it was, so there was no need for anything else.

Angela didn't expect a reply. *He said it might take some time and…* Her stomach cramped. She knew Clitherow had been in control of several investigations into the Ferals, all of which had gone nowhere for want of evidence, and she'd just asked her brother to look into one of her cases. The Ferals were leading a charmed life with a level of immunity that could only come from someone well placed in a senior position. She hadn't discussed his reasons for being mixed up with them and now she was realising just what she'd done.

She picked up her regular phone and called Stacey. 'Maybe…'

There was no answer.

She tried the burner again.

Same.

Was she too late?

Chapter 4

Tom Gregory stared around at the blank walls of the cell they'd thrown him into. He'd never been in any kind of trouble before, but he somehow knew that all his hopes for a scholarship had unceremoniously ended.

It seemed like hours before the door opened and a uniformed officer escorted him to an interview room.

The officer pointed to a small table and said, 'Sit.'

Tom had done as he was told and saw his reflection in a large mirror opposite the table. *Aha,* he thought. His experience of watching crime shows on the telly told him it was a one-way mirror and there would be people on the other side watching his every move and noting his body language.

A few minutes later, the detective who had arrested him arrived with a young woman only slightly older than Rebecca.

The detective pulled out a chair for the woman and said, 'You can have fifteen minutes before we start the interview.'

The woman nodded, and the detective left the room.

'Tom Gregory?'

Tom nodded.

'My name is Angela Carter. I've been appointed as your lawyer until you can find someone else you prefer. Do you know why you have been arrested?'

He'd nodded again and said, 'It wasn't me.'

The lawyer made a jotting on her legal pad. 'They say they have substantial evidence that puts you in the timeframe for your teacher's murder.'

Tom nodded. 'Doesn't mean I killed her.' He'd looked directly into the eyes of the young lawyer. 'Have you been doing this long?'

The lawyer's face flushed.

He'd asked for a pen and paper.

She'd torn a sheet from her pad, slid it across the table and handed him a Bic.

He'd written down an address and telephone number. 'Call my dad. He'll know what to do.'

The lawyer nodded. 'I already have, and he says it's all down to you. We don't have much time. They'll be back soon, and they'll be asking you questions. Do you want me to be with you when they do?'

Tom shrugged.

'Shall I take that as a yes?'

The door opened, and the detective returned with another officer. He'd pressed a button on the recording device at the end of the table. Announced himself and named his colleague. He pointed up at the at a camera mounted on the ceiling. 'This interview will also be videotaped.'

Tom shrugged.

The detective began asking questions to determine Tom's whereabouts at the estimated time of the murder, and the lawyer made very few comments. Everything seemed cut and dry.

Tom had no alibi to speak of and there was plenty of evidence of him going out of his way to be in the vicinity of his teacher for several months, even to having her stay overnight, many times, at his home.

'My dad should be getting me a proper lawyer,' he'd said.

The lawyer seemed to rankle at his summary dismissal of her abilities, but she'd remained outwardly cool and unruffled. 'If that is what you really want, Tom, so be it.' She'd handed him a card and stood to leave. 'Call me if you need more help, and I think you are going to need all the help you can get.'

He'd tucked the card into his pocket and stood to be led back to his cell.

The police claimed the evidence was stacking up against him and unless he could throw some light on his alibi, the chances of him going to the US were dwindling fast.

He heard a sound outside his cell. 'Hello?' he called.

The slide opened and a pair of eyes peered in.

'I need to let my folks know where I am.'

'Already been done. DCI Clitherow will be seeing you in the morning. He'll bring you right up to date then.'

***

Angela Carter waited patiently in the interview room while her client was collected from his cell. She scanned the notes she had taken earlier and jotted down a few more than memory joggers.

The door opened and a police officer escorted in a haggard-looking Tom Gregory.

'Take a seat next to your solicitor.' The officer removed the handcuffs and hitched them on to his belt. 'The DCI will be here in a minute.'

Angela thanked him and spoke softly to Tom, 'I know you don't want my help, but if anyone is to help you,' she tapped her notes. 'They'll need a lot more than what's in here.'

Tom nodded. 'There isn't any more I can say, other than the last person I saw with Rebecca was DCI Clitherow. I started keeping tabs on his movements after she turned up at school with a bashed-up face. I think he's been stalking her. He's even watched my parent's house the times she stayed overnight.'

'Have you heard anything from them?'

Tom shook his head. 'The cops say they've been informed. You said they say I'm on my own.' He shrugged. 'Whatever any of that means.'

Before they could speak further, the door opened and Clitherow entered with a female officer. She took a seat at the table and pressed the record button before introducing them as DS Morton and DCI Clitherow before outlining the proposed charges. 'Do you understand?' she said, when she finished speaking.

Tom turned to Angela.

'My client is having difficulty understanding the charges, given he was nowhere near the victim when the crime took place.'

'So, *he* says,' Clitheroe said and focussed his attention on Tom. 'Where were you between the hours of eleven thirty am and three fifteen pm on the day you were arrested?'

'I've already told the other detective that.'

'Yes, but I want to hear it for myself and the tape.' He pointed to the box at the end of the table. 'Where were you?'

Tom looked at Angela.

She nodded.

'I was riding around on my bike.'

'Anyone see you riding around on your bike?' Clitherow said.

Tom shrugged.

'Exactly.'

'I'll need some more time with my client.'

'Go for your life,' Clitherow smirked. He pointed to the door, and the female officer followed him out.

When they were alone, Angela said, 'Right, Mr Gregory, you'll need to sharpen your act if we're going to make progress.'

'How long have you been a lawyer?'

'Okay… Are you saying you don't want to use my services?'

Tom blushed. 'You don't look much older than Rebecca.' He squirmed in his seat.

Angela brushed away his remark. 'Did you like her?'

Embarrassed by her comment, he said, 'Okay, I suppose. I'm sorry I didn't mean…'

Angela nodded and forced a tight smile. 'But?'

'She was my teacher. She wasn't interested in me beyond that.'

'You said she stayed at your house. Do you know how that might be viewed?'

'Nothing happened. Nothing ever happened.'

'But you were alone with her on many occasions.'

'You can ask Mum and Dad. They knew her. They were long-time friends of her family. Nothing ever happened. I would have risked everything, and this scholarship was a fantastic opportunity. It won't happen now, will it?' Tom scowled and hunkered down.

Angela wrote a few words on her pad and said, 'Did you kill Rebecca Connolly?'

'No! Ask him that.' He nodded in the direction of the door. 'I'm convinced he was stalking her.'

'You weren't even the slightest bit jealous?'

'No. I needed her help. I even got some of the basketball team to keep an eye on her.'

'Keep an eye on her?'

Tom squirmed again. 'Not like that. I saw him following her, and I asked my mates to watch over her. Fuck, miss. She was important to my future.'

'Okay, Tom. I'm going to see if I can get you bailed.'

He nodded. 'Mum and Dad?'

'I will be speaking to them again, but the charges are serious and that limits my flexibility. Understand?'

Tom nodded again.

'Do any of your friends use a GoPro?'

He shrugged.

She passed him her pad with a fresh page exposed. 'List their names and addresses, phones. Anything you can think of that might be useful.'

Tom picked up the pen she gave him and began to write. He'd written half a page of text when the door opened.

'That's it, ma'am,' PC Morton said.

'As I see it, the only evidence you have is circumstantial and weak at best. I'd like my client bailed with immediate effect.'

DCI Clitheroe's face jerked at the mention of bail. 'We'll see about that, Madam. Your client is about to be charged with murder. I think he will be very lucky to leave this station other than in a truck to the remand centre.' Clitheroe took his seat and gestured to the female officer. 'Lock him up.'

Before the officer could speak Angela Carter stood and said, 'Then I'll require your written explanation as to why you are refusing this request, and I will see you in court tomorrow morning.'

'Sir?' Morton said.

'Okay, bail him, but on a tight leash.' Clitheroe stood and stormed from the interview room.

DS Morton struggled to hide her smirk and fluttered an almost unnoticeable wink at Angela before leading Tom to sign for his bail.

Angela tapped Tom on the shoulder and said, 'Come on. Let's get this over with and then you can go home to your family.'

With the formalities out of the way she offered him a lift home and he accepted. 'Thanks, miss. I'm sorry about.' He shrugged. 'You know…'

'You said you understood the bail conditions. Do you?'

'I think so.' He held the paper they had given him. 'It's all on here.'

'You'd better not let me down, and you'd better start trusting me. Okay? I don't believe you did this, but to prove it I'm going to need a lot of cooperation from you.'

'Miss.' He nodded.

She stopped outside his house and said, 'Would you like me to come in with you?'

Tom shook his head.

'Well, you're eighteen, Tom, so I don't need your parents' permission to act for you but…'

He nodded again. 'Okay, miss. Come on then.'

Tom walked to his front door with Angela in tow. He pushed his key in the lock and turned it.

The door opened immediately and a man in his mid-forties stood glowering. 'They let you go then...'

'I haven't done anything, Dad.'

'That's not what the police say. And they've been here, ransacking our home.' He held out a sheet of paper that had the word SEARCH WARRANT in bold print. 'Your mother's petrified... After all we've done for you.' He looked over Tom's shoulder and nodded towards Angela. 'She your next victim?'

Angela Carter stepped forward and thrust her card at the man, who was clearly upset.

He attempted to brush it away.

'I have been appointed as your son's lawyer, Mr Gregory and, as it happens, I believe your son is completely innocent...'

Gregory butted in. 'That's not what the police say. They say they have more than enough evidence to charge him.'

'So why haven't they, and why is he standing here, on the doorstep of his home, on bail that they couldn't refuse.' She nudged Tom towards the door. 'I don't need your permission to act for your son, but I thought it might be a good idea to get to know you and see how we can work together in his defence.'

George Gregory stepped back reluctantly and muttered, 'Here goes my superannuation, I suppose.'

Angela matched his mutter with a murmur. 'Well, you can always cough up for a silk...' she spoke louder. 'Never mind, Tom. I'll call you tomorrow to make a time for a talk in private. Okay.'

'Dad! I need her help!'

Gregory huffed and stood back from the door. 'I suppose you'd better come in then, Ms Carter, and what you have to say had better be good.'

Chapter 5

Stacey was in bed when James Carter answered a call on the burner he kept for the purpose of security. As he did, he looked at the phone that would receive calls from Angela. There was a text. She knew what she'd done and there was nothing more he could do to recover.

'You there, Carter?'

'Yeah, sorry, boss. Look, I had no control over what happened. I'm worried that if my sister knew what I was doing, who else? I've told them I'm crook and I'll be away for a few days, so we'll have some time up our sleeves.'

'You're kidding. We'll need to start the whole thing again and that could take years to fix up.'

'Hold on, boss. While I was in favour, and I'm not yet entirely sure I'm out of the loop, I placed listening devices in all the places they talk. There is a large importation of ice going ahead within the next few days. They think I'm having medical treatment, but I'll be overseas with my family and still in touch with the team.'

'Any idea of a date and time?'

'About a week. I can't be closer than that. We'll get the word via the headphones, and then it'll be on for one and all.'

'Not happy, Jim. We've spent a shitload of cash on this exercise for it to go belly up, just because your sister wanted a fraternal chat.'

'That's not quite how it was, boss, but we're still good to go.'

'You'd better be.'

The call ended with a click, followed by silence.

'Who were you talking to?'

'Mulligan. He's a bit pissed about Angela compromising me, but he'll get over it, and be a trifle shocked when we turn the key on Slippers.' He slid in between the sheets and Stacey kissed him on the lips.

She then pulled away, rolled away, and said, 'Goodnight.'

'I thought?'

'And you thought wrong. Maybe when we've had a bit more time together, and I've had a chance to warm to you again.'

***

The meeting with Tom's father was in no way cordial. George Gregory seemed to have it firmly fixed in his mind that his son, Tom, had brutally murdered his tutor, and nothing Angela could say would deflect him from the direction he was taking.

'Very well, Mr Gregory, you leave me no choice in my actions. I'll see you tomorrow, Tom. Shall we say ten am? You have my address.'

Tom nodded sullenly and headed up the stairs to his room. He heard Angela's voice one more time as the front door closed behind her, then he heard his father growling at his mother. He couldn't make out much of that conversation, but he could tell it was heated.

***

DCI Peter Clitheroe was sitting in his executive leather chair, leaning back, with his eyes closed, pondering his options, when Jackie Morton tapped on his glazed wall.

He signalled for her to come in, and she nodded courteously before speaking.

'Spit it out, girl!'

'DNA, Sir.'

'What about it?'

'Forensics have found traces of DNA evidence in their swabs of Ms Connolly's body. The DNA is a partial match to that of Tom Gregory.'

'Gotya!' Clitheroe spluttered. 'Bring him in, Jackie. Let's see what we can wring from the twerp.'

PC Morton closed the door and returned to her desk to pass on Clitheroe's message. The response was mixed, but they were under no illusion as to where they would be going next.

***

Despite all the actions of the last day, Tom Gregory was trying his hardest to concentrate on his schoolwork. Being just eighteen years old and the prime suspect in the murder of someone who he'd become attached to was making it harder than it should have been.

Miss Carter seems to be the only one on my side… His thoughts were shattered like a sheet of glass being hit by a brick when the sirens screeched, and cars squealed to a halt outside his home.

He heard a loud banging on the front door, followed by his mother's wail as the police pushed their way in.

'Where is he?' the lead officer yelled.

'Who?' his mother whimpered.

'I'm here,' Tom said as he made his way towards the sounds.

A constable stepped forward, turned Tom around and cuffed his wrists.

'Not enough evidence, hey?' The lead officer grinned as the constable led him to the waiting patrol car.

'Call Miss Carter, Mum… Please.'

Tom fell into the back seat of the patrol car and the constable who had cuffed him pushed in beside him. 'You're gone, kiddo. DNA doesn't lie.'

Confusion filled his already cluttered mind. *DNA? How could there be DNA?* Tom knew what DNA was. *Anyone who watches crime shows knows that, but don't they need to associate it with bodily fluids?* He thought.

When they arrived, he was literally dragged from the police car to the interview room and made to sit.

Clitheroe joined them with a big grin on his face. 'Your smart-arse lawyer is waiting for you. The conversation should be quick, then we can get on with revoking your bail and throwing you in the can…' The knock on the door silenced him.

It opened to reveal a stiff faced Angela Carter complete with her notepad. She glared at the officers, who all stood to leave, then she closed the door and dropped a folder of papers onto the desk. 'Forensic report. I'm going to have to ask you again, did you or did you not kill Rebecca Connolly?'

He responded, 'I didn't do it.'

'They are revoking your bail based on the new DNA evidence and you will see a magistrate who will probably send you to a prison with a remand centre. All is not lost, but do you want me to remain as your solicitor?'

Tom nodded. More words were pointless.

Clitheroe returned and stunned the room with the announcement that Tom's guilt had subsequently been well and truly established from the DNA of a two-month-old male foetus discovered during the autopsy of Rebecca's body. He sneered at his prisoner. 'Just a friend, hey.' Clitheroe then turned to DS Morton. 'Lock him up, Sergeant. Court tomorrow morning. Shouldn't take long it's all pretty much cut and dried now.'

Angela Carter's jaw dropped with the revelation. 'I'll be there for you tomorrow, don't worry.' She rested her hand on his shoulder and whispered, 'Just because she was having your baby, it doesn't mean you killed her.'

Tom demonstrated his despondence with a shrug.

***

Once again within the confines of a cell, his mind whirled. Though he'd not yet enjoyed the pleasures of a female body and though he did know the basics of the birds and the bees, he was stung by the naïve thought he might have somehow made Rebecca pregnant merely by being with her. He lay back on the skinny, too short, bunk and found himself becoming aroused as he imagined the soft warmth of her body.

Then the thoughts of his future career crawled through his mind. *If they send me to prison for murder…*

The thoughts were intolerable, and his captors had provided him with nothing to take his mind off them. They had taken his belt and the laces of his trainers, and the cell was devoid of anything that might enable him to shut down his terror permanently.

'Help!' he yelled. 'I've done nothing.'

The hatch opened and a pair of eyes appeared. 'You'd better shut it boy, we don't like cold-blooded killers of young ladies, and where you're going, you won't want the word to get around.' The hatch slammed shut.

Tom curled into the foetal position and struggled to repress the tears that followed in a torrent. As they dried up with the dawning of the reality of his situation, he recalled his pleasant evenings of study with Rebecca and how, at the end of each session, his smiling dad would enter carrying a tray of his speciality, cinnamon laced hot chocolate. The four of them would sit and talk and sip hot chocolate until their eyes began to droop, and it was time for bed. He'd never felt so happy. *Why did it go so wrong?*

Rebecca had always slept in the room next to him. *I never heard a peep out of you because I was always fast asleep within seconds of my head hitting the pillow. You always said you slept well too, and sometimes… I wish I'd had the courage…* He cast the thoughts from his mind and tried to sleep.

***

The court proceedings were short and formal. The Magistrate listened carefully to the police prosecutor and asked if Tom had anything to say, which he didn't.

Angela Carter spoke for him, but the bench was adamant that there was sufficient evidence to warrant a trial. The next step would be for him to be remanded in custody until a date to be set at some time in the future.

There was no indication of an actual date and Angela promised him she would do all she could to save him from the fate that was stretching out before him. The potential of a successful and lucrative career had been ended all because he had tried to improve his education.

The doors of the prison transport slammed shut to reinforce his unhappy position, and he could only hope that the young woman acting as his lawyer wouldn't also succumb to pregnancy in his presence.

Despite his request that she didn't, Angela called her brother to tell him of the disaster that had befallen Tom Gregory and thanked him for his offer of help. 'I'm so sorry I hope I haven't mucked up your case against...'

Jim cut her off. 'Don't mention his name. There will be breaking news soon.'

'What about Tom? I feel I've let him down badly.'

'Let me finish what I have to do. Then we can talk about where we go from here. Please don't call me again, just wait to hear from me.'

Chapter 6

Angela heard little over the next few weeks, and she was on the verge of giving up. Her visits to Tom, in the remand centre, were wearing her down and there was still nothing in his demeanour that indicated he was a killer. In fact, quite the contrary. She'd tried to trip him up on several occasions, but nothing changed. He steadfastly refused to admit to even touching Rebecca. Not even an occasional handshake or an accidental brush of hands while they were working.

According to Tom Gregory, Rebecca was fully aware of the risks she was taking during their tutoring sessions, and she'd always distanced herself by standing or sitting opposite him.

One of the most concerning things were the bruises Angela had begun noticing during their meetings. He'd shrugged them off as sporting injuries. The prison hierarchy had apparently recognised his talents, and he'd been given the task of assembling and training a basketball team to work off his frustrations.

None of his excuses cut it with Angela. She recognised the results of punches. She'd seen enough of them over the years.

***

The weeks had been frustrating for James Carter as well. Though the gang had accepted that his short absence was more to do with helping a bimbo with an abortion than anything else. On the few occasions he'd been ready to blow the whistle, circumstances always seemed to change.

Today, however, it was go-go-go. Clear video evidence of Clitheroe accepting a bribe would have been enough, in its own right, but the accompanying audio left his colleagues in no doubt that Clitheroe was about to involve himself in a major importation of methamphetamine.

The scene had been set and Clitheroe's team were in the process of setting up detours and roadblocks to prevent access to the drop off point. Ostensibly, the roadblocks were for a serious police incident and the news media had been advised that the road might be closed for several hours.

What Clitheroe's team didn't know was that James Carter's team were also there. Armed with assault weapons and sophisticated recording equipment, and ready to make their move.

Jim scanned the coast with his binoculars and caught sight of a large motor cruiser heading toward the shore. He grinned at Jesse, who signalled the gang to be ready to unload the boat as quickly as possible.

Two clicks of static in Jim's earpiece told him the members of his team, hiding off the beach, understood and were ready. He clicked back twice to acknowledge.

Half the team moved to observe Clitheroe's patrol cars setting up their roadblocks with officers in high vis jackets turning motorists around.

It was just another hassle trying to get to work for most.

The boat dropped an anchor and a group of Ferals set out in rubber boats to unload waterproof boxes before returning to toss them into a large four-wheel drive.

James Carter grinned when he saw the overweight figure of Clitheroe step out of a vehicle and shake hands with Jesse, the lead bikie. *They'll both be seriously pissed when they find me facing them over an interview table.*

As soon as the boxes were loaded into the transport, Jim clicked twice more, and a small army of camo clad individuals appeared from the dunes.

The Ferals began scattering, and Clitheroe stumbled over the soft sand as he tried to make a run for it and fell into the arms of one of Jim's team.

A PC snapped the cuffs around his wrists and said, in a loud voice, 'Well-well, I never thought I'd get to cuddle with one of Australia's finest, DCI Clitheroe himself.'

Several more vehicles arrived in convoy and the captives were loaded for the return journey. More sirens could be heard on the coast road. They were followed by loud voices, as Clitheroe's team of road blockers were neatly stored in their own allocated paddy wagons. They'd be kept separate from the beach mob, and James wondered how different their stories might be.

***

Angela felt a warm glow roll over her as she watched the media's abbreviated review of her heroic brother's work, superimposed over his crew wrapping up their arrest.

Sadly, none of this would help her client and she could only hope that Clitheroe's arrest might point to some future relief.

Her phone buzzed.

'Hi, big bro, just been watching you on the telly.'

'I'm going to be busy for a couple of days, Ange, but then we must get together and discuss your man's case. Something has come up and you probably ought to know about it.'

Angela wished he had said nothing because she would now lie awake at night worrying about what their next move might be. *Perhaps Clitheroe had said something during his arrest.*

So far, the circumstantial evidence had pointed to Clitheroe being equally in the frame for Rebecca's death. Perhaps he'd got word of her pregnancy and killed her in a fit of jealousy. The potential for consequences was huge. She pulled out Tom's file and went through everything, word by word, day by day, time by time.

Nothing Clitheroe had said during interviews provided any clues to his guilt. Nothing even pointed to him as being vindictive, and while he was probably skating on thin ice when it came to the evidence he had collated, Tom had no answers to any of his questions. And so, his trial followed a straightforward course with technical experts for and against.

Clitheroe was under suspension and took no physical part in the trial. His statements were backed up by other officers who were not involved with the drug importation and the experts all confirmed the DNA evidence.

Ten Years Later

Chapter 7

As Angela Carter tidied her nine-year-old son's school uniform ready for the arrival of the school bus, she caught a news report. The body of a young woman had been found not far away in remnant bushland and she sucked in a sharp breath.

'What's up, Mum,' Oliver said.

'Nothing. You should be fixing up your own clothes by now.'

He grinned and ran from her grasp.

Angela felt wistful as he joined his school friends, and she wondered how Tom Gregory was holding up. She pushed the thought from her mind and readied herself for her trip to the city.

Tom Gregory was her first and only failure, and she'd been advised by so many of her contemporaries that getting involved would only make things worse for everyone. She'd given of her best and though, to this day, she still believed he was innocent, there was nothing and no new evidence that could be used in an appeal.

The last time she had seen Tom, was when her son Oliver was two years old, and she'd discovered her then husband, George Hanrahan, was screwing half the office females. The breakup was hostile, and she'd spent thousands of much needed dollars reinforcing her home following several violent incidents. Thankfully, he overstepped the mark with another married woman whose husband served a relatively short prison sentence for rendering Hanrahan mentally incompetent.

Her phone buzzed. 'Hi Jim, how's things?'

'Lunch, Saturday. Bring Oliver. Stacey's decided it's time we had a family fun day, and the weather's looking great.'

'Just the six of us, then?'

Jim laughed. 'Hey, have you heard that Slippery is due for release on parole next week?'

'No. I hadn't, and I don't really care, but if you do the crime, you should at least do the time.'

'Yeah, well, you're not alone there. Heard any more about that young bloke you defended? The one who got life?'

Angela shook her head before realising he couldn't see her. 'No.'

'Well, anyway. See you Saturday?'

'I'll check my diary and let you know.'

'Go on, sis. It'll do you good, and young Oli.'

She pressed end and slumped into a chair. She could so easily avoid a day of mayhem. Her recent promotion to junior partner of the legal firm Locke, Keyes and Associates meant there were always activities available to trump private functions at weekends.

Angela picked up her car remote and slung the long strap of her briefcase handbag over her shoulder. *But it'll be good to see Jim again. I've left it far too long, as usual.* She made her decision and knew it would at least be fun for Oliver to meet the other kids.

As Saturday loomed, she began to have doubts about the day. Even when they were kids, they'd gone their separate ways and how, more often than not, family meetings would degenerate to shouting matches. *Just go along and keep your mouth shut, girl,* she thought.

The day arrived and Stacey welcomed them into the mayhem that was a kid's party in full swing.

'How many kids are here?' Angela said.

'Most of Jack's class and a few from Andria's playgroup. Drink?'

Angela nodded. 'G&T please.'

Stacey went to get the drinks and a middle-aged man homed in on Angela.

'Hello,' he said. 'You're the lawyer that defended my son, aren't you?'

At first Angela didn't recognise the man, and it was a few seconds before it dawned that he was Tom Gregory's father. 'Mr Gregory, of course. I didn't recognise you immediately.'

Gregory smirked and appeared to be on the verge of speaking when James excused himself and led her away.

'Phew, thanks for saving me.'

'Yeah, sorry about that. Stacey knows him from the gym they both use. He's apparently very popular with the younger females and he likes to promote himself as an eligible bachelor.' James paused for a moment, pointed out the window and said, 'That's his pride and joy. What was your first impression when you met him?'

Angela glanced at the black BMW Z4, shrugged, and said, 'Want the PC answer or the truth?'

'Truth will be good for a start.'

'Okay, a creepy, narcissistic, sociopath would go some way towards explaining my first view... and the car shouts mid-life crisis.' She didn't get to finish because a smirking Gregory appeared with their drinks on a tray.

'I've been downgraded from guest to skivvy,' he chortled.

'Haha,' Angela nodded towards her brother in the hope of dropping a hint that she wished to speak to him.

'Ah, yes, the man who brought down Slippery Clitheroe. He was Rebecca Connolly's uncle, you know.'

The shock of the admission caused Angela to involuntarily suck in a deep breath. 'Really?'

'Yes. Her father was killed in a traffic accident years earlier, and it almost did her poor mother in. We tried our best to help out, and when Becky offered to tutor Tom, we thought it would be good for both of them. Big mistake, hey.'

Angela felt her skin crawl. The man seemed to be needling her in a precise way. 'It was very sad about Tom. I still believe he's innocent and I'm sorry I couldn't be of more help.'

'I love your naïveté, Ms Carter. Thing is. My stupid son did a bad thing. The evidence was there and now he must pay the price.'

'Do you ever contact him?'

'Ha.'

'If you'll excuse me, I have a few things to discuss with my brother. Thank you for bringing my drink.' She put the glass down without touching the liquor and left it when she walked away. As she did, she noticed Gregory turn to direct his smarm towards a couple of the younger mothers.

She found James in the garden. He was pushing two kids on separate swings, and they were both yelling, 'Higher!'

As soon as he saw her, he stepped away to the groans of the swingers. 'Sorry, I didn't want to get involved with your friend.'

'He's not my friend, and neither did I. Did you know that slippery was Rebecca's uncle?'

'Never came up. Why do you ask?'

Angela shrugged. 'It's the first time I've heard of it and Tom never mentioned it.'

'Maybe he didn't know.'

Angela shrugged again and murmured, 'Curiouser and curiouser.'

'Why do you say that?'

'Her parents were allegedly friends of Tom's family. I would have thought it was common knowledge, and given Slippery was the SIO, there might have been just a smidge of conflict.'

'From what I saw and heard. Slippers went right by the book on the murder case. Even more so than usual.'

'Didn't you think that was a little odd in its own right?'

'To be honest, Ange, at the time I had so much on my plate with the undercover work.'

Angela shrugged. 'Thanks.' She made a mental note that first thing Monday morning, she'd go over all the trial material and the evidence offered up. She then noticed Gregory handing his business cards to the two mothers. *Well, it's not illegal, I suppose.* She interrupted her brother's swing pushing again, and said, 'That body they found, it's been on the news.'

'What about it?'

'Similar MO perhaps?'

His eyebrows raised involuntarily. 'I can't discuss the modus operandi, sis. The investigation is still underway.'

'But you can think about it. Say thanks to Stacey for me. Young Oli's had a ball.'

'We must do this again.' He leaned towards her, placed a kiss on her cheek and whispered, 'Right now, I have some thinking to do.'

Oliver seemed a little miffed at being dragged away from the party, but he quickly settled down after he clambered into the car.

'Have a nice day?'

'It was okay. I knew some of the kids from school, and the others were mostly nice.'

His word drove a spike into Angela's chest, and she realised that her work was keeping them apart when they should be having the best of times. 'Would you like to have some of your friends over?'

Oliver shrugged.

'Okay, we'll see what we can do.' She felt her choice of words seemed to indicate the prelude to another heavy workload might do exactly the opposite. 'I'll be quite busy over the next few weeks. Think you can manage?'

Oliver shrugged.

'I promise.'

He shrugged again.

Angela knew he'd be okay. They'd sit at the same table while she worked on cases, and he did his homework. She enjoyed the look on his face while he puzzled over problems and wondered if he felt the same about her, and at least having him there made her contain her language.

'You know, before you were born, I lost a case, and it meant that a young man with huge prospects was jailed for life. I believed he was innocent, and I still do. I'd like to see him released from jail.'

'Why did you lose?'

'The evidence was too strong.'

'What is evidence?'

'The only facts available to determine the truth.'

Oliver nodded slowly. 'So, if the wrong facts are made available, you might be jailed for something you didn't do?'

Angela was taken aback by the lucidity of his response. 'Got it in one.'

'Are you going to look for some evidence that will help get him out of jail?'

Angela couldn't help but smile. 'Would you mind?' She slowed and pointed the car into the driveway of their home.

'You'd be famous.'

'I sincerely hope not, but it would be good to try.'

As he clambered out of the car, he reached into his jacket pocket and pulled out a squashed cupcake. 'You didn't get much to eat at the party, so I kept it for you.'

'Thank you, darling.' She rolled her eyes before suppressing a tear and quickly unlocking the front door.

'That man you were speaking to?'

'Hm?'

'I heard the other kids saying he is a bit weird, and sort of creepy.'

'They might be right.'

Chapter 8

The Monday office was almost deserted when she arrived. Apparently, the partners had a golf day that went on longer than it should have. Fortunately, it had become the routine that few, if any, appointments were made for Mondays. It also meant that Angela could get on with things without disturbance.

'Can you dig me out the original copies of the files on the Tom Gregory case, Sheil?'

Her clerk, Sheila, grinned. 'Didn't think you'd be able to keep your hands off it for too much longer.'

'Well, keep it to yourself. Okay?'

Sheila touched her fingers to her forehead in a fake salute. 'It is *all* on the database, you know.'

'I know but… I want to feel the real paper and… well, you know?'

Sheila stood from her desk and headed towards the archives room.

Angela returned to her office and pulled up the trial transcripts. She knew she'd have a major job on her hands, and that she'd need to deal with it word by word, line by line.

***

James Carter scratched his head. How the hell Slippery wangled parole was beyond him. He was a senior police officer who had surrounded himself with a deeply corrupt team and involved them *and* himself with a gang, to import a massive amount of crystal meth. *They should have thrown away the keys*, he thought.

Seeing his sister again had helped him focus on the innocence of Tom Gregory. Even after all these years, she'd remained convinced of his innocence. Yet it was DNA evidence alone that had put Tom at the scene and the tests confirmed, without a doubt, that the child she was carrying was his. It was something he had forcefully denied both at interview and in court.

He shook his head as he made his way to the evidence storage area. DNA is usually the clincher, and that's where I'll need to begin. The poor kid didn't get much of a chance. Even his father dumped him the moment he'd been arrested. Tom had no alibi on the day Rebecca Connolly died and it didn't take much for Slippery to distance himself from the evidence that Tom gave, and that made Tom the last person to see her alive. Now there was another suspicious killing.

At Angela's request, he'd checked Slippery's alibi. He'd denied that Tom could have seen him driving Rebecca's car with her in it on the day of the murder. His team had even backed him up, that he was in the office on that day.

Problem number one; some of the other investigating officers were a part of Slippery's drug import team, and they had all gone down with him. It was a major scandal at the time and the chances of getting much out of them now would be slim at best. He knew he'd be starting from scratch and that would put him at odds with Slippery's successor.

The last thing he needed was another scandal.

***

Tom Gregory was stunned when the prison officer opened his cell door and told him he had a visitor.

'It's that lawyer who got you locked up. Be nice, hey.'

'Miss Carter?'

The officer shrugged and led him to the legal visitors' meeting room. He pointed to a chair and said, 'Sit.'

A few minutes later, Angela Carter was escorted into the room. The prison officer closed the door and left them alone.

'Miss Carter, I thought…'

'That I'd forgotten about you, Tom?'

He shrugged. 'So why are you here?'

'I want you to tell me as much about your relationship with Rebecca Connolly as you can. I want you to leave out nothing. This will be between us and no one else, understand?'

Tom nodded. 'It won't make any difference. Back then, no one believed anything I said.' He gave another hopeless shrug and said, 'It wasn't that complicated. She was helping me get better grades so that I could take up the scholarship in the USA.' He grimaced. 'Look at me now.'

'On the day she was killed you said you saw DCI Clitheroe take her keys and then drive away with her and that was the last time you saw her alive?'

Tom nodded. 'They said she was having a baby. Is that why he killed her?'

'You still believe it was the DCI?'

Tom shrugged again. 'They found *me* guilty.'

'And I found a copy of a statement from DCI Clitheroe that explains his relationship with Rebecca. Did you know he was her mother's brother?'

'She never mentioned it,' Tom said.

'He claims that on the day of her murder, he had taken her to a cemetery to put flowers on the grave of her father. It was something they did every year. There are also security videos showing everything that happened near the grave on that day.'

'So why didn't he drive her there in his own car and drive her back?'

Angela flipped through her file. 'Nobody asked that question. But the cemetery security videos clearly showed them arriving in her car and him leaving in a police vehicle. Rebecca was seen standing at the graveside for some time after he departed. She then left in her own car. And that's the end of it.'

'They said the baby was mine. I know I was only a kid at the time, but I knew enough to know that couldn't be possible.'

'Well, the DNA evidence confirmed the child was yours, so you'll need to come up with a better explanation than just knowing it couldn't be yours.'

Tom shook his head as though trying to knock his neurons into some kind of logical thought. 'I never had sex with her, miss.'

'Tell me about the times she used to stay the night at your home.'

'I loved those sessions. I reckon I learned more in them than any of the others.'

Angela raised an eyebrow.

'Yeah, well, you can think whatever you want. You obviously don't believe me, so you're probably wasting your time.'

'I do believe you, I honestly do, but I need to find out what happened that might have caused her to become pregnant, if it wasn't you. The DNA evidence points to you. So how come?'

Tom put his face in his hands. 'I also visited her at her home, but we played everything straight. We both knew that any hint of scandal would have ended her career as much as it would mine.'

'Did you want to have sex with her?'

'Miss, I was a hormonally charged eighteen-year-old, and she was a beautiful woman not much older than myself. I can't say I didn't get urges, but I never touched her, ever.'

'So, tell me more about the nights at your home. You've already told me they were special, and maybe you can understand where I'm coming from. Tell me everything that happened and leave nothing out.' She placed a small recording device on the table. 'I don't want to miss a thing.'

He nodded.

Angela looked at her watch. 'We only have fifteen minutes before they'll kick me out. So, start talking.'

Chapter 9

Angela listened attentively to everything Tom said, how his dad used to make them all his special hot chocolate treat. And how, even after being hyped at the end of a session, he would sleep like a log.

'You all had these special hot chocolate drinks?'

'It had become a tradition and Rebecca once commented how well she, too, slept after our sessions, and I never heard a squeak from her room, ever.'

He detailed the lunch time sessions and how Rebecca used to prepare snacks, in advance, to save time. 'She was just a naturally kind person, and I can't imagine why anyone would want to kill her.'

'Well, someone did, Tom, and you were the one they found guilty.'

'I'll admit that I might probably have been guilty of stalking her in away, but it was only because I thought DCI Clitheroe was acting strangely.'

'Hmmm, it seems the DCI was also stalking her. You said he used to park outside your house, and you even saw him watching when you had your daytime sessions.'

Tom shrugged. 'She came to school one day with her face all smashed up. That was never mentioned in court.'

'How long before she died did that happen?'

'About a week. My dad said he'd dropped in on her to pay her some money for the coaching she was giving me. He said she looked like she'd been hit by a bus. He wasn't half wrong, and I thought it must have been the DCI. That's when I got my friends to keep an eye on her.'

The door to the visitor room opened and a prison office called time on the meeting.

'I'll do some more work on this and try to visit again very soon,' Angela said, before he was led away to his cell.

She passed through the security and returned to her car with her mind whirling. Before she started the engine, she called James. 'I've just left a meeting with Tom Gregory. Can we get together for a chat?'

'I'm a bit snowed under at the moment, sis. Tomorrow, okay?'

'I'll buy you lunch.'

'You're on.'

***

James didn't want to meet up with Angela, and today would be filled with reviewing evidence of a still unknown gang trafficking young women. His police work had become intense and was taking its toll on him. His family life was suffering again, Stacey was getting toey again, and the current case involved long hours of unproductive surveillance sessions. 'Hey. Ho,' he muttered as he pushed open the interview room to be greeted by a lawyer and his client.

He recognised the female suspect instantly. She had aged considerably since he'd last seen her. Thankfully, she showed no signs of recognition, which was a relief. 'Ms?' he looked down at his notes.

The lawyer interrupted with the suspect's name, 'Roxanne Santos.'

'Well, Ms Santos, you understand that this interview will be recorded.' He went through the routine "rights" procedure and pressed a button on a device. 'You are not yet charged with anything and, depending on what you tell me today, you may or may not be free to go. Do you understand?'

'No comment.'

'Okay, Ms Santos, if that's the way you want to play it.' James said, 'I'm charging you with aiding and abetting a human trafficking enterprise...'

He was about to continue when she blurted, 'I did nuffin, and you have no proof I did.'

'Like I said, where we go from here is largely up to you...' He was disturbed by a knock on the door. 'Come in, PC Fellows.' He announced her name for the tape and said, 'Ms Santos here says she has no involvement with the operation.'

'Really.' Fellows pressed a button on a remote and a screen lit up. A few seconds later, a security video played. It showed the suspect performing a sex act with a muscular male whose face was off camera. 'Do you know who he is?' Fellows asked.

Santos flushed. She was about to say something when her lawyer tapped her arm, and she said, 'No comment.'

Fellows opened a series of images. 'Do you recognise any of these women?'

Jim was watching her, and a slight smirk crossed her face when a particular photo appeared. It was a young woman asleep on a dishevelled bed. Her face obscured by her hair, and her underwear was in disarray, leaving little to the imagination for anyone who viewed it.

'You know her, don't you?' Jim said.

Santos looked at her solicitor, who nodded. 'She had a website, sleepingsandy.com or summink like that. That's a tame one. There were once heaps of videos of her. She must have been making squillions on the web.'

'Do you know her?'

'Only from her porno work I've never met her. Anyway, I heard she gave it up and found herself a bloke. She's made nothing new for years.'

'What about the others?'

'Nah, they all start to look the same after a while.'

'But you do remember this Sandy person?'

'Word had it she was a local chick who was friendly with a senior cop.' She shrugged.

'Are you aware that some of the people in those pictures have mysteriously disappeared or have no contact details?'

Santos shrugged again. 'There were a few girls making those sleeping movies. Mostly just posing shit, but Sandy went the whole hog. Wait a minute, I did hear that she was a schoolie making a few bucks on the side. About the others…' She looked towards her solicitor, who nodded. 'I can't say nuffin about the ones who disappeared. How would I know where they went?'

Fellows switched up another picture. 'Know her?'

Santos shook her head.

'Interesting.'

'Whatever rots ya socks.'

'I spoke to her yesterday. She knows you. Remember the Ferals gang?'

Santos shrugged. 'No comment.'

'You did pole dancing stints with her at their clubhouse. At least you did until you went to seed.'

Roxanne scowled. 'I dunno know what you're talkin about.'

'That's okay. Your friend is giving us heaps of info, so we might as well charge you and get it over with.'

DC Fellows stood to leave, and as she reached for the door, Santos blurted. 'She knows nuffin.' She looked at Jim with pleading eyes. 'They'll fuckin kill me if I talk. You know that.'

'If you talk, we can offer you protection. Do you really think they'll believe you've said nothing while you were in here?'

Santos' face burned as she turned to her solicitor.

The lawyer shrugged. 'What have you got to lose, other than your life?'

'Shit!' Santos had begun shivering and scratching at her arms.

'And you need a fix?'

She nodded.

'Tell me who your supplier is, or is he also your pimp?' James said.

She shook her head.

'Take her back to the cells, DC Fellows. Let her have a safe night's sleep before we turn her loose in the morning.'

'Wait! If I tell you who he is. What's in it for me?'

'Can't promise anything.'

Roxanne pointed to the screen and then her mouth. 'The bloke with the muscles. He runs a system.'

Fellows and James leaned forward in their chairs.

'We're all ears Roxanne,' James said.

***

Angela stopped to pick up Oliver on the way home from school. 'Have a good day?'

'S'pose.'

'Shall we get a takeaway for dinner?'

He shrugged.

'Okay, what's up?'

Oliver shrugged again.

'Something happen at school?'

He shook his head.

'Okay, something *did* happen at school. Is it something I should be aware of?'

He said nothing for several minutes as his face changed colour from white to pink and onwards to red.

'Have you been fighting?'

He shook his head.

'Right, you can tell me when you're ready. Okay?'

Oliver nodded. His lips were pursed as though he were trying his hardest to not blurt out a secret.

Angela reached out and patted his shoulder. 'It's just you and me, Oli.'

He spontaneously burst forth, 'They're saying you lost a court case and sent an innocent man to jail.'

'Oh gosh. That was before you were born. It was the only case I ever lost. I told you about that, remember? I'm still regretting it.'

'They say he killed his schoolteacher because she was a…' he paused, 'a slut.'

'A what!?'

Oliver shrugged. 'The whole school knows. She had her own website.'

'You do mean Rebecca Connolly?'

Oliver nodded.

'I think you need to stop listening to that kind of talk. From everything I knew about Rebecca, she was certainly not that kind of girl.'

'They say she was sleeping with half the school's staff. I'm not a kid anymore. I know what that means, mum.'

'You are a kid, Oliver. You are just nine years old. Do your teachers know about this?'

Oliver shrugged.

'Well, tomorrow I'll pay the head a visit. Maybe he'll have some answers.'

'He's a she, Mum.'

'Well, okay. That's fine too.'

Chapter 10

I thought we were having takeaway,' Oliver said when Angela parked her car in the driveway.

'We'll have it delivered. I'm sorry. I forgot.'

He slung his backpack over his shoulders and waited at the front door. 'Pizza.'

'Okay, I'll call the order in as soon as we get settled.'

Before Angela called the pizza shop, she rang her brother. When it started ringing, she went outside. She didn't need Oliver hearing what came next.

'Hi sis. Can't you get enough of me?'

'Oliver says there are rumours going around at his school.'

'What's new about that?'

'They know I defended Tom Gregory, and that I lost the case. Oliver's now copping a heap of flak from his classmates.'

'Hardly a police matter. Have you taken it up with the school?'

'I'm not sure I'm the right person, given my history. Anyway, the rumour has it that Rebecca Connolly was sleeping with half the school, and making porno videos on the side that she sold on the web.'

'It's hardly a crime. She was an adult at the time and free to do anything she liked... The videos didn't include school kids, did they?'

'I don't know. All I've got is the word of a nine-year-old kid, who is being bullied because of something I did. And now there are reports of another body. A young woman about Rebecca's age.'

'Sadly, there's not much I can do about rumours. If you can dig up some evidence, that might be a different matter. As far as the body that was found, Mulligan is handling that.'

'Well, I guess that's it then. Still good for lunch?'

'I'll call you in the morning. Slippery's being released later today, and I want to know where he goes.'

'Good old Slippery Clitheroe. There are a lot of coincidences around him aren't there: first, we discover that the DCI not only had a connection with the Ferals, and Tom Gregory's family, but he's now a convicted corrupt cop. Enough DNA evidence to convict Tom was found on Rebecca's body. Then to cap it all, she's discovered to be pregnant, by Tom, who says he never touched her.'

'From what I've seen from the case notes, Slippery followed the book in that investigation. You'd be hard pressed to pin anything on him after all this time, Ange.'

'Well, if you can't help me, I'll have to go my own way.'

'For Chris'sake Ange. These people are dangerous. They'd cut your throat as quick as looking at you.'

'Well then, you'll have another murder to follow up on.' Angela ended the call and before he could reply, she switched her phone off.

She waited a few minutes before switching it on again and calling the pizza shop. There was only one pizza Oliver liked, so no consultation was required. After making the call, she switched her phone to silent.

Oliver returned from his room as she ended the call.

'That was Uncle Jim, and I've ordered the pizza,' Angela said.

'The cop?'

Angela nodded.

'Have you dobbed me in?'

'For what?'

Oliver shrugged.

'I told him about the rumour, but there's nothing he can do, so you'll just have to suck it up and get on with things.'

'They reckon she let people do things to her in her sleep. How weird is that?'

'Have you got much homework?'

'Nah, why have you?'

'I need to do a bit of research, so if you can find yourself something to do after we've had our pizza, that'll be good.'

Oliver shrugged and slumped in front of the TV.

Sometime later, the doorbell rang.

'That will be dinner. Hungry?'

Oliver shrugged.

Angela paid the pizza kid and opened the box on the table. Oliver grabbed a slice, returned to the couch and grabbed the TV remote, while Angela put a slice on a plate and took it to her study.

She Googled Rebecca Connolly and returned heaps of information about her murder and subsequent trial. There was even a video of Oliver's father saying how disappointed he was with his son, and finishing his tirade with, 'We didn't bring him up to be like that and I blame the crap we get via the TV. We gave him every freedom and the opportunity of a lifetime, and he blew it.'

Angela muttered under her breath, 'What an A-hole.'

Another video showed George smiling and shaking hands with Slippery Clitheroe, the DCI in charge of the homicide investigation. *How odd*, she thought. She continued through the various news reports that showed up, and even videos of herself entering and leaving the court. 'You've put on a bit of weight since then, Angie baby.' that triggered her into thinking about an old song by Helen Reddy.

She began to hum the lyrics, and the words found their way into her thoughts. *How true that is about yourself, Angela. You've pulled your head right in and have hardly any friends.* She reached the lines about lovers in her bedroom, daddy tapping on the door, and the boy with evil on his mind. She knew the earworm would stick with her for the whole night and chase any logic away. She loved Helen Reddy's music, but it always had that effect on her. 'Shit.' She shook her head in an attempt to clear the thoughts.

Next, she googled George Gregory, expecting nothing, but hoping it would drive away Helen Reddy. Instead, she again found heaps of stuff. George and Gregory were obviously popular names back in the day. Angela trawled through until the search diversified to the point where nothing much related. Then she saw it. No names were mentioned, but the text was to do with a long-ago court case involving a young boy who was caught in the act of sexually assaulting his next-door neighbour's daughter. She was unconscious after he plied her with drinks and the girl had fallen pregnant. There were obviously no pictures, both were well underage, and their names had been suppressed.

'Oh God…' Angela tapped Jim's number on her phone.

'Give it a rest Ange,' he said.

'I can't. I've just seen something I can't unsee, and I need to ask you a question. Just one, then I'll leave you alone, I promise.'

'Go on.'

'Do you hear of many women being sexually assaulted when they are asleep or drunk?'

'Happens all the time.'

'What about a teenage boy assaulting his next-door neighbour's paralytic daughter?'

'Are you asking me this for a reason?'

'I did a search for George Gregory…'

'And?'

'No names were mentioned. I just wondered…?'

'You're drawing a long bow.'

'What if the child Rebecca was carrying was not Tom Gregory's?'

'The DNA was conclusive. It's done and dusted, so that won't work. Sorry.'

'Okay, well, thanks anyway.'

***

James Carter pressed end on his phone and returned to the table to finish his dinner. 'That was Angela. She still has a bee in her bonnet about Tom Gregory.'

'Someone should tell her to forget it. He was convicted of murder fair and square, and you should switch your phone off at mealtimes. It's not fair to the kids,' Stacey said.

'Sorry, next time.' His appetite had by now evaporated and he blurted, 'Shit!'

'I beg your pardon?'

'Something Angie just said. It might tie in with a case I'm working on.'

'How?'

'I can't say right now. I'll head to the office after dinner. If I don't, I won't get a wink of sleep.'

'Well, don't stay up too late. We don't seem to get any alone time lately.'

'Sorry Stace. This is stuff I can't do at home. I'll try to be quick.' He picked up his car keys and excused himself.

Chapter 11

Disappointed with her brother's attitude, the matter played on Angela's mind. Tom had never spoken of drinking on the nights Rebecca stayed over. In fact, the only drink he mentioned was the hot chocolate treat made by his father at the end of each session.

'How involved *is* Clitheroe with the Gregory family?' She took a bite out of her now cold pizza and grimaced. Her phone rang. She answered it. 'What now, Jim…?'

'Ange I…?'

'You've changed your mind?'

'No, but you said something that might relate to an interview I had with a witness. Can I come around now? I'm in my car, on the way, so please say yes.'

'I thought you said it was cut and dried.'

'Let's talk when I get there.'

'See you soon then.'

James stopped at a bottle shop and picked up a chilled SSB. A few minutes later, he was at Angela's apartment.

When she opened the door, she looked down at the bottle. 'Hmmm, Semillon Sauvignon Blanc, my favourite. What's this, bribery?'

'Not quite. Is young Oliver around?'

'He's watching telly.'

'Can we go somewhere private?'

'Oliver, Uncle Jim's here. Will you be okay while we do some stuff in the study?'

'No worries, mum. Just keep the noise down, I'm watching a movie.'

'Cheeky monkey,' James grinned as Angela pulled the door shut.

She pointed to a small settee. 'Take a pew.'

'We won't be disturbed. I hope?'

'Why? What are you planning, big bro?'

James opened his briefcase and pulled out a series of stills. He lay them on the small coffee table and said, 'What do you think of this?'

Angela sucked in a startled gasp. 'At first glance, pretty disgusting.'

'I expected that, but these are evidence that has come into our possession from another direction. Remember you mentioned that kid assaulting his neighbour's daughter?'

'Sleeping porn? Surely most of that is rigged, right?'

'I would have thought so…'

'But…?'

'What if it wasn't?'

'Rebecca?'

'Pull up your browser. I'd like to try something.'

Angela shrugged and clicked on her browser icon. 'All yours.' She stood and offered him the chair.

'I hope we find nothing, but just make sure young Oliver is safe, and turn down the volume so we don't get any shocks.'

Angela did as he asked and popped out to check on Oliver. 'Good movie?'

His shoulders twitched into a shrug and his jaws crunched on the contents of a packet of crisps.

'Okay, we shouldn't be too long.' She returned to the study to see her computer screen displaying a porn movie that James was watching intently. 'I see…'

'I don't think you do.' He backed out of the site and logged in again.

'sleapingbiuty.com. We had a witness say she thought there was a video doing the rounds about a young woman being sexually assaulted in her sleep.'

'Shit! Are you thinking what I'm thinking?'

'The witness told me the site name was sleepingsandy.com, but she wasn't sure. I tried that but got nothing, so I Googled different spellings of sleep.'

'And that came up?'

'Her face always seems to be obscured by something, so I doubt the videos will be of any use as evidence. She would have to make a complaint if she knew it was her.'

'How would anyone be able to commit this kind of assault on a conscious person without their knowledge?'

James logged into the site again and it displayed several pages of thumbnails. 'This might be bugger all. There is nothing to identify the woman, and nothing to say she wasn't compliant.'

'Oliver said he was being ribbed about Rebecca…'

'Exactly. If we can find something that links that gossip to fact…'

Angela reached over and scrolled through the thumbnails. 'There's hundreds of them and they don't look like the same model is being used in each case.' She stopped at a thumbnail depicting a dark-skinned girl.

'Do you remember saying that Tom Gregory had said his dad made special hot chocolate drinks at the end of each session?'

Angela nodded slowly.

'Back in the nineties there was a case were a bloke drugged and raped twenty-four women. What if?'

'Tom's trial was ten years ago. We'll be lucky to trace anything back that far.'

'I found this near the top.' James scrolled back up to the top of the thumbnails. 'See that tattoo?' he pointed to a small bird on the ankle of the woman. 'The latest body is that of a young woman of about Rebecca's age, and she had a tat just like this, in exactly the same place.'

'Did Rebecca have any tattoos?'

'Nothing in her file.'

'So where does this take us, other than an evening of salacious porn viewing?'

'I don't know. I'm going to pass this on to our IT mob. They have ways of finding things we could spend a lifetime looking for and miss completely.'

'Mum,' Oliver tapped on the study door and James closed the lid of the laptop.

'We'll be a little longer.'

'Can I watch another movie?' he said, pushing open the door.

Angela looked at her watch. 'No, it's getting late, and you have school tomorrow. It'll keep and we're nearly finished here.'

'That was a bit too close for comfort.'

'Yeah, I don't want him getting ideas.'

'Okay, I'll follow this up tomorrow and see where it takes us.'

***

Angela saw her brother out and then cleared her browser history. Whilst Oliver rarely used the study computer, it was probably better if there was nothing he might inadvertently stumble upon.

She warmed some milk, made two mugs of hot chocolate, and handed her son the largest of the two. 'Might help you sleep.'

Oliver shrugged and sipped at his drink before smirking.

'What's that about?'

'They reckon that's how they got to video the teacher.'

'Who?'

'The movie makers. They reckon they used hot chocolate with drugs in it.'

Angela shook her head. 'Enough. Finish your drink, and then it's bedtime for you.'

Oliver did as he was asked and headed to his bedroom, but Angela was worried about his attitude and sent a text to James.

I Think we need to check out the rumours doing the rounds at Oliver's school.

James flicked a quick reply.

I'm with you.

***

Stacey was asleep when James arrived home, and he slipped into bed without waking her. He could understand her attitude to his work. She'd lost him for months while he was undercover, and now he was getting involved with something that was likely to take him to all the wrong places again. That, and a sleepless night, was assured, as his mind began working overtime.

Clitheroe was convicted in a different case, but I'm convinced there was something that should have rung bells and I missed it.

Roxanne mentioned something that should have clicked immediately. She knew a senior police officer at the time of the sting, and she might know even more. If I can get her to my answer my questions, and maybe a start would be to talk to Slippery. He had close connections to the gang at the time they busted them and why stop at drugs?

The alarm clock wrenched him from his sleep and his bleary eyes focussed on the time. He leaned across and kissed his wife. 'I need to be in early today there's a lot going off.'

'What's new,' she said, 'and who is Roxanne?'

'Roxanne?'

'If I didn't know better, you spent half the night interrogating her.'

'Shit. Was it that bad? She's a witness, and she might have a connection to Tom Gregory's situation. I can't say any more.'

'Angela's finally worn you down.'

'Not quite, but she's uncovered information and scuttlebutt that might point to some jiggery pokery at the time of his arrest.'

'That ought to please Slippery Clitheroe.'

'Yep, and he's swung parole. He's due out today.'

Chapter 12

The first thing James Carter did when he arrived at work was to head for the cyber division. It was at the other end of the building and a place he rarely visited.

He knocked on the door and walked in, to a bunch of nerdy looking uniformed cops, in what looked like a version of the once hated cube farms. Their heads were all bowed, their fingers dancing on keyboards, and their eyes glued to computer screens.

He peered over the first divider and asked who was in charge.

'Over in the corner, sarge.'

James followed the man's pointed finger to a slightly larger cube where he saw the top of a dark-haired ponytail. 'Her?'

The officer nodded.

The cube was built like a labyrinth and as he weaved his way through, he recognised the person he was aiming for.

Detective Sergeant Jennifer Crawford had been the key to apprehending several paedophiles over the years and had been involved with the closure of many of their evil rings.

She looked up as he approached. 'Ah. I heard you were here. I wondered how…'

James felt his stomach twist. 'Jen…I…'

'G'day, Jim, what's serious enough for you to drag your carcass into my territory?'

He suddenly felt nervous. They'd had a fling in the police

academy that went a lot further than a few kisses and cuddles and continued long after they left. He rolled his eyes.

'How's Stacey keeping? You behaving yourself?'

The twinkle in her eye told him she too had memories of their time together and it was an episode he did not wish to reopen. 'I need you to look into some stuff I've come across as part of another investigation.'

'You're involved in the human trafficking thingo, aren't you?'

James nodded. 'You know about that?'

Jennifer shrugged and tapped the chair alongside of hers.

As he sat, he felt her aura reach out to overwhelm him and he moved the chair to distance himself.

Her face turned towards him, and he noticed a tight smile on her lips. 'It was a long time ago, Jim,' she said. 'Don't worry, I'm over it.'

Unconvinced of his own degree of over-ness, he nodded. 'I'm working on something that still seems to have a smidge of Clitheroe lingering. He was involved with the case of Tom Gregory. Do you remember that?'

'Vaguely.'

'Well, young Tom. He was only just eighteen at the time, has lost ten years of his freedom on the evidence provided by Clitheroe, who was on the verge of being commended for ridding the world of another sexual predator, slash murderer.'

'That I remember.'

'So, information has come to hand that someone is circulating videos of young women being assaulted in their sleep. Have you come across anything like that?'

'Have there been any complaints?'

'Not that I can find, but that doesn't mean it's not going on.'

DS Crawford turned to her computer and said, 'What's the site?'

James handed her a note with the details. 'This is only a preliminary perve. I didn't want to go searching every site on the web, but Tom Gregory's lawyer is my sister, and her son has been getting ribbed at school. Some of the kids have heard about her failure in court and they seem to know stuff that hasn't crossed into our territory. If you get my drift.'

DS Crawford reached the site and was peering at the screen. She made a few notes and pulled up another program. 'This will, hopefully, tell us where the site is hosted. If it's in some obscure place, we might have difficulties going further.' She smiled. 'Ha! Right here in good old WA. Seems whoever is involved, he or she, doesn't have any worries about being caught. There is, of course, no law that prevents people from viewing this stuff in the privacy of their own home.'

'What if the acts are performed on people who don't give their permission? What if they are underage or drugged before the performance and are genuinely unconscious?'

'Then we might have a case, but…' She pointed to a text listing on her second screen. 'Some of the videos on this site go back over ten years and *I'm* not aware of any complaints in that time period. Certainly, nothing has crossed my desk in the last few years.'

'Is there anyway of identifying the actors in the scenes?'

'From what I've seen so far, their faces are obscured in some way.' She pointed to the video that was playing. 'This one goes back to about the time of Tom Gregory's trial. Here's another one from about that period.' DS Crawford paused. 'Ha! This one has a tattoo. See. Now all you need to do is find the girl with the birdy tattoo and ask her if she gave her permission to be filmed. Good luck with that, my friend.'

'Yeah, she'd be too old to be the kid they found dead recently.'

DS Crawford clicked on another thumbnail, and the same young woman appeared in a similar pose. This time, a hand reached out to adjust her clothing. The model didn't move. 'Either she's fast asleep, unconscious, or just a very good actor.'

'Reckon she's out cold?'

DS Crawford responded, 'Looks like it to me. Tiny tatt on the ankle, like that earlier one, so it is probably the same person.' She started the video again and stopped it when the hand appeared. This time, they both noticed the high-end wristwatch. 'Not too many of those around, Jim.'

'I know that watch, Jen. Slippery had one just like it. Rumour had it he took it from a dealer in exchange for going easy on him.'

'Do you know who the dealer was?'

'No. Like I said, it was a rumour.'

'Clitheroe is due out soon, isn't he?'

'Today, but how he wangled parole might be a pertinent question down the track.'

'Okay Jim. Leave this with me and I'll see what I can find on this and similar sites. I can't promise anything, but if there is something shady going on, you can bet they'll shoot themselves in the foot somewhere along the way.'

***

The things Angela had seen over the last few days were bothering her, and when James called to tell her, he'd handed things over to Jenny Crawford, she knew there might be repercussions if Stacey found out. Particularly given that Jenny was his girlfriend long before they'd become an item. She decided it might be best if she did her own research and avoid Jim's involvement as much as possible.

She cleared a few of the things that were sitting on her desk and then pulled up her browser. There were two sites mentioned by her son and the second one she had looked at with James. The first seemed to be inactive, but that might have been due to a typo when entering the URL. She tried sleepingsandy.com again, and this time it went through.

This time, the female in the scene was clearly recognisable from her face. It was Rebecca Connolly. *So maybe Oliver's school friends are right.* She called James.

'I'm a bit busy right now can I call you later?'

'I think you should see what I've just found. Remember that site that didn't seem to exist? Well, maybe you did make a typo. I have it up on my computer now and the star of the show is defo Rebecca Connolly. Whoever made the movies hasn't even tried to conceal her identity.'

'Do you think Tom Gregory might have run across this and spat the dummy?'

'I doubt he'd have known anything, Jim. He wasn't that kind of kid. Basketball was his passion and Rebecca was a means to an end. I don't think he even had a girlfriend.'

'Send me a link to the URL I'll pass it on to the cyber division.'

Angela's email left her computer before he'd finished speaking.

'Got it. That was quick.'

'There is a heap of stuff to go through, whoever did this was prolific.'

'I've forwarded the link to the cyber division. If anyone can find anything, Jenny Crawford will be the one.' He ended the call and Angela knew she'd need to speak with Tom Gregory as soon as possible. If he could throw any light on what she'd discovered, it would be a bonus. She rang the prison and made an appointment for a legal visit two days on. By then, something else might have turned up, and she sincerely hoped that none of it would point the finger at her client.

She couldn't resist taking another peek at the site. And scrolled through several of the thumbnails. She stopped when she saw one with only buttocks. When she reran the selection, it started with Rebecca being slowly undressed.

Next, a hand slapped lubricant onto her body, then she saw a knee lift onto the bed and soon after, Rebecca was completely obscured by thrusting male buttocks. When whoever it was finished, he left the camera running while he collected a bowl of soapy water to wash away the residual evidence. He towelled her dry, and a voice said, 'And the good thing is that no one will ever know, Becky, except you, in your dreams. Sleep tight and we'll meet again next week.'

The voice was too familiar, and it sent an involuntary shudder through Angela's body. She knew him. 'You poor girl. No one deserves what he's done to you.' She copied the link to a thumb drive.

> Sorry Jim, I've found something else. I daren't send it, so I'll drop it around.

In frustration, she powered down her computer, told her receptionist she wasn't feeling well and was leaving for the day. She wasn't lying. Everything about that video had made her feel sick, and she knew she would not be free of it until Rebecca and Tom received proper justice.

Chapter 13

The voice was familiar but not enough to tie it to anyone in particular. The male body was out of focus which meant it would be difficult to pick up on physical attributes. Angela played it again on her home computer and then began scanning through the many thumbnails to see if there was anything else.

It soon became obvious that someone would need to trawl through the entire site, on the off chance that another shot of the man would appear. Angela didn't feel up to that, and she hoped Jim, and his cyber division might be a better bet. She called his office.

'I saw the video. Fairly gruesome I thought. Have you any idea who the male might be?'

Angela replied angrily, 'No! I hoped your people might be able to come up with something. The one thing I can say for certain is that the male figure is not Tom Gregory.'

'How can you be so sure?'

'He was barely a kid at the time, more toned physically, and a fraction of the weight of that actor. Also, the voice is familiar, and it isn't Tom's. I think someone needs to go through all those videos to see if there is anything that can be considered viable as evidence.'

James said, 'I'll see if I can talk Jenny Crawford into a session but you're asking a lot of us. Tom was found guilty based upon the strong DNA evidence provided by DCI Clitheroe's team. So far there is nothing that points to the murderer of Rebecca other than that evidence. Sorry Ange, I'll probably be needing much more if I'm to pull the curtains aside.'

She pressed end. *I hoped it would be easier than this.* 'So, it looks like you're going to be trawling through the filth on your own Angela. Better get to it before Oliver arrives home.' She took something out of the freezer for dinner, made herself a coffee and began her marathon.

Most of the videos were a standard format, a sleeping woman. The website said she was someone called Sandy, but it was definitely Rebecca Connolly. She could be no one else.

She remembered the first video they had found and the unusual watch on the wrist of the perpetrator. 'If that can be tied to the voice…' Her phone rang. 'Hello, Jim.'

'Jenny says she can put someone on the trawl, but for how long…?'

'Thanks so much, Jim. I thought I might have to do it all myself. Remember that one from the other site — the watch — any ideas?'

'I know Clitheroe had something similar but for all we know these videos might be consensual, so unless we find something concrete that says they aren't, we won't get very far.'

'Well, someone filmed himself in flagrante delicto with Rebecca. She became pregnant at some time and soon after ceased to exist. The link I sent you should tell you that someone else might have had a hand in that other than Tom Gregory.'

'Still doesn't prove the man in either of the films made her pregnant or killed her.'

'Time to pay a visit to Tom, maybe he can cast some light.'

'He's probably your best bet, Ange, and if his memory of the time is returning, he might be able to come up with something useful.'

Angela Carter ended the call feeling disheartened, but he had said try Tom Gregory, to see if he can come up with anything. She made a screen grab of a few scenes in the video. *They're blurry and movement scarified, but Tom might recognise something.* She printed the stills and slid them into an A4 envelope, before hiding them in a file in her briefcase ready for her prison visit.

***

James had a little more success with Jenny. Although she had offered one of her team the job of scouring the site, she'd also made a point of checking a few of the thumbnails herself. 'Hey, Jim, take a squiz at this.'

He scanned the papers she'd lain on his desk. 'So, the site is owned by a consortium. How do we find out the consortium's members?'

'It is in hand as we speak, might take a few days for an answer but if the domain is hosted in Australia, we might be able to get a warrant. Are you up for that?'

'We'll have to make it official…'

'Have you got enough to do that?'

'I'll need to think about it, I'm already under the pump on this trafficking case, and this is something I don't need right now. I'll see what my sister can come up with and let you know.'

'Your call, Sweet Cheeks…'

He heard the chuckle in her voice as she left his desk. Sweet Cheeks was one of the names she'd used, in private, when they were an item, he'd always rankled at it, and it made her laugh. Strangely it also invoked a memory of the good times they'd had together, despite her deliberate provocation.

Jenny Crawford had apparently remained single since they parted and word had it, she was still carrying a torch for someone. Until now he'd kept her at arm's length, and he now needed to put all those thoughts from his mind and call Stacey.

Bad move. She was in the worst possible mood. Everything that could go wrong had. The school had been on the phone about a fist fight his eldest had got into, and his daughter had hit a teacher when she tried to split the fighters up.

'I'll pop over to the school and sort things out,' he said.

'Someone had better because I'm just about up to here with being the only parent in this family.'

***

On the way to the school, James picked up some flowers and Stacey's favourite chocs then he summoned up his courage and confronted the head teacher who introduced herself as Jane Parker.

Parker said, 'It seems that Jack was confronted by one of the other boys whose father had been arrested for a DUI. He knew Jack's dad was a police officer and decided to repair—she waggled her fingers in the air—the "reputational" damage. Then Andria joined in and when a teacher tried to break up the fight, she smacked her in the jaw with a full thermos, it broke one of the woman's teeth.'

James felt horrified, neither of his kids had ever shown any violent tendencies. 'But it *was* Jack who was provoked?'

'It seems that way, but one of our staff has been injured, and you, better than anyone, will understand the ramifications of that, Detective Sergeant Carter.'

James nodded. 'Where are my kids now?'

'I called your wife to collect them. Regrettably, I've been forced to suspend them.'

'I've just spoken to her on the phone, and she said nothing about them being collected or suspended.'

James called Stacey. 'Are the kids at home?'

'I told them you'd be picking them up.'

Jim Carter felt a chill deep inside. He turned to the head. 'My wife says she told the school I would be collecting them. So here I am.'

'Apparently they were collected one hour ago, so Mrs Carter must be mistaken.'

'Who handed them over?'

The head opened her mouth to speak when Jim's phone buzzed with a text tone:

> If you want to see your kids alive again, drop your investigation into the Connolly killing.
> You have twenty-four hours to confirm you have closed the investigation before body parts will begin arriving in your post.

The texters phone was unidentifiable. He showed the message to the head. 'Think this beats your teacher's broken tooth, Ms Parker. I want the person who handed over my children brought here now.'

The Head's face had turned an ashen white, 'Oh my God.'

'You're wasting your time invoking him or her. Get that person here ASAP or I will arrest you for aiding and abetting, the kidnapping of two innocent children.'

The woman pressed a button on a microphone on her desk. 'Georgia Hawkins. My office please.' She shrugged and gave a weak smile. Her desk phone chirped. 'Yes? What do you mean she's left for the day?'

Her face began to redden as he listened to the one side of the conversation.

'Casual? I didn't know we had any casual staff.' Sweat began beading on her reddening forehead. 'I need her address. There is a policeman here, Sergeant Carter. He needs to speak to her... I'll hand you to him.' She handed the phone to James.

The voice at the other end said, 'Sergeant Carter, Ms Hawkins handed your children over to your wife about two hours ago. She has now left for the day, and I understand she is heading directly overseas for a holiday.'

'My wife has not collected my kids. I said, and she told this school that I would be collecting them.' He turned to the head. 'You have a problem, ma'am. I'll require all your security videos immediately. If there're any difficulties, I can arrange a warrant.' He punched a number into his phone. 'Sorry, boss. Both my kids have been kidnapped from their school within the last two hours. One of the perpetrators might be heading for the airport. I don't know where or when she is flying but her name is Hawkins…'

'Georgia Hawkins,' the head interrupted.

'Georgia Hawkins, but it's probably a false name, anyway. I need back up here. I'm calling this a crime scene and I'll need a warrant to search the place.' He ended the call and turned to the wilting woman. 'No one leaves this school until my team have cleared them. Understand?'

'But I have…'

'All your haves, and those of your staff, are cancelled until further notice Ms Parker.'

The first of urgently skirling sirens abruptly ended their conversation.

Chapter 14

Upon hearing the news, Jenny Crawford was not backward in coming forward. She offered to check the security videos personally and assist in any way she could. It was her area of expertise and she'd often found things in footage that no one else would pick up.

'If the perpetrator is in those videos, we'll have her banged to rights in a flash, mate. Go home to your wife. She'll be needing you more than we do.'

James knew she was right, but a red rag had been thrust in his face and he had no intention of standing down for anyone. He nodded to acknowledge her comment and left the building. As soon as he was clear, he called Angela.

'All good?' she said.

'No. I'm on my way home to be with Stacey. Some bastard's taken Andria and Jack. I intend finding them and I might need your help.'

'Shit, Jim. What's going on here?'

'I wish I knew. I have someone trawling through security videos, but I've no idea what they'll come up with.'

'You called *me*. Is this related to Tom Gregory?'

'Got it in one. It has been suggested that I stand aside from that case. And I'm the only person other than you, and Jenny Crawford who knows what I'm doing.' He copied the text to her.

'Gosh, they don't seem to be mucking about do they.'

'They've given me less than twenty-four hours to cancel an investigation that isn't even officially underway. I've already received a warning about digging into the Gregory case and this is going to make things much worse. Add to that my own workload and I'm likely to disappear down the crapper.'

'Can we meet?'

'I'll have to speak with Stacey first. She's at the end of her tether.'

'I'll meet you there. Maybe I can help.'

'I don't think that's a good idea, Ange. Let me talk to her first, then we will need to get together and discuss our options.'

'Okay, I'll be by my phone waiting for your call. Meanwhile I'll get the papers together. Let's see if we can find someone to point a finger at.' Angela ended the call as James was parking his car outside his home.

Stacey's face was frozen into a block of sweat and tear dripping granite. She pushed him away when he tried to give her a hug. 'Don't fucking touch me,' she sobbed. 'You've let *my* kids be kidnapped from under your...'

'Hey! Easy on, they're my kids too you know.'

'I'd never have guessed.' She slumped into a chair and began to weep convulsively.

James thought it better if he let her get it out of her system and boiled the kettle. 'Here, cuppa. It might help, and you should know that people are already out there looking for them.'

Stacey blew her nose and took a sip of her tea. 'Do you know who picked them up?'

James shook his head. 'Jenny Crawford is trawling through the school's security vision. If anyone can spot something she will. The airport is on notice and if she's there, they'll find her.'

'She?'

'Georgia Hawkins, mean anything to you?'

Stacey started to shake her head, then abruptly stopped. 'Georgia Hawkins?'

James nodded.

She took his hand and led him into the study where she booted her computer. Once it was up, she engaged Facebook and searched for Georgia Hawkins. An arm long list of names appeared together, each with a circular pic. There were also many without mugshots.

Stacey listed her friends in another lengthy list. This time she was able to find a Georgia Hawkins, but the friend had no image. A quick check of the profile showed there was almost nothing on the site to show it was in regular usage.

'Troll page,' James said.

'I don't even remember befriending her.'

'It's easily done by accident.' He nudged her aside and pulled up her home page. 'How many times have you contacted her?'

'I've no idea. I don't even know who she is.'

'Maybe this Georgia has been able to garner enough information about you, to enable her to approach the school.'

'So now it's my fault.'

'I don't mean that, but I need to meet up with Angela to go through all the papers she has in relation to the Tom Gregory case. I can't use the official channels because of my personal connection. Should I invite her here?'

Stacey nodded.

James called Angela. 'You're on. How soon can you get here?'

'I'm on my way.'

***

DS Jenny Crawford yawned. Trawling through security videos was not the most entertaining of pastimes, and this was no different. There was barely any activity showing, besides the odd child or adult briefly passing through the arcs of visibility. She'd double checked the slots that related to the time that the kids were collected but there was nothing of any significance that could identify a suspicious human. It was only then that she noticed a discrepancy. There were no videos covering a ten-minute period. The time stamp simply jumped. 'Ahah!'

Her yawning ceased. She called the school. 'I don't have a contiguous series of videos. Ten minutes worth are missing. Can you think of any reason for this discrepancy?'

Parker spluttered, 'I can't, but there *was* a brief power outage during the morning.'

'Time?'

'I can't say exactly. It just went off and came on again soon afterwards.'

'Think hard, Ms Parker, the lives of two of your students are in grave danger.'

'It's possible that it might have been around the time of the children being collected but I can't say for certain. There was no indication at any time that there was a need for caution.'

'Are there any battery-operated cameras that might not have been included in the vision collected under the warrant?'

'I'll check and get back to you.'

'I will also require all mobile phones to be handed in, both children and adults. Someone will be with you shortly. No omissions for any reason. Understand?'

'I'll see what I can do.'

'This is not a request, Ms Parker. Every phone and camera.' DS Crawford immediately texted James to advise him of the progress, but there was no response. She then phoned Synergy to check on official outages. There were none reported, so the power only affected the school. *Someone must know enough of the electrical set up to close down the whole school's service.* She wrote a note in her book.

***

The doorbell rang and Stacey checked the entry video. It was Angela. She sucked in a deep breath and opened the door to the woman who might be the primary cause of her children's disappearance. 'He's in the study.' Her voice flat as she pointed to the half-open door.

Angela wasn't sure how to react to Stacey, her hostility was more inflamed than usual. She nodded and joined her brother at the computer. 'Stacey seems pretty intense.'

'How would you feel if *your* lad had suddenly been taken, with a note advising body parts would be forwarded after 24 hours?'

Angela laid out the file on the table. 'This is all the case notes relating to the trial of Tom Gregory.'

James began flicking through them but struggled to find anything that would point the finger at anyone in particular. He handed them back to Angela. 'We need to find something that might identify that male. When are you next seeing Tom?'

'I made an appointment for early next week but that was before all these videos turned up, and now you have a limited time to track down the kidnappers, so I'll try to get into see him today.'

'See if he can recognise anything. He was closer than anyone at the time.'

'You can keep the papers. They are only copies. I'm not sure what you'll find in them but you're welcome. If Tom comes up with anything I'll let you know.'

Chapter 15

The prison administration seemed deliberately awkward, but Angela finally got through to them that Tom Gregory might be the only person who might be able to help in regard to the kidnapping.

She arrived one hour later and passed through the security system. Eventually Tom Gregory arrived looking puzzled.

'I wasn't expecting you, miss.'

'I have something to show you.' She opened her file and handed him the stills one by one. As each picture appeared his face turned proportionately redder.

He scrunched up the papers, looked up, and glared at Angela. 'Is this some kind of sick joke?'

'We discovered these following a tip off. James Carter's kids have been kidnapped, and he's been given twenty-four hours to stop any investigation into the death of Rebecca.'

'So!'

'So, is there anything you can add after seeing these pictures? Anything you can say that might help us track down her killer.'

'It was me. The court said so.'

'I've never believed that, Tom.'

'What you did or didn't believe, didn't help.'

She pointed at the pictures. 'Anything?'

He shrugged and flipped through the now crumpled stills.

'Could be our spare room.' He pointed at a small strip of wallpaper that was visible above the bed's headboard. 'Mum liked wallpapering. She bought a job lot just like that. I always hated it, but it was only used in the spare room. The bedhead's like ours too. So now they'll have enough evidence to make sure I stay in here.'

She pulled out the clip with the buttocks. 'That you?'

He shook his head. 'Don't recognise it either but then in here you learn to not perve on other blokes' arses.'

'Tell me something about the nights you had sessions with Rebecca?'

'Just that. I'd try to work out the math problems she gave me, and at around nine o'clock my dad would turn up with four hot chocolates and end the session. Mum, Dad, Rebecca, and me, would sit around chatting and drinking the stuff, and we'd all be in bed by nine-thirty. Exactly the same routine for weeks and weeks.'

'You said you slept well and never heard any sounds from the spare room that was right next door to yours.'

'That's what I said. That's what it was.'

'Did your mum hear anything?'

'She didn't say.'

'Your dad?'

'He was always full of himself on the morning after Rebecca's sessions and she'd get annoyed when he'd joke about her dreaming of her boyfriend. I assumed he meant the bloke who kept parking outside.'

'DCI Clitheroe?'

Tom shrugged.

'How well did your dad know Clitheroe?'

'I didn't think he did until the trial, then they seemed to be almost like old buddies.'

'You know DCI Clitheroe was caught up in a drug importing ring?'

'I heard something. Didn't help Rebecca, did it?'

She flipped the pic with the watch. 'Recognise that?'

'It's like my dad's but that isn't his hand.'

Angela collected all the photographs and slipped them back into her file. 'You've done well, Tom. Thank you for your help.'

He nodded and stood to leave, in the company of one of the guards.

As soon as she left the prison, she called Jim on his burner. There was no answer, so she sent a text:

Need to speak urgently!!!

She looked at her watch it was mid-afternoon, and they were running out of time. Instead of heading home she made her way to James' house, to be greeted by a tearful Stacey.

'He's getting nowhere, and his boss has pulled him off the search. Someone else is looking for my kids and no one is talking to me.'

'Who is that?'

'His ex fucking girlfriend. Why would she care?'

'Name?'

'DS Crawford.' She handed Angela the card Jenny had given her.

Angela rang the mobile number on the card and a voice answered, 'Crawford.'

'DS Jenny Crawford?'

'What can I do for you?'

'My name is Angela Carter…'

'I'm quite busy, Ms Carter, may I call you back.'

'I'm Jim Carter's sister…' She heard an anguished sigh at the other end.

'We're doing all we can, Ms Carter, and this is taking me away from another investigation. I'll call…'

'Don't hang up I have information that might be important.' The frustrated huff at the other end was irritating.

'What information?'

'Are you at work?'

'Yes.'

'I'll be there in five.'

***

James Carter felt his teeth grinding, as he waited for the prison doors to open and spew out the day's discharge of ex-cons. He was waiting for one in particular. An ex-DCI who was once his boss. His intention was to take him to the office for questioning about his current case, and he'd rather be sticking pins in his eyes, but he knew Jenny would be doing her best with the search for his kids. He looked at his watch, time was getting away from him and he also knew the text was from someone who had zero conscience.

Another half hour passed with no Clitheroe. He called his contact in the prison.

'There's been a slight problem, Jim. Mr Clitheroe found himself at the wrong end of a shiv, just before the evening meal yesterday.'

'Is he okay?'

'Well, he certainly won't be any more trouble once they screw his coffin lid down.'

'Shit! Dead?'

'Dead as.'

'Who did it?'

The voice laughed.

'Great.'

'Sorry, chum I wasn't there.'

James texted Jenny Crawford.

Have you heard the news?

That Slippery's shuffled of this mortal coil? It's all around the office. I've had Angela on the phone. She's found something rather interesting. She's with me now.

I'm on my way.

Your sister's here. Go home to Stacey, sweet cheeks. 💋 🖤

James rolled his eyes. The last thing he needed was to be the filling in a feminist sandwich, but he needed the firsthand information, and he wouldn't be getting that at home.

***

While they waited for James to arrive, one of Jennifer's staff knocked on the door of the meeting room. She popped her head around and said, 'We think we have a suspect.'

DS Crawford said, 'Show me what you've got.'

'It's a typical security camera shot, fuzzy at best, but clear enough to show a car being driven by a woman we know as Lorraine Partridge.'

'Lorraine Partridge. Are they Jim's kids in the back?'

'We think one is. We've put out a call and there's a car heading to the airport with some better pics of Partridge. The AFP have been alerted and they say there's a good chance of stopping her, but only if she tries to get through passport control.'

'The school said she was heading overseas but that could mean anything. We need to find that car and Lorraine Partridge.'

The officer dropped a sheet on the desk. 'Her current address. Someone's on the way right now.'

Angela felt her heart quickening. 'Think we'll get lucky?'

'Who knows? The airport might be a ruse. She could be anywhere, and so could Jim's kids.'

Angela glanced down at her watch. 'The time stamp says it's six hours since they were taken.'

'Yeah, it's a long time for the kidnappers and the blink of an eye for us.'

The door to the meeting room flew open and James entered. 'They said you have something?'

'All we have is the car on video from six hours ago. Everyone is looking for it and so far, no one of interest has left the country. Go home Jim.'

He looked down at the still of the car. 'Lorraine fucking Partridge?'

Jenny covered it. 'Go home, you idiot, Stacey will be frantic.'

She was too late covering the still, James had snapped a pic of the car using his phone. He turned around and marched forcefully out of the room.

Chapter 16

The day was shaping up as a disaster in more ways than one. James Carter had lost his opportunity to interview Clitheroe, and his kids had been kidnapped by a known criminal. At least he had the details of her vehicle and the approximate direction she was heading in. As he was about to drive from the station yard, he saw his sister waving furiously. He pulled over, and she grabbed the door handle, before hoisting herself into the car.

'Sorry Jim, they're my family too.'

James said nothing, just gunned the engine and flicked on the flashers.

'There is a whole lot more to this than meets the eye big bro. Tom reckons the screen dumps from the porno videos infer they could have been made in his parents' spare room.'

'His mother's dead, so she'll be of no help.'

'His father is still alive. Maybe after we find the kids, you should be questioning him.'

James shrugged, tooted the siren to move people out of the way and wove through the traffic. 'Right now, I have only one priority, Lorraine Partridge, if she had some connection to Clitheroe, she might be able to answer the questions I wanted to ask him.' He fell silent as the airport turning loomed, then he spoke again. 'Border Force will stop her if she tries to leave the country by normal means.'

'What do you mean by normal?'

'Well, if there is a private aircraft involved it might be more difficult.'

'Private planes are expensive. Big money involved you reckon?'

'Whoever made the porn that featured Rebecca Connolly, might be finding him or herself on the wrong side of a murder charge at minimum. That's if we can't make the associated assault charges stick.'

'You know that someone with a fat butt has featured in one of the videos?'

'Any identifying features?'

'Well, Tom Gregory doesn't recognise it. Apart from that, the video was dated before Rebecca was killed.'

They both fell silent as they approached the airport terminals. There was no sign of the vehicle that James had snapped but he pulled into the drop off area, and left the lights flashing when he clambered out of the car, to run leading Angela through the doors.

Then his shoulders slumped. The terminal was relatively quiet and there were few travellers wandering about. He turned and retraced his steps to his car.

Angela was no longer with him she'd shot up to the second floor and was searching about frantically. Then she noticed the observation windows and peered through. A woman was leading two children to what looked like a small dark blue passenger jet. It had no markings, but she took a photo with her phone and ran back down the stairs to rejoin her brother. She was too late, his car was heading away from the terminal. She texted the photo and said:

Blue private jet—Hurry!

James was already heading in the direction of the private terminals when he received the text and saw the blue aircraft taxiing towards a runway. The airport was well out of his jurisdiction, but he swerved through a gate that was closing, hit the switch for his top lights and gunned his engine.

The jet was moving slowly as it negotiated the other parked planes then began to pick up speed as it closed on the runway.

The illegal entry of a local police car, with flashing lights and sirens blaring did not go unnoticed as it pursued the blue plane. Within a heartbeat, several AFP SUVs arrived and were attempting to cut him off.

James outdrove them and followed the aircraft at high speed until it stopped at the end of the runway in preparation for take-off. He heard its engines increase and steered his vehicle directly in front of it.

The engines slowed to an idle and James' vehicle was surrounded by the AFP. The SUVs discharged their passengers who stood off with their weapons drawn, each with its red dot laser sight wobbling on James Carter's chest, each ready to shoot if ordered.

James stepped out of his car and raised his hands in the air. He knew he'd blown his chances when he was disarmed and cuffed.

'Detective Sergeant James Carter. You should know better.'

'My kids. They are on that plane.' Its engines began to rev up.

'That isn't really an excuse is it chum.'

'You have my phone, check my texts. They are with a woman of interest who may be associated with a freshly deceased human trafficker.'

The leader of the group spoke quietly into his radio. A moment later the aircrafts engines slowed to an idle, the boarding door opened, and a set of steps lowered to the tarmac.

Three of the AFP contingent boarded and soon afterwards a loud voice preceded two muted shots from within the superstructure.

James was helpless. Had Partridge shot his kids?

***

Angela was almost hyperventilating when she saw what was happening on the tarmac and two TV crews had already parked their vehicles near the gate and were setting up to record their scoop for tonight's news.

When she saw the men board the plane and heard the shots ring out, she had her answer. She could only hope that Oliver was safe in his classroom and far away from here. Then she saw an ambulance arrive and medics rushed up the aircraft's steps.

She could feel her heart pounding when she noticed James, in cuffs, sitting on the ground with his back against a black SUV and an AFP officer standing over him with an assault rifle aimed at his head. She called Jenny Crawford and left a message on her voice mail.

Angela was beginning to wish that she'd left well alone, instead of opening a huge can of worms that might ruin several lives. She looked up and saw two stretchers leaving the plane. Both occupants appeared to be adult, and she breathed a sigh of relief. *At least it's not the kids.*

A few moments later a woman, dressed as cabin crew, led a number of children down the steps to a waiting AFP vehicle. Their heads were covered, and Angela couldn't recognise them.

Jim looked up and saw the same. She heard him say, 'Shit!'

She heard the leader's radio squawk, and he detailed two more of his team to board the plane. He then turned to James and said, 'Big mistake Detective Sergeant. A couple of those kids were being escorted by their aunt to be with their father in France. She's now dead and so is one of mine.'

'Who shot who?'

'The aunt was armed. The manifest was in order. Her papers were all in order as were those of the kids. I think you'll be having some questions to answer matey.'

***

Angela tried to call Jim's burner. She had no luck. It was off. She found a payphone and called his office. Jenny Crawford was unavailable. She escalated her call to the Senior officer.

DI Mulligan said, 'It's what happens when you break all the rules. Sorry, I'll see what I can do but…' The line went dead.

Angela felt the same. All she'd tried to do was help a young bloke prove his innocence, and she'd wrecked her brother's family in the process. She hailed a taxi and directed the driver to the school to collect Oliver. *At least he'll be okay tonight.*

'You look like you've had a bit of bad luck, lady,' the taxi driver said,

She didn't answer as she dabbed the tears from her eyes.

'Just heard there was a shooting on a private jet. Fed cop killed and a woman. Several little kids are now going into care. That should make their lives good. No?'

'You know a lot for a taxi driver.'

He pulled out an earpiece and said, 'Cop network.'

Chapter 17

It seemed everyone knew what was happening except for her. The taxi stopped at the school gates and Angela asked the driver to wait while she collected her son. It was early afternoon, so she'd need an excuse. While she walked through the gates she pondered her plan, and glanced around as her taxi drove off and another replaced it. Nothing was making sense. *Taxi drivers don't do that.*

The school doors closed behind her, and she made her way to the head teacher's office. 'He has a medical appointment I'm sorry I clean forgot.'

'Hmmm. I'll get my secretary to collect him for you. A bit of notice in future, would be good, Mrs Carter.'

Angela didn't bother to correct the salutation she wasn't in the mood for crass explanations that had nothing to do with anyone but her.

After a few minutes Oliver appeared his face creased with puzzlement.

'Sorry, Oliver, I forgot.'

He shrugged.

Angela pulled a wad of notes from her bag and handed them to the head. 'Would you please pay the taxi for me I'll leave by the rear entrance. This should more than cover his fare from the airport along with a healthy tip.' She tried to downplay her anxiousness with a bright smile. 'Come on, Oliver.' She glanced down at her phone to see if there were any messages. There were none. It was as though everything before now had never happened.

'Where's our car, mum?'

'At the police station,' she lied. 'I had to go there earlier to check on a client.'

'Oh.' He didn't sound entirely convinced.

***

James Carter knew he was likely to be in the deepest of the deep crap and it didn't help that he still hadn't found his kids. He was now alone in an AFP interview room, awaiting a grilling over today's escapade. He hoped Angela was okay and felt guilty about leaving her in the lurch without transport.

The door opened and two men in civilian clothes took seats opposite him.

The first spoke, 'My name is Walker, Superintendent Walker Australian Federal Police. What were you playing at DS Carter? You don't have any jurisdiction on federal property, and you certainly don't have the right to prevent aircraft from taking off with legitimate passengers. Now one of my men is dead, another is wounded and a passenger on the plane was also shot.'

'Sounds like you were having fun, superintendent.'

'Don't get funny with me chummy. You are in it up to your neck, so I suggest you tell us in your own words what your intentions were.'

'Simple. About seven hours ago, my kids were taken from their school by a person with a known record. I received a text to say I would be receiving body parts by post, if I didn't shut down an investigation that isn't officially underway. I tracked that person to the airport. The rest you know.'

'You have a name for this person "with a known record"?'

'I know her as Lorraine Partridge. She is wanted in connection with a human trafficking organisation, which sort of makes sense, when you realise, she was able to con my kids' school into handing them over. I saw her board that aircraft with two children of similar ages to my kids.'

'The names of your children?'

'Jack and Andria Carter.'

'Ages?'

'Jack's nine, Andria's nearly eight.'

'These are some of the passports we confiscated.'

James took the documents from Walker and opened each in turn. None had photographs that resembled his children. He shook his head in disappointment. 'General ages are right but none of passport photos are of my kids.'

One of the men waiting, behind Walker, said. 'There were several more children on the plane.' He held up another bundle of Australian passports.

'May I?' James said.

The man handed them to him.

James flipped through the pages of each. Stopped and put one on the desk. 'Jack. Although it's not his name on the photo page.' He continued until he had checked all of them. 'No sign of Andria. She must be going a different way.'

Walker turned to his assistant, 'Get this kid and bring him here. Try not to scare the shit out of him.'

The man left.

'Well, Sgt Carter. Let's hope this child is yours. Have you any idea where they were taking them?'

James shook his head. 'I wasn't privy to that information. If they have been deliberately separated, I need to be looking for my daughter...'

The man who left earlier returned with a boy. As soon as the boy saw James his face froze.

'Do you know this man?'

'Is he in trouble?'

'Depends.'

'Where is Andria, Dad?'

'I don't know, Jack, did they say where they were taking you?'

Jack shook his head. 'Will she be okay, Dad?'

'I don't know mate, but I'll find her I promise.' He looked across at the Superintendent, his eyebrows raised.

'This trafficking mob you are after, are they the ones who have threatened your kids.'

'I wish. Fact is, I have no idea who kidnapped them and made the threat of posted body parts, but I agree there must be a connection, given what we have all discovered today.'

'What's the investigation, they've asked you to shut down?'

'Like I said, there isn't an official investigation. My sister defended a murderer nine years ago. She still believes he is innocent, and she asked me to do a bit of background checking. Next thing I know, my kids are taken, threatened, and here we are.'

Walker turned to look at his team. 'Anyone got any objections.'

There was a general negative rumble from the group.

'Okay, DS Carter you're free to go, take your son home to his mother. Then pull your head in and leave the rest to us.'

'No fucking way, I found my son. I will now find my daughter.'

'Suit yourself but if we cross swords again, you might find yourself on the losing end. Your choice DS Carter.'

James held his hand out. 'Keys to my car, please.'

One of Walker's men removed an evidence bag from a carton. He handed the bag to Walker.

James took it from Walker and ripped it open. 'Thank you for your hospitality,' he quipped, as he left the room holding Jack's hand.

When they were in the car Jack said, 'I didn't say anything, Dad. That woman, the one who got shot, said something about Andria going for a train ride with the rest of the girls.'

'Did she say where?'

He shook his head. 'Will Andria be okay, Dad?' his eyes were wet, and he was close to losing his cool.

'Don't worry, I'll find her, son.' James was already thinking about train services. There weren't that many out of WA, and none of them needed passports.

He dropped Jack to his mother and, after she calmed down, said, 'I'll be out and about for a while. Don't try to call me, I'll call you as soon as I know what's going on.' He gave her a hug then did the same to Jack. 'Look after your mum for me, okay?'

Jack nodded.

'If you can remember anything more about today. Tell your mum. Okay?'

Jack nodded.

He turned to Stacey. 'Keep the door locked. My service pistol is in the bedside cabinet. It's fully loaded but I hope you won't need it.'

Stacey's eyes filled with tears. She grabbed him tightly. 'Find her, Jim.'

He pushed her away gently, and pulled the door shut behind him.

Chapter 18

As he walked to his car, he texted Angela:

I have Jack. Andria is still missing.

Meet me at the East Perth Terminal, West Parade side. I'm heading there now.

A few seconds later his phone vibrated:

♥ 👍 I'm on my way.

Angela was waiting for him when he arrived, and waved as his car entered the car park. 'I had no idea this would happen Jim,' she said as they met.

'No one could have predicted it, Ange, but Jack said that the woman who took them said Andria would be taking a train ride.'

'Did she say where?'

'No, and she'll be of no help. She didn't make it through a stand-off with the AFP.'

'These people mean business then?'

'Which is a bit scary when you think about it. I'm thinking someone doesn't want the truth to come out about Tom Gregory's guilt, or otherwise. Where is Oliver?'

Angela nodded to her son who was waiting to the side. 'He's not going anywhere without me for a while.'

'Might make things difficult having a young'un in tow.'

'There's no one I can leave him with, and I don't trust his school after what happened to you.'

James nodded. 'He can stay with Stacey and Jack. We'll take him there when we've checked out this place.' James launched himself from his car and grabbed Oliver's hand. 'You'll be staying with us for a few days matey.' He opened his door, put him in the back and said, 'Keep your eyes peeled, mate. If you see anything or anyone odd, bang on the horn.'

Oliver looked smug, as if this was a real adventure and he was going to make every second count.

James led Angela into the station, found some timetables and opened one. 'The next and only train is three-fifteen, The Prospector to Kal. We have about an hour to wait so we should split up and check out any likely passengers arriving.'

'What if they know about the incident at the airport?'

'Then they won't appear, and I'll need a new plan. Jack said something about a train ride and there's no guarantee this is it.'

'Give me your keys. I'm not leaving him alone in the car.'

James shrugged and handed them to her. 'Okay, if I see anything I'll text you.'

Angela hurried away from him and made directly for his car. Oliver was alert his head swinging around looking for anything and everything. As she unlocked the car, she noticed a minibus with dark tinted windows pull into the disabled parking slot. Nothing happened, so she waited and watched. While she waited, she texted James:

> Minibus in disabled parking slot, just arrived, no
> movement as yet.

Got it.

Eventually the door slid open, and a uniformed female disembarked. She was accompanied by a heavily built man who began shepherding small children into a double conga line. The kids, all girls, were all dressed in what looked like school uniforms and their faces seemed dull and pasty.

Perhaps they are not happy about the journey they are heading on. Angela thought. Then she muttered, 'Too bloody easy. It can't be.' She didn't recognise any of the kids. They were of the same age as Andria, but in their uniforms, and in the lines they all looked alike. She watched as they followed the woman into the station concourse, with the man bringing up the rear, and she began to have her doubts.

James had seen them too.

Angela watched as he skirted the entrance and disappeared. As far as she knew he wasn't armed, and she had no idea if the people leading the children might be. *They might even be a genuine school group going away for an exchange.* Then she remembered the day Oliver left for a summer camp, with his school friends. She didn't let him out of her sight until he boarded the train. Along with all the other nervous parents, and she remembered pressing her nose against the window to see his excited face smiling back. It wasn't until the rail car was about to move that she stepped back and dabbed at the tears. Angela wasn't alone that day other parents were just the same. It was his first trip away from her, and she'd felt empty.

Her reverie was burst by the sounds of someone shouting. She signalled Oliver to duck and wait until she returned.

***

James Carter followed the group discreetly. He couldn't tell if his daughter was among them. If she was, he would need to tread carefully. The kidnappers had already threatened to cut off body parts, so, if this group *was* them…

The woman led the children to the Booking Centre where they waited outside until she had arranged whatever they might need. A few minutes later she reappeared clutching a wad of tickets.

The train would be leaving in thirty minutes, so he needed to act quickly. He watched as they entered the station and headed for the platform, then he approached the booking clerk holding out his police ID. 'Those tickets you issued. Where are they for?'

The clerk looked at her screen and began tapping on her keyboard.

'Can't you remember? It was only a couple of minutes ago.'

'Sorry. All the way. Kalgoorlie.' She shrugged.

James called his boss. 'I think I might've found my daughter.'

'Where?'

'Possibly with a group of kids about to board the Prospector for Kalgoorlie.'

'Backup?'

'Might help, there's a male and a female. I have no idea if they are armed.'

'Have you identified your daughter?'

'Not yet. I haven't been able to get close enough without raising suspicion… Shit!' He saw Angela approaching the woman.

She smiled and said, 'What beautifully behaved children.'

The woman smiled back but said nothing.

'Would you mind if I took a photo? My friend is a schoolteacher, and she tells me horror stories.'

The woman scowled, nudged her aside, and the man moved in between as they escorted the kids to the waiting train.

The body language was enough to further fire Jim's suspicions, and he began to walk as quickly as he could without drawing attention to himself.

Angela hadn't moved since she was nudged aside. He saw her looking about until she noticed him. She gave a slight shrug and shook her head.

James heard a siren approaching it might or might not be the backup, but he knew if the people with the kids were doubtful, something bad could easily happen. He decided to approach the group as if he was simply curious. Maybe something would come of it. Maybe not.

'G'day, Madam. DS Carter.' He flashed his ID then pulled a photo from his jacket. 'I wonder if you might have seen this little girl around the station. She's gone missing and we're asking everyone.'

The woman spoke in a thick accent that James could not identify. 'No. I have seen no one who looks like this.' As she turned away and looked over his shoulder, her face softened with a look of relief.

It seemed that someone else had just boarded the train at its rear.

The woman reached into the briefcase, she was carrying, and exposed a small pistol. The man drew a larger weapon and there was nothing James could do but raise his hands.

The siren grew louder. Then it stopped.

Angela had watched with horror and her mind was in a whirl as the events unravelled before her eyes. *This is not my speciality.* She boarded the train and took a seat while the man and woman ushered the children aboard.

She felt the slight jerk as the carriage moved. *Kalgoorlie here I come.*

She nodded to James as she passed him standing on the platform with several of his colleagues, who had just arrived. *What a pointless exercise*, she thought. The police can simply board the train at the next stop and arrest them. Then she noticed the kids were all seated in a full rail car, and any shooting would be a disaster.

She texted James:

No sign of Andria in this group.

The moment she sent the text, she saw another woman leading Andria down the train towards her. She was about to send James another text when the large male grabbed her phone and crushed it under his foot.

'Tebe eto ne ponadobitsya.'

She had no idea what he had muttered, but it sounded Russian, and she had a good idea of what he meant.

Chapter 19

No one in the carriage seemed to have noticed what had happened. They were all engrossed with their phones, tablets and regular reading material. Now she'd been earmarked, and it would be almost impossible to act without drawing further attention.

The next stop would be Midland. She could see the police moving from the platform, with James in the lead, and without a phone, there was nothing she could do to alert him. The guardians were armed, that much she knew, and she knew that Andria was now in the same group. She could see her sitting, droopy eyed and blank faced, next to the woman who'd boarded with her. Not just Andria, all the children seemed to be away with the fairies. *They must be drugged or something.*

The man's eyes flickered on to her and back to the front. She was being watched, and he was letting her know that a wrongly interpreted move might have serious consequences. Then she remembered the burner James had given her it was at the bottom of her handbag.

Angela rummaged around and found it then she pulled out a tissue and faked a sneeze.

The man looked up and turned to face her. She faked another sneeze. He smirked and then seemed to forget she was there.

Angela tapped on the SMS icon and texted the number James had given her:

> Andria on train, kids appear drugged and there is no
> indication of where they are taking them.

She had no idea if he'd receive the message and she had to trust that he'd use his discretion.

When the train slowed for Midland station, Angela could see no one. She could only hope that her message had arrived and prepared herself for whatever might happen. She noticed a few potential passengers waiting on the platform next to their luggage when her burner buzzed with a text.

She sneezed again and reached into her handbag. He'd got the message. A wave of relief passed over her, but anything might happen when the train eventually halted.

It slowed down, its brakes squealing tormentedly until it stopped moving to allow those waiting to board. None entered her rail car, which was a relief, but she could see them shuffling further down the train. There was no sign of any police and she felt helpless.

The train clunked into motion again and she saw a ticket inspector slowly making his way down the aisle towards her car. She knew the kids, and those controlling them, had tickets, but *she* didn't. Then she saw him. A tall man in a suit was walking through the rail cars in the direction of the inspector.

The man stopped him and led him back the way he had come. *What is going on?* she thought.

The pair disappeared, and all was quiet except for the rumble of the wheels on the tracks.

Angela breathed and the lung full of air, she was holding in, came out as a sigh. *Now what?* The children all seemed to have fallen asleep as had the big man of the group. She tried not to stare at the two women who were excessively alert. Their eyes darted back and forth, and the one who had arrived with Andria had shaking hands.

The woman stood and woke each of the children from their sleep. She also thumped the man's shoulder.

He woke up with a grunt and as she turned around to retake her seat, he took a long swig from a hip flask.

Probably Vodka, Angela thought. Par for the course no doubt. Angela had no fighting or basic self-defence skills, and she knew, drunk or sober, he would be a major challenge.

The tall man reappeared and caught her eye.

Why me, she thought, shaking her head slightly. Then she felt the burner vibrate. She sneezed again and reached into her handbag. A message from Jim:

> The tall man is Raymond. He's aware of the situation.
> He knows they are armed and there will shortly be a
> stop while the train is split. A broadcast will be made to
> advise passengers that all is well.
>
> Don't worry. We have it in hand.

Angela turned her head towards the big man. His eyes were drooping again and this time she saw the butt of an automatic pistol, with its barrel jammed down the side of his pants. *Highly professional,* she thought, *not.*

She tapped a reply to James:

> One large male full of vodka. He is armed and sleepy.
> Two women both appear high on something, and they
> are on full alert. The kids all appear drugged. If shooting
> starts?'

Angela heard a linking door slide open behind her and saw James.

He was wearing a waiter's jacket, and he winked, more a flutter of his eyelid than anything as he made his way down the carriage and handed a small card to each of the passengers, with the exception of the group.

One of the group's women held her hand out for a card and she heard him speak softly.

'Sorry, Ma'am. Special for our frequent travellers. It's for a free coffee in the buffet car.' The woman sneered and ignored him.

One by one the carded passengers stood and headed down the carriage in the direction of the buffet leaving the group, and Angela, as the only remaining passengers.

She muttered, 'Thanks a million bro,' as she heard the brakes sing when the train began to slow again.

A voice over the PA system said, 'We apologise for this short interruption to your journey. There has been a minor disruption on the line ahead and for your safety we will be diverting down a branch line to skirt this damage. You may notice the train stop and start and move forwards and backwards whilst this occurs. Thank you for your patience.' The two women exchanged glances and glared at Angela.

She shrugged as though it was completely normal practice. 'Happens all the time on this line,' she said.

The man felt the movement too and looked up from his sleep. He turned towards Angela who shrugged again as he reached for his hip flask and clattered it over his pistol butt as he lifted it to his lips.

One of the women called to him, 'Enough, Serge.'

'Da!' he said and took a long swig.

The clanking and the moving back and forth of the railcar encouraged the man to stand and peer out of the windows. There was nothing to see but bush and a second run of lines parallel to the ones they were on. The train jerked, and he flopped back into his seat.

'Some damage on the line Serge. They say it won't take long.'

'Da!' he took another swig, reached into the small bag he'd boarded with and removed a litre bottle of Vodka that he spilled over his hands as, he refilled his flask. He then muttered something that sounded like. 'trakhat tebya,' before slumping into a stupor.

Maybe he won't be such a problem, Angela thought.

A few minutes later the shunting seemed to have finished and the tall man in the suit, accompanied by the ticketing inspector, clambered up from the tracks.

'We apologise ladies and gentlemen. This car has received some minor damage in the shift. We will assist you to leave in an orderly fashion and transfer you to another car.'

He walked through the car to the opposite end and opened its door. 'This way please.'

The drunk was oblivious to the goings on, and remained snoring peacefully while the women led the children to a ramp that had been prepared.

The ticket inspector followed the kids and the moment the two women were outside the train, he slammed the door shut.

Angela held her breath when she heard the first shot and gasped when it was followed by a warning. The man opposite grunted and opened his eyes. As he reached for the pistol in his waist band, he stopped as James pointed the business end of a Glock against his head.

James then reached down, removed the weapon, and handed it back to a man in black who was holding an AR15.

'Keep an eye on him, he probably has a backup. If he can remember where he put it. On your feet, matey.'

The man lumbered shakily to a standing position. From then it was all systems go. He swung around and struck James with a right hook that almost knocked him off his feet. The man with the AR stopped him from falling and put a round in the drunk's chest.

'Trakhat tebya,' he shouted and kicked out, striking the man in black, square in the testicles.

James had recovered and jammed his Glock against the drunk's throat. 'Settle down, Sunshine.'

The man suddenly slumped down to half an arse on the seat then collapsed to the deck where James cuffed him.

Chapter 20

Through the window, Angela could see the body of one of the women being photographed by a police officer. There was no movement and Angela assumed she was dead. She left via the same entrance as the women and looked around. Her body was shaking from its adrenalin infusion, and then she saw Andria sitting quietly, aside from the other children.

'Andria?' she said.

There was no reply, she seemed to be stoned out of her mind, as were the others, judging by their blank expressions.

'Shit!' She grabbed the sleeve of a medic and said, 'These kids have been drugged with something. They need to be hospitalised.'

The man nodded and pointed to the fleet of ambulances that had begun arriving on the service road. 'Don't worry, they'll be well looked after.'

Angela sat on the ground next to her niece, put her arm around her and hugged her tightly but received no response.

***

Having disarmed and cuffed the drunk, James dragged the man's bleeding body to the door furthest from the kids and yelled for assistance.

As paramedics lifted him onto a stretcher, he began rambling in a Russian like, language. Most of what he said seemed to be profanities and threats against those who had brought him down.

The other woman, the one Angela had spoken to at the station was standing erect, head held high with her wrists in plastic ties and snarling, what sounded like more Russian obscenities, at her guardians.

It was over. James had his son and his daughter back, almost unscathed. Angela was safe and the only passengers injured were a woman and her drunk companion. 'What happens next,' he muttered.

He headed back into the railcar and caught the eye of Angela.

'All good?' she said.

He nodded. 'Andria will need to be seen by the doc. We think all the kids have been given a strong narcotic that makes them compliant. No one's talking so it might not be quick. I've organised transport to take you home.'

'I think I'd like to stay with your daughter, Jim. A familiar face might be just what she needs right now, and you're obviously too busy.'

James rolled his eyes. 'There's more to this than you can see. It's right on the edge of the trafficking investigation and far too close to walk away from.'

'I see. So, we start looking into Tom Gregory's false imprisonment, and it tips the edge of one of your investigations, so it's dropped.' She could feel her face warming. 'I might remind you, that the reason we are here, is that someone didn't want us to dig deeper into Tom's imprisonment. What is so important about Tom's case, that it fired these people up? Two are dead another is injured, and a child has almost died at the hands of your team. Fuck you, Jim.'

'I'm sorry you feel that way, Ange. Can I at least ask you to call Stacey for me?'

'Shit. You're almost as bad as the A-holes who took Andria.' She gave the little girl a squeeze. 'My phone was smashed by the drunk and all I have is your one-number burner, remember?'

He reached into his pocket and pulled out a smart phone. 'It's yours. I'll get a new one.' His expression switched to pleading.

She'd known him long enough to know how he could manipulate people, but she also knew how worried Stacey would be. 'Okay, I'll call her, but I'm staying with Andria. Okay?'

He nodded and dropped to the ground without closing the door.

***

The next thirty minutes zipped by as paramedics loaded zombie-like children into the ambulances. Angela followed Andria into hers and saw a Media crew filming at a distance. She couldn't hear what the reporter was saying, but she had a good idea. She made a call, but Stacey's phone was not answering, then a message bank option asked for details. She said nothing and pressed end. 'If I'm going to speak to your wife, Jim, it won't be via a message bank.'

As the ambulances wove their way from the service road to the highway, she heard radio talk back from the cab. It was faint but clear enough to understand that they would be heading back to Perth. She tried Stacey again. This time she picked up.

'Jim, about bloody time. What's happening? Have you found them? No one is calling and I've been by the phone all day.'

Angela let her finish her rant before speaking. She switched to loud speaking. 'It's Angela Carter, Stacey. Jim is tied up with the police stuff. I'm with Andria now.'

'Can I speak to her?'

The paramedic shook her head.

'I doubt she'd know who you are. The people who took her had five other children with them and they have been subjected to some kind of narcotic. The medics don't know what it is, so all the kids are on their way back to Perth. Hopefully by then they will have learned something.' She heard Stacey gasp. 'How is Oliver?'

'Fine, Oliver's unflappable. He thinks it's just another adventure.'

There was a short pause.

'Can I at least speak to her? Let her know I'm here.'

Angela held the phone to Andria's ear and heard Stacey's voice. Andria's eyes flickered as if in recognition of the sound, but she said nothing.

'Sorry, Stacey, she's as good as out cold. I think we were very lucky to find her before...'

'Can I speak to Jim?'

'I haven't a clue where he might be. You might be able contact him via work.'

'Where are they taking her?'

The paramedic said, 'PCH. At least an hour from Northam and we're twenty minutes from there.'

There was no answer.

'Did you get that?'

The line was dead, and Angela noted that the signal was non-existent. 'Great.'

***

DS Jennifer Crawford listened intently to the voice at the end of the line. It was making little sense. She knew that both of Jim Carter's kids were safe, but the voice was insisting differently. Her intent was to keep the speaker on the line while the comms people sussed out the location. She saw a thumbs up across the room and the man at the end of the thumb walked over and dropped a map on her desk.

'Shit, Mick, that's Jim's address.' She tapped his number on her smartphone and Angela Carter answered.

'Hello.'

'Who am I speaking to?'

'Angela Carter. Jim gave me his phone. Mine got damaged.'

'Where are you?'

'Halfway between Meckering and Perth,' the Paramedic offered.

'Did you get that?' Angela felt lightheaded and sweat began to bead on her forehead. She was trapped in a vehicle that would take longer than an hour to reach Perth. Now her own son was in danger and there was nothing she could do.

'Hello…' Crawford's voice penetrated her fug.

'Hello. Sorry, what you just said…'

'There is no one at Jim's house. I don't know whether that's good or bad.'

'I've not long spoken to Stacey, but she was definitely with both boys, at her home.'

Chapter 21

Stacey Carter was a lot smarter than everyone gave her credit for. As soon as she heard the phone line cut off, she bundled the boys into her car and headed for the nearest servo where she filled the tank and pointed the car towards the east. 'We're going for a drive, boys, hope you don't mind?'

There was no reply. They were both bashing away at their tablets, engrossed in a game that only they could comprehend.

Eventually she turned onto Great Eastern Highway and locked her cruise control onto the speed limit. She'd already lost fifty percent of her points and Jim had been of no help. She tapped his number in her phone. The traffic density had lessened the further out of town she drove, and she saw no evidence of a police presence. When the operator answered she said, 'I can't contact Sgt Carter on his mobile. Would someone pass a message to him… I'm his wife and I have the boys with me. We're heading out to meet them along Great Eastern Highway.' She pressed end.

As she left the township of Mundaring there was even less traffic, but while she maintained her speed to within the limit and felt the slip stream of an open-topped car fly past her in the same direction. It was an eighty limit, and he was travelling well over a ton. The car was familiar. She'd seen it only recently. *Then it was being shown to a couple of the younger mothers at the "fun day"*. She did the wiggle thing with her fingers, in her mind. *Why is Tom Gregory's father in such a hurry?* She shrugged and continued at the speed limit. Stacey was on the lookout for a convoy of ambulances, not a poncy twat in a flash car.

She passed through Sawyers Valley and when the limit increased to 110kh she lifted her speed. It was then that she saw the Z4 again. This time it was on the hard shoulder, and she recognised him, even though his head was turned down and away from her, as though he was studying something on the passenger seat. She ignored him and continued with her more important business.

The Lakes came and went with no sign of any ambos and the boys were still engrossed in their game when, once again, the Z4 drew alongside.

Gregory beamed a smile.

Stacey flicked her hand in an acknowledgement but otherwise ignored him.

Next, he pulled ahead slightly and began to edge into her lane forcing her to move over.

Stacey slowed, Gregory shot ahead, and she remembered his creepy needling of Angela, about his son, at the party. *Now he's trying it on with me.* She pulled over into a parking area at Bakers Hill. 'Anyone want a pie?' The boys were ambivalent. 'Okay.' She called Jim's phone.

***

Angela saw the name and felt her stomach fall through the floor. She answered, 'Stacey? I...'

'I have the boys with me. We're heading your way and guess who is shadowing me?'

'Sorry?'

'George Gregory, in his poncy beamer. He's tried to edge me off the road once.'

'What's up with him?'

'I've no idea. He's a real creepy guy. Maybe he knows something

108

we don't.'

'Where are you?'

'Outside the pie shop.'

'We're almost there now.' She turned to the paramedic. 'Andria's mum is at the Bakers Hill pie shop. Can we stop when we get there?'

She nodded. 'Suppose it can't do any harm,' and signalled to the driver.

***

'About time, Sweet Cheeks.'

'What!'

'I guess you haven't heard. We had a call from our mutual "friend", and I managed to keep him on the line long enough to triangulate his location. He was at your house. We sent a car, but no one was there when they arrived.'

'Shit.'

'I've had a call from your sister. It seems she's in an ambulance with your daughter and they're heading to Perth. Also, Stacey left a message saying she was heading out to meet the ambos.'

'She okay?'

'Your guess is as good as mine, Jim.'

'Can you organise a Russian interpreter? One of the women in the group is dead, and the other is refusing to communicate so I'm bringing her in. Without an interpreter we'll have no hope. The male is incapacitated in one of the ambulances heading in convoy to Perth and he'll be incommunicado for the foreseeable future. I thought the alleged traffickers were being controlled by a local gang. *So why the Russian-speaking mob?*'

'There's plenty of evidence of the Russian mafia indulging in trafficking, Jim, but once they're behind their own country's borders there'll be Buckley's chance of tracking them. The kids on the plane were all boys. All girls on the train, and there's no indication that they are connected, or even if they were heading to the same destination.'

'Can you run a check of missing children, Jen? There were five girls, between five and eight years old. They've all been subjected to some form of narcotic and are on their way to PCH. My daughter made six, and my son is with his mother.'

'I'll get someone on to it.' The line began to beep with an incoming call sound. 'Got another call, buddy, wanna hold while I check it out?'

'Go for it.'

It was Stacey. 'I have your man on the other line, Mrs Carter. Is there a message I can pass to him?'

'Yes. There is. I'm being pestered by a man called George Gregory, in his Beamer. He's even tried to run me off the road once. I'm waiting for the ambulance and my daughter, at the pie shop in Bakers.' A black Z4 turned in and stopped alongside her. 'Shit he's just parked up right next to me.'

Jennifer heard the line go quiet, she switched back to James and said, 'It seems George Gregory is making a nuisance of himself at Bakers hill, Are you able to…'

There was no response.

***

Gregory stepped out of his car and tapped on the window. He finger-waggled an instruction to lower it so they could speak.

Stacey lowered her window a couple of inches. 'What do you want? I'm waiting for my husband.'

'I just wanted to say hello and apologise for cutting you up earlier. You look a little frazzled, can I buy you a coffee?'

Stacey almost gagged on his treacle-like smarm. 'No thanks. Apology accepted. Bye-bye.' She closed her window and continued to ignore him.

He tapped again and waggled his finger again.

Stacey was about to press her down button when she saw an ambulance turn into the car park. Instead, she gave him the bird before stepping out of her car, slamming the door and pressing her remote to lock it. She wasn't sure whether he'd deliberately attempted to block her way, but she shoved him aside anyway, and waved to the ambulance.

It stopped, its rear door opened, and Angela Carter stepped down. 'She's in the back. Do you want to continue on with her, to the Hospital?'

Stacey didn't answer, she simply clambered up the steps and rushed towards her daughter.

'I'll take that as a yes then.' Angela called, before she noticed Gregory sitting on the boot of his low-slung vehicle and leering at her. She saw the boys in the back of Stacey's car and followed her into the back of the ambulance. 'What's he doing here?' she thumbed over her shoulder.

Stacey shrugged. She was more interested in her daughter than Gregory.

'If you give me your keys, I'll take them home.'

Stacey didn't reply.

The driver said, 'We need to keep moving, miss.'

Stacey handed her keys to Angela with an apologetic expression. There was no need for words, but Angela smiled sympathetically and said, 'Well, if you need anything, let me know. I have Jim's phone, mine was smashed.' She held up the device. 'Okay?'

Stacey nodded through tired and teary eyes.

Chapter 22

It wasn't until Angela Carter slumped into the driving seat of Stacey's car that she realised the mistake she'd made. Angela had barely driven a car with a manual gearbox and the gearstick was almost a mystery to her. The three pedals only added to the confusion.

Jack attempted to come to the rescue. 'I can drive, Aunty. I know what to do.'

Gregory tapped on the window. 'Have we a problem?'

'No. *I* do not,' she snapped, knowing full well she'd be going nowhere without a driving lesson or two.

Jack Carter clambered between the seats, into the front passenger seat and pointed down at the pedals. 'Clutch-Brake-Accelerator. It's not that hard, Aunty.'

'Okay, smarty pants. What do you suggest?'

He pointed at the gear lever knob. 'It's in neutral, see?' he grinned impishly. 'So, it's safe to start.'

Angela inserted the key and started the engine. 'Got it.' She could almost feel Gregory's breath on her cheek, 'Now what?'

Stacey had parked the car parallel to the highway so it could easily move forward or backwards into clear space.

'Press your foot down on the clutch pedal.'

Angela did.

'Now put the car in first gear.' Jack covered her hand with his and moved the gear lever. He tapped the hand brake. 'As you take your foot of the clutch pedal, press gently down on the accelerator and let the handbrake off.'

Angela shook her head. 'Why doesn't everyone drive automatics?' Luckily, she had actually driven a manual, but that was long before she qualified as a driver of an automatic. She racked her brains for the technique she'd learned all those years ago and decided to give it a go.

The car lurched forwards, and she slammed her foot on the brake. Its tyres screeched, and the boys laughed.

'It's not that funny.'

Gregory tapped on the window, 'Would you like me to drive you all home?'

Angela concentrated hard and recalled the actions she needed that would soon become muscle memory, *God willing*, by the time she reached her home. The car moved forward, and she lined up to cross the highway. There was no traffic.

'Go, Aunty!' Jack yelled, and the car lurched forwards, tyres squealing as it stabilised into the right direction.

'Probably a good idea to change up, Aunty.'

Angela scowled and when she managed to perform the manoeuvre without crashing the gears or the car, she bared her teeth into a grin. 'Thankfully there aren't many stops along the way, Jack.'

'You'll be right Aunty. Your mum's a great driver Oli.'

'Yeah right.'

The mood had changed from one of fear into one of relative comfort and when she saw the Z4 closing in the rear view. She decided to ignore it.

***

James Carter called in to the station again. 'I'm bringing in a suspect for questioning and I'll need that Russian interpreter, I think that might be the language. It sounds like it.'

'No worries, sarge I'll pass the message on. Thought I'd better let you know. We have had a report of your wife's vehicle being driven erratically on Great Eastern Highway, the other side of Sawyers Valley. Hope everything is alright.'

'How long?'

'Couple of minutes.'

'I'm not far behind I'll check it out.' He flicked the top light switch, increased his speed and it wasn't long before he saw Stacey's car. The driver seemed reasonably competent, and the reported erratic driving had passed. He also saw the Z4 too closely tailgating her car. He flicked on the flashers and tooted the siren.

The Z4 pulled out to overtake and gunned his engine.

James reported the incident on the radio and flashed his wife to pull over. The woman in the back of his was cuffed and going nowhere so he felt safe to exit. He stepped out and walked to his wife's car.

Angela lowered the window and thumbed towards the back seat. 'Where's Stacey?'

'She's accompanying Andria to the Perth Childrens Hospital.'

He looked back towards his car. The front passenger door was open, and his suspect was no longer there. 'Shit! See you later, sis.' He ran back to his car, confirmed she'd left the scene and immediately called in her disappearance on the radio.

Today was looking like a succession of disasters and he knew there would be hours of paperwork required to explain his failure to secure a prisoner, who was now at large, somewhere in the region of Sawyers Valley.

James retraced his steps to his wife's car and Angela lowered the window. 'Thanks, sis. Sorry I was a bit abrupt.'

'Can I take the boys home now, officer?' She tried to conceal her smile.

'I wish it were so funny, Ange, but I've just lost a key witness in the kidnapping.'

'Stacey's in an ambulance, heading to PCH. Your wife and daughter probably need you more than the cops right now.'

James nodded. 'Drive carefully, Ange,' he said knowing he had no choice but to hang around in the hope that the woman would show herself. He watched as his sister cleared the township before returning to his car to await his back up.

***

He heard the sirens before he saw the squadron of police vehicles in the distance. The one person he didn't expect was a Superintendent, who alighted and approached him.

'You've done us proud Detective Sergeant so proud, in fact, you are suspended until further notice.'

James' jaw slackened. 'Suspended? Why?'

'I have no intention of discussing this with you on the roadside, but you may avail yourself of the vehicle while we find your missing prisoner. Meanwhile…' He held out his hand.

James handed him his ID.

'Service weapon?'

'I'm unarmed.' He walked up the road a short way, turned, and saw the others fanning out to begin a search. The Z4 appeared from a side road, and he could see there were two people in the car.

James ran back to the group and advised that the prisoner he had lost was now in a BMW Z4, heading towards the city.

The superintendent stared at him as though he'd crawled from under stone. 'Go home Mr Carter. You're not required here.'

James returned to his car and followed his instructions, at least until he was out of sight of the task force, then he turned on his flashers and gunned his engine.

There was no sign of the Z4, but he knew who owned it and he made his way towards the last known home of George Gregory.

***

'He must be in a hurry,' Angela said to the boys, as the police vehicle shot past her. To her it was just another cop in a hurry, and she hadn't noticed it was her brother at the wheel.

She drove to her home and commanded the boys to get themselves into the shower while she ordered a takeaway. She heard them grumbling that they weren't dirty, but they were hungry, and it was now late in the day. The poor kids had not had as much as a snack since morning.

When they were cleaned up and fed, Jack squeezed into a pair of Oliver's pyjamas that were probably a size too small. He said, 'That was my dad in the cop car that overtook us.'

'I didn't notice,' Angela said. 'Let's hope he manages to catch the people who took you and your sister, Jack.'

'He will, Aunty. My dad's the best.'

Angela felt her face colour and a moistness well in her eyes. There is one boy, and another called Tom who will never be able to say that about their father, she thought.

Chapter 23

The thought rattled around in her head long after the boys were in bed. Angela often pondered being a single mum and all the things she needed to be proxy for. Her ex had shown no interest in Oliver. And Tom was disowned by his father the moment he became a suspect in Rebecca Connolly's murder. *How could a dad do that?*

It seemed that since his wife had passed, George Gregory had become a notorious creep, drawn to anyone of the female gender below the age of fifty, though his preference seemed to lean towards teenagers. Then her mind began to work on the events of the last few days. The fancy sports car and his trying to run Stacey off the road. Then him tailgating her until Jim appeared on the scene when he just took off at speed without any reaction from a police officer. *Is he protected? Am I missing something here?* she thought.

The boys were safe and in Oliver's bed, Stacey was with her daughter and Angela felt a head aching fatigue from the events of the day. She looked at her watch, *ten PM, and time for bed.'*

***

The girls were all admitted by the PCH ED and tested for the narcotic agent that had kept them in such a state of compliance. None of them could give their names or had any memory of their homes or of their parents. Not even Andria who had been with her mother for most of the trip home. She'd simply slept or stared blankly ahead.

Stacey was allowed to accompany Andria into the ED and sat next to her while blood tests where processed. As she was the only parent in the room, a doctor eventually approached her.

'Mrs Carter?'

'Yes,' she answered.

'We've tested all the children and can find no trace of any known narcotics.'

'So, where to from here?'

'We will need to keep them under observation until such time as whatever it is works its way through their systems.'

Stacey felt her stomach churn. 'How can this be? What are the long-term effects?' She could feel anger rising and tried to remain calm.

The doctor was as reassuring as he could be, and said, 'We have requested some specialised diagnostic assistance but that might not be available until tomorrow.'

'So, my child must remain a zombie until then?'

'I'm sorry. If it could be sooner, it would be best for everyone. There simply isn't anyone available right now.'

Stacey had heard of parents going ballistic when the medics couldn't instantly fix their precious offspring and she was trying hard not to put herself in that category. She at least knew that Jack was safe and with his Aunty Angela. 'May I stay here with her?'

'Of course.' He pointed to a police officer. 'They assure us there will be around the clock protection while they are here, and we have made a special ward available so they can all be together.'

Stacey nodded. His genuine sincerity had the effect of lowering her blood pressure to the point where she could still operate coherently. 'Thanks.'

A porter arrived to push Andria's cot to the ward and Stacey followed. She'd not seen the other children until now and she gasped when they were wheeled in.

'We will monitor them closely throughout the night and there is a bed for you to rest on.' He pointed to the small divan that had been placed next to Andria's cot. 'If you need anything, please don't hesitate to call one of the nurses.'

She felt her jaws tighten and tried not to grind her teeth. *How could anyone do this to children? Andria is only seven years old.* 'How dare they.'

Whatever the narcotic that had overcome them was, the kids were all exhausted and quickly fell into a deep sleep.

Stacey kissed Andria on her forehead and assured her she would be next to her until she awakened. She then stretched out on the divan and allowed sleep to win over.

***

The home of George Gregory was as he remembered it. He parked outside, walked briskly to the front door, knocked and waited.

A young woman, of around Stacey's age, opened the door. 'I'm not religious and I'm not buying anything on my doorstep.'

James Carter apologised and asked if he could speak to George Gregory.

The woman laughed. 'Who the hell is he?'

'He doesn't live here?'

'Not for the last five years at least. I'm busy are we done?'

He nodded. *Well, it was worth a try.*

James Carter drove the police car to the station, handed over the keys. He collected his private vehicle, drove straight home and into his garage. He closed the door Tand when he walked into his house through the adjoining door, it felt cold and unwelcoming. It was still his home but all the elements that made it that, were missing. Stacey and he had been through a couple of rough patches, *undercover has that effect.* Now he was missing her far more than he could have expected. She *was* his home, and the kids. Well, they were almost the furniture. He found a burner in his bedside cabinet and called his regular phone. There was no answer. He had no idea where his sister would be so she might just be out of range. No matter how well the Telcos marketed their products, there were gaps everywhere. Fifteen minutes later he tried again and heard a sleep confused voice.

'Hello...'

'Ange?'

'Yes.'

'Everything okay?'

'I think so. You woke me.'

'Sorry. Would you look in on Jack for me?'

He heard a grunt and a clattering as though someone was struggling to motivate themselves through the fog of sleep.

'Ange?'

The line had gone dead.

***

DS Crawford put down the receiver and made a note on her case file. Jim Carter's phone was with his sister, but she needed to contact him. The hospital had advised her that kids he had rescued were all suffering from some kind of narcotic induced trance the cause of which could not be identified by the hospital. Her boss had advised her that DS Carter had been suspended until further notice. It was of no help to Jennifer Crawford.

She'd been on shift since early this morning and fatigue was beginning to cloud her judgement. *Time to go home, Jennifer.*

She made her way to the carpark and found her car. Then she had a thought. *Maybe he's gone home.* James didn't live far from the station, and she decided to make a detour and check if he was okay. Her conscience warned her that contacting a suspended officer was the wrong thing to do. It was so unfair and though she knew everything that was once between them had long gone, she'd also felt the heat when he was close by. She shrugged and drove into his vacant driveway.

There was a light on towards the rear, so she gave the door a policeman's knock and immediately wished she hadn't. She saw him backlit from the rear light as he approached the door and felt a shiver of regret as he drew closer.

'Jen. What's happened?'

'Nothing. I'd just heard you were suspended, and the hospital called to say they couldn't identify the narcotic that was affecting the kids.'

James shrugged. 'Stacey's there with Andria, Jack is staying with my sister, and I'm here in limbo.'

'You're okay though?'

He shrugged.

Jennifer sensed the tension that was building up in her friend. She reached out to touch him on the arm and suddenly they were in an unintentional embrace that led to a kiss powered by memories of a long-long-ago time. She pulled away and apologised. 'Sorry Jim I...'

His face had then crumpled, and tears began pouring from his eyes. 'I didn't mean...'

Jennifer Crawford had never seen the man she once loved break down, even in the worst times of their relationship. 'Hey mate. Let's have a cuppa, hey?'

He sobbed as he stood back to allow her in. 'The bastards tried to take my kids...'

'And we'll find them, and they'll go down for a long time.' She followed him into his kitchen, side stepped him and picked up his kettle. 'Sit.'

He plonked down onto a chair with his knees beneath a small rectangular breakfast table.

Jennifer imagined his family sitting around it, having breakfast. She only ever ate breakfast alone, and no one had entered her life since they'd parted.

'You shouldn't be here Jen.'

'I know.' She placed a cup in front of him. It still had the teabag in the hot water.

He smiled. Took a deep shuddering breath and said, 'If Stacey saw that she'd have a fit.' He smiled, squeezed it dry, stood, and dropped it in the small bin before returning to the table.

Jennifer had deliberately sat on the opposite side. Almost, it seemed, as if she was preparing to interview a suspect.

'You got me banged to rights officer.' James said and began to laugh at the irony.

Chapter 24

James was awakened by the light streaming through his bedroom window. He looked over at the tousled pile of dark hair on the pillow next to him and almost said, 'What have you done to your hair, Stace?'

Jennifer turned to face him, and he felt the warmth of her naked body as she moved close, and their lips touched.

Sometime later he looked at his watch on the bedside table. 'Shit!'

Jennifer was no longer there. *Was it just some kind of erotic nightmare?* He immediately knew the answer when he imagined her long black hair scattered across the pillow. 'Christ!' He heard the kettle from the kitchen as it came to the boil.

A few minutes later Stacey pushed open the bedroom door and said, 'They're keeping her in for another day, but they're hoping there will be minimal effects from the narcotic, and they'll keep the samples to have them retested until they find out what it was. I see you had a restless night.'

'You could say that. I've been suspended.'

'What does that mean in real terms?'

'I'm no longer a cop until they decide I'm dinkum again.'

Stacey seemed to sniff the air and said nothing for a few moments, then. 'Will you still be paid?'

James shrugged. 'At least you'll have me around the house and under your feet for a while.'

'What will happen to the other kids?'

He shrugged again. 'Suspension has, sort of, taken me out of the loop.'

'Can you live with that?'

'I'm coming to grips with it.'

'I'm going around to Angela's, to get Jack. Will you be alright on your own?'

'I'll do my best. Then perhaps we should all go into the hospital and reunite our little family.'

***

Jennifer Crawford sat down in front of her computer and pondered her future. Last night had invoked things that she thought she had long since extinguished.

She could have so easily joined him in his bed and reignited the flame, the existence of which she'd struggled to disavow. They'd drunk their tea. They'd chatted for what seemed like hours until he'd calmed down and eventually escorted her to the front door.

'Thanks,' he'd said and leaned in to kiss her cheek. She knew it was only to be a friendly, thank you, kiss and it shouldn't have turned into something more.

When they finally separated, she'd said, 'This is totally out of order, Jim.'

'I know,' he'd said, and they kissed again.

She'd so wanted it to continue, yet she hated herself for allowing it to happen. She opened the word processor on her computer and selected the "Request for Transfer" document. It didn't take as long to complete as that last kiss. Where she'd go from here was anyone's guess, but she knew it needed to be as far away from Jim Carter as she could possibly make it. She finished the form and as she dried the tears from her eyes, she posted it. In her mind she said, *Au revoir, my love, goodbye.*

***

After Stacey left to head for Angela's, James rang his phone again. It was his intention to warn his sister that Stacey was on her way, but his call went directly to the message bank. He tried Jennifer, but she too wasn't answering calls. He called the main line for the station and asked to speak to his senior.

The person on the switch said, 'Sorry, Sarge. He's not taking any calls, but I have a note here that says, particularly from you.'

He'd only been suspended for twenty-four-hours and already he was climbing the walls with frustration. He'd promised Stacey, he would accompany her to the hospital and that meant he was effectively trapped. He went to his study, logged in to his computer and discovered he was barred from the police database. 'Well, Mr Google, it's you or nothing'.

He started with a search for narcotics that might have a similar effect to the one that had been used on the kids. There was nothing showing up in any of the English-speaking sites and as he scrolled through, he discovered a site exclusively written in Cyrillic. It was impossible to make any sense, so he tried a dark web AI site, he'd discovered when he was with the bikies, and found a similar website with an English translation. It made reference to a number of narcotic products found only in the Eastern Bloc. Regardless of the translation all the product names were in Cyrillic. It didn't help, and to make matters worse the standard of the translation used appalling grammar. He persevered and eventually found a product that was recommended for the temporary control of prisoners.

It stated that they would be fully awake, but passive and obedient while under its influence, and an antidote--another Cyrillic word—was required to return them to a normal status.

'Prisoners? That infers adults and there is no mention of it being used on children.' He screen-dumped the information, printed several copies and headed for his car. Before he left, he texted Stacey:

I have a lead on a possible drug. I'll see you at the
hospital.

He waited for a reply, gave up and started the car. 'At least she'll know where I am.'

***

'My office DS Crawford.'

Jennifer followed DI Mulligan as he wove his way through the labyrinth of desks and into the glass partitioned area that functioned as his office. She fully expected a blast for her transfer request.

Instead, he was sickeningly pleasant. 'Well-well, Jenny, my sweet.' He smirked. 'Got just the place for you.' He slid a sheet of paper across his desk. 'That far enough away for you?'

She looked at the name of the police district he was planning to assign her to and rolled her eyes.

'The current Sergeant has called in crook so you can leave tomorrow. It's only temporary of course, but…'

'Warakurna? Where the hell's that?'

He handed her a map, with the station location circled, and a travel document that would see her on a plane to Leonora early tomorrow morning. 'Your onward conveyance will be waiting at the airport.'

'I, sort of, hoped I might have a few days to clear my desk.'

'Maybe you should have thought about that last year, DS Crawford.'

Last year? All she could recall was shoving him away when he drunkenly tried to grope her during a function. She remembered his leering, booze reddened face and knew she should have done something about it at the time, but she'd decided to give him the benefit of the doubt. To progress it then, would have been career ending anyway, and she'd just handed him the opportunity to punish her. 'Thank you, sir. Goodbye.'

'I have every confidence in you DS Crawford. I trust you won't let me down.'

Let you *down, arse-wipe.* Jennifer wove back to her desk with a cardboard box and began filling it with the detritus of a two-year posting. She breathed deeply to control the regrets and emotions that where swirling through her mind and when she'd finished, she simply walked from the room, went straight to her car and dropped the stuff in the boot.

No one spoke. Either they were unaware, or simply didn't care.

Jennifer toyed with the idea of calling on James for a last hurrah. Just as quickly she put that out of her mind and remembered her first assignment as a young constable in a remote outstation. How she grew to love the small group of indigenous friends she made during her stay and suddenly, she felt warm inside. *You can do this and...* She thought of that last kiss with James and her heart finally broke.

'He's all yours Stacey,' she sobbed. 'I'm well and truly out of your hair now.' Jennifer drove to her home, in no mood to pack, but she knew she'd need things that wouldn't be readily available where she was going. *Tonight, will be a long night.*

Chapter 25

He made his way to his daughter's bedside, and a nurse asked him who he was. 'I'm her dad, James Carter.' He reached for his police ID before remembering he no longer had one. 'My wife Stacey was here with her, last night. She said that no one had a clue as to the narcotic used.'

The nurse nodded. 'We're hoping it will simply pass through their systems and they'll be as right as rain in a few days.'

He handed her a copy of the screen dump. 'I found this, but the names are all in Cyrillic and I can't make head nor tail of them other than an antidote is required to normalise behaviour. Somehow, I think this, or something like it, is what the kidnappers used. So waiting for it to wear off might be a long haul.'

'I'll show it to the doctor maybe…'

'I've several copies. Maybe we'll need someone who can understand Cyrillic text.'

The nurse nodded and left the room.

James sat next to his daughter and tried to speak softly in words she might understand. Her eyes were fixed directly ahead, and she made no response. He persevered until he felt a hand on his shoulder. He turned to see Stacey and Jack. 'Nothings working.'

Their embryo conversation was interrupted by a medic. 'Mr Carter?'

'Yes.'

'This document?'

'I found it on the dark web. Whatever they're drugged with, it seems to have a similar effect to what we are experiencing.'

'According to this it says we will need an antidote.'

'Exactly my view.'

'It's a Russian product and would be unlikely to be available here.'

'I guessed that too.'

'And we're not even sure that this is the same thing that was administered to the children.'

'Yup, so what are you going to do?'

'I wish I could answer that question, sir.'

James turned to his wife. 'It's going to be down to me. I have a couple of ideas, but I'll be completely off grid. Will you be alright?'

Stacey nodded. 'I don't know why, Jim, but I've always trusted you… Take care.'

Her words jangled in his mind especially so close after his encounter with Jennifer, but he found his car, started it and had not a single idea where his quest might take him. He called Jennifer's mobile.

There was still no answer, he got the message bank but didn't leave a message. He tried Angela who answered on the phone he had given her.

'Hi Jim, I found a charger that works, and I promise I'll get a new phone soon so you can have yours back.'

'Can I come around there? I need to throw some ideas around with someone.'

'Sure. See you soon.'

***

He parked his shiny Z4 in the spacious treble garage of the home he'd constructed after his wife died suddenly, five years earlier.

Since then, George Gregory had never been short of money, and yet he never seemed to go to work.

This house was built to his specification on a larger than average block in the area known as Peppermint Grove and while he knew his "A list" neighbours had their suspicions. He couldn't hide the fact that he was the father of a young man, in prison for the murder of a schoolteacher. Thankfully, he had long ago made sure that everyone was aware that Tom, his son, was well deserving of the rap.

Apart from that and the occasional late-night visitors, he gave no one any cause to complain, and he was happy to allow the rumour to prevail that he was in foreign currency trading. This also helped explain away the expensive-looking satellite dish discreetly mounted at the rear of his property.

Since Tom's imprisonment, his connections had grown, and his internet business had taken off in a dramatic way. Cash simply gushed into his offshore accounts and lodged were no one could trace their sources. Many of the transactions were in US Dollars and came from eastern European countries but his biggest customer was Russian, and this particular client had provided him with all the specialised tools he needed.

George Gregory looked after himself very well, loved the high-end sports vehicles and had already preordered the replacement for his Z4, a Lamborghini Revuelto which would not even start production until the following year.

George especially loved the late-night visitors who arrived in the nearly opaque windowed limousine parked alongside his Beamer. No one had ever seen any of these visitors leave but that was none of their business. George was now a privileged member of a society who never asked awkward questions of each other.

He flicked a leaf from the fender of the Z4, pushed aside the neat tool rack, pressed the button marked C on a gold plate and entered a small lift that the never-to-be-used-tools conveniently hid.

***

She heard the car roll onto the gravel driveway and told her son to find something to do while she had a private conversation with his uncle James.

Oliver headed straight to the lounge and fired up the TV. He was rather pleased to be home from school at his mum's request, and he was under strict instructions to tell anyone who called, that he had COVID.

Angela embraced James when he entered. Somehow, this had brought them closer than ever. 'How's Stacey?'

'At the hospital with Andria. They're waiting for the drug to wear off.' He handed her a copy of the screen dump. 'According to this an antidote might be required.'

'The name of the drug is written in a Cyrillic font.'

'The people on the train were Russian speakers…'

'Shit. You don't think…?'

'I wish I knew.'

'One of my colleagues speaks Russian. I could ask her.'

'I'm not sure if I want this to go beyond our circle. Those kids were, in my opinion, caught up in trafficking. The boys, probably to an eastern bloc country to be sold as adoptions. The girls… I'll leave that to your imagination.'

'Is that why they were travelling separately?'

'I'm certain of it. That text threat I received, about my kids, was to ostensibly to stop an investigation into the Tom Gregory case. I'm sure it was more of a red herring and to do with delaying it until the kids were out of the country.'

'Are you saying that the person who sent the text knows what I'm doing in that regard?'

'I've no idea, Ange.'

'Do you think George Gregory might know something?'

'Stacey said he tried to run her off the road, although it might just have been poor driving.'

'And he aggressively tailgated me. Remember? Then, when you put your flashers on, he was off like a bride's nighty, and you didn't even follow him.'

'I was more concerned about you and the boys. Jack didn't seem to have been subdued by anything, but all the other kids were, including Andria.'

'Maybe the body parts promised were to come from him?'

'Well, he's safe for now, but I've been suspended so technically I'm no longer a cop. I've told Stacey I'm going off grid for a while. She's been there done that, and she might not like it, but I can't wait for someone else to care about my kids.'

'What can I do?'

'Nothing. Just be my fall back,' he handed her a burner and held up a similar phone. 'I picked these up on the way here. They aren't traceable to you or me and we'll only use SMS for comms. If you get a call, you'll know I'm in big trouble. The number will allow the cops to locate the phone. You'll know what to do when the time comes.'

Can I ask where you'll be going?'

'No, but you can ask your colleague if the Cyrillic for the drug is sold under any other name and also the antidote. If you happen to get a positive answer, pass it on to Stacey. She'll pass it on to the medics who are treating the kids. Make up a story and don't even hint why you are asking.'

'Can I ask a question?'

James nodded.

'Do you think Tom Gregory is somehow involved with this trafficking?'

'I'm thinking, like you, that he is a completely innocent player.'

Chapter 26

The lift descended silently, and its door slid open to reveal a carpeted corridor the likes of which might be found in a cheap hotel. There were four doors on each side, each with a digital locking system that required a six-figure code.

George Gregory did an eany-meany-miny-mo and selected the third door down on the right-hand side. He tapped the code into the lock and pushed open the door.

'Hello my dear,' he said.

The young woman, spread eagled on the bed, did not respond. He removed the drip from the cannula and covered the device with a fold of the sheet. 'Don't worry I'll connect you back to your food supply later. Never were much of a talker were you, Zoe? Still, you will enjoy my penal servitude, won't you?' He smirked at his little pun as he dropped his trousers and slid out of his jocks. 'Sadly, this is the last time you'll have the pleasure of me. One more visitor will soon complete my consignment, and then you'll be off to your new lives.'

George enjoyed the prep as much as anything and as he set the camera and adjusted the lighting, he felt his libido stir. Next, he would adjust her minimal clothing and video himself touching her. Of course, he knew she wouldn't be responsive, but his viewers wouldn't care, especially when he pulled her face towards him and opened her mouth to receive him.

When he finished, he wiped her face and touched up her make up. Then he readjusted her night wear and lay next to her, to await further arousal, and the conclusion of his fantasy.

He wasn't worried about himself being caught on his camera, he'd gain as much pleasure watching himself later, and this section would be edited out before its publication on his popular dark web platform.

When he'd finished with Zoe, he tapped on the wall of the next room. 'Your turn tomorrow, Gina, nighty night, girlies.'

It was still early when George ascended to his apartment and luxuriated in his personally designed shower, before dressing and returning to the garage. Tonight, he would cruise the streets of Perth and select the final element of his consignment. He checked the vial in the glove box. 'Enough for at least three more.'

***

After the relatively short flight to Leonora DS Crawford located the waiting land cruiser and tapped on the window. 'Hey, sleepy head.'

The face of the young constable was familiar, and his grin lit up when his eyes opened. 'Hey, boss. They said we had a good looker comin. They didn't say it was you.'

Jennifer rolled her eyes but couldn't help smiling. She'd known Mickey for years and one of the good things was his ability to handle the press. It meant she wouldn't need to show her face if there was a problem. He was the go-to for journos who'd been handed the poison chalice of an indigenous story, and he'd always be trotted out when there was a need to front a camera. His enigmatic face and calm yet larrikin voice made any story an easy shoot. 'Keep your cool, Mickey, you know you're not my type.'

PC Mickey Krakauer couldn't help himself either, a wide smile was his normal status. 'Hop in boss. We gotta long drive ahead.'

Jennifer hoisted herself into the passenger seat and turned towards her old friend. 'If I'd known I'd be working with you, I wouldn't have felt so bad about this posting. How've you been Mick?'

'Nuttin much, boss, *you* know. Yourself? How's that fella you were knockin round with, Jimmy, wasn't it?'

Jennifer shook her head, 'Nah that ended years ago.'

'Fark, boss, and I thought you two were in it for the long haul.'

Jennifer stiffened her expression. 'From now on its DS Crawford to you, PC Krakauer. Okay?'

Mickey's face crumpled slightly from her remark. He started the engine and headed for the road. 'Sorry DS Crawford.'

'Oh, for fuck's sake Mickey. Why do you think I'm here? Not a word to anyone. You're the only person I've told, and If you hadn't picked me up no one would be any the wiser, capisce!'

His wide grin reappeared. 'My lips are sealed, boss.'

'Much happening?'

'Nah quiet as. Usual drunks, but we've gotta team of wimmin sortin dem out. The old sarge got sick, so she's been taken to the city for treatment. Dunno when she'll be back though.'

'I'd have thought you'd be a sergeant by now.'

'Ha! Maybe one day. That run in with a spector Clitheroe in Hedland, few years back, sorta put the mockers on me makin sarge.'

'Well, he made DCI and got caught with his hands in the trouser pockets of a bikie and ended up in the slammer.'

'Ha!' Mickey's grin widened. 'When does he get out? I'd like to be there for that.'

'Bit academic unless you'd like a drive to attend his funeral. He had bit of a contretemps with a shiv the day before his release…'

'Aw shit. Couldn't have happened to a nicer fella.' Mickey laughed and then fell silent.

Neither spoke again until they hit the dirt road that would start the next part of their journey to the community of Warakurna.

***

'Walking dead?'

'That is the direct translation of those Cyrillic words. they are pronounced khodyachiye mertvetsy, Ms Carter.' Alice Bowman replied.

'What about this one?' Angela handed her a second sheet of paper with the Cyrillic Возвращение к жизни inscription.

'Back to life. It does not to me sound like a drug.'

'Nor me.'

'I am so sorry I can be of no further assistance, but next time I write them, I will ask my relatives if they have heard of such things.'

'Thank you so much, Alice, you've been a great help.'

The translations of the Cyrillic made plenty of sense or at least as much sense as using the words "pain killer" for any number of drugs. If we can't get hold of the back to life component, the kids might be locked out for the forceable future. Angela tapped a message to James:

'Walking Dead and Back to Life.' They are the direct translations. Somehow, I think a visit to the local pharmacy will be unhelpful.
Soz.

Tks

*****

There was only one place he could go to get answers, but that was now out of bounds to him. He called Jennifer Crawford's private phone.

There was no response, so he left a short message. 'Hi Jen. The drugs used on those kids translated directly are Walking Dead and Back to Life. Any chance of you speaking with the two Adults we arrested on the train. Thanks.' He was beginning to realise his suspension was a lot more serious than he first thought. *I can't even get into the system to do a bit of poking around.* 'Shit!'

He had an idea. He was already considering that Rebecca

Connolly's death might be linked, even tenuously, to the bikie case that had seen the demise of DCI Clitheroe, and there were several officers involved with Slippery when he went down. The next thing would be finding them. Even though he could remember some of those names, it would be a long shot. Rebecca's death was ten years earlier.

He accessed his computer and entered Craig Fullerton in the white pages search.

Nothing.

He followed with DS Jackie Morton. She was Jen's predecessor, and he swallowed the lump in his throat.

Nothing.

He went right through the list of remembered names and drew a blank on all of them. *They can't all still be inside. If Slippery managed to scrape out early…?* He decided to take a risk and call the prison that was once the home to ex DCI Clitheroe.

He drew another blank.

Next the women's prison. Perhaps Jackie's still around. At the time, he remembered being surprised that she'd allowed herself to get caught up in Slippery's shenanigans.

He took a risk and identified himself as a police officer and eventually a voice said:

'She was released two months ago.'

'Do you have an address for her?'

'I can tell you the name of her parole officer.'

'Go ahead.'

'Imelda Krakauer. She operates out of the Northam office.'

He thanked the speaker and called the Department of Justice in Northam, only to be told she worked from home at Meredin. The speaker gave him a mobile number and ended the call.

The name rang another bell, Mickey Krakauer, he'd fallen foul of Clitheroe over something quite petty, but it led to a stoush that Mickey lost big time. It didn't seem to bother Mickey that his career was virtually ended, he was a proud indigenous officer who preferred policing in the regions, anyway. *I wonder how he's doing these days.*

He pushed the thoughts of Mickey from his mind and tried Imelda's number.

She answered immediately. 'Department of Justice Ms Krakauer speaking.'

'Hi. DS Carter, Imelda. I've been given your name as the parole officer supervising Jackie Morton. I need to ask her a few questions…' The line went dead.

Shit. She's now likely to call the office in Perth. That will set the cat among the pigeons.

His phone rang. He answered it cautiously 'Jim Carter.'

'Imelda Krakauer, DS Carter. Sorry I'm in a bad reception area. You said you need Jackie Morton to answer some questions. You know she hasn't been released from prison long?'

'That's why I'm calling you. She was involved with a case that DCI Clitheroe was managing, or rather driving. I was one of the team who broke up the racket.'

'Jackie's trying to pick up her life again, sergeant, we've spoken about the shemozzle that she got caught up in and she's keen to put it behind her.'

'I knew Jackie at the time, we were old friends, and I was gobsmacked at what happened. The reason I need to speak to her is about something else. Even if you are present when we talk. She has nothing to fear from me.'

'I'll ask her, we have an appointment for tomorrow morning.'

'Great, thank you. I'll await your call.' The line went silent, and he knew he was still not off the hook if she decided to follow up with his station. Tomorrow he would take a drive in the country and be close by if and when Imelda returned his call.

If she didn't call, he would ask questions around the traps. Someone would know her.

Chapter 27

The dirt road was decidedly lumpy, but Mickey had a grip on the wheel that ensured they'd stay on it even at the speed he was driving.

'Don't need to worry about radars out here, hey, Mickey.'

Mickey grinned back at her. 'I'm part of the land, boss. She look after me.' He braked hard and skirted around an emu with a clutch of stripy chicks in tow that had attempted to challenge his beliefs.

'Yeah right.' Jennifer said.

'We missed'm din we.'

Jennifer shook her head, but the ice had been broken. 'You remember Jim Carter.'

'Thought it were all over wid you an him.'

'Not that. He was investigating a bikie racket that involved people trafficking and drug importation.'

'Yeah, I eard about that.'

'He's just got himself involved with the rescue of some kids who we suspect were being trafficked to the eastern bloc somewhere.'

'Shit?'

'He was only involved because his own kids were taken, and there was shooting. Whoops! Shit, Mickey.'

Mickey wrestled with the wheel, 'Sorry boss roadkill, shoulda seen it.' He slowed markedly for a while before speaking again. 'Jimmy got em though?'

'Yes. He managed to rescue his son by parking in front of the jet the kids were in, but his daughter was being taken somewhere by someone else. She was drugged with something weird. His son was okay, but he said he'd heard the females, including his sister, were going by train. We caught them near Merredin. Their captors were Russian, and the little girls were all drugged.'

'Shit. Jimmy Carter were a good bloke he din't deserve that. I remember hearin some goss about a young bloke being sent down for killin his teacher around that time. Wasn't Jimmy's sister the one who lost him the case?'

'No one was satisfied with that outcome, and we've just turned up some porn in which the teacher was the star. It was Slippery who was driving the case against him.'

'I member that. I weren't allowed near it, but I knew stuff that was goin on. That kid's dad was in Slippery's inner circle and word had it dey shared girls like lollies. No evidence though. I heard the kid was a shit-hot basketball player too.'

Jennifer turned and stared at Mickey's profile his eyes now locked firmly on the road ahead. 'They shared girls?'

'That was the goss, boss.' His face turned slightly towards her. 'I was already in deep shit with Slippery, so I kept my ears open, an me gob shut.'

'By girls, you mean…'

'Goss said anything between fourteen and twenty-five. No proof, mind.'

'When we get to the station, I'll need to look at some stats, will that be possible?'

'You'll be the boss-cocky, boss. Sorry I mean boss-chooky…'

Jennifer grinned. *I don't think this posting will be quite as bad as I expected*, she thought.

***

The women George was looking for were, in the main, barely women. He knew the places they hung out, how they dressed and how they made themselves up to look a minimum of five years older than their actual age. His clients liked them to be as young as possible and be adherents of the current fashion for bodily depilation. Fourteen years old was his own preference, and he felt a twinge of arousal as recalled his session with Zoe. She would fetch a good price. A couple of the others were marginal, but tidied up they'd pass muster.

The Z4 was a major attraction to the girls, and he always promised his target a ride in it. Those promises were never kept, but the limo that arrived to take them to a top table party easily fitted that bill. They'd be served champagne and wouldn't know what hit them until they were awakened in an eastern European brothel where they'd be fully schooled before the next part of their journey.

He only needed one more to fill his quota. The client was prone to toey-ness if he didn't come up with the exact goods, on time, and he was already a tad behind the eight-ball with the children he'd provided to fill a special order. Their parents should have remained totally in the dark, having been advised that their babies had been selected by a religious organisation to do a two-week course in choral singing. At least two weeks would pass before their disappearance would be noted. It was such a shame that the fools responsible for escorting them out of the country had screwed up so royally. Thankfully it was after the payment had been transferred to his account in the Bahamas, and so far, he'd kept himself at arm's length from the shippers.

The greatest consolation from their slip up was the cop on his back being suspended.

Thankfully, he still had high-level connections with the police force, and he knew where all their metaphorical bodies were buried.

The effects of the narcotic, provided by his client, could not be reversed without an antidote which would normally be administered on arrival at their destination. Until then they would effectively remain as voiceless zombies.

He steered the limo into the underground carpark of the prestigious hotel, where tonight's target would be waiting. He shrugged on his tuxedo jacket, flicked off a long auburn hair, and then hauled himself from the low-slung vehicle to make his way to the private lift. This would take him directly to the Presidential Suite. From there he would call his target and give her instructions.

George Gregory almost quivered with the anticipation of her delivery to the sixth cellar bedroom of his home in the Grove where she would be treated to a session of his avant-garde movie making. Later, and from a remote location, her phone would be used to send her family and friends a text advising them she would be away with a friend for a short while, and they were not to worry.

The hotel had been informed that their guest was a person of substance who valued the maximum privacy, and staff would not be required for the short duration of his stay. The bill had been paid in full and the account that paid it, no longer existed.

***

He hadn't heard anything from Imelda by mid-morning so he decided that perhaps Jackie might be keeping a low profile. His first stop was a place where he could pick up a burner or two, then he headed in the direction of Merredin, he'd be there by midday. Plenty of time for Imelda to call him if Jackie came good, and he could live in hope.

He almost jumped out of his skin when, about half-way there, his phone began to squawk. He pulled off the road and took the call. It was Imelda.

'I spoke to her, but she's adamant. She doesn't want anything to do with the police. She says she's done her time and wants to be left alone. Sorry, DS Carter That's the best I can offer.'

'Thanks anyway, Imelda. If you do get to speak with her, tell her I'm on her side.'

'No worries…'

Before the line went dead, he heard another woman's voice say, 'Thanks.'

Imelda was with her as they spoke. He pressed recall and was answered, with a harrumph.

'She doesn't want to speak to you DS Carter…'

He cut her short. 'Tell her it's Jimmy Carter. My kids were abducted by a Russian cartel. They're safe but others aren't. Jackie might be able to answer some questions that might help me find them.' He knew he'd stretched the truth a little, but he'd no real choice. He heard Imelda's muffled voice passing the message.

'Hi, Jim. Sorry, I can't help you. I've been inside for the last ten years. Give me a break.'

'Can we at least have a chat over a coffee? You know DCI Clitheroe was murdered?'

'Shit. Look I have a life now… Shit… When?'

'I'm on my way to Merredin right now. Imelda can sit in with you. Please, Jack?'

He heard a scuffling sound as if the phone was being handed around.

'How long. DS Carter?'

'I'm about 30 minutes away.'

Muffled voices.

'We're at her home.' Imelda followed with Jackies address.

'See you soon.' James felt his heart pound. *She might be a complete waste of time but she's the only one from that time that I've found.*

Chapter 28

He struggled to maintain his speed at the legal limit, the last thing James Carter needed while under suspension, was a speeding ticket. At last, he found the address and stopped several blocks up on the opposite side of the road. He was in his own car, but knew he'd be picked as a cop by any busybodies peeping through their curtains.

A late model Hyundai was parked in the drive. *Imelda's. She's still there.*

Feeling a sense of relief that he wouldn't be alone with Jackie, he opened her front gate and walked as casually as he could to the door. The policeman's knock was not appropriate, so he tapped lightly with his fingertips on the glass.

The door opened to a woman who had aged to an almost skeletal appearance. 'Jack?'

She nodded. 'We're out the back.'

Shocked at the deterioration of his old friend, he followed her through to the simple patio and nodded to Imelda. Although they'd never met, she could be no one else. 'Ms Krakauer. Thank you for seeing me.'

'I can't stay for long Mr Carter.'

'I hope this won't take too long too.' James turned to Jackie. 'How have you been?'

'How do you think, Jimmy? Can I get you a drink?'

'I'm fine but don't let me stop you.'

Jackie nodded to Imelda, 'Coffee?'

'I'll make them, you speak to your friend.'

The moment Imelda was out of earshot, Jackie snarled. 'Fucking bastard…' Then her lips formed a tight humourless smile. 'She said they took your kids?'

'They're as safe as they can be, but I need to ask you about your time with Clitheroe.'

'Sounds like you had us as married.'

James laughed, 'You were far too good for the likes of Slippery, Jack. There were rumours though. Remember that kid who got sent down for murdering his teacher?'

'Tom Gregory… I remember him clearly. He was no killer. I had my doubts and suspicions from the start, but Clitheroe had the case solved and put to bed PDQ. There was supposedly irrefutable DNA evidence, and he was loving every minute of it.'

'I heard a rumour that Clitheroe and Tom's father had a special relationship. Did you get any of that?'

'It was all around the station, but you were on another project at the time. Or at least that's what everyone thought. Then Clitheroe got caught with his hands in the bikie's till.'

'Tell me about the rumours.'

'The word had it, he was making internet porn with Tom Gregory's father. They used to make the movies and share the girls. There wasn't a shred of evidence of course and no one really believed it, but Clitheroe was such a twat so anything could be true.'

'There might be evidence now.' He opened his briefcase and lay out a selection of the stills Angela had collected. 'Sorry they're a bit explicit.'

She pointed at a print. 'Slippery's watch. I'd know that anywhere. Mind you it could be anyone I suppose.' She flipped through, stopped at the buttock pic, and pointed to a small scar just above the man's waist. 'That's Slippery's arse. The scar is from an injury he got when he was in Hedland. They reckon another cop gave him a bit of a beating. Nothing was ever done about it, but afterwards my mate, Mickey Krakauer, was defo in his black books.' She mopped away a stray tear, stopped talking and turned towards Imelda as she returned with a tray and three coffees.

'I fixed you one anyway, Mr Carter,' Imelda said.

'Is Mickey Krakauer your lad?'

Imelda nodded. 'Hardly ever see him these days, he's out in Woop-Woop somewhere. Why do you ask?

'It seems Jackie has identified him as a potential witness, Imelda. I think we might need a bit more time,' James said.

Jackie nodded enthusiastically. 'Take as long as you want, Jim. Just as long as that lovely wife of yours doesn't come gunning for me.'

Imelda rolled her eyes and frowned. 'Is my boy caught up in this?'

'Don't worry, Your Mickey was kept as far away from Clitheroe's business as it was possible. They hated each other,' Jackie said, turning back to James. 'Another rumour was that Tom Gregory's dad killed the teacher. Then, as soon as the DNA evidence turned up, Tom became the prime suspect, and his father disowned him. There was a young lawyer involved, if I remember correctly. She tried to get Tom off.' Jackie shrugged.

'My sister,' James said. 'She's still burning over it.'

Suddenly the skeletal face of Jackie Morton exploded into tears. 'I did time for something I didn't fucking do, so I know exactly what that kid went through. I got dragged into that drugs haul believing I was there to legitimately control traffic and keep travellers out of the danger zone.' She glowered at James. 'And you, you bastard. You were the one who pulled the pin.'

He nodded. 'And Slippery made sure everyone went down with

him.'

***

Angela Carter Googled the stats on people who had disappeared in the last twenty years. It seemed that something like three in five missing persons were never found and a large proportion of them were female and under eighteen years old. The figures weren't up to date so things might have changed but the numbers didn't lie.

A young woman had been found murdered only recently, and the MO was strikingly similar to that of Rebecca Connolly, but it couldn't have been Tom. He had the alibi of custody for the last ten years.

If Clitheroe was involved with Rebecca's death he too was out of the loop for the new victim. She knew there was convincing evidence that Rebecca had fallen pregnant to Tom. It had been confirmed in the court by a prosecution expert. Yet Tom had denied everything, and she believed him. She still did. So how could he be the father of the embryo that was discovered during Rebecca's postmortem. There was much more to this than what appeared on the surface.

Angela's problem was that she was on the nose with the police and even her own brother had kept her at arm's length for many years. She perused the case notes for the umpteenth time. *There must be something that doesn't add up.*

Jim had mentioned a sergeant Jenny Crawford and how she had helped him via her connections with the cyber division. Her number was in Jim's phone. She called it.

The call went directly to voice mail, so she called the station and asked to speak directly with her.'

'DS Crawford is no longer working here. Is there anyone else who can help?'

'Thanks, no there isn't.' *Jim had said nothing about her moving.* She couldn't call him. She still had his phone. Angela sat back and concentrated her mind. The key people at the start of this affair were Clitheroe and Tom. Tom's father had forcefully disowned him from virtually the moment he had been arrested. His mother had died several years later, and George Gregory was still out and about in his flash chick-puller car.

Stacey answered her phone in a quiet voice. 'Hello?'

'It's Angela Carter. Remember when I came to your little soiree with my son, Oliver?'

'I remember you didn't stay long.'

'I know. That's the reason I'm calling. I left after running into George Gregory. When he learned I was his son's solicitor…'

'Ah. You still think he's innocent even after all the evidence.'

'I'm more interested in locating George. I'd like to have a chat with him. Maybe try to patch things up, you know.'

'He's a slime ball, but he seems to know everyone who is anyone.'

'Where is he these days?'

'I heard he built himself a McMansion in Peppy Grove. I don't know where he gets his money, but he seems to be raking it in these days.'

'Do you have an address?'

'I think he left a card after the party. He claims he's in foreign exchange or something like that. Sorry, I can't help you now, I'm still at the hospital with Andria. She's showing no improvement and I'm worried sick.'

'Okay, I'll try the hard way, take care of yourself.'

Almost as an afterthought Stacey said, 'Thanks for finding them and for looking after Jack, Angela.'

'It was a pleasure, but I think he's probably better off with his grandies. And Oliver is now being spoiled rotten by my parents.'

They ended the call and Angela googled the white pages for George Gregory.

Chapter 29

'There were no entries for the Grove. There can't be too many Z4s around. I wonder…'

Every avenue seemed blocked to her, and tracing a vehicle's owner from its model was nigh on impossible… *Unless.* She googled the "BMW Z4 owners club" and found a Facebook page.

There were plenty of proud owners pictured next to their shiny steeds, but no George Gregory. 'Damn!' She scrolled through the various entries and saw a familiar face. He was a student at the same time as she, and he was even invited to her wedding. 'Ha! Bernie Higgins.' He'd hardly changed, except for the paunch that extended over his belt. 'Well-well.' He was pictured standing next to his bright and shiny, red charger, outside his recently opened restaurant in Claremont.

Angela found the number and called the restaurant. 'Bernie Higgins, please.'

'One moment, I'll see if he's here.'

Angela waited, listening to several repeats of the menu that had nothing on it that sounded particularly appetizing. A voice answered.

'Higgins?'

'Bernie? Its Angela Carter. Remember me?'

The voice became animated. 'Hey, Angie. It's been a long time. How did you manage to track *me* down?'

'I saw a pic of you with a flash car outside your very own restaurant. You gave up the law then?'

'It was never for me, so when my dad fell off the perch, I decided to set myself up in the hospitality business. Bloody Covid nearly killed us, but we survived. Enough about me. So, what are you up to these days? I'd heard you'd split with your bloke.'

'Yeah well, you know…'

'So…?'

'Do you know a chap named Gregory, George Gregory?'

'George?' He laughed. 'He's a bit hifalutin for me these days. He doesn't eat in my place. I think we're a bit down market for the likes of him. Why do you ask?'

'I defended his son, sadly I lost the case, and the kid went to jail for life.'

'Ah yeah, I remember that. Weren't you working at that big mob of lawyers, Locke and Keyes, wasn't it?'

'Still there for my sins. Would you know George's address by any chance? I have some information for him.'

'Hang on. I'll check my contacts.'

A few minutes later he responded. 'Here we go.' Bernie rattled of an address in the Grove. 'I'll text it to you.'

'He's certainly moved up a notch since I knew him,' Angela said.

'In FX I believe. At least he was the last time I had the misfortune to speak to him.'

'No love lost then?'

'Makes my skin crawl. But hey, that's just me.'

Angela didn't bother to tell him that was exactly how she felt when she met Gregory. 'Thanks Bernie.'

'Pleased to have been of service. Pop in sometime when you're next in the area. The grub's simple but fresh and tasty.'

'Will do.' She rolled her eyes, ended the call, tapped Google Maps and entered Gregory's address.

It was only a short drive on the mapping app, and she was surprised how low key "the mansion" appeared. She looked at the time on her watch. It was now late afternoon and probably no one at home. 'Oops. Spoke too soon.'

The automatic gate across the gap in the high wall surrounding Gregory's property opened and a white stretch limo slid out.

By the time Angela realised what was happening it was alongside her, but she couldn't see the driver for the heavy tinting. *Might have been hired for a function*, she thought, but decided to tail it to see where it went.

Fortunately, it wasn't hard to follow, but she kept as far back as possible. It was heading to the city, and she followed it into the underground car parking area of a new hotel that had recently sprung up. Glitzy place, as she recalled from the ads on the TV, but she couldn't remember the name.

As she took her ticket she noted its name, The Arete Hotel. The limo cruised around the outer lane of the car park before stopping in an extended glass partitioned bay alongside what looked like a small lift. She parked her car and waited.

A few minutes later she saw him.

George Gregory was the driver of the limo, and he stepped out of the car to make directly for the elevator. Then she lost him as its door closed. 'Bugger.' *But if he's in the hotel, he should be findable.*

She headed to the same lift and found it had a security key-controlled access under a metal plate that said, "Presidential Suite". Further across the carpark there were a pair of public lifts to the hotel reception. She took the one to the reception and made her way to the desk.

A receptionist raised her face with a disdainful look. 'Madam?'

'I understand Mr George Gregory is staying here can you put me through to his room please, I have an important message for him.'

'One moment, madam.' She tapped her fingers over her keyboard, looked up and said, 'No one of that name is registered in this hotel.'

'But I just saw him enter a lift labelled the presidential suite, in the car park.'

'One moment please, madam.' She tapped away on her keyboard again and then her eyes lifted and moved to someone in the foyer.

Angela turned to see who it was and noticed two uniformed security officers heading in her direction. It didn't at first register that they might be heading for her, and she turned back to the receptionist.

The woman raised her eyes again, and this time looked over Angela's shoulder.

She sensed their aura before she heard one quietly say. 'Please leave the hotel, ma'am. The person you are seeking is not here.'

'I just saw him. I'm a lawyer and need to speak to him. What is the problem?' She felt the hand of the larger of the two men close tight around her upper arm.

'It will be easier for you if you do not make a scene, ma'am.' He guided her away from the reception desk in a careful but gentle manner. 'Do you have a vehicle in the carpark?'

She nodded.

'Very good.' He walked her to the lift, pressed the down button, and waited for it to arrive.

The smaller man positioned himself directly behind her and all three stepped into the lift.

Another woman rushing to catch the lift was edged back by the larger man.

Angela was beginning to feel nervous. It wasn't the behaviour she'd expected from a high-end hotel, but it seemed she had no choice. She was being given the equivalent of a high-end bum's rush.

The guards escorted her to her vehicle and waited while she sat in it and closed the door. They then stepped back. One spoke into a small radio device before and waving her away.

She picked her ticket up from the passenger seat, but the barrier lifted as she approached, to allow her to leave without payment. 'Very smooth. Obviously, George has some cred.' She mumbled as she drove away.

'Interesting.' She couldn't phone James, so she entered a few lines of text into his notes app and decided to call on him at home.

Stacey opened the door. 'He's not here, sorry.'

Angela handed her the phone he'd given her. 'Mine was smashed in the train incident and Jim lent me his.'

Stacey took the phone and said, 'Can I offer you a cuppa? You look like you've had a bit of a day?'

It was the first friendly act of Jim's wife and she felt she couldn't refuse. 'Thanks, that *would* be nice.'

Stacey led the way to the kitchen and started the kettle. 'I hoped he'd be home more since they suspended him. Fat chance.'

'It's all my fault, Stacey. I asked him about Tom Gregory and things began coming to light.'

Stacey handed Angela a cup of tea and placed her own on the table. She didn't offer milk or sugar which was fine.

'I gave up milk and sugar in tea years ago.' She smiled. 'How is Andria?'

'No change. I'm scared she'll be stuck that way, but the medics expect her to recover spontaneously… maybe. I hope so. At least Jack's okay. It was all just a big adventure for him.'

Angela took a sip of her tea and rolled her eyes. 'I so needed that.' She paused for thought and then said, 'I saw Tom Gregory's father enter that flash new hotel in town. He was driving a stretch limo.'

'I thought he ran around picking up young girls in his beamer. Maybe he's upping the ante.'

'I asked for him at reception and got the weirdest response I've ever experienced. Then I was almost immediately escorted from the building by their security people.'

Stacey shrugged.

'Well, I thought it was weird, anyway.'

Chapter 30

Jennifer Crawford breathed a sigh of relief when Mickey's headlights lit up the walls of a weatherboard house as he turned into its driveway.

'This is yours, boss. See yas in the morning.' He clambered out and grabbed her bag from the boot. 'Travellin light then?'

Jennifer sighed. 'I don't need much, these days, Mick.'

Mickey handed her a set of keys. 'There's a vehicle in the garage.' He pointed to a Zincalume shed. 'It's been detailed and filled with juice. Night, boss. If you need anything, give me a call.' He handed her one of his police cards that had his mobile number written in biro. Then he slid back into the vehicle they'd arrived in and drove off without another word.'

Jennifer opened the front door to the scent of lavender and when she switched on the light, she noticed the place had been given a serious spring clean. She found the kitchen, and as she filled the jug, she noticed the colour of the water bordered on brown. She checked the fridge. It was stocked with basics and several bottles of imported water.

Jennifer needed a shower badly, but the colour out of the tap put her off. She went to the bathroom, anyway, and turned on the shower which quickly heated to a steaming flow of fierce water. 'To hell with it.' She dropped her clothes to the floor and left them where they fell before stepping into the hot rain and, for the first time in days, felt relaxed.

Later, she found the fridge that had some steaks, bread and frozen veges, while a small pantry had a rack filled with spuds and carrots. She looked through the window to the primitive patio and saw a gas barbeque. 'That'll do.' She lit it and threw one of the steaks on the grill. The aroma made her feel even more hungry so rather than go to any trouble she grabbed a couple of slices of bread, spread them with tomato sauce and mustard, and waited.

'You've only been here five minutes and you're turning into one of us.'

Jennifer was shocked at the sound of the voice and turned to see who it was appearing through the gloom. 'Beg yours?'

'Clarrie Collard, I'm your DC, and you'd be DS Jenny Crawford up from the big smoke.'

Jennifer extended her hand.

Clarrie took it. 'We're a bit casual out here and when Mickey said there was a big dick from Perth coming up to take over from the sarge, I thought I ought to take a squiz.'

'Sorry about the dick part?'

Clarrie laughed and marked a score in the air with her finger. 'So, what brings you here?'

'I needed a change.'

Clarrie smiled. 'I might not be that crash hot, but I am a detective y'know.'

Jennifer placed her steak on a slice of bread covered it with a slice and halved it. She indicated that Clarrie might like the other half.

'Nah, girl. You had long drive. Feed yourself and tomorra night you can join me and my bloke for a proper tea.'

'Bloke?'

'You'll see. See yas in the office tomorra.'

Jennifer watched as her new colleague left, the way she came in, and then she took her first bite of her sandwich. *That isn't half bad,* she thought, and ate the lot. It had filled one gap at least, and as she crawled in between the fresh clean sheets, she mused, *I suppose, from now on I'll be doing the washing.*

Sleep came quickly but the raucous screeching of her alarm brought her back down to earth, with a thud.

***

James fanned out the photos. 'The goss about Slippery and George Gregory, and the porn?'

Jackie pointed at the prints he had spread across the table. 'Now if that's evidence, we didn't have it back then. If we had that, plus the goss, we might have made a dent in him. But Slippery ruled the roost and there was an even bubble of white noise that surrounded the commissioner.' She sorted out the buttocks pic and pointed to the scar. 'That's defo Slippery's ass. Maybe Imelda's boy might know something.'

Imelda picked up the picture and grimaced. 'Mickey might be a bit of a tearaway, but he wouldn't be into this.'

'He might know something that could put us on the right track. My daughter was kidnapped by a mob of people traffickers, and she was drugged with something that can only be reversed by an antidote. Unless I can get to the bottom of these rumours and convert them to fact, I might as well bang my head against the wall, and I don't have the time.'

Imelda found her phone and tapped on a number. She pressed the speaker button.

'Hey, Mum. Who's died?'

Imelda shook her head. 'Sorry I don't call you much these days but...'

'You don't even return my voice mails.'

'Yep, yep, but I have a bloke here who wants to speak to you. You should get along. He's a cop too.'

'Hey, Mickey.' James called to the phone. 'We were in the

academy together and met a few years ago, in Hedland. Jimmy Carter, Remember?'

'Look, mate, I drove her here that's all.'

'What?'

'Your ex…'

'What the hell…' Carter looked at the faces opposite him and wondered what he was getting himself into.

'DS Crawford. She'll be in the office soon and you can speak to her yourself.'

'Hold up Mickey. Are you saying Jennifer Crawford is with you in Warakurna?'

'She arrived last night.'

'Shit, mate. That's not the reason I called. I'm with your mum, and a friend of yours from way back, Jackie Morton.'

'Look, DS Carter. I'm here for a reason, and that is, I don't want to bring back all that crap, there's too many bad memories. Hi Jack, how long you been out?'

Jackie ignored his question and said, 'He needs your help, Mick. His kid was kidnapped and drugged. He was hoping you might have picked up some intel back then, that might give him a lead.'

'Well, how's this for a lead? You were framed, Jack.'

'Surprisingly, I know that, Mick, but we need to get inside the minds of the bastards who framed me, murdered Rebecca Connolly, and maybe a few more.'

'Look no further. Slippery Clitheroe and his mate George Gregory. I heard Slippery's dead, but George shouldn't be too hard to find.'

James rolled his eyes. 'Any ideas?'

'We can talk up here but I'm not coming into the city. You probably know that I'm carrying a bit of baggage with some of the old school, and the phone connections are a bit dodgy.' As if to prove his point the line went dead.

James turned to Jackie. 'Fancy a drive in the country?'

Her eyes crinkled as though he'd stirred a distant happy memory. She turned to Imelda.

Imelda nodded. 'Just keep in touch, you know the rules?'

Jackie nodded. 'I won't let you down, Imms. I promise.'

'Pick you up tomorrow then. We'll probably need a cut lunch and a water bag.' He stood ready to leave and noticed that Jackie's whole demeanour had lifted.

She looked at her phone. 'Shops are still open.'

'I'll give you a hand, Jack.' Imelda said and patted her on the knee.

James headed for home. He needed to have a serious conversation with his wife, and she was not going to like him being away for an unpredictable length of time.

Chapter 31

As expected, Stacey's views of him heading to Woop-woop with an ex-female cop, who'd just been released from jail, were somewhat jaded. He leaned on his elbow and faced her, with his head resting on his hand, and tried to explain why he needed to do it, but to little avail.

'You've got yourself suspended and now you want to make matters worse by getting involved in an investigation that, truly, has nothing to do with you.'

'It does. The person I'm going to interview is a cop who was close to the suspects back in the day.' James knew things were tough for Stacey, especially with their daughter in hospital under observation and not knowing what eventual outcome of the Russian drug might be. 'I'm hoping the guy I'll be seeing, might remember a few things. He wasn't on Slippery's Christmas card list.' James shrugged. 'No one else is interested. They're all too worried about their pensions.'

Stacey turned towards him. 'How long have we been together?'

He did the mental calculation leaned forward and kissed her on the lips.

'You will take care won't you. Oh, I forgot Angela came around and returned your phone.'

'I've been managing with a burner, but it'll be good to have my contacts again.'

'She's almost as screwed up as you. Must be a genetic thing.'

'She feels guilty about Tom Gregory, Stace. Ange believes he was framed and I'm coming around to her way of thinking.'

'If he didn't kill her, who did?'

'That's the burning question and with Slippery Clitheroe dead, it'll be even harder to get to the truth.'

'When Angela brought your phone back, she said she'd seen George Gregory driving a stretch into that posh new hotel. When she asked about him, she was "escorted" from the building by their security.'

'So, Gregory has some cred?'

'Well, Angela doesn't like him. Who is running the trafficking case now you're suspended?'

James shrugged. 'I think it's only ever been me and I'm thinking Angela might have been on the ball, right from the beginning.'

***

George Gregory was relaxing in a spa in the extensive Presidential bathroom when he heard the knock at his door. He pulled on a bathrobe and dripped through to open it.

'Your guest is in the front bar, sir.'

'Thank you.' He lifted a small white envelope from an occasional table and said, 'See that she gets this.'

The man bobbed his head in a vague bow, took the envelope and pulled the door shut behind him.

George looked at himself in the mirror and dropped his robe to expose his toned body. He smiled and sensed a flicker from his nether regions. 'Down boy. The night is young.' He reached into the bar fridge and extracted a bottle of cheap Champagne. It had already been doctored, *and she won't know the difference.*

A few minutes later Gregory was dressed and heading down in the lift, to meet his evening's entertainment. She was standing next to the limo, her short skirt leaving little to the imagination. Her add-on eyelashes giving her the look of a deer in the headlights.

'Hello, Georgie,' she gushed.

He opened the passenger door of the limo. 'A little gift to help get you in the mood, my darling,' he said as he popped the champagne cork and followed her into the rear. 'Sorry. I'll be driving.' He handed her a chilled flute and smiled. 'I can indulge when we arrive.' George then stepped out and took the driver's seat, started the engine and said, 'There's usually a few, hence the limo, but hey, all the more for us.'

The girl giggled and took a good gulp of her drink and relaxed into the plush seat, ready to be driven in style to a posh party.

By the time George arrived in his garage the deer in the headlights was well and truly focussed on an unknown fate. He opened the door for her, led her to his lift and pressed down. As the lift moved downwards George lifted her skirt for a peep and slid his hands between her legs. She didn't flinch.

He knew the drug would allow a sort of semi-normality, for a limited period, before it slammed its recipient into the living dead state. He had a small emergency stock of what his clients called the "Back to Life" antidote, but he'd never used it and he saw no reason to. The client had already provided enough to get them walking when the time was right.

He led her to the room where he'd have his fun, make his movies, and then, along with the others, she would be dressed in a travel outfit before, one by one, they'd be escorted to the limo and driven to a private airstrip to board a private plane for onward shipment.

For George Gregory, this was the most tedious and risky part of the operation. What happened after they left his care was none of his concern.

He pushed her limp body onto the bed, Activated the camera to record him stripping her and re-dressing her in night attire. From then on it was to be a repeat of the last session but he couldn't contain himself and prematurely ejaculated.

'Not to worry my dear the night is young.'

***

While James waited for Jackie, he checked his phone for messages. There weren't any. *This suspension really sucks.* He checked his notes app and saw something new. It was a message from Angela:

To James from his ditzy sister

I followed George Gregory from his home to that brand new Arete Hotel. He seems to have access to the Presidential suite which has its own private lift.

I think it might be worth checking out.

Also, he has a very low-key mansion in Peppy grove. If he has anything to do with Rebecca's death, I suspect you might find some evidence there.

I'll call you when I get a new phone.

It was too late to change his plans and even if he wanted to, Jackie had just dropped into the passenger seat after first popping an Eski onto the back seat.

'I was joking when I said we'd need a cut lunch and a water bag.'

'Well, I've been away for a while so I'm looking forward to a picnic in the country with a handsome dude.' She grinned. 'The look on your face.'

They both laughed.

There would be plenty of time to catch up during the long drive to Warakurna and as they settled in for the haul, Jackie said, 'Jenny Crawford? There was talk of you two being an item.'

James shrugged. 'That was a long time ago and I've got a couple of kids and a bolshy wife on my back now.'

'That's what worries me. I saw your face when Mickey mentioned her name.'

'It's all ancient history.'

'That's not what I heard.'

James turned the radio volume up and tried to concentrate on the road.

Chapter 32

Angela had an uncomfortable feeling in her gut when she left Stacey. James was heading into the country and the person she believed to be the lead perpetrator was cruising around in either a Z4 or a stretch limo. She decided to head for Gregory's mansion and do her own surveillance. She'd parked almost opposite the entrance gate, and it was late afternoon when she saw his limo slithering goanna-like down the street.

The gate slid opened, and the goanna slipped in.

This might be my only chance, she thought, and quickly exited her car to run through the gate just before it was about to click shut. From there she watched the limo head towards a large garage door.

Now she felt nervous, but she knew she needed to get inside the mansion, and that would be technically a breach of the laws she'd sworn to uphold. Angela ducked low and followed the slow-moving vehicle as it slid under the door.

The Z4 was parked to the left, and she scooted in behind it to peer over at the limo and its occupants.

Stifling a gasp, when the driver's door opened, she watched as Gregory opened the passenger compartment and led a dozy looking teenager to the wall. When he placed his hands on a section disguised as a tool rack she heard a tinkle, as though something small had fallen to the floor. The tool rack slid to one side to expose a small lift. *He certainly likes his little lifts*, she thought, as the pair stepped inside before its door closed.

Angela stood and noted that there were two buttons on the lift panel, the dark one indicating up, the other, illuminated, told her it was travelling down. She could do nothing but wait, and hope if there was security video, she'd managed to squeak past its all-seeing eyes.

The down light went off. The lift had reached its destination. *What next?* The question in her mind was manifold. She was not trained in surveillance and did not know what might happen. *Would Gregory return to his car and leave? Might he do whatever he was planning and return to the lift to head back up? Or would he spend the entire night with the young girl, filming her embarrassment for his next soiree on the world wide web?*

She could hear no sounds emanating from the building, not even the flush of water through pipes. *You're trembling, you're not scared, are you?*

She murmured, 'If you don't mind, yes, I am. I am very scared.' In the silence, her murmur sounded with the volume of a fishwife's cackle. *Shit.*

Approximately one hour passed and Angela's knees were feeling the strain of crouching behind the low slung Z4. The up light illuminated. She ducked lower and heard the crack of one of her joints. The door didn't open again, but the light went off briefly before the up light illuminated again and then went out.

No one left the lift. She waited for almost thirty minutes. *Nothing.* 'Right… Let's see what you're up to George.' Angela straightened up and steadied herself before moving quickly to the lift. She scanned the floor around the lift for whatever it was she heard drop, with no success, then she pressed the down arrow and the door opened immediately. She stepped inside and felt it move. It was surprisingly deep and would easily take a full sized bed. The door opened, and she found herself looking at what might have been a budget hotel corridor.

It was softly lit, carpeted, and had six doors. Three on each side. She stepped out. The lift door closed behind her and there was nowhere to hide if George decided to return.

Angela felt for her phone, and a chill ran down her spine. *I am completely incommunicado.* She stiffened her resolve and tried the first door.

It was unlocked.

She opened it and knew that if George did return, she'd be a dead person walking.

The semi naked girl on the hotel type bed—the only item of furniture in the room—was out cold. Angela checked her vitals and realised she was still alive. She prised one of the girl's eyes open. Her pupils moved with the light, but she was otherwise comatose: *six doors? Maybe six girls. Stretch limo? Their transport?* Then she noticed the drip connected to a canula. *Crikey.*

She stepped outside and saw that the lift lights were dark and tried the next door up. Another girl. Same condition. She tried the next, and the next, same. She tried the last door on the left.

This girl was still woozy. There was no drip, and she realised she must be the one she saw him bring home.

'Can you hear me?'

The girl nodded.

Angela grimaced when her hand fell on the cold sticky liquid on the light sheet that covered the girl. She reached into her pocket and removed a tissue to soak up the residue. *Not exactly forensic but might be a start.*

'Can you stand?'

Tears trickled from the girl's eyes.

'Can you at least try, if I help you?' Angela took her by the arms and attempted to sit her up. It worked. She swivelled her around, so her legs were over the side of the bed.

Then she heard a voice approaching. It sounded like it might be a loving father talking softly to his daughter. It was difficult to catch every word but what words she could catch were in no way fatherly. She pushed the girl down and onto her back, said, 'Stay,' and looked for somewhere to hide.

The only obvious place might be under the bed, but the gap between the base and the floor was narrow. Unless…

***

Jennifer made herself a light breakfast showered and headed to the garage for her new corporate transport. When she opened the door, she laughed. 'Fucking detailed, you said, Mickey Krakauer. Wait until I see *you* again, Constable.'

The ancient and crumpled dual-cab-ute's door squealed in agony when she dragged it open. The inside was littered with chocolate bar wrappers and a faint whiff of stale chips and onions assailed her nostrils. 'Great.'

She brushed away the wrappers and inserted the key, turned it, and smirked when the diesel rattled into life. 'Well at least you had the courtesy to start.' The fuel gauge was showing empty. 'I thought you said you'd filled it… another black mark, Mickey.' He'd given her some directions, and she followed them to the ancient weatherboard building that was the police station.

As she drove into the yard, she saw Mickey and a bunch of uniformed officers all grinning from ear to ear. Then she saw Mickey reaching out to collect cash from each of them.

'Hey boss we got enough for a few tinnies thanks to you.' He handed her the keys to the four-wheel drive they'd driven up in. 'Can I have my car back now?'

She knew she'd been set up and could only return his infectious grin with a smirk as she followed them into the building.

Clarrie Collard was frowning. 'You gotta watch them buggers, Sarge, they's got too much energy for their own good. Cuppa?'

Jennifer nodded and found a desk that she thought might be appropriate for the rank of DS. As she lay out her personal items, she saw Clarrie taking the teacups into a separate office.

'Hey, boss. This your desk.'

***

Angela Carter didn't get the opportunity to test the hidey hole.

She felt a hand on her shoulder and a voice said, 'Why, Ms Carter, Angela isn't it?'

She felt the prick of a hypodermic through her pants and turned to see George Gregory.

Gregory grinned, 'You're a bit old for me, but my viewers might like a change.'

Angela struggled to remain focused on the face, swimming in the ether, before her eyes.

'Don't worry you won't remember a thing and when you wake up, you'll be in a brand-new country making brand-new friends. I'm sure you'll like it I've had no complaints from my younger travellers.'

Angela's mind was still active, but her body had ceased to respond. All she could think about was that she had no phone. This little exercise was an impromptu excursion into the world of the man she believed had answers to the question, 'Who killed Rebecca Connolly? Was it you?' she mouthed.

Gregory stood over her body and tutted. 'Pity it's the voice that always goes first. I never get to hear their squeals of ecstasy.' He reached down and grabbed her legs to straighten her out in readiness for the unveiling.

'You'll need to be patient with me, Angie. This young lady was first in line. You can even watch if you like.'

Angela felt her stomach cramp. The drug couldn't prevent her urge to vomit, but she couldn't move, she was on her back, and she knew if she vomited, she'd be dead. *What the hell have I done, James?*

Angela could hear Gregory setting up his camera and then visualised him manipulating the girl's outer attire before seeing it fall to the floor. He began softly cajoling the girl before the buzzing began.

'You *do* like this don't you?' His pants dropped to his ankles, and he stepped out of them.

His jocks slithered down his legs, and she recalled the video she'd seen on Jennifer's computer. She tried to move. And remembered the purpose of the Living Dead drug wasn't to immobilise completely, at least not at first. She twiddled her toes. They moved. She tried her hands and found she could move them. It felt like the time she'd got paralytic drunk, in her uni days.

Gregory was grunting and snuffling on the bed, but she'd have no chance of tackling him in her current state. She looked around the room. It had been set up like a hospital ward, and an oxygen bottle stood next to the bedside table. It didn't seem to be connected to a piece of equipment, and it might do.

Chapter 33

James had reached the halfway point in their journey and stopped on the fuel ramp outside the Tjukayirla Roadhouse. He woke Jackie from her car sleep. 'Hey, kiddo, we're halfway.'

She stared at him and said, 'halfway to where?' Her eyes rolled as she looked around at the landscape and sat upright. A few seconds later her mind clicked into gear. 'Shit I thought I was still in my cell.'

'Nope, they say this place makes great burgers though, and we need fill up with diesel.'

Jackie nodded. 'Sorry I was…'

He climbed out and began filling the tank. 'Would you like to go inside and organise some eats, we can put it all on this bill.'

Jackie nodded and shuffled towards the building.

While he was filling, he ignored the rules and checked his phone for messages. There was only one, and he didn't recognise the number:

> Angela, it's your mother. Are you alright? You said you would pick up Oliver.
>
> Can you please call me?
> Your Mother
>
> PS: dad is getting worried.

There was one bar of signal which might not be enough. He tried anyway.

'Is that you James?'

'I just got your message, mum. Have you heard from her?'

'No. It's most unusual for her not to call.'

'Have you noticed you called my number?'

'Of course. She said you'd lent her your phone. Can I assume she's returned it to you…'

The connection dropped and James recalled the message she'd left in his notes app. 'Shit!' The single bar had gone to bed for the night, so he followed Jackie into the roadhouse.

She smiled and waved from the table she'd selected.

James paid for the fuel and the meals and asked if they had accommodation.

The attendant looked at her computer and said, 'We only have one budget room available.' She described it as a twin single with use of the separate ablution facilities.

'I'll take it, just one night.' He handed her his credit card and then joined Jackie at the table. 'We have to share a room. Sorry.'

Jackie's face froze. 'Share. Shit! I…'

'You'll be okay. I'm knackered and even if I wasn't, I have a wife who'd kill me.' He looked at his phone and noticed it had bars. He recalled his parent's number. 'Sorry, mum. I'm right out in Woop-woop at the moment. You were cut off.'

'Well, there's not much to say is there?'

'Did she say if she has a new phone yet?'

'We haven't heard from her since that message. Don't worry, Oliver can stay for as long as he likes but if you hear from her can you tell her I'm worried?'

'Yeah sure, mum.' He ended the call.

'Problems?'

'I'm not sure. My sister defended Tom Gregory. She lost, and he was sent down for life. That was ten years ago, and she's still stewing.'

Jackie nodded. 'That kid was defo framed but Slippery controlled the evidence.' She pointed to herself and mouthed, *just like me*.

***

'Here ya go, boss. Lucky for you it's been a bit quiet around here. Peggy worked her guts out just so the cancer could get her, poor bugger.'

'They said she was just a bit crook and that I'd only be here pro tem.'

'They lied, boss. Peggy was stuck here for eight years. They reckoned she'd upset summon in the big smoke.' Clarrie pushed a mug of tea across the desk. 'You planning to be here *that* long?'

Jennifer shrugged. 'A few people might like that, Clarrie.'

'Dun worry, boss, we'll look after ya.'

'Right and thank you, DC Collard. Would you get everyone together so that I can introduce myself?'

'No worries, boss.' Clarrie took a sip of her tea and relaxed.

'Now, DC Collard.'

Clarrie almost choked on her tea but stood and said, 'Right away, boss.'

A few minutes later her office was packed. With a variety of young officers in various shades of brown.

'Thanks for coming guys, and gals.' She acknowledged Clarrie, and another PC, who smiled.' Jennifer had never given an introduction speech before so she was unaware how they might take her. She started by thanking them and particularly Mickey for his unusual form of welcome. 'Good job I'm only a sergeant and not brass, hey, Mickey?'

Mickey looked down at his feet and mumbled a half-hearted apology for the car.

Jennifer smirked. 'I'll try to speak to you all, one-on-one, over the next few days otherwise you know what you have to do.' As the room cleared, she called to Mickey.

'Boss?'

'This business of DS Carter…?'

'No worries, boss.' He drew a long, imaginary, zip across his lips, knowing her world was about to be tipped on its side.

Alone again, Jennifer used the quiet time to run through the current cases. Most wouldn't attract the skills of a towny DS, but it was all she had, and she began welcoming the simplicity. The day passed quickly, and the re-initiated thoughts of James Carter began to wane. She'd made a clear break, and she was always at her happiest working alone.

At the end of the day, she returned to the lavender scented shack, luxuriated in the smelly shower water, and poured herself a glass of chilled red wine. Tea with Clarrie hadn't eventuated, so it looked like an early night might fit the bill. Then just as she relaxed back into her chair, headlights lit up the opposite side of her room.

'Shit, what now?'

'Hey, boss get your glad rags on. The bloke's keen to get a squiz at the new de-tective.'

The way she said it sounded like "nude detective".

Clarrie corrected herself. 'Sorry, boss I nearly said the dick word.' She pushed open the door. 'You okay?'

Jennifer stood, grabbed the bottle of red from the fridge and said, 'These *are* my glad rags. Wadda we wadin for?'

They could have walked the short distance to Clarrie's place, but out here, no one walked and certainly not at night.

Clarrie's bloke was waiting in the doorway when they arrived. He was holding a glass of chilled beer, and he grinned when he saw his wife haul herself from the brand-new Land Cruiser. 'She look's a beaut, babe. A goer as well, I hope.'

Jennifer strained to smile. *That didn't take long.*

'Well, ya berra not break this one, Collard.' Clarrie waved towards Jennifer. 'This here's my new boss, so you'd berra behave yourself, mister.'

'Hello, Mr Collard, thanks for the invite.' Jennifer paused, Clarrie had never said she was married to him, only that he was her bloke. 'Should I call you that?'

Collard laughed. 'Only she calls me that, everyone else calls me Fatso.'

'But you're…'

'Yeah, built like a bloody racing snake.' He rolled his eyes, before they crinkled up in laugh lines. 'Now we're on speakin terms, you can call me…' he leaned over and whispered in Jennifer's ear.

Gerrard? He doesn't look like a Gerrard. Her face must have told the story. 'Okay, Ge…' And before she had the chance to finish, he'd escorted everyone out of earshot, and on to the patio.

Clarrie caught her eye and nodded to the side. 'What did he say his name was?'

Jennifer whispered, 'Gerrard?'

Clarrie snorted. 'You'll get used to him. He got wicked humour.'

'So, what *is* his name?'

Clarrie shrugged. 'How should I know, why d'ya think I calls 'im, Collard?' As she showed Jennifer to her place at the table Collard winked.

Chapter 34

Angela cranked her head stiffly around and dragged herself towards the bottle. She could hear the lustful blathering's of Gregory as he went about his rape and her strength grew along with her anger. She reached the bottle as he was reaching his climax and used it as a prop to help her to her feet.

Although unsteady. She managed to swing the bottle and bring it down on his head with all the force she could muster. Gregory roared and fell silent. The last thing she saw was blood flowing and the last thing she heard was the oxy bottle clattering to the floor alongside her.

She had no indication of the passing of time. It was the weirdest of sensations and then the girl on the bed began to moan.

Angela struggled to her knees. Gregory was flat out across the girl and blood was still leaking from his head. *Have I killed him?* If she had, she knew it would have been acting in the defence of another. He was in the act of raping a girl who couldn't be much more than fourteen. 'Hey,' she said. 'Can you hear me?'

The girl moaned, but it was incoherent.

Angela tried to stand but her legs seemed paralysed and all she could do was support herself with the edge of the mattress.

The girl seemed peaceful but also unable to move.

Angela remembered the drips that were connected to the other girls but she, nor the girl on the bed, had anything. The horror of what might happen, crossed her mind. The other girls were being kept in stasis, waiting for something to occur. Gregory had mentioned a flight to somewhere. Were they in a state of preservation until that time came? If so, how long did she have before she'd need the same.

No one knew where they were, so there could be no knight in shining armour rushing to the rescue. Gregory was out of things. Maybe even dead. She tried to stand again but her world turned black.

***

After dinner James and Jackie availed themselves of the ablution facilities. He'd given her the key to the donga-style room, assuming she'd be finished first. He waited for her to return and after a lengthy delay he decided there must be something wrong. He returned to the ablution block and called her through the door. 'You okay, Jack?'

There was no response.

'Shit. I'm a suspended cop, out bush with a parolee, who's probably already blown away all of her conditions. Perhaps this wasn't such a good idea after all.' He headed to the roadhouse and told the cashier that his friend had gone off somewhere. 'She has the key to the room, and I can't get in.'

The girl pressed a button on a PA mic and said something that sounded like, 'Lock out. Someone to reception.' She looked up at James. 'Happens all the time, mate. Tempers sometimes get a bit, well, you know.'

The door opened and a man who looked to be in his mid-sixties and wearing a battered white Stetson, entered. He said, 'Who's locked out then?'

The girl pointed to James and rolled her eyes.

'Come on mate, let's see what gives.'

James followed him to the cabin and waited until he found the master key.

The door opened and he could see Jackie curled up under the covers of one of the beds. She'd turned out the lights and was snoring quietly.

He said softly to the man with the key. 'Thanks.'

'No worries, bro,' the man murmured back and returned to wherever it was he had come from.

James gingerly climbed into the second bed and fell almost instantly asleep.

The sleep didn't last too long. The piercing scream from the bed next to him ended that.

He switched on the light and saw her clutching her bed sheets, her face locked in terror. She was sweating profusely and jabbering incoherently. Then just as suddenly she stopped.

Classic nightmare, he thought. He waited for a while before speaking. 'That sounded bad?'

Jackie flinched and turned towards the voice. 'Who the fuck…? Bastards. Fucking bastards.'

'Can I get you a coffee or something?'

Jackie shook her head. 'Sorry I woke you up, Jim. I can't shake the bloody things.'

'What is it you see?'

Jackie's eyes flickered and closed into a peaceful sleep.

It was no help for him. His mind immediately flew to his sister, the message from their mother and Angela's apparent disappearance. He had zero control. There was nothing he could do to respond in any way to the things whirling through his mind.

He opened the note she'd written:

To James from his ditzy sister

I followed George Gregory from his home to that brand new hotel. He seems to have access to the Presidential suite which has its own private lift.

I think it might be worth checking out.

It's a very low-key mansion in Peppy grove. If he has anything to do with Rebecca's death, I suspect you might find some evidence there.

I'll call you when I get a new phone.

The go-to person would have been Jenny Crawford, but she was as far away as him. If I call the station, they'll get all het up over my checking out stuff while I'm suspended. There was no one he could immediately think of who might be available to help. Then he had an idea. He had no choice but to ask the one person who would be the most resistant and probably the least able to cope.

'Stace, it's me.'

'It's three am.'

'Sorry… It's just that Ange has gone missing. She left Oliver with our Mum, and mum called to tell me she hasn't collected him. I have a note on my phone from her that says she's been surveiling George Gregory.'

'So?'

'So, she wouldn't be doing that unless she had good reason.'

'So, what can I do about that. I can't go rocking around town with a kid in tow at this time of day. I said *a* kid because you might not remember that your daughter is still in hospital, with no change to her condition. Angela is a mature woman, a lawyer no less and she should be able to read things better.'

'If Gregory is involved in some way with this human trafficking case, he might also have a connection to the antidote they mentioned.'

There was a long silence before Stacey spoke again. 'You can't do anything because you're under suspension. Why not call that ex-girlfriend of yours?'

'DS Crawford has been transferred.'

'Oh really, DS Crawford is it now?'

'Stace… I'm really sorry to wake you at this ungodly hour but there is a distinct possibility that my sister is dead or at least in some kind of captivity.'

There was another long silence. 'Do you have an address?'

'A very low-key mansion in Peppy grove, is all she said.'

'I don't think even google maps could find that. How did she? Has she contacted anyone recently who might know more than us.'

'Shit.' He pulled up the call records for his phone and found an outgoing call to an unfamiliar land line. He dialled the number and reached a voice mail.

'Thank you for calling, etc, etc.'

It didn't help. He checked the text messages. *Maybe something in there.* The same number came up. *Maybe she'd booked a table.* The message said:

> Hey babe good to hear from you again. We really
> should hook up. The address is…

'Ha! Well done, Stace. I think I have an address.' He read the text to her.

'Okay, I'll take a drive out, after I drop Jack at school. Now if you don't mind, I need my beauty sleep.'

'Love yas.'

'Bugger off.' The line went dead. James rolled over and fell into a deep sleep.'

***

It had been a pleasant evening with the Collards. Clarrie seemed to have the culinary side of things well sorted, and Gerrard's stories kept her entertained with much, heard-it-before, eyerolls from Clarrie. *I guess you'd need to be self-sufficient to live out here. I wonder if I'll make it to that stage.* Though she was awake, the raucous alarm still sent a shiver through Jennifer's body. 'Hey-ho, hey-ho, it's off to work we go.'

She breakfasted, showered, and dressed in the one uniform she had brought with her. As a detective in the city plain clothes were the norm, but everyone seemed to wear a uniform of sorts out here. She hitched up her utility belt and checked her Glock before slipping it into the holster. Though she rarely had the use for a Taser, she checked the charge. *At least I can look like I know what I'm doing.*

The drive to the station was a little less odorous, the little tree someone had thoughtfully hung on her mirror helped. This time there was no sniggering welcome committee as she disembarked. 'Clarrie around?' she asked of no one in particular.

No one replied.

The light morning wind was kicking up little willie willies from the dusty yard and she half expected to hear a lonesome whistle or the sounds of a banjo, or even a Jew's harp, as she pushed in through the door.

Clarrie dropped the receiver on the rest. 'We gotta a coupla visitors comin tonight, boss,' she said. 'Think you might knowem.'

Jennifer cranked her head. 'Might?'

'City folks. They're at the Tjukayirla Roadhouse so they'll be awhile.'

'You said I might know them?'

'One is a crook cop, just out on parole, the other has been suspended for poking his nose where it wasn't supposed to be poked.'

'Helpful.'

'Jackie Morton and Jimmy Carter.'

Jennifer felt the blood drain from her face. 'What the fuck…?'

Clarrie shrugged. 'They've come for Mickey. Think he might know sommat.'

'Have you told them?'

Clarrie shook her head. 'They'll find out soon enough. If I tell Mickey, that city folk are comin here to ask him questions... Well, you know... Anyway, probably won't be til late. Jackie can bunk up with us. Can you look after this Jimmy bloke?'

Jennifer said, 'You take Jimmy, I'll take Jackie.'

'Sorry, it's not me. Collard don't like other blokes in the house that aren't related.'

'Isn't there somewhere else they can stay?'

Clarrie shrugged.

Jennifer sat at her desk and opened the daily file of minor cases. 'Might be a murder before the end of the day.'

Chapter 35

She waved goodbye to her son and drove to the hospital to check on her daughter. There had been no change in her condition and the medical staff had connected her to a drip to maintain her fluids and nutrition. Stacey kissed the benign little face and left with a heavy heart.

'How dare someone do this to my child?' She plodded back to the car park and keyed in George Gregory's address.

'At least it isn't too far away.' She allowed the GPS to direct her and quite soon she was on the street outside the house. 'Well, you did say low key. She looked up and saw Angela's car parked on the street almost directly opposite the closed gate. 'Shit.' She called her husband but there was no reply. She left him a text message:

> Found the place. Angela's car is outside. The house is
> secured like a mini-Alcatraz, and I don't think I'll be able
> to get in.
> Sorry

She sent the message and then decided to explore the possibilities. The electronic gate had a pad that contained no digits. 'Must be a remotely operated gismo.' A letter box next to the pad was empty. She walked up and down the wall that contained the electronic gate. There was no other access.

'If at first...' Stacey walked up the street to the next-door neighbour's house. It had a gate with a video intercom. She pressed call.

'Hello. What do you want?'

'I'm trying to contact Mr Gregory, but I can't find a way to let him know I'm here.'

'One moment please.'

A woman, who looked to be in her eighties, arrived at the gate and looked Stacey up and down. 'You're not a police officer?'

'No, I'm just a friend, I haven't heard from him for a couple of days and that is unusual.'

'Hmmm… He keeps very much to himself. A friend you say?'

Stacey nodded. 'I thought of calling the police, but I was worried that George might not like their involvement in his affairs.'

'Hmmm.' She reached into the pocket of the old-fashioned apron she was wearing. 'Sorry, been baking. Great grandies are all due birthdays, and you can't get decent stuff in the shops these days.'

Stacey beamed her most patient smile and accepted what appeared to be a remote-control device.

'He gave me this for emergencies a few years ago. I've never used it so it might not work. Give it a try and let me know. You can pop it in the letterbox when you're done.' She pointed to a slot in the wall with a small door beneath it, then the gate closed and locked itself again.

Stacey walked back to Gregory's gate and pressed the single button in the device. She heard a motor begin to whir then the gate slid sideways and silently into a cavity in the wall. She stepped over the threshold and walked along the gracefully curving drive to an elegant entrance. By the time she reached it the doors to the garage were rolling up to expose two vehicles and space for a third. One she recognised immediately, George Gregory's Z4. The other was a white stretch limo she'd not seen before.

Stacey looked around the garage but could see no sign of a door leading to the house. She thought it odd, but returned to the front door, at the top of a rise of three marble steps. There was an antique polished brass doorbell, which seemed a little pointless, given the entry security. She pressed it and heard a ding-dong tone from deep inside. She waited. Nothing happened.

Stacey tapped James' number on her phone and listened to it ring several times before a woman's voice then answered.

'James Carter's phone. He's not here at the moment may I help you?'

'Who am I speaking to?'

'DS Jennifer Crawford, Senior Officer Warakurna Community.'

Stacey's phone fell from her fingers and cracked as it hit the stone floor of the portico. She looked down at her shattered device and could hear the faint, tinny sound of a voice emanating from its speaker. She stamped her foot on it to shut off the sound. Picked up the pieces and returned to her car, after first tossing the remote control over the old lady's gate. 'Bastard, cheating, fucking bastard.' She shouted through tears and was in no condition to drive, but she wanted to be as far away from here as was humanly possible.

***

Mickey Krakauer's meeting with Jackie, was somewhat more relaxed than that between James and Jennifer.

'Hi,' he'd said. 'Sorry it's so late, but.'

'They've put you up with me. I didn't ask for it and I'd like you to get over whatever business you have with Mickey and get back out of my life ASAP, capisce.' She handed him a towel and a bar of soap. 'That's your room. Good night, Detective Seargent.' Jennifer pushed open her bedroom door and pulled it shut behind her.'

'Sorry Jen,' he called after her. 'I didn't know you'd transferred before it was too late. Good night.' He found the shower freshened up and crashed on the tiny single cot in the spare room. She was so close he could smell her once familiar scent and sleep would not come easily tonight.

Jennifer's alarm was too far away to be effective, and his appalling night had left him in the deepest sleep when he should have been awake.

He heard her thump on his door. 'I don't care if you want to stay in bed all day, but I need to get to work.'

'Sorry Jen, give me a minute. I'll quickly shower and be with you.' He saw her gathering her things and ignored her as he passed to get to the bathroom. On the way he dropped a file and his phone, on the table with her stuff.

Jennifer didn't speak. The last thing she wanted to admit, was the awful night she too had experienced. She waited while he showered and when his phone rang, she'd picked it up in an auto response.

***

The old woman, who lived in the house next door to George Gregory, was startled when the remote-control device clipped her head after it passed over the wall. 'Hey!' she shouted. She was too late to catch the number plate of Stacey's car as it turned at the end of the street.

She went inside and picked up the handset of a landline phone on a small antique table. She'd never had a call to make contact with the police but this time she had been angered by the crass lack of concern shown by the woman who could easily have deposited the unit in the post box as she'd requested. She dialled 000 and waited.

'What state are you in?' A voice answered.

'Beg yours?'

'What state are you in please?'

'Don't you know?'

'What state ma'am?'

'Western Australia, of course. I'm at...' she rattled off the address. 'That is in Peppermint Grove. Just so you understand the importance of my call.'

'What is the emergency, Ma'am?'

'A woman has just thrown next door's gate controller over my wall. It hit me on the head.'

'Do you need an ambulance?'

'What?'

'Do you require police, ambulance or fire?'

'Police of course. That is why I'm calling you.'

'Thank you, ma'am.'

A few moments later a gruff sounding male voice said, 'Someone threw something over your wall and it injured you, is that right?'

'Next door's gate controller to be precise.'

'How is that an emergency?'

'Well, I don't know who she is. She might be a burglar or something.'

'She?'

'Youngish woman, maybe early forties, said she wanted to contact Mr Gregory, but couldn't get in. I told her to put the controller in the post box when she'd finished. Instead, she…'

'Madam, I do not believe this requires an urgent response. I'll pass your details to one of our patrols who will get to you when they have an opportunity.'

The line went silent.

'Ha! Not good enough my friend.' She dialled another number.

'Violet, hello, my dear. It's been a long time since you last called. Is everything alright?'

'No, it is not, Robert. I have just made an emergency call for help, and it has been dismissed as being unimportant.'

'Oh dear. Tell me what has happened. I can't promise. Things are very tight at the moment.'

She retold the story and when she mentioned George Gregory's name the tone of the voice at the other end, changed.

'Did you say George Gregory?'

'That's right. He's my next-door neighbour.'

'Like I said, I can't promise but I'll look into it. How have you been?'

'Just get your people here, now, Robert. You might have a fancy rank but you're still a police officer.'

'Yes, Aunty Violet.'

The line went dead again, and as Aunty Violet returned to her gardening chores of pulling up the new shoots that the professional gardeners had missed. She tutted as a number of police sirens sounded in the street outside.

'Well done, Robert, I'll put in an extra rock cake for you,' she said as she walked to her gate and opened it to see what appeared to be a SWAT team gathering around the Gregory gate.

One black clad man approached her, 'Are you the one who called in the emergency?'

She nodded smugly.

'Do you have this remote-control device?'

She reached into her apron pocket and handed him the device.

'Go inside and close your doors.'

Violet nodded and went to her first-floor bedroom where she could glimpse some of next door. She'd not felt so excited since her husband died and she discovered he'd left her several million dollars.

***

The SWAT team opened the gate and began calling out "Armed Police…!" as they swarmed around the perimeter of the house.

The garage doors were now open, and the two males and a female officer assigned, were staring, in awe, at the cars.

'Sarge?'

'Found something?'

The male officer held up a scrunchy of the kind teenage girls hold back their hair with. 'Just like my kid's.'

'Evidence bag.'

'Sarge.'

They carried on scouring the garage but found nothing of note.

'Weird init, Sarge?' the female officer said.

'What's weird?'

'Posh house, posh suburb, posh cars. Heavy duty physical security, but no CCTV and no way to get into the house from the garage.'

The sergeant shrugged.

A commotion from outside stopped them in their tracks.

'That's it, false alarm. Withdraw and return to base.'

The SWAT team dispersed into their transport and the senior officer placed the remote control in Violet's letterbox slot. He would have a forthright conversation with the man who activated them, on his return.

Chapter 36

When James returned from the shower, Jennifer was clutching his phone with an anguished expression on her face. 'Something wrong?'

'I'm so fucking sorry, Jim. I didn't ask for any of this shit.'

'What's happened.' He reached out and took the phone from her. 'Has somebody called me?' He checked his recent calls and saw the name Stace. 'Is she alright?'

'I don't know. The line went dead as soon as I mentioned my name.'

'Christ!' He tapped the number but there was no response. 'Did she say anything?'

'I think she just hung up the phone. Did she know you were coming here and that I'd be here?'

He shook his head and tapped the number for his parents. 'Mum. I have a problem. Stacey just called and I think she might be in a bit of a state. Could I ask you a favour…?' He ended the call and turned to Jennifer. 'I only found out that you were here after I'd set out. Jackie reckons Mickey might have information about the Connolly murder. She knows a few things, and she reckons that between them, they might be able to open up a couple of leads.'

'I'm so sorry if I've upset Stacey, Jim. I came here to put clear air between us. I didn't expect…'

He looked into her eyes and saw the thin line of wetness

beginning to form on her lower lids. James Carter wanted nothing more than to reach out and… He was too late.

Jennifer's phone rang. She pulled back the bed sheet and rummaged on the bedside cabinet. 'Hello?'

'Everything alright, boss?'

'Shit! Sorry, Clarrie. Overslept. I'm on my way right now.'

He curled his arm around her naked waist and felt her shiver. 'We'd better get a move on.'

She turned to watch him as he dressed. 'We've really fucked up, this time, Carter.' Her face stiffened as though she was deep in thought. 'I didn't,' she said.

'Didn't what?'

'I didn't find someone else. I couldn't.' Jennifer grabbed her clothing and ran to the bathroom.

James heard the shower start the moment his phone buzzed.

'You don't deserve that girl, you disgust me.'

'Mum?'

'Most men would have checked into a cheap motel but not you.'

'What are you talking about?'

'Your wife went out of her way to help you, and this is how you treat her?'

'Went out of her way?'

'You mean you don't know.'

He knew what he'd just done but. 'Has something happened?'

'She visited that creep, Gregory's place. Next thing the armed response group are all over the TV news reports.'

'Shit. She never mentioned that.'

'Probably because your girlfriend answered her call instead of you.'

Jennifer was tucking her shirt into her trousers when he looked up. Her hair still wet from her shower and her face still flushed from their lovemaking. 'What now?' she mouthed, without making eye contact.

He muted the phone. 'Stacey went around to Gregory's and sparked of a full scale ARG operation.'

'Shit! Well, he is best mates with the Commissioner, but that's not what I meant.'

'I wish I knew, Jen.'

She picked up her bag and keys and headed for the door.

'I'll take my car. It might be better if we're not seen to arrive together.'

Jennifer nodded and climbed into the four by four.

***

'Speak slowly and clearly Mrs Carter. You are not under arrest, but we need to know why you visited the house in Peppermint Grove yesterday?'

'My husband asked me to check on his sister. She hadn't collected her child from their mother's place, and she hadn't made contact to say why.'

'Why would that make you cause a disturbance at Mr Gregory's home? His neighbour was so upset she dialled 000.'

'Her phone was damaged during an incident on a train and my husband had lent her his. Because she couldn't call him Angela left a message in his notes app. It was to tell him that she suspected Gregory's house might contain evidence relating to the murder of Rebecca Connolly.'

'That case is closed. The perpetrator is in prison and your husband is currently under suspension. Where is he now?'

'I don't know but his sister's car was parked directly across the road from Gregory's place when I was there.'

'Can you describe it?'

'A metallic red Rav 4.' I'd show you a photo of it, but I dropped my phone, and it was smashed.'

'Why was your husband's sister, sniffing around the home of

George Gregory?'

'She said she suspected he was maybe the murderer of Rebecca Connolly and that he might also be a part of a human trafficking ring...'

The officer laughed out loud. 'You do realise who George Gregory is? He mixes with the elite of Perth and is a good friend of the commissioner, himself.'

Stacey shrugged. 'Anyway. There was no one there. The house seemed deserted except for the two cars in the garage. A BMW Z4— I know he drives that—and a white stretch limo.' She shrugged again. 'Why not ask the commissioner to give Gregory a call. Maybe he can answer your questions.'

***

Jackie had a tight smile on her face when James walked into the small office, they'd been allowed to use as an interview room.

Mickey Krakauer was sitting opposite her, trying not to make eye contact.

'Right, you two. What can you tell me about the rumours that surrounded DCI Clitheroe?'

'You mean you don't know, Sarge?' Mickey blustered.

'I know some stuff, but I want to hear everything you have. I know he gave you a rough time, and I'd rather be speaking to him personally but fortunately or maybe unfortunately, he's joined the choir infernal.'

Mickey smirked.

Jackies eyes rose to the ceiling.

'As I heard it. There'll be no comeback on this?' He paused.

James nodded. 'I'm under suspension Mick, I'm not even a cop at this moment in time.'

Mickey nodded. 'Rumour was that Slippery was in league with a few high-fliers, and they used to share girls. By that I mean barely legal or even way too young.'

'That's a significant accusation, Mick. Have you anything to back it up?'

Jackie interrupted. 'I have.'

'Oh?'

'That Rebecca Connolly. The one who was found dead, and the kid was blamed.'

'Go on.'

'She was Slippery's—sorry DCI Clitheroe's—niece. He used to take her to visit her father's grave once a week.'

'That's common knowledge.'

'Well, the story has it that Clitheroe and George Gregory had an arrangement. He would leave her at the cemetery and George would collect her to take her home, where she would provide his kid with extra tuition.'

'We know that.'

'It's never been proved but, after a few beers one night, Slippery allowed it to slip out that he and Gregory used to take turns with Rebecca after the family had gone to bed.'

James raised his eyes. 'Well, she was an adult. That really doesn't count if it was consensual, and someone would surely have noticed.'

'Who said anything about consensual? I heard that George used to drug the whole family at the end of the session. Hot chocolate laced with Rohypnol. But, one night, Gregory got the mugs mixed up. Instead of his wife being knocked out, he was, but not before he was caught by his wife trying to mount Rebecca. The poor woman was unconscious and there was a camera set up over the bed.' She smirked. 'Then slippery turned up for his share.'

'Shit,' Mickey said, 'Remember when Slippery tried it on with you in Hedland?'

Jackie nodded. 'Sorry Mick, I couldn't stop him. I could barely keep my eyes open. Then you arrived on the scene. All hell broke loose, and you stabbed Slippery in the back with a screwdriver.' She reached for a tissue. 'You changed after that.'

Mickey reached across the table to take her hand. 'I thought...'

'Well, you thought fucking wrong, constable. Slippery was going to throw the book at you but...'

'Shit.'

'Yeah, shit, and it's cost me my career and time in the slammer.'

James hadn't expected this sudden outburst. He was expecting a long and tedious picking away until something coherent emerged. 'So, you're saying that Slippery drugged you, and he and Gregory used the same technique on Rebecca?'

'Slippery was spitting chips when he arrived at the office the next day. He called me in and said...' Jackie's face cracked, and she began to sob.

'Take your time, Jack,' Mickey said.

He threatened to have you charged with stabbing him if...'

'He'd have left it a bit late.'

She emitted a humourless laugh. 'He could pull strings, Mick, and you'd already been cast aside.'

James raised his hands in a defensive position. 'Hey, guys. How does this move us forward?'

'She collaborated with Slippery to save me.' Mickey pointed at Jackie, stood and walked around the table to lift her from her seat and crush her in an embrace that ended in a passionate kiss.'

'Well, now you know.' Jackie said when she came up for air.

'That's why you were so standoffish?'

'I had to keep my distance, Mick. I'm sorry. It hurt me as much as it did you.'

Clarrie arrived with a tray laden with coffee and biscuits. She stared at Mickey and Jackie, still in their embrace. 'Shit, must be sommat in the water out here, but Collard aint drinkin it.'

Chapter 37

Angela Carter felt death must be imminent, she could barely breathe, and her swollen dried-out tongue was sticking to the sides of her mouth. She tried to move, but none of her muscles seemed to work. She was paralysed, she knew that, but her mind was still very much alive.

She tried to move her eyes to see if there was anything that might help her to break her malaise. All she could see were a pair of feet sticking out from the top of the bed.

She remembered what had happened, and when the feet moved, she knew her situation had just changed for the worst. Angela hoped she had killed him. Instead, she was the one as good as dead, and she had no idea how long she had been in this state.

The feet stopped moving and a loud groan sounded from where the head end might be.

Holding her breath wasn't an option. *Shit, where is everyone?* She heard the door to the room open. *Is this one of his accomplices?*

'Christ! Better get in here sarge.'

'What is this place some kind of Botox lab?' another voice said.

'Well, whatever it is we now have what seems to be an attempted murder.'

'Dissatisfied client?'

Angela saw a face close to hers. 'Did you hit him with the bottle?' The face had a hand connected that pointed to the oxygen cylinder.

She tried to answer but nothing came.

A voice spoke into a device. 'We have what looks like an attempted murder.'

…

'Mr Gregory, the commissioner's friend.'

…

'A woman early-forties, maybe.'

…

'There is also several of what appear to be comatose patients in other rooms. We'll be needing some ambulances.'

…

'Roger that.'

Angela saw, what appeared to be, police officers lifting Gregory from the bed, and it sounded like they'd carefully laid him on the floor beside her. She wanted to cringe away. She couldn't.

***

Clarrie had been gone for about thirty minutes when Jennifer poked her head in. Deliberately ignoring James, she said in a forceful tone, 'PC Krakauer. We have a problem.' She waved him out of the room. 'Sorry folks there's been a shooting a few kays up the road. I'm sure you can keep yourselves amused.' The door closed.

James looked across the table at Jackie. 'You were close?'

'Two fucking close for Clitheroe.' She smiled brightly for the first time. 'The water must be doing him some good, he looks so healthy.'

'Country living you reckon?'

'You and her?' Jackie nodded to the door.

'None of your business.'

Jackie grinned. 'I was right then.'

Clarrie interrupted them. 'Sorry again. DS Carter. Head office on the line.'

James followed her to the land line and lifted the receiver. 'Carter?'

'Your suspension is revoked. Get your arse back here quick smart.'

'Boss?'

'They've found your sister.'

'Angela?'

'Do you have another?'

'Is she okay?'

'No, and it looks like she'll be charged with attempted murder as soon as she recovers. Higher if her victim dies, which is on the cards.'

'Victim?'

'Get yourself back to Perth ASAP. There is a flight leaving the Warakurna Community this afternoon.'

'My car?'

'Your problem.'

James returned to the room and slumped in his chair. 'They want me back. Suspension over.'

'That's good news, isn't it?'

'Well, if what you said is true, and I'm not, in any way, saying it's not. I will be on the afternoon plane from here, so I'll need you to take my car and get back to Perth. Set up a recorder and save anything you can remember, as you drive.'

'What about Mickey?'

'I'll need him too, but I'll need to clear that with Jen... Um... DS Crawford.'

Jackie seemed to ignore his slip, deliberately. 'Thanks for what you're doing Jim. I'd never have seen Mickey again if it weren't for you. If there is anything... anything I can do, please don't hesitate to...'

The two-way radio had suddenly become active. They both headed towards the sound.

'Fucking ambush, Jim. Mickey and Jen are both holed up and

under fire.'

'My suspension has been lifted, where are your weapons?'

'Follow me.' Clarrie led him to a locked and reinforced door. 'Technically...'

'You up for this Jack?'

She nodded.

'Couple of Glocks, a shotty and a rifle. We won't be close enough for tasers.'

Clarrie looked over James' shoulder. 'She's on parole. I can't.'

Jackie shrugged. 'Okay Jim, you sign for the weapons, and I'll just come along as a first aider/impartial observer.' She turned to Clarrie who retreated.

From what Clarrie had said there wasn't much time. James checked the weapons and ammunition. When satisfied, he loaded them into his vehicle and the pair prepared to set out and meet their fate.

'Yeay!' Jackie said. 'Crim one day, shootout the next.'

'You do remember the rules?' James said as he loaded the pump action.

Jackie rolled her eyes, clicked in the magazines, and racked both Glocks. Then she reached for the rifle to do the same.

Clarrie unfolded a map, pointed to the location and handed him the keys to the police vehicle, standing on the road outside. 'Good luck guys I'll try to get you some back up when I can track the buggers down.'

***

Stacey Carter gave up. She'd tried several times to reach her husband's phone and had left him several messages. All of them apologetic for her mistrusting him. The police had released her on a caution and had advised she might be in serious trouble if she were to visit Gregory's place again.

She switched on the TV news and saw Gregory's house with a

journo, front and centre, talking about the police raid, and the finding of six mid teen girls and a middle-aged lawyer who was accused of attempting to kill the homeowner.

The reporter said that all the females were in no condition to speak. Stacey picked up the handset of her land line and called the officer who she had spoken to earlier.

'Please stay out of this Mrs Carter. We are doing everything we can to discover what is going on and there is nothing more for you to do.' He was about to hand up when he heard her voice screaming down the phone.

'My fucking daughter is in hospital! She was drugged and they say she may never recover!'

'Madam…'

'The drug is believed to be Russian and causes its victims to Zombify! There is an apparent antidote and I believe you will find it in George Gregory's house…!'

'Madam, Mr Gregory was attacked by your brother's sister…'

'I would have made sure the bastard was dead.'

The line went silent but for the sound of a muffled voice. A minute later a new voice came on the line.

'Mrs Carter. I should tell you that I am DI Mulligan, and I am involved with the search of the premises. Now, this antidote?'

'James took a series of screen dumps relating to a drug and its antidote, but no one knew where it might be obtained.' She paused. If you can give me an email address, I'll scan what I have here, and send it to you. Maybe you can check if there is anything like it in that house.'

Mulligan rattled off an address and Stacey sent the images.

A few minutes later her phone rang.

'Hello?'

'Mrs Carter?'

'Thanks for that, but it's all in Russian.'

Stacey rolled her eyes. 'Of course it's in fucking Russian, that's where it's fucking made. Find some drug supplies with Russian names and you might just get somewhere. Do I have to teach you your fucking job. And, while you're at it, there are five little girls all in the same boat as my daughter. If you remember, it was my husband who was involved with their rescue and your mob suspended him.' She slammed down the phone in a fit of anger and tried James' number again.

This time he answered. 'Hi Stace, I can't speak for long I'm on my way to a local incident...'

'I've just had some moron cop in my ear. Aren't you supposed to be on your way home?'

'Sorry, there's been a shooting and a couple of officers are holed up, so it's all hands to the pump. Hopefully I'll be on the afternoon plane so I should see you soon.'

'I sent him your screen dump of the Russian drugs and he complained it was in fucking Russian.' She heard the rooftop siren kick in as the line went dead.

Chapter 38

As soon as James flicked the siren, the group of individuals using their cars as cover turned their weapons towards his vehicle. He heard the clank of a bullet as it ricocheted off the roof.

'Shit, Jack. Head down!' He could see the shooter and the gun smoke still drifting around his head. He steered the car directly for the man and put his foot down hard on the throttle.

The whole gang began shooting in their direction, but, luckily, their marksmanship was the equal of their bravery. They leapt into their vehicles and stirred up a ton of dust as they revved their engines to go nowhere, fast.

He stopped and, using his vehicle as cover, called to the drivers to give up.

One had become irrevocably bogged the other was sideways across the road.

'Throw down your weapons and step out of your cars!' He raised the shotgun to his shoulder and sighted down the barrel.

Jackie did the same with her rifle, her aim on the bogged car.

James saw a movement by a rocky outcrop. It was Mickey waving furiously.

'Stay down Mick!' James yelled.

'It's DS Crawford, she's hit!'

Mickey's words struck James like a sledgehammer. He fired a round at the gang vehicle, and its occupants immediately stepped out with their hands in the air. He pumped in a new cartridge and turned the weapon to the other vehicle, but he didn't need to pull the trigger.

When he was sure they were all disarmed, he approached and made them lie face down while Jackie used plastic ties to cuff them.

'Hey, Jimmy. Fucking help me, here!'

James radioed for an ambulance then jogged towards the outcrop with his shotgun at the ready. Jennifer was stretched out on her back and a large bloodstain had spread across the sand. Mickey was speaking softly to her when he arrived. He dropped to one knee.

He whispered close to her ear, 'Hey, what's all this?'

She coughed up some blood and beckoned him close. 'Sorry my love. It's better this way.' In her hand was a crumpled and bloodied sheet of paper. 'Some… links… they might help…' her head flopped to one side, and blood trickled from her lips before she lay still.

'Shit, Jim,' Mickey said. 'I tried.'

He patted the constable on the back and called to Jackie. 'If one of those bastards should even blink, you have my permission to blow their fucking brains out.' He turned to Mickey. 'Give me a few minutes mate.'

Mickey nodded and left his friend to return to the woman he'd been missing for longer than he could remember. She'd rolled up her sleeves and he could see the prison tattoos standing out on the taut brown skin of her forearms as she held her rifle ready for action. 'Love the tats, well no I don't, but no matter I love you, babe.'

'Jackie smiled let's not drop our guard, hey, big fella.'

The sound of a siren filled the air from somewhere within a distant dust cloud. For one man his world had ended, whilst for another it had just begun.

James Carter's phone vibrated. He rummaged in his pocket. 'I'm surprised there's a signal here.' He looked at the screen and saw there had been several calls from Stacey and one from Mulligan. He opened the doors of the vehicles and manhandled the cuffed gang into the rear. Then he opened the boot of the nearest car and found twenty-five reasons for them being there. He opened the other boot. It was stocked with cases of spirits and more of the white bags.

There was another vehicle further down the road. Its tires were flat, its windscreen shattered, and its passengers were both dead from head shots. James checked its boot and found several leather holdalls. He unzipped them one after the other and saw more cash than he could hope to earn in an entire lifetime.

He watched the ambos wheel their stretcher back to their vehicle and slide its shrouded cargo inside, there was no hint of ceremony.

James called in his findings then he, and his colleagues watched in silence as the ambulance retreated slowly within another dust cloud.

'What next Jen?' he mumbled. 'You asked, and you got your answer.' He could feel his shoulders begin to shudder involuntarily and he fell to his knees on the rough ground.

***

Detective Inspector Mulligan grunted as he slammed down the receiver. 'Bloody cheek. Bloody sergeant's wives telling us what to do. Not good enough.' He called through to the outer office. 'When DS Carter gets here, tell him I want him in my office. Immediately.'

A voice called back. 'He won't be here until late if he's flying in from Warakurna, boss.'

'What the fuck's he doing there?'

'Dunno sir, he was suspended, remember?'

'Well, first thing in the morning then.'

A female voice piped up, 'Just heard there's been a shooting out there, boss. DS Crawford, they reckon. So…'

'Is she okay?' Mulligan called.

'DOA, sir.' A moan was followed by a sniff.

'What did you just say?'

'She's fucking dead y…' The voice cut itself off, probably to avoid continuing with, 'you fuckwit.'

'Shit!' Mulligan picked up his phone from his desk and scooted from the office.

After he'd gone, the office fell silent for several minutes.

'Anyone know if she has someone… family?'

There was no answer. It was as if they all knew.'

***

Jackie Morton said nothing as she drove the police vehicle back to the station building. She didn't dare cast a glance at the man beside her, lest she'd crack up and make a complete fool of herself, but she couldn't stop the tears though, and her dusty face had pale rivulets all the way from corners of her eyes to her chin.

In her peripheral vision she saw his face turn slightly towards her. 'Don't, Jim. Please. I'm barely holding together as it is.'

'I have to get that plane back to Perth,' he said, and handed her the flight details Clarrie had given him before they set out.

Jackie pulled to the side of the road and found the paper map in the door slot. She pointed at the airfield and looked at her watch. 'According to this, your plane leaves at 1330. We'll need to go straight there from here. You okay with that?'

James shrugged. He'd travelled light, and he'd have everything he'd need at home.

'You can't go like that, mate. Have you looked at yourself recently?'

James adjusted the rearview and saw the shirt he was wearing was covered with blood. He tapped on his phone. 'There's no signal.'

Jackie picked up the shortwave mic and called in their position. 'DS Carter needs to be at the Giles airfield in just over one hour. He can't travel covered in blood can someone…?'

Clarrie answered, 'I'll get someone to pick up his stuff from

Jenn's place...' There was a gasp. 'Sorry... He'll meet you at the airfield.'

'Thanks Clarrie. Get that, Jim?'

James nodded. 'Thanks Clarrie,' he called, and then closed his eyes. He'd be home in something like seventeen hours. Then he'd have to face Stacey, and he wasn't sure how that might pan out with his current emotional overload. She'd known that he'd gone to a place where his former lover had been transferred. What she didn't know, was that he'd lay in her arms all night after making love for, unbeknown to him, the last time.

He could still taste her scent and as he looked down at her dried blood on his shirt, he knew he would never be able to put her out of his mind nor the corrupt office politics engendered by Slippery Clitheroe. If it hadn't been for Slippery's actions, Jennifer might have been his wife, instead of Stacey.

'Hey, Jim?'

He turned to face Jackie, who was staring directly ahead with her eyes firmly fixed on the dirt road.

'There was nothing you could have done, mate.' She reached across the car and rested her hand on his shoulder.

He turned to face her again. 'There is something I can do.' He pulled the bloodstained paper from his pocket. 'She'd been listing sites that traffickers use. They're all dark web shit, and you can bet your life that George Gregory will feature large in their dealings.'

'His hangers on will already be closing ranks, Jim.'

He nodded. 'But you have the knowledge, and Mickey knows more than he's saying. You both have an axe to grind, and I'll be happy to be the whetstone.'

'I'll do anything you want.'

'I want only the truth and nothing but the truth, Jack.'

'As soon as I get back from dropping you off. I'll speak to Mickey. Don't worry, ultimately this is going to hurt some people much more than it hurts us.'

The airport loomed on the horizon and Jackie pointed to a four by four, with its roof lights flashing. 'That'll be Clarrie. She's made good time.' She pulled alongside the vehicle and Clarrie stepped out with a bag in her hand.

'I hope I've got everything and there's at least a change of clothes.' Clarrie reached out and drew James into a hug.

Mickey was in the passenger seat. He waved but didn't leave the car.

'Mickey's a good bloke, Jack.' James said.

She nodded towards the car. 'If you want. I can get myself back.' she sucked in a deep and tremulous breath 'It's been a long time. I just hope it hasn't been too long.'

Clarrie drove James the remainder of the way to the airport. On the way, she said, 'I didn't want to say anything earlier, but there's been some movement and I'm feeling you'll need to drive things hard.'

'Movement?'

'I guess you'll find that out when you get home.'

Chapter 39

While he waited for his flight to be readied for take-off, James tried Stacey on their land line. This time she answered.

'Where are you?'

'Waiting to board a plane at Warakurna. Short flight to Yulara, then about four hours of hanging around and about 8.5 hours to home via Adelaide, I hope. Any news of Andria?'

'Still locked in. Angela is too. They found her in Gregory's house, she'd hit him with an oxygen cylinder, and they'll be charging her with attempted murder as soon as she recovers consciousness.'

'I've had a message from Mulligan. He's making noises about me getting back to the office.'

'Does that mean you're no longer suspended?'

James laughed. 'I guess that will depend on whether I hit the bastard or not.' He paused for perhaps longer than he should.

'You okay?'

'We'll need to have a long talk.'

'You can say that again. How is Jennifer?'

He paused again. 'There was a shootout, drugs. She was caught in the crossfire.'

'Shit, is she okay?'

He felt his voice crack as he said, 'No... She's... She's fucking... Dead... Shit, Stace. I didn't want any of this to happen.'

Stacey's voice softened. 'Come straight home, hun. Mulligan can wait.'

'There is too much to do. Jen gave me a list of sites that need looking into if we are to find that antidote and I owe it to her to make the most of it. I know I'm going to be up against it trying to get a second search warrant for Gregory's place and I'll need to use every trick in the book.'

'Jen is it…? Your family are more important, I hope.'

'If I don't crack this, two members of my family might die with some filthy paedo's drug in their system. Did you get any response in respect to the screen dumps?'

'Mulligan sounds like he's shit scared of upsetting someone…'

'So, there you have it. If we're to find the drug, Andria and Angela need, we can't afford to be reticent. Personally, I don't care whose toes I tread on from now on.' He felt a tap on his shoulder.

'Boarding, sir.'

'I'll have to go, Stace. We're boarding.'

'Come straight here…'

'Okay.' He pressed end, walked to the light plane, waiting on the dirt runway, and handed his bag to the pilot who jammed it in the luggage compartment in the aircraft's nose, before James clambered into the cabin. There were ten people on the plane and from experience, the acoustics, would prevent all but minimal conversation. For that he was thankful.

The doors closed, the twin props started, and the aircraft taxied into position at the end of the runway. James peered out of the window and saw Clarrie and Jackie standing next to their vehicles. They wouldn't be able to see him but the fact that they waved as the plane began to move lifted his spirits, in a strange kind of way.

The pilot made a couple of announcements, they didn't sound like a panic, so he settled down for the ear-wearing trip to Yulara.

***

The flight from Yulara was a little more comfortable than the trip from Warakurna and he tried to get a bit of shut eye. With no direct flight he was stuck with a trip via South Australia which added time to the journey. It turned out that shut eye wasn't a possibility, instead he had hours to think through the events of the last few days.

He tried to think only of Stacey and his kids, Jack and Andria, but the more he tried, the harder it was to forget Jennifer. They'd been drawn to each other right from the start, as recruits at the Police Academy. It hadn't taken long before they had moved in together as an almost unbreakable item.

Their first assignment as junior cops had them working together in Port Hedland, which is where they met Mickey Krakauer. Mick was slightly ahead of them in seniority but all three hung out together and backed each other up. Then Jackie joined the team, and they were complete. At least they thought they were.

Inspector Clitheroe had different ideas. James and Mickey regarded him as a half-arsed wannabe, but the two girls felt his misogynistic pressure, constantly.

Jennifer told James that he'd tried it on with her a couple of times, but she was adamant nothing more than drunken fumbles happened, and she didn't want it to go further. On the other hand, Jackie had to cope with a full-on rape by a senior officer, and that was when Mickey stepped in and tackled the man. At first it was a leave off order and Clitheroe had laughed, knowing he had won.

Next, Mickey was on a transfer to a country station. He was given only two days to sort out his affairs and when Clitheroe made a sneering comment, he copped a broken nose. The subsequent fight led to the pair of them rolling about in the vehicle workshop before Clitheroe locked Mickey in a choke hold. He was foundering until his hand fell on a heavy screwdriver and Clitheroe only stopped choking when its crude blade ripped through his skin and narrowly missed one of his kidneys.

Had it gone further they might have both been dismissed from the service. Clitheroe said nothing, and two days later Mickey was a PC in a remote Aboriginal community. Several years passed before Mickey and Jackie resumed their relationship back in Perth.

Jackie was under the command of the newly promoted DCI Clitheroe, and he never let her forget what he had over her lover.

Jennifer Crawford and James met again much later and instantly resumed their affair. Without warning Jennifer was on a transfer list to a regional station.

That was when Stacey came into James' life. They married and had two children. He was promoted to sergeant and went undercover on an op. Life seemed good until his sister almost broke his cover to ask him to investigate the strange happenings with Tom Gregory.

The whole of his life seemed to have been misdirected by DCI Clitheroe, and so when he discovered the man was involved in corrupt activities, it was a no brainer.

His sleepless reverie was shattered by the captain announcing the flight had begun its descent to Perth Airport, and James felt his guts twist. He would soon be in his home with the woman who had clearly been his second choice of partner. He loved her dearly, but could she continue to love him…

James had only an overnight bag, so he had no need to wait for the carousel to disgorge luggage. He made his way to a long queue for taxis. *Take your time folks*, he thought, *I'm in no hurry*.

James dropped his bag alongside his feet and prepared for the shuffle, when he noticed someone had picked it up.

He was about to say something when she closed his mouth with a kiss.

'My car is just there… Come on, you look like total shit.'

'Jack?'

'He's with your parents.' She lowered her eyes and poked him in the ribs. 'We have some catching up to do.'

James looked down at his watch. It was three-am. 'We'll need to be quick then… I have things to do that can't be delayed any further.'

Stacey led him to the car, threw his bag in the boot and slumped into the driver's seat. 'I'm so sorry about Jen.'

James nodded. Now was not the time for that discussion.

He seemed to have only slept for milliseconds when the alarm ripped him awake, and he turned towards his wife. 'I'm sorry. I'll have to go.'

She nodded and kissed him on the forehead. 'Find the bastards, Jim. This is now far too personal for an A-hole like Mulligan to have his way.'

While he showered for the second time in as many hours, Stacey threw his clothes in the washing machine and made him some toast and coffee.

'Thanks.' he said as he spread vegemite on his toast. Then he noticed her eyes were moist. He reached across the table and touched her cheek with his hand.

Stacy smiled, and a tear broke cover. 'The blood should come out of your shirt…' She stood, wiped away the tear with the back of her hand, sniffed, and began busying herself with kitchen stuff.

Chapter 40

He was finishing his coffee, when a toot from a siren told them they had visitors.

'Sorry,' Stacey said. 'I told them you'd be ready to go about now.'

James stood, put his hands around her waist and pulled her to him. He kissed her on the back of the neck and said, 'Wish me luck.'

She swivelled and kissed his lips. 'You have me, and you know exactly what you need to do, so you don't need luck.'

The ride to the station was mostly in silence. The young constable who'd been handed the job had obviously decided that any conversation with this, particular, DS might be career limiting. 'We're here, sarge. DI Mulligan said you were to go directly to his office.'

'Without passing go and then directly to jail, no doubt.'

The constable gave a confused shrug and said nothing.

'We'll see.' He returned sympathetic nods as he walked through the ground floor reception area to the lifts and pressed the button for the second floor. While he waited, he felt a presence. He turned towards the person who had approached.

'They say you were with her when…'

James raised his eyebrows.

'Before she was sent away, Jen put together a complete dossier…'

'DS Crawford?'

The woman nodded. 'The one thing Jen knew better than anyone else, was her way around a computer system. I think she'd known something was up even before you approached her.'

'So?'

'So, I want to help. If you'll let me.'

James looked up to the ceiling. 'I have to get past… You know who first.'

She smiled. 'You know where to find me.'

The lift door opened. He stepped inside and realised that she hadn't followed him. He reached out to stop the doors from closing, but she'd gone. Evaporated like a will-o-the-wisp.

***

The lift jerked softly to a halt, and the door opened to the corridor that would lead him to what? He had no idea what Mulligan was up to, but he had no choice than to confront his boss.

James Carter knocked on the door and was about to walk in when he heard the word, 'Enter.'

Mulligan was behind his desk a cup of fresh coffee sitting steaming next to a virginal blotter. He looked down at his watch. 'What time do you think this is Detective Sergeant?'

James looked at his own watch and said, '0930, sir. Is there a problem?'

'I stated first thing in my communication.'

'Well, here I am, sir.'

'You have been reinstated. The business you were involved with before you went bush is on hold until further notice.' He slid a manilla file across his desk. 'Your new assignment, DS Carter. Try not to stuff this one up.' He made a back handed wave as if summarily dismissing him from his presence.

James picked up the file and opened it. 'You have to be kidding me.'

'I beg your pardon, DS Carter. I don't think I heard the word, sir, and why are you still here. You have work to do.'

'Too bloody right I do.' He picked up the file and pulled the door firmly shut as he left. *You know where to find me she'd said.* There could only be one place and he strode to the lift, rose to the next floor, and marched directly to the cyber division. This time he didn't knock on the door, instead he pushed it open and looked across the sea of heads.

One head stopped bobbing immediately.

James made his way around the labyrinth until he located the young officer.

She smiled. 'You found me then?'

He slid onto the seat next to her. 'Okay. I should just warn you that…'

The officer stayed him with an envelope. 'Open it later. Meanwhile, take a look at this.'

James pocketed the envelope and stared at the screen she had energised. 'Jen…?'

'She was my boss, but she was also my friend… They say you were with her when she… You know,'

He nodded and reached into his pocket for the crumpled bloodstained note. 'She gave me this.'

'Is that her…?' Mandy said.

James nodded.

'Bastards!'

'We can't blame her murder entirely on them…'

'She wouldn't have been there if it hadn't been for…' She turned to glare into his eyes.

'You got me banged to rights on that one.'

'She was really upset one morning then she slapped in a transfer request and that was that. Now she's dead but I hold Mulligan to blame.' Mandy opened the file he'd placed on her desk. She covered her mouth but couldn't help her laughter. 'He's not serious?'

'You tell me.' Before he could say anything else another officer of similar age approached Mandy's desk.

She tapped her watch and said, 'We have to go, babe.'

'Sorry,' Mandy said, 'It's our first. It's due any day and we want to be together for the final ultrasound. This is Jean.' She slipped his bloodstained note into the file.

It was only then that he noticed that Jean's uniform was struggling to disguise a significant paunch.

Before he averted his gaze Mandy said, 'They've let her do light duties.'

'Well, don't let me hold you up.' He was stuck. His vehicle was still in Warakurna and wouldn't be back until Jackie arrived. He walked out of the station and caught a taxi to his home.

'Didn't expect you so soon.' Stacey said.

'My car is still in Warakurna, and I need a set of wheels pro-tem.'

'I'm not planning to go anywhere for a while, but I do need a new phone. Mine got broken.'

James kissed her, and said, 'I'll grab you a burner until we can make an insurance claim on your Android.' He picked up the keys to Stacey's Hyundai and said, 'I'll call you on the land line if there are any problems.'

***

Clarrie told Mickey she'd cover for him if he needed to go back to Perth and assist James. He didn't need much persuasion, and he set off in James' vehicle, soon after DS Carter's plane took off for Yulara, with Jackie riding shotgun on the long drive to Perth. It would be a two-to-three-day drive at least and would give them a chance to reconcile the relationship that was stolen by Clitheroe.

Neither spoke for many kilometres but they held hands like a couple of newly minted lovers. The occasional head turn, and a smile was enough.

'Did I tell you, you're looking absolutely fabulous, Mick?'

'You too, babe, but we need to start putting our heads together soon.

Jim Carter's going to need all the help he can get.'

'Ha!' Jackie pulled her hand free. 'Ten years in the slammer don't do anyone no good, but you're right, Mick, us getting all doe eyed aint gonna help no one.' She opened the screen of her phone and selected the voice memo. She then plugged its charger into the USB port and noted the charging symbol had appeared. 'That way we can just leave it on.'

'Anything that comes to mind, that's what he said, and I've got plenty to say about Slippery.'

'Jail was crap, Mick. Made Slippery seem like a good bloke.' She reached out and took his hand again. 'I had to do things…'

Mickey slowed, drove off the dirt road and onto an area of cleared bush. 'We all know what goes on in those places. You're out now. Everything that happened in there is behind us. We're gonna have to start all over again. Okay?'

Jackie nodded and was about to speak when a top end Land Cruiser roared past them at a speed far too high for the road condition.

It disappeared in a huge red dust cloud.

'Where are the cops when you need them,' Mickey said.

Out of some long and distant habit, Jackie had spoken the rego number aloud. It was picked up by the voice memo and converted to text. 'You can dob-em in when we get to the next stop, officer.'

'Yeah right. Leonora, here we come.'

Chapter 41

He'd almost forgotten the envelope, and he pulled it from his pocket.

Stacey looked a little askance, 'What are they up to now?'

James ripped open the envelope, and a smile curled across his lips. 'You little beauty, Jen.'

Stacey's eyes flashed. 'What?'

'It's a warrant to search Gregory's place from top to bottom and it's been signed off by the deputy commissioner.' He held up a handwritten note also signed:

> In strictest confidence,
>
> To whom it may concern,
>
> Detective Sergeant James Carter is to proceed with the execution of this warrant. He is authorised to utilise all personnel as required and is to report directly to me.
>
> Arthur Bertram Deputy Commissioner

A separate handwritten note in the envelope said:

> This has gone on too long, Jim. Whatever it takes, get to the bottom of it or both our necks will be on the block.
>
> Arty

'Who's Arty?'

'We signed up together at the academy. He had the creds for fast track, but he's a good bloke and Jennifer had his ear…'

Stacey interrupted him, 'She won't go away, will she?'

'She's dead, there's no coming back from that.' He turned towards his wife. 'Yes, we had a thing going in the early days, but it was long before I met you.'

'It didn't go away though, did it?'

James looked down at his hands. He wanted her to stop talking, because every word she said twisted a knife in the wound that had been Jenny Crawford. It wasn't working, and he felt his shoulders convulse. He tried to speak but all that came out was spluttered gibberish.

He felt Stacey's head press against his and her arm curl around his shoulder.

'Just us now, Jim. Please. I can't be doing with other stuff, and we need to get Andria free of the shit they've pumped into her.'

He looked into her eyes.

She nodded questioningly.

'Just us. I promise.' Stacey's unwavering faith seemed to spur him. 'Mickey Krakauer and Jackie Morton are bringing my wheels back from Warakurna.'

'Wasn't she the one who went down with Clitheroe?'

'Yep, and she was well and truly framed for it. She's carrying a nice fat grudge and so is Mickey. They both have an incredible knowledge of the goings on back then. Up to now they've been forced to it keep bottled up, but the cork is about to come out.' He kissed her on the forehead turned and walked out.

***

'I know that car, Jack.' Mickey picked up the phone and stared at the rego number, then he pointed out through the windscreen at an angle of 45 degrees. 'It's gonner get rough for a little while, but I know a route that I'll bet they don't.'

'Cross country, I'm impressed.'

'You might not be by the time we get there.' He checked the tanks one was low, but the extension was full to the brim. 'As long as we don't get a flat, we'll be good.' Mickey's driving was fast but skilful until he came to a poorly maintained dirt road. Then he bumped over the rough edges, turned right into the bush, and settled to a steady speed.

'Who are they?'

'You don't need to know. But as sure as eggs is eggs, they are soon gonna discover we've slipped their tail. Who'da thought it, hey. Fancy losing a tail in the middladabush.' His face widened into his classic Mickey grin. 'No one said we couldn't have fun.'

'Hey, we've gotta signal.'

A number of notations flashed up. They were mostly Facebook crap but there was a text from James Carter:

> Hey Mick,
>
> We've got the go ahead for a search of Gregory's place.
> I'd like your help. How long will you be?

Jackie held the phone for him to read the message.

'Text him back and say we were being followed, but we lost them. Give him that rego and say, next stop Leonora, about one hour. Then another 11 hours allowing time for a feed.'

Jackie keyed in the words as he said them and showed him the phone.

He nodded. 'Send it. You good for a nonstop?'

'Right now, I'm good for anything. Tell me when you want a break, you're the one who's driving nonstop.'

'We'll have a bite at Leonora, I know a place that does great pies. Then you can take over for a while. Let's see if we can get to Jim by early tomorrow morning.'

Jackie curled her knees under her and leaned her back against the door. 'Nighty-night then, big fella. Wake me when we get there.'

The dirt road Mickey had returned to, was slowly disappearing along with the light and he felt a little guilty about his estimated arrival time. He had the option of belting it and risking disaster, but he'd only just got his girl back and there was no way he was going to lose her again. He'd many years' driving experience on bush tracks and he knew how to do it safely.

It was midnight when he hit the main street of Leonora, and his favourite pie shop was closed. He turned left onto the Goldfields Highway and left Jackie sleeping while he filled up at the BP Servo. He grabbed a paper, some drinks, chips and snags, and a couple of bars of chocolate. He used the paper to stack everything on the centre console, then bit into a sausage and set off in the direction of Kalgoorlie. Three hours, then another six to Perth.

As he cruised into Menzies, Jackie stirred. 'Where are we?'

'Menzies.'

'You were supposed to wake me.'

He pointed to the cold sausage and the shrivelled chips on the greasy newspaper. 'Sorry, I reckoned you'd need the sleep more than the grub.'

Jackie picked up the cold sausage and bit into it. 'Not too bad.' Within minutes she'd scoffed the cold chips and washed them down with warm Coke. 'You really know how to treat a girl, Mickey Krakauer.'

'That's what they all say.'

Jackie found one of the chocolate bars and it set her off into a feeding frenzy until she finished them all. She saw Mickey's face turn. 'Don't get much of that shit inside, Mick.'

He laughed. *She can eat as much fucking chocolate as she likes.*

***

James returned to base and made his way directly to the desk of Mandy Stevenson. 'How did the ultrasound go?'

'All good.' She smiled and flipped a photograph.

'I remember those.' He pulled out Arty's note and showed it to her. 'Looks like our girl pulled strings.'

'Shit.'

'Welcome to the team. I have Jackie Morton and Mickey Krakauer on their way from Warakurna and I have a warrant to search Gregory's place that I intend to execute first thing tomorrow. There will be data and software, and all the stuff you are familiar with. While you go through that, we'll be going through the other stuff.'

'I'll need to clear…'

He held up the note from Arty. 'You're now cleared by order of the deputy commish. See you at six am.'

Mandy looked at her watch, closed her laptop and slipped it into a soft leather case. She then picked up a small, framed photograph and placed it in a pocket of the case.

James had noticed the picture of Mandy and a young man earlier but said nothing. 'Your brother?'

'In a way. A close friend and colleague, he was killed in an IED incident in Afghanistan.'

'You where…?'

Mandy said nothing, but stood, and wrapped her utility belt around her waist. She tied the bottom of her holster around her lower thigh and said, 'Well then Sarge, I'll be needing an early night and then we'll do it for Jen.'

Eyes followed them as they walked from the cube farm. So rarely did anyone wear arms in cyber division it would soon get around that something was afoot, and time was of the essence.

James made another call to complete his team then he headed to the hospital to see first his daughter and then his sister.

Andria was connected to a drip and apparently sleeping peacefully. Her nurse said that all her vitals were as they should be.

He raised his eyebrows.

'Well, as near they should be without…'

James nodded she looked so peaceful, and he wondered if she'd remember any of this later. 'The other kids who came in with her?'

The nurse said, 'All pretty much the same. We are still waiting for your mob to tell us who they are.'

'It's in hand.' He replied. 'My sister is in a similar condition.'

The nurse nodded. 'So I heard.'

James left and found Angela flat on her back on a hospital bed, with her eyes staring directly ahead as if she was dead.

'Ange?' He thought he detected a slight movement in her eyes. 'Can you hear me?' The movement occurred again. 'Gregory?'

The movement occurred again. It was barely noticeable, but he had to be certain.

'Eyes left for yes, right for no.'

'Are you Angela Carter?'

Her eyes flicked left.

'Your favourite snack is tinned salmon sandwiches?'

Her eyes flicked right.

He grinned. 'This might take a while.'

Her eyes flicked left.

'Did you try to kill George Gregory?'

Her eyes flicked left.

Their eyeball conversation continued for several minutes before a nurse interrupted them. 'I need to bathe her eyes, she can't close them, and you should leave her to get some rest.'

James nodded. Their painful conversation had yielded only limited information, but it was more than when he started. He now knew that the Antidote needed to be his primary target of the search. He held up the paper with the translation she had obtained.

Her eyes flicked left.

'Do you think the antidote will be found somewhere in Gregory's house?'

Her eyes flicked left.

As he walked from the hospital, he noticed that a text had arrived from Mickey's phone. It was late, but he knew what he needed to do.

Chapter 42

It was between Menzies and Kalgoorlie that he again saw the vehicle that had been tailing them. 'Any news of that number?'

Jackie checked the phone and shook her head.

'My belt is on the back seat. Reach it for me please.'

Jackie struggled over the seats and grabbed the belt.

Mickey leaned forward. 'Hand me the Glock.'

She did as he asked.

He rested the weapon between his thighs, 'Now text Jim and see if he's got any info on the number.'

She was about to hit send when his text arrived:

> Sorry Mick, I've only just seen this. Give me a
> few mins.
>
> Jim

Mickey continued as though nothing had happened, and he wasn't even certain that the car just ahead of them was the one tailing them. The rego number was the same and when he looked in the rearview mirror he realised why.

An identical vehicle to the one ahead was hugging his rear. It had all the ingredients of a disaster waiting to happen. 'They've pulled a swifty, Jack, and I think they've upped the ante.'

Mickies phone tooted. It was a message from James:

> Defo bogies.

You'll need to watch yourselves. It's not an official
police vehicle. There are two of them and they're out
your way on a "covert" police operation. I think it might
be directed at you, but I can't find more info, everyone
is being super cagey.

'How's Jack holding up?'

She's good, Jim. Mick has his Glock but if they're
cops?

Tell him to use his discretion, Jack.

Thanks.

You're welcome.

The text stream ended with a smiley face emoji.

'He says you to use your discretion, Mick, whatever that means.'

Mick pulled off the road and waited for what was to come. 'It'll look real good on tonight's news. "Sneaky cops in gunfight, in the goldfields".'

'I wonder if they'll let us have a copy of the report for my scrap book?'

'You keep a scrap book?'

The car in front didn't even slow down but the one behind swung out and pulled directly in front at an angle to prevent Mickey from extricating himself.

A face appeared at his window and Mickey ignored it.

The face's hand knocked on the window and indicated it should be wound down.

Mickey gripped the Glock and lowered his hand to his side before reaching over a and pressing the down button with his left hand.

'Licence.'

Mickey handed it him with his left hand.

The man took his licence and walked to the car across the front of Mickey's. A few moments later he returned. 'I have reason to believe this car is not yours.'

'And you would be perfectly correct.'

'Are you being some kind of smartarse?' He glared across the vehicle and locked his eyes on to Jackie. 'Well, well, well. What have we here? A car thief and his moll. Does your parole officer know about this, Ms Morton?'

'Well, you obviously do. So, I assume she does too.'

'Both of you, out of the car.'

Mickey obliged by opening his door and putting a round from his Glock through the man's knee. He then stepped out of the car and showed his squealing victim his police ID. 'We were warned that there were a couple of bogus cops picking on innocent tourists, so what do you have to say about that.'

The man's partner had exited their vehicle, and he was aiming a police issue weapon.

'You too? I think you'd better get, your man here, to Kalgoorlie hospital. That is if you don't want him to bleed to death.'

'You'll be in big trouble for this PC Krakauer.'

'So, you do know who I am and that's why you know about Jackie here. Pick him up and get him to hospital. How you explain a cop's bullet in his leg is your problem. Right now, I have urgent business in Perth, and your antics are slowing me down. Oh, and just by and by, I know who you two are and that your mate Slippery Clitheroe is out of circulation so he can no longer protect you.'

The man looked puzzled.

Mickey grinned. 'Get him to hospital, make your report and we'll see who wins, Detective.' He walked around the car. 'You good to drive, Jack?'

She stepped out, walked around, snatched Mickey's ID from the clutches of the wailing wounded and clambered into the driver's side. 'As a matter of fact, my parole officer *is* aware.' She slammed the door put the car in reverse and then drove around the askew vehicle.

'You did well, Jack.'

'Pricks.'

'I shouldn't have shot him.'

'Slippery shouldn't have screwed Rebecca Connolly, but he did.'

Mickey sent another text to James:

> Bogies buggered, boss. Might have some explainin to do.

> We'll be at Kal soon then full bore to Perth.

James replied with a thumbs up emoji before his eyes closed and he dropped into a deep sleep.

***

As the working day began, raised voices could be heard throughout the various police departments.

Fury at the issuing of a warrant was high on the list of DI Mulligan's list of gripes. He'd steadfastly avoided that next step and the raid on Gregory's property was listed a rescue mission to save him from a deranged lawyer. He'd taken care of the riskier side of the raid and the girls were all in hospital, but now he would be forced to approach his immediate superior to advise him things might be about to get out of hand.

George Gregory had credibility at the highest level both with the upper echelons of the police force and the government. It was rumoured that the Premier had even dined at his home on numerous occasions.

Mulligan picked up his desk phone and tapped in a number.

'What's happening, Mulligan? I've heard there was a shooting on the Goldfields Highway.'

'The least of your worries, sir. I reinstated Carter at your request and now he has obtained a warrant to search Mr Gregory's home.'

'We can't stop that?'

'Yes sir, we can, but the search is underway as we speak, and it seems those involved have the protection of a tactical response group.'

'I'll make a call.'

'Yes, sir, that would be good.' Mulligan rested the receiver and then his head in his hands. He was a green young PC when the Connolly murder was being investigated. He'd made a decision to gravitate towards those who were favouring Tom Gregory's incarceration and he'd even "arranged" evidential items at the behest of DCI Clitheroe. Fortunately, Clitheroe was caught red-handed in a drug sting and that meant Mulligan was able to cover his tracks.

Then Detective Sergeant Carter's sister became a thorn in his side, but she'd lost the trial. Tom Gregory got life and now Mulligan owed his father, who had played a significant role in his promotion. He visited the Archives, reached into the pertinent filing cabinet and removed the case notes. Next would require a careful adjustment of the contents to remove any papers that might indicate his involvement in anything that might point to a conspiracy to pervert the course of justice. His next move would be to obtain another search warrant to override Carter's.

***

At Southern Cross, Mickey reached into his travel bag and retrieved a small plastic tube.

'What's that Mick?'

He dismantled his Glock, opened the tube and slipped out a duplicate Glock barrel then reassembled the weapon with the new component. He held up the barrel for Jackie to see. 'Any ballistics, assuming they find the bullet, will be harder to track to this gun. The one I've just inserted is my original police issue.'

'Shit.'

'Yup.' He slipped the old barrel into the tube, 'I switched them before we left, just in case. I can lose the used one later if I need to. Take a break. I'll finish the trip.' He extricated himself from the car and swapped seats with Jackie.'

It was mid-morning when Mickey parked outside the Gregory mansion and was confronted by a heavily armed officer. He showed his ID, and the man communicated the details. The gate slid aside, and Mandy Stevenson reached out to shake his hand.

'We've been waiting for you two to show your faces.' She turned to Jackie.

'I don't have an ID.'

Mandy smirked. 'Jim tells me you're the one with all the creds, though.' She indicated that they should follow her and led them into the garage. 'Sneaky chap, our George.' She slid aside the tool rack to expose the lift and said, 'Jim's down below. I'll be upstairs if you need me for anything. Have fun.'

'Hello, anyone here,' Mickey said as the lift arrived, and the door opened. He didn't have long to wait for a reply.

James carter's head popped out of the second door on the right. He waved them along. 'Not much here, unfortunately. It's been cleaned out. I think if we're going to find anything significant it will have to be in the main house.'

Jackie had slipped on a pair of bootees and nitrile gloves and pushed in through a door at the end of the corridor. The incumbents of the rooms had been moved to a hospital environment where their drug induced state could be monitored professionally. Jackie grimaced, the floor had a spot of blood on it, and she flashed back to Mickey's shirt after Jenifer died.

She sucked in a deep breath and then, despite her time in prison, her professional training came to the fore. All the blood told her was that Gregory had suffered an attack with an oxygen bottle. It was still laying where it fell. She ran her hand over the mattress and searched for transferred debris such as hair. It wasn't just hair that she found. Two curly pubes almost side by side next to a dried stain. She leaned close, sniffed and grimaced again. 'Jim! I think I have something here.'

DS Carter and Mickey Krakauer arrived within a couple of seconds of each other.

'Show me,' James said.

Jackie pointed to the residue and the curly hairs, and said, 'Someone went off half-cocked and shot his load. Should be a nice serve of DNA in that lot.'

'If it belongs to Gregory…'

'Maybe your sister was acting in the girl's defence,' Mickey said.

Jackie followed with, 'Means the sicko can't say that Angela attacked him on a whim.'

'Wrap up the mattress for now, then let's start a search for the antidote. Several kids' lives are at stake, and we don't know how long they'll survive in the Zombie state.'

Jackie photographed the evidence, bagged and sealed it, then marked it with PC Krakauer, the date, and the time.

James' phone rang, and he answered it.

It was Mandy.

'Found something?'

'Not yet, I've just received a call from one of my colleagues. A woman has just walked into the Wanneroo police station and attempted to self-immolate.'

'Shit. What brought that on?'

Her eight-year-old child has been missing for about two weeks. When she reported it to the police, nothing happened, and then her husband mysteriously drove his car into a tree. He died at the scene.'

'Are you saying…?'

'Maybe one of the younger girls is her daughter?'

'Does your friend have her contact number?'

'It won't help unless you speak Spanish. She's from Argentina, on an accompanied corporate sponsorship deal with her engineer husband, and because of the time factor she is now only on a temporary visa and cannot work. To make matters worse, she has received a letter from immigration advising her that her visa is about to expire, and she must leave the country.'

'And her daughter is missing?'

'Hardly surprising she chucked a wobbly.'

'Mandy, get your colleague to organise an interpreter ASAP. Let's get this poor woman's questions answered and ask a few of our own. I also want photos of all the girls in the hospital. It strikes me that given this case has been allocated such a low profile, someone with connections might have something to lose.'

'On it. I've stalled a bit on the computers, anyway. It seems that Gregory employed some sophisticated software security, hopefully I'll crack it soon. The one thing that is patently obvious, is the lack of CCTV coverage at Gregory's place.'

The call ended.

James addressed Jackie and Mick, 'Well, you two, it's time to pull the house apart. I'm looking for anything that looks like Russian text. Do you understand?'

'Cyrillic, boss?'

'Smartarse, Mick. I'll be happy with phonetic translations if there are any.'

Mickey grinned, followed Jackie into the lift, and pressed the up button.

Chapter 43

The follow up from Mandy was not good. The woman had survived her attempt at self-immolation, but she was in a hysterical state when admitted to the hospital, where Mandy was advised she would be unavailable for interview.

'Am I hearing things correctly? There are 11 children who are apparently missing, and a priority search has not been initiated.'

'Hey, boss I'm just the messenger here. I'm with you in all respects and I think a kind of divide and separate rule has been applied.'

'How?'

'Keep it low profile and if anyone reports a missing kid, it is the only missing kid in the entire world. Imagine the press take on eleven, and these are only the ones *we* know about.'

Get me a list of all missing children, their parents contact details, and make sure those kids in hospital are photographed.'

'I'll need help.'

'Leave it with me.' As soon as the call ended Carter rang the Deputy Commissioner.

'Jim? How are things going?'

James relayed the recent events and mentioned the South American woman. 'I was lucky that I was able to identify my kid and do something about it, but her kidnapping was directly associated with my unofficial investigation. We now have eleven unidentified children who, in my opinion, were about to be shipped overseas for the purpose of who knows what. I hate to be the one to point fingers, sir, but…'

'Point all you like Jim. I have had my suspicions for some time, but until now the evidence has been thin on the ground.'

'Can you name names?'

'I'm hoping I can leave that to you. So, what is the real reason you called?'

'I need some additional support staff. I've pulled in Mandy Stephenson, but her skills will be wasted without some leg work.'

'How many?'

'Six would be a good starting point. They don't have to be whiz kids, just capable of asking a few questions and reading through papers.'

'Where can I send them?'

'I'm making Gregory's place my base while we rip it apart, metaphorically of course.'

'Done. How can I get to speak with this poor woman?' he paused. 'What? Jim… Wait.'

James was about to relay the name of the doctor Mandy had given him, when Arty cut him off.

'Another search warrant has been issued. I'm not sure what's going on, but you'd better make it quick and find what you're looking for before they get there. They might have better luck finding what they want, than us finding what we need.'

***

Jackie Morton sat herself in a plush armchair to stare around at the opulence that was George Gregory's home. *To search this thoroughly will be a major task,* she thought, but Jackie had her own way of searching that utilised a kind of primordial sixth sense. Like a radar aerial she would move her eyes around, taking in every detail of a room, while thinking. *Where would I hide something I didn't want anyone to find? Is it hiding in plain sight or only just out of eyeshot?*

Mick was elsewhere, and he too had his own way. She could hear cupboard doors opening and closing, drawers sliding open and slamming shut.

Jackie was putting herself inside Gregory's mind and seeing the world through his eyes. She was almost at a point of resonance when it popped into her field of vision. A simple wooden block with dimensions of approximately thirty centimetres by twenty by ten, on the polished marble mantle of an ultra-modern fake-fire feature.

She stared at the block, willing it to give up any secrets it might have. When it didn't, she stood, picked it up and caressed it with her hands. There was no obvious lid, so she tipped it left and right, and heard a dull thud from within, not unlike those small hard balls rolling about in a fancy golf club bag.

Further study led her to believe it might be a high-quality puzzle box of some kind. The simplest solution would be to drop it onto the polished marble floor and hope it shattered. Jackie's solution would be less simple but much better forensically. She returned to her chair with the box, rested it on her lap and closed her eyes.

After a while, she leaned back into the chair and began caressing the box's exterior. She knew that the key would be the lightest touch driven only by the deepest of her thoughts. It was a technique taught to her by her mother and her mother's sisters. She closed her eyes and waited for her success.

'Euripides,' she hooted when the lid slid to one side.

'Shouldn't that be Eureka?' Mickey said as he walked in on her.

'You say what you want to say, Mickey Krakauer, and I'll say Euripides.'

Inside the box were a number of brown glass bottles about the size of old-fashioned eyedroppers. 'I think we might have it, Mick.' She held up one of the bottles. 'Weird characters. Cyrillic enough for, you reckon?'

'Would you want that stuff injected into you without a confirmation?'

'If my only other option was to die?' she shrugged, and messaged

James.

***

The Deputy Commissioner called Mandy and asked if she would accompany him to the hospital. 'I'm a bit of an old duffer, PC Stephenson and somehow I think this might call for a bit of feminine finesse.'

'I wouldn't say that exactly, sir, but I agree that a lighter feminine touch might work better than a pair of size fourteens.' She hoped she hadn't overstepped but heard him chuckle before the call ended. She picked up a DNA test kit, then printed off a set of recently taken photographs.

He'd agreed to meet her away from the office and was behaving in what, in the eyes of his compatriots, might be considered a treasonable manner. He flashed his lights and pulled over.

Mandy dropped into the passenger seat. 'Personal car, sir?'

Arthur Bertram grinned and nodded towards the back seat. Dr Anna Maria Caltabiano, meet Mandy Stephenson. Anna will be our interpreter.'

Mandy nodded an acknowledgement. And no one spoke again until they stepped out of the car at the hospital carpark.

Arty identified himself at reception and made the entrée.

The receptionist raised an eyebrow at the seniority of the officer she was required to deal with.

'It is vital that we speak with this lady. I understand she has been through a great deal of trauma, but she might be critical to finding who, if anyone, took her daughter.'

The receptionist made a call, looked up and said, 'Someone will be with you shortly.'

After a long wait, Arthur Bertram glanced at his wristwatch. 'I wonder what longly might mean. If this is shortly?' he said, as he was about to step forward to speak to the person on the desk again.

'Sir,' a man in a tweed suit interrupted the brewing storm. 'Would you please accompany me?'

Bertram growled and waved the two women ahead of him. 'We wouldn't be asking but this lady is critical to an investigation into several missing children. Can she see?'

The man nodded.

'Can she speak?'

'With some difficulty. Fumes…'

Bertram nodded. 'You got that Anna?'

Anna Maria nodded.

The man led them to a private room and ushered them in.

The nurse, in attendance, scowled.

The man spoke softly to the woman who responded with a slight nod.

Anna Maria took her seat in a visitor's chair, leaned close, and spoke softly, in Spanish.

The woman's lips formed a tight smile, and she turned her head.

Anna Maria reached for the photos Mandy had printed. She spoke softly again and showed her each photograph.

Her eyes barely moved until they almost burst from her head. She began to rant in Spanish while Anna Marie tried her best to calm her down.

She showed the photo to Mandy and Arthur. 'Her daughter.'

'We'll need DNA samples for certainty.' Arthur nodded to Mandy.

'I brought a kit just in case.'

'Better to be safe than sorry. Anna, explain that to her and tell her, her daughter is safe and in good hands.' Arthur stood and spoke quietly to Mandy. 'I want all these photographs on tonight's early news. Get the older girls snaps up as well. Fuck the repercussions.'

The man in the tweed suit raised his eyebrows at the profanity.

'You got a problem with that?'

The man said nothing.

Chapter 44

James was in no doubt of the actions he needed to initiate. First, he would explain to Angela and hope she would have no objection to receiving the so-called Antidote. He grabbed the box and asked Jackie to accompany him.

She agreed.

'You'll be okay, Mick?' James asked.

'Aways, boss. I got plenty to do here.'

'Then find what we need, and we'll keep you posted.' His phone buzzed. 'Yeah?'

…

'Shit, sorry I was a little abrupt, but I think Jackie's found some antidote. Don't know how good it is, but I'm heading over to ask my sister if she'll be a guinea pig.' He pressed his speaker to loud and whispered, 'Arty.'

'Well done, Jim. That might be just enough. How are the other's going?'

'Jackie Morton is coming with me, while Constable Krakauer and his newly arrived team will be going through the Gregory place with a fine-toothed comb.'

'Better move quickly there are other interests homing in. Any problems, you have my number. I think we are about to stir up a bull ant nest.'

The call ended, Jackie puffed out her chest and grinned. 'Just like the old days, Jim, I'm feeling good for the first time in years.'

They piled into his car and he put the blues on as they exited the car park. He turned to Jackie. 'We should be chasing a pardon for you, if we can work it through.'

'That would be good but I'm not holding my breath. It's been a long time since I truly felt free.'

FS Hospital loomed ahead, and James parked in a doctor's spot. There were several empty, and he didn't have the time nor the patience to trail around looking for somewhere to leave his car. Instead, he left the flashers on and jammed a police business card under a wiper.

James knew where to find his sister, and he led Jackie to the lift. 'As soon as we get there, I'll talk to her as best I can. We've a sort of eyeball sign language that seems to work, but I think our biggest problem will be dealing with the staff, I'm not sure they'll be happy sticking a needle full of unknown gunk into one of their patients.'

Jackie followed him clutching the wooden box. 'I guess this box might be a bit of a barrier, given everything else is in throw away plastic containers.'

They arrived at Angela's room. Nothing had changed she was still flat on her back, with a drip feeding her the minimal sustenance she needed to maintain life.

James pressed the nurse call button and while he waited, he began the tortuous eye twitch language they had used previously. He pointed to the wooden box in Jackie's hands. 'We think this might be the antidote we've been looking for.'

Her eyes looked directly ahead.

'Are you prepared to give it a go?'

Her eyes twitched left.

He pulled the copy of the screen dump, they'd used to obtain the initial translation, and showed her the two Cyrillic names. 'Is this the one your friend said was the antidote?'

Her eyes twitched left.

'Are you still prepared to give it a go?'

Her eyes twitched left.

A nurse entered and said, 'did someone just press the call button?'

'I did. This lady is my sister and I have what might be an antidote to the drug that is subduing her.'

'I'll need to find a doctor.'

'I hope you won't be too long. If this works for Angela, it might well save the lives of twelve children.'

The nurse scurried out, and they waited again.

'How have you been? Good?'

Her eyes twitched left, and James thought he detected the tiniest of quiver of her lips.

Nothing mattered. She had given him her permission. And now all they needed was a doctor who might be prepared to take a risk.

Ten minutes passed and still no one had arrived.

Jackie touched him on the shoulder. 'Leave it with me, Jim.' A few minutes later she returned with a kidney-shaped stainless-steel bowl containing two syringes. She lifted the lid of the box and filled both syringes with 100ml of the liquid.

Before he realised what she was doing, she'd injected the contents of one syringe into her thigh.

'Shit, Jack!' James said.

'Well, if I die, you're fucked, and no one cares a crap about me, anyway.'

He put his arm around her shoulder and said, 'Well, I do.' He led her to a visitor chair and made her sit.

The nurse returned and said, 'There is no doctor prepared to authorise the injection of an unknown substance into a patient. I've been asked to ensure you leave immediately or I'm to have security remove you.'

'I've just injected myself with it and I'm not dead yet. Nor am I experiencing any problems.' Jackie stood and moved to the bedside of Angela. 'If they won't do it, I will.'

Before the nurse could react, Jackie had emptied the entire syringe into the canula's piggyback point.

The nurse tapped on the screen of her smart phone and screamed down the line. 'We have a major breach. Angela Carter's room, I need security immediately.'

James sat on the side of the bed and held his sister's hand. For all he knew, Jackie might have ended her life. He felt her fingers tighten around his. 'Hey, sis. Are you coming good for us?'

Her lips parted.

Jackie smiled. 'And I'm still alive and kicking.'

Two burly security men burst into the room.

James held up his police ID. 'Can I help you gentlemen?'

They slowed and turned to the nurse.

One said, 'No one mentioned cops.'

Angela said, 'I'm starving.'

The nurse said, 'Shit,' and adjusted Angela's bed to raise her back.

James called Mandy. 'The antidote has had the desired effect on my sister. She's able to speak.'

'The kids!'

'We'll need to check dosages but get them fixed up ASAP, can you call Arty for me? I think he likes you and his gravitas won't go amiss.'

'All the photos are to be published on national TV. Hopefully parents who are waiting for news of their kids will come forward.'

'Better hope there are no anti-vaxers among them, hey.' He turned to speak to Jackie, but she'd slumped over on the chair and seemed unconscious. 'Jack?'

There was no response.

The nurse smirked.

Angela slid her legs over the edge of her bed and attempted to stand.

***

The moment Mandy ended the call with James she called Athur Bertram to give him the news. He sounded depressed. 'Sorry, sir, I thought you'd be happy.'

'I am, but certain folks believe that privacy is more important. Their privacy, I'm thinking, but whatever, they are refusing to sanction the exposure of the photos to the media.'

'Pity that. Given I personally took those photos with my personal iPhone. They are my copyright, and I've already shared them.'

'Okay, share them with my account and get Jackie Morton to post them all over social media. One; she's not a cop. Two; she has an axe to grind. Well done, PC Stephenson.'

Mandy called James to relay the news. Our pal is getting the collywobbles. They've slammed a privacy order on the photos but he's still being supportive.'

'Shit, can they do that?'

'They're my photos, taken with my camera.'

'The deputy commissioner has asked if Jackie could post them around. She's no longer a cop, and it gives us a degree of separation.'

'I'd ask her, but she jabbed herself with the antidote shit and is now unconscious.'

'Angela?'

'Angela won't shut up.'

'Put her on.'

He handed his sister his phone.

'Hello.'

'Good news, hey.'

'I'll probably be in here for a couple of days.'

'If I send you some photos, can you post them on your social media? And then share them with the news outlets. The more the merrier.'

'Consider it done.'

Jackie moaned and almost fell from the chair she was in. 'Shit, what the hell happened? One minute I'm firing on all cylinders then I'm out of it.'

'How much sleep have you had over the last few days?' James asked. 'Whatever, we'll need to get this muck into all those kids, and we'll be up against the same resistance as we met here. If we can get parents to respond and show them Angie's recovery… We might…'

Chapter 45

The first parent to be advised of the antidote would be Stacey, and James needed to be the one. He escorted Jackie to his vehicle and made her comfortable in the passenger seat.

Still woozy from lack of sleep she slumped back, and her head fell forward as he clipped her seat belt, then started his engine and pointed it towards the exit. He lived about twenty minutes from the hospital and, given recent events, he wasn't sure how Stacey would handle him returning home with a groggy female in his car. He couldn't telephone in advance, her phone was irreparably damaged, so he'd need to wing it.

When he parked in the short drive, he said nothing to Jackie. Anything he did say would be wasted and if her snoring didn't attract Stacey's attention, nothing would.

He turned the key in his door and heard a dozy voice.

'Who is it? Is that you Jim?'

He found her stretched out on the settee with daytime TV at the lowest volume. 'Hey. We're nearly there.'

Stacey sat up instantly, as though she'd been touched with a cattle prod.

'Sorry, I couldn't call you, but we think we might have found the antidote.'

'Is she okay?'

'Not yet. We'll be posting photos of the kids we've found, on all the social media channels and there will be permissions required for the antidote.'

'Why can't they just use it?'

He reached out and took her hand. 'Come.' She meekly allowed him to lead her to his car. 'This is ex-PC Jackie Morton. She jabbed herself with the antidote to ensure it was safe.'

'Is she alive?'

'She's been on the road nonstop for forty-eight hours, but she was able to find and open the container it was in.'

Stacey was staring at him incredulously and shaking her head. 'And you want me to allow our child…'

'Help me get her into our spare room. She needs sleep.'

Suddenly Stacey was businesslike and between them they dragged the semi lifeless Jackie to lay her on the bed. Stacey covered her with a duvet and said, 'I think an explanation is required.'

'First, you should know that since Jackie injected her, Angela is recovering. We will need to give our permission for Andria to be treated and for her photo to be posted on the news channels. Someone is trying to suppress all publicity and we need to let the other parents know their kids are safe.'

'How many?'

'Five of Andria's age and six in their early-teens.'

'I haven't seen much on any of the news channels.'

'They've only been reported individually on localised radio and TV stations, but we need to show the country that there may be many more in a similar situation. Jackie should sleep for a while so let's get back to the hospital and give our permission to have Andria treated with the antidote.'

Stacey nodded. 'Then we should pick up Jack from your parents. I think they're getting a bit antsy.' She slumped onto the passenger seat and waited while James took his place in the driving position. 'I'm so sorry about Jennifer, Jim.'

James felt his face colour. 'She was a colleague, killed doing her duty. Let's leave it there.' He crunched the gears into reverse and edged back out onto the road, half thinking her next words would be "Methinks thou doth protest too much". She didn't.

***

Mandy Stephenson posted the pictures to Facebook, Snapchat and TikTok under fake profiles. She then shared the Facebook post to the major media outlets with a short text mentioning that they were all reported missing and have since been found under the influence of an unidentified narcotic. She didn't go into detail but requested that all the photos were shown on their various channels with a number to call.

She was stunned by the number of likes she received within seconds of her post, and even more surprised by the number of contacts via PM. There were now far too many claimants to be the parents of the kids, and she realised that she had an even bigger problem. 'Shit. How do I make sense of this without compromising the privacy of the actual parents?'

She was able to reduce the claims significantly by a simple check of police records, but there were either many parents with missing children or far more missing kids than parents seeking their whereabouts.

She called James Carter. '

'Besieged by parents Mandy?' He chuckled.

'It's not funny, Jim. There is a heck of a lot more parents missing their kids than those we've found.'

'All the boys were returned safely. For some reason they'd been convinced they were all going on a big adventure sanctioned by their parents. If my kids hadn't been taken, we wouldn't have found any of them before they were flown somewhere. For, whatever...' He paused, 'And that was all down to Angela.'

'Angela tracked the older girls to Gregory's place and look what happened to her.'

'I'm beginning to think Gregory is small fry,' James said. 'It seems, he might be the one who fulfils the orders and arranges for shipment, but we need to find the people who use his services and create the demand.'

'Has anything turned up in the search?'

'All the computers were scooped up in the first raid run by Mulligan. There isn't any physical paperwork, and all the documentation is digital. If those computers have been interfered with in any way…?'

'What about that box that Jackie found? My experience teaches me that folks who are apt to act a little, shall we say nefariously? Might like to keep a little failsafe for pointing a post-nicked finger with.'

'I'll ask her when I see her next. We're about to head into the hospital and try the antidote on my daughter.'

Mandy held up both hands with her fingers crossed. 'Where is Jackie now, Jim?'

'Asleep in my spare bed.'

'You're not one of those people who leave a key under the mat?'

'Why do you ask?'

'Because Jackie might be in great danger.' She heard his voice muffled by something, maybe his hand. *'Jim?'*

'Stacey says there is a key to the back door. It's stuck in the soil of a planter, next to the door.'

'Well, let's hope we're the only ones who know about that. Keep me posted if anything positive happens with your daughter.' Mandy didn't wait for further acknowledgement. She ended the call, grabbed her utility belt, and ran through the office. Then, skipping the lift, she took three steps at a time down the fire stairs. 'Let's hope I'm not too late,' she panted, as she threw herself into her car and started its engine.

***

James wasn't surprised when he came up against opposition to the use of the drug contained in a small brown bottle with Russian writing on it. 'Fact is, doctor, if you are not prepared to try to save my daughter's life then I might have to take matters into my own hands.'

The doctor continued to protest, but James loaded the same syringe that had been used to resuscitate Angela. He had no idea what a child's dose might be.

'Wait.' Stacey said. 'I'm her mother. The decision should be mine and mine alone.'

The doctor nodded. 'But I must continue to protest.'

'Look, doctor. These children are part of a consignment that the consignee valued highly. To inject them with something dubious would be tantamount to throwing a brand-new shipment of expensive jewellery under a steamroller.' She turned to her husband. 'Do it, Jim, but only a half dose.' She stayed his hand, before climbing onto the bed and folding her daughter in her arms. 'Sorry if this doesn't work Andy.' She kissed the small face before nodding that she was ready.

James filled the syringe, estimating half the amount Jackie and Angela had received. He pushed the syringe nozzle into the canula's piggyback point, as he'd seen Jackie do to his sister, and pressed the plunger slowly. 'It's done. Now we wait.'

'Mummy? Mummy, where am I?'

The sudden sound of a tiny voice in the hushed silence of the hospital room, startled everyone.

Stacey's eyes filled with tears, and she hugged her daughter as if she was never going to let go. 'Say thank you to Daddy.'

'Thank you, Daddy.'

'The other's, doctor?' James asked.

The man had slumped into a visitor's chair. His dilemma

obvious. 'What if…'

'What if they all die and their parents never get to hear their voices again?'

Reluctantly he stood, nodded, and said, 'Follow me.'

***

Mickey's team had checked every possible location for something that, apart from the obvious, might point to George Gregory's legitimate reasons for imprisoning six early-teen girls. Denied the opportunity to interrogate the man or the computers that might answer the hundreds of questions he had. He was stumped. He called James to advise him of his lack of progress.

'Hey, Mick.' James sounded upbeat. 'Just injected Andria with the antidote and…'

'There's nothing here, boss. It's been a complete waste of time.'

'Tell you what, Mick. Get the blokes to go over the whole place again. We'll never get another chance like this, and we need something that will overcome Gregory's perceived high-level protection.'

Mick felt dejected. He knew there had to be something, but it wasn't showing its face in the Gregory mansion.

Chapter 46

DI Mulligan put his phone on the rest and his head in his hands. 'Once, just fucking once, that's all.' He began pondering the words from the phone call he had just received. There was a party. He was invited and, being at a loose end, he went along. Everyone who was anyone was there and all from the top echelon. And there were girls, lots of them, and all young and seemingly willing.

He shook his head. His boss had just instructed him to begin cleaning up potential witnesses and put his most senior DS out of action for the second time in less than a month. This time he was expected to make it a permanent arrangement which could mean only one thing in Mulligan's mind.

Mulligan reached into his pocket, switched on the burner phone he kept for this purpose and tapped in a number.

'What?'

'Job, take it or leave it.'

'What kind of job?'

'Wet.'

'Usual terms?'

'What else.'

'When?'

'As soon as you can get off your arse. Yesterday if possible.'

'Send me the details.'

'Get a pen and something to write on.'

'Can't ya text it?'

'No.

'Okay. Go for it.'

Mulligan read out the address of James Carter. 'Everything about this must be deniable. He has family they are all on the list.'

'You can leave cash in the usual place. You'll hear about it on the news, and late payment means… well, you know what it means.'

Mulligan put down his phone and closed his eyes. She was *fourteen years old. They swore all the girls were eighteen plus.* He'd lived with the expectation of a comeback one day and working with Clitheroe had helped keep the dogs at bay. Now he was on his own and his powerful owners were demanding their payment in kind.

The last time he had used this contact, a small magnetic charge was affixed to the victim's fuel tank. Forensics reconstructed a device designed to detect a vehicle's specific movement. The car had exploded in flames and incinerated its occupant just as it entered the traffic flow. He wondered how the Carters would disappear.

***

A twilight gloom was well established when Mandy arrived at James' home. She parked her police vehicle away from the property, fastened her utility belt around her hips, checked her Glock and affixed its tactical flashlight, *just in case*, and then she made her way around to the rear. She didn't expect the back door to be wide open and there were no sounds coming from within.

She withdrew her weapon from its holster and brought it two-handed to her eyeline in the aiming position. There wasn't much room in the laundry area, so she mainly focussed on the opposite side where a door led to the main house.

Mandy listened but could hear nothing. Not even the sounds of someone snoring. Without alerting the intruder there was no way she could let Jackie know there was someone acting suspicious in the house, so she moved quietly like a cat and, with Glock at the ready, inspected each room.

So far there was nothing to indicate anything out of the ordinary. *Perhaps the back door was never shut.* With only two rooms to check. It was becoming too dark to see clearly, so she flicked the switch on the torch as she approached what seemed to be the master bedroom.

There was no reaction to the sudden light, so she edged closer to the door and froze. Her beam had illuminated what appeared to be a trip wire, stretched across the jamb at about 150mm above the ground.

Mandy backed off and looked at the other bedroom doors. they too had trip wires. *This is focussed,* she thought. *Jim and Stacey aren't here but if Jackie is to wake up…*

She'd slowly turned around to head back to the laundry when she heard the thumping of feet and saw a shadowy figure running from the property. Mandy followed at pace, but the figure dropped into a high-end vehicle that might have been a black Mercedes. She gave further chase on foot but was too late to record the rego.

Mandy had seen a similar tripwire set-up once before. The unfortunate officer called to investigate never knew what hit him and the charges brought the entire building down. But that was in Afghanistan, where IEDs were commonplace.

She stood back from the house and made a call.

Fifteen minutes later an armoured vehicle arrived, and several officers spilled on to the drive.

'PC Stephenson. Tell me what you know.'

Mandy explained the circumstances and advised of the potential booby traps. 'Of course, all this might be an elaborate ruse to deflect us.'

The man nodded. 'They might also be detonated via a call to a mobile, so we'll need to move quickly.' He murmured into his radio before saying, 'The blokes will go door to door, and we'll close down the street.'

'What if…'

'Yes… The intruder might detonate remotely but if we don't evacuate who will take responsibility for the carnage that might result.'

Mandy nodded. Of course, he was right, but that didn't help Jim and his family. She backed away and carefully circled around to the rear of the property where she believed Jackie's bedroom might be.

There were no lights on inside the house and she pointed her torch through each of the bedroom windows. What she eventually saw made her gasp. Jackie Morton was flat on her back on the bed. A parcel of some kind was resting on her chest and it was completely wrapped in red tape, leaving no clue as to its functionality.

Jackie made no movement to acknowledge Mandy's presence as she shone her torch around the window frame that was a sliding affair behind a fly screen.

She whispered through the gap, 'Try to be patient the bomb squad are in attendance.'

Mandy didn't expect an acknowledgment, and she didn't get one. She pulled a small pocketknife from her utility belt, easily cut out the fly wire, and reached in and around to release the window lock.

***

She felt like she was undergoing the recovery from her worst ever university hangover and her eyes were unable to focus on anything she attempted to engage. Angela Carter knew she was in a hospital bed, and she knew something had happened to her but, apart from the hangover memories, her mind was a blank.

A nurse approached, attached a monitor and said, 'You've had a good long sleep. How are you feeling?'

'Like shit. Who am I?'

'Angela Carter, according to your brother. He tells us you're a lawyer and a good one. Does that help?'

'I'm not sure. The last thing I can remember is collapsing to the floor. I can't remember where.'

'Well… you might have your brother's friend to blame for being here and communicating.'

'Friend?'

'A Ms Morton. Ring any bells? She jabbed herself with the same stuff before she injected you and then she collapsed.'

Angela shook her head. Then she shook it again as if trying to clear cobwebs from her brain, 'I feel bloody awful.'

'But you're alive and, according to your big bro, in a strong position to close a missing person case that might have been running for years.'

Angela's mind upshifted into overdrive and her neurons at last began kicking in. 'Where is he?'

'They are both with their daughter, Andria. She was only the second person to receive the jab.'

'Is she okay?'

'Better than you, I think.'

'When can I leave? I have things to do that can't wait.'

'The doctor reckons a couple of days, but…'

***

With the window now open, Mandy Stephenson shone her torch around the room. No trip wires were visible, but that didn't mean they weren't there. Against all her better judgements, she gingerly clambered over the sill and lowered herself to the floor inside the room.

Jackies eyes seemed to follow Mandy's movements as she visibly checked the device for detonators or switch mechanisms. She didn't dare touch anything until she was positive there were none and she knew that what was left of the bomb squad would be seriously pissed off if she accidentally blew them to kingdom come.

Before taking up police work, she was army and had been posted to an IED detection and suppression squad in Afghanistan. Now right before her eyes was a crude variation on a theme.

The package on Jackie's chest was probably operated by a tilt switch, and even the slightest movement might spell disaster. She could hear the muffled sounds of the bomb squad outside the door. They would be tracking the trip wires that seemed unconnected with anything in this room.

Whoever had set this up had little time for finesse and might have expected the first blast to trigger a movement to set off bigger charges.

Mandy approached the bedside with caution and lowered herself to one knee. 'Silly question I know, but are you awake?'

Jackie blinked her eyes.

'I think the house has been booby trapped, but the good news is, that I don't think they are connected to the device on your chest. The bad news is that it might be triggered wirelessly or by a movement detector. Do you understand?'

Jackie blinked.

'I want you to stay perfectly still while I do another visual examination.'

Jackie blinked.

Mandy shone her torch, peered closely at the package and, after what seemed like an eternity, she said, 'Fancy taking a big risk?'

Jackies eyes widened and moved from side to side.

'The device isn't fixed to you. How would you feel if I carefully lifted it off your chest?'

She blinked.

'Okay. This is the plan.'

Chapter 47

Angela stood unsteadily and tottered around the room, using the walls and furniture for stability. 'I need the clothes I was wearing when I came in.'

The nurse pointed to the steel locker at the side of the bed. 'They'll be in there.'

Angela gripped the bed rail, lowered herself to one knee and pulled open the door to find her clothes neatly folded and stacked. She pulled them out and heaved herself up to the bed before reaching into the pocket that held the tissue, she had used to collect the evidence of Gregory's ejaculation. 'Can you get me a clean plastic bag?'

The nurse nodded and returned with a dressing disposal bag. 'It's sterile so I hope that will be clean enough.'

Angela placed the tissue in the bag and sealed it before dressing. Then she put the entire bag back into her pocket. She knew there would be some DNA contamination but hoped that at least it might be clear enough to hold Gregory for his crimes. *Strange that young Tom was convicted using DNA evidence and wouldn't it be nice to confirm that the killer was someone else.*

When she'd finished dressing, she requested that she be discharged and, after a protracted hoo-ha, the treating doctor acquiesced.

The taxi to home seemed to take forever, and she handed the

driver her credit card.

It bounced.

She tried again.

It bounced again.

'Wait here, I have some cash inside.' She walked up to her door, turned her key in the lock and was immediately thankful that she'd had the nous to install a reinforced door following the breakup of her marriage.

Knocked flat by the blast, the door protected her from the shrapnel field that peppered the taxi.

Her brain was still fried from the drugs, and it took Angela some time to realise what had happened. Eventually, she picked herself up and turned to see the poor driver banging the sides of his head with the heels of his hands. The door had also saved him from the worst of shrapnel that had punctured his now flat tyred car, everywhere but where he was sitting. She approached the car. 'Do you have a phone?'

He pointed to his ears and waved his hands as if to indicate he was deaf. Blood trickled down his forehead and when he managed to understand her signals, he handed his phone to her.

It was working, so she called first, for an ambulance, and then James.

'What happened?'

'My ex just saved my life.'

'I thought he was locked away at The Governor's pleasure.'

'He is. Let's talk about that later. Someone has just tried to kill me, and he almost killed the poor bloke who was driving the taxi. How is Andria?'

'She's as well as can be expected. We're hoping for the parental approval to try the antidotes on the others.'

'When I was in Gregory's house and before I hit him over the head, I collected a sample that will contain his DNA. I still have it, though it's probably contaminated.'

'Where is it?'

'Right here in my pocket. I will give it to no one else but you.'

***

Mandy Stephenson touched Jackie Morton on the shoulder and whispered. 'Don't even flinch, hold your breath as long as you can and wait until I give the word to move.'

Jackie blinked.

Mandy carefully cupped the package in her hands and slowly raised it from Jackies chest.

Both women knew they were as close to a violent death as it was possible to come, and Mandy knew the risks more than anyone.

She raised the package carefully until it was at shoulder height. 'Now slide off the bed, away from me.'

Jackie complied and as Mandy slowly lowered the package she said, 'Go straight out of that window and hit the ground.'

Jackie followed the instructions to the letter and prostrated herself as far as possible away from the house.

A few seconds later she was joined by Mandy who covered her ears with her hands.

The blast that followed was nowhere near as loud as expected, but it would have been more than enough to kill Jackie, if still mounted on her chest.

They waited in silence until the team from the bomb squad hurried around.

'What the hell happened?'

Mandy sat up and shrugged. 'Find anything in there?'

'Couple of significant charges on trip wires. Big enough to kill and they would have made enough of a bang to make someone jump. Whoever set the charges intended no one's survival.'

Mandy breathed out a long sigh.

Jackie grabbed her into a tight hug.

'The bad news is, there is nothing left with prints, so it'll be hard to track down the bomber.'

***

George Gregory opened his eyes and looked around the room. It was unfamiliar. Then he realised from the TV and the equipment rail, he was in a hospital room. He found the patient handset and pressed the call button.

Nothing happened.

He pressed again.

Same.

He pressed again, and this time waited until a harassed nurse pushed in through his door.

'Good you're awake. I'll get the doctor.'

'Fuck the doctor, get me the Premier. Now!'

The nurse took a deep breath and said, 'I'm not your personal servant, I'll get the doctor. What you do next is up to you.' She pointed at the phone at his bedside, exited, and closed the door behind her.

Gregory felt his face reddening with anger. He pressed the call button again. When nothing happened, he pulled the VS sensors off his body and sent the monitor into an alarm state.

Several minutes later the nurse returned with a woman in different coloured scrubs.

'Mr Gregory. It's good to see you awake and full of beans,' the woman said in a soft Irish accent, before signalling to the nurse who reattached the sensors. 'You are not doing yourself any favours by being obstreperous…'

'Get me the Premier on the phone.'

'When you are well enough, you can do that for yourself. Right now, you're quite badly concussed and I'm not prepared to allow my staff to be pressurised or intimidated by anyone. Do you understand?' She signalled to the nurse who pressed the plunger on the syringe she had attached to the piggyback point on the cannula in Gregory's arm. 'Okay, Mr Gregory, the nurse has given you a light sedative that will help you relax. You need to rest.'

The doctor was about to leave when Gregory said, 'You'll both regret this. I know people in high...' His eyes closed before he finished speaking.

'The police say they want to speak to him as soon as he awakens, 'the nurse said.

'Do you have a number?'

The nurse pulled a standard blank police card from her pocket and handed it to the doctor who looked at the handwritten name, nodded towards Gregory and said, 'He sounds like a belligerent sod. Check his wound, go by the book, and then you'd better give this DS Carter a call.'

'You were very lucky, matey,' the nurse said to the unconscious Gregory. The x-rays showed no fractures and there was no evidence of bleeding on your brain.'

Gregory said nothing.

While the nurse re-dressed his wounds and checked his vitals, she noticed a small black tattoo high on his bicep. She looked closely. It was a black dot slightly larger than one cm in diameter. From its top a black squiggle extended, to end with some short lines in a star formation. It looked like an old-fashioned image of a bomb. She shrugged and returned to her station.

***

James answered his phone to the hyper vocals of Mandy Stephenson.

'Hold on, PC Stephenson. Calm down. What did you say had just happened?'

'The bomb squad are here. Someone booby trapped your home, there has been some minor damage, and Jackie Morton is in shock.'

'George Gregory? Where is he?'

'I don't know. I thought he was in the same hospital as your sister.'

'Okay, I'll call you back.' He ended the call. 'Sorry Stace there's been a development. I'll have to go.'

Stacey groaned. 'I'm staying here. Jack is with his grandies and while they are getting a bit grumpy with the arrangement, I think they'll be okay.'

'I'll try to call in on them when I get a minute.' He headed for Angela's room and pushed the door open to find her bed empty. James pressed the nurse call and was greeted by a face he didn't recognise.

'She's checked herself out, sir. She was advised against it but… She is a lawyer and…'

'Thanks.' He ran down to his car and with top-lights and sirens, drove at speed from the car park.

Angela's home wasn't far and when he arrived, the police were stretching crime scene tape across the end of her road. He parked and waved his ID at the tapers. 'What happened?'

'Bomb detonated when the owner turned her key in the door.'

A fire engine was on standby, and he ducked under the tape to see his sister leaning against the low wall that defined the limit of her property.

A medic was applying dressings to small wounds when he approached.

'Hey, Ange what happened?'

She pointed to the taxi. 'He copped it worse than me.'

The taxi driver was on a stretcher and being lifted into the ambulance. As she spoke.

'My door was booby rigged. I was lucky. I'd installed a heavy duty one after I busted up with Hanrahan.'

James stared at the damaged door. It'd been ripped from its hinges, and Angela looked like she'd copped it full on.

Chapter 48

Both DS Carter and his sister. Any idea who it might have been?' DI Mulligan said, as he began writing.

'No, sir.'

'Where is Carter now?'

The officer shrugged.

'Find him, and when you do, tell him I want him in my office immediately.'

'Right you are, sir.'

Mulligan switched on the evening news to see a cut from Angela Carter's house. The narrator was describing how a high-powered charge was used to blow off the door of a local solicitor's home. The explosive was known, and the police believed they would soon be making headway in the discovery of who had set off that, and another bomb that had detonated in a police officer's house. No one was seriously injured, and further information would be broadcast as it became available.

'Shit… You were supposed to get rid of them not give them a little scare.'

'Why are you calling me?'

'You were given a job, and you failed on both accounts,' Mulligan said.

'Maybe you can do better yourself. You know what my fee is, or you might just find my next job is closer to home.'

Mulligan shrugged. 'Better watch your back.'

'I'm quite capable of that and I'll await payment as agreed.'

***

James bundled his still dizzy sister into his car, returned both her and Jackie to Royal Perth and checked them in to the ER Department. Having done that he visited his parents-in-law to give them the news that Angie's son Oliver would be staying with them for a while longer.

His next move was to head for his office to pick up the tabs from his absence. When he arrived at his desk, he found a pile of case files with a post-it-note stuck to the top:

MY OFFICE. DI MULLIGAN!

Well, that's a surprise, he thought. He looked at his watch and decided tomorrow would be soon enough.

***

The sedative began wearing off and Gregory opened his eyes. His head was sore but everything else seemed fine. He reached down to the locker in his bedside table and found his street clothes. There was some evidence of blood from his injury, but he felt it was not enough to stop him.

He lowered his legs over the edge of the bed and steadied himself as he dropped to the floor. Within minutes he was dressed and ready to leave. He peered out of the door and saw no one in the corridor. Although he was now in his street clothes, he decided to don the hospital shift he'd been wearing. He would be less conspicuous in that.

Gregory's major problem was transport, he had no cash, and he had no idea if the cops would be at his home. Thankfully he still had one connection he knew he could rely on. The row of Telstra payphones near the exit meant he could call anywhere for free. They were all deserted, and he chose the nearest to the exit.

'DI Mulligan?'

'Francis, so good to hear your voice again.'

'Who is this?'

'A good friend of yours. I have just been released from FS Hospital and I need a lift home.'

'Fuck off we're not a taxi service.'

'Ah. I see. You are choosing to be uncooperative.'

'Who are you?'

'George Gregory, Francis. We have some unfinished business to take care of, so your help would be most appreciated.'

'I have no idea what you are talking about.'

'Perhaps my son, Thomas. He's serving time for murder, but you know that don't you, Francis.'

'You do the crime you do the time.'

'Well, you'll understand it when I say that a certain Angela Carter is stirring things up. Pick me up old chap. We'd better have a drink and discuss our mutual future.'

'I have no future with you. You're a person of interest in a human trafficking and child porn ring. I could send a car around to arrest you if that would help.'

'Oh, golly gosh, what fun and I'll be able to show them the pics of you with your little friend. Clearly you seemed to be enjoying it more than she was, if I remember correctly. Not to worry, I'll call an Uber.'

'Wait!'

'Look, old chap, I've had a tiresome time and I want to go home.'

'Fiona Stanley Hospital, you say?'

'I'll keep my eyes open for you. Thank you so much, Francis, that would be super.'

***

After a rough night James Carter was well and truly ready for Mulligan. He knocked loudly on his door and strode in just as Mulligan put the phone down from a call.

'What do *you* want?'

'I'm here at your request, sir.'

'Forget it I have to go out. There is plenty of work on your desk that should keep you busy for a while.'

'Very well, sir. I'll be with the Deputy Commissioner should you need me.'

'What!?'

James dropped a copy of the letter he'd received. 'That ought to be enough to update you with my progress on certain matters. Meanwhile I'll also be updating him.'

Mulligan scanned the letter, and the blood drained from his face. 'He has no right...'

'Thank you, sir. If you no longer need to see me, I'll get on with the business assigned to me by the Deputy Commissioner.' James stepped back through the door and as he pulled it shut, he turned to see Mulligan frantically pressing buttons on his phone.

On the subject of phones. He left a note on his desk to say that he would be back in one hour and left to purchase cheap replacement phones for Stacey, Angela and himself. *There'll be time for updating when this mess is cleaned up.*

As soon as his new device was active, he called Mick. 'How did you go?'

'Nuthin, boss. The only find was the antidote and you know about that.'

'At least it seems to have worked. Where are you now?'

'Royal Perth. Jack's had a bit of a scare and...'

'I know. I'll see you there as soon as I've seen Stacey.'

'Your spare bedroom's a fucking mess, sarge.'

'Thankfully Jackie and Mandy seem to have survived. They said she shifted the bomb while Jackie escaped.'

'Yeah, and if it had gone off while she was holding it there would have been a bigger mess.'

'She should get some sort of award.'

'Yeah, maybe when it all settles down.' He pressed end as he turned into his drive.

Stacey came out to meet him, and he handed her, the new phone. 'It's a burner but it'll be enough until we get sorted.'

'I hate setting up phones and then I have to learn how they work all over again.'

'It's all done.' He turned the power on. 'I've loaded my number and Angela's. Mine the same and I've got one for her too. New numbers but we can get our old ones set up at some stage.'

'Thanks.'

'Sorry about all this.'

Stacey grimaced and her eyes flooded. She sobbed for a few seconds and said, 'At least Andria is well. They are keeping her in for a couple of days observation. The other kids have all responded well to the antidote and their parents have been alerted.' She breathed out long and hard. 'This has to be ended Jim. The people who did this to our children are pure evil.'

James nodded. 'Will you be okay for a while, I promised I'd look in on Jackie and Angela.'

'I can come with you. We can grab a takeaway on the way home.'

'You know something? I'd really like that.'

Chapter 49

Frank Mulligan parked in the drop off slot at the hospital entrance. He had no idea how long he might need to wait for Gregory, but he was pleasantly surprised when a man with a bandaged head, wearing a hospital gown, headed his way.

'Home, James, or should I say Francis, and don't spare the mules.'

'If we don't do something, and soon, the shit will hit the fan big time.'

'I know and you're the person best placed to sort things out,' Gregory said.

'Are you aware the deputy commish has taken an interest?'

'Why would I? We have bigger fish on our side. I hear your friendly bomber has been showing his hand again.'

Mulligan shrugged. 'Nothin to do with me.'

'Oh right, so that copper dyke is an independent operator?'

'She was lucky.'

'Luck didn't come into it. That bint was handling bombs long before she became a cop, and she has the medals to prove it. You'd better hope your bomb squad have cleaned up all the bits or she might find out who your little friend was, quick smart.'

'Are you saying Mandy Stevenson was in bomb disposal?'

'Not long but she took to the job as easy as.'

'You knew her?'

'Not intimately. PTSD got to her. She gave it all up when one of her buddies found a bomb, he couldn't fix.'

'Will she be a problem?'

This time Gregory shrugged. 'I suggest you don't let her get too near to the action,'

'Easier said than done. Carter has had her transferred to his team.'

'Then untransfer her and give her some tedious work to do.'

'It won't be that easy, he has the ear of Deputy Commissioner Arthur Bertram.'

***

Angela was sitting up in her bed when he arrived.

'You're looking good,' her brother said.

She gave a noncommittal nod and said, 'What next?'

'You said you had some evidence from Gregory's place.'

Angela reached into the bedside cabinet and pulled out the plastic bag. 'This is evidence that Gregory was doing stuff to at least one of the girls at his mansion. Unfortunately for him he went off half cocked, as it were. The contents of that bag contain remnants of his semen. You should be able to extract his DNA from it.'

'We won't be able to use it. It wasn't collected under the warrant, and all the other contents were cleared by the cops who found you.'

'I had a feeling you'd say that, but I didn't expect you to use it other than to put Gregory under stress. Your people did find the antidote to the zombie drug, and that search was under your warrant. Why would Gregory have an antidote to the drugs used to keep those kids compliant?'

James shrugged.

'Why were they kept compliant in the first place and what about those kids on the train? Same drug, and I saw Gregory leaving with the Russian from the train. She's wandering around as free as a bird and if this doesn't shout human trafficking, I don't know what

265

might. Your boy was found with others on a private plane, the flight plan of which said it was bound for Asia. Who knows what they were going there for, and the manifest didn't mention passengers, did it?'

James could see she had a point, and with Mulligan's attitude the investigation could easily disappear into someone's filing cabinet, never to be seen again. He dialled the deputy commissioner on his direct line.

'Jim, how're things going.'

He updated him on the present situation complete with Angela's postulations.

'Smart cookie, your sister. Get that DNA tested, let's see what it produces. Also, while you're at it get Tom Gregory's DNA re-tested too. Let's see if there is anything that might lead us down another path.'

James ended the call and turned to Angela. 'When Tom Gregory's DNA was used to identify the father of Rebecca Connolly's child, was George's tested too?'

'Why would they test his? All the circumstantial evidence pointed to Tom Gregory as her killer. The DNA was close enough to clinch it, as far as Slippery and his cohort were concerned. The judge believed his experts and Tom went inside.'

'But you never believed it from day one.'

'You think...'

'I'm not sure but there are things at play that point to interference by someone. Clitheroe's dead so we can't talk to him and there seems to be a poorly managed death curse becoming associated with the case.'

'Death curse?'

'Slippery Clitheroe was shivved the night before he got out of jail. Someone tried to blow Jackie to bits along with my family. Jen Crawford was shot, though I don't think that was related, I hope.

Your house was bombed and, had you not fortified your front door, you'd be dead, and an innocent taxi driver would have been badly injured.'

'Why would George Gregory have six drugged teenagers in his house if he wasn't up to mischief? All that porno stuff needs to be analysed too. Before I was knocked out, he had cameras set up over those beds. Were they there when I came to?'

James shrugged.

'And where did all the footage go?'

'No matter what, everyone involved with this is in serious danger. I'll speak to Arty and see if he can arrange some protection.'

***

George Gregory shrivelled into a spoiled-child-grump, as Mulligan drove in silence. Eventually the gates slid open, and Mulligan's car eased through. As soon as he stopped Gregory stepped out and looked at his open and empty garage.

'Where are my cars?'

'How would I know,' Mulligan said. 'Maybe they've been taken by forensics for testing. I'm sure you'll get them back.'

'This isn't good enough.'

'Then you'd better talk to that bigger fish you mentioned.'

'Phone!'

'Sorry, maybe you should let yourself in and use your house phone.'

Gregory fumed as he stamped towards his front door and tapped on the keypad.

Nothing happened. He walked to a small garden rockery, picked up a stone, and flung it at his door with all the force he could muster. The toughened glass shattered into star like shards held together by the tough core, and he achieved nothing.

'That's what security does for you,' Mulligan sneered.

Gregory marched to the garage and shoved aside the tool rack to

267

expose the lift. He keyed a code into the call unit and the lift door opened. Mulligan stepped in beside him and he pressed up. His first stop was to the room with the artificial fireplace. He reached for the box that was on the mantle. There was nothing. 'What happened to the wooden block that was here?'

Mulligan, who was now behind him, said he was unaware of a wooden block.

'It was on this shelf.'

'Would you like to report it missing, sir?'

'Report it missing? I would like to report its theft. This is disgraceful.'

Mulligan made a note on his phone. 'I'll see to it. It may have been taken as evidence.'

'Evidence of what?'

'You tell me, sir,' Mulligan replied.

Gregory said nothing, he was already planning his next move and the people he would be squeezing had far more clout than a lowly DI.

***

Mickey Krakauer was feeling nervous as he looked over the shoulder of Mandy Stephenson while she scrolled through the web footage.

She said, 'We need to find the stuff that was in the cameras at Gregory's place. It all disappeared when the first police team entered his place to find those girls and Jim's sister. Gregory was out of it, thanks to an oxygen bottle, so he's unlikely to be of much help.'

'So, you reckon one of ours must have known about Gregory's activities,' Mickey said.

Mandy nodded. 'Mulligan would be a good starting point, but I'm thinking he's small fry and I don't think he was on the initial raid.'

'So, who was on that raid with sufficient knowledge of Gregory's operation to think of half inching the camera kits.'

Mandy shook her head. 'We can't just ask around that would attract instant failure.'

'Maybe Jim can get hold of a list of attendees, I'll ask him when I can raise him.'

'Gregory's place is particularly interesting for what it doesn't have. He has zero protection other than shatter-proof glass and coded locks. There is no CCTV security which is unusual for the area, given most of the residents are paranoid about being caught with their pants down, and they have more security that you could point a stick at.'

Mickey laughed, then his face hardened. He tapped on his phone and waited for an answer. There was none. 'Jim's still not answering.' He turned back to the screen and said, 'Maybe the cameras were directly linked to a cloud storage facility. I can't imagine someone like Gregory carrying a load of memory sticks around with him.'

Mandy gave a whoop. 'Shit! You know, I should have thought about that. But how to find it?' She shuffled through the file on her desk, then she stopped. 'Wait!' She stood and almost ran from the office to return a few minutes later with another file. She opened it and breathed out with relief. The bloodstained note was still there. 'I remember putting this in Jim's file.'

Mickey's face paled, and he slumped onto a chair. 'That's Jen's blood. I was with her when…'

'Oh my god, I'm so sorry, Mick, I didn't know.'

He wiped aside a tear and said, 'Even more reason to get these bastards. She wouldn't have been there if Jim and her hadn't accidentally got together over this case. Did you know that they had a history that was totally fucked over by Clitheroe?'

'I didn't know that.'

'Clitheroe has a lot to answer for, but thanks to a shiv we can't now question him.'

Mandy grunted, pulled up her Tor browser and began keying in code from the list. There were several addresses, and she had no knowledge of what they were or where they might take her. Most seemed to be hard core, bestiality, and paedophilia. She saved the link to the paedo site, winced at the content, and quickly moved on.

Eventually she stumbled on some of the footage that Angela had made stills of. 'I think we might be getting somewhere.' She clicked through various thumbnails until she stopped with a gasp. 'Christ, Mick. Take a look at this.'

Chapter 50

George Gregory sent Mulligan away with a dismissive gesture. 'Get back in your box, DI Mulligan. I need to think.'

Mulligan did as he was instructed and left the premises. He knew there was a storm brewing but how big and how dangerous he couldn't imagine. He took his time driving back to the station and stopped off to collect a takeaway for lunch. *I might even get the time to eat it,* he thought.

He'd no sooner picked up his lunch and walked back to his car, in the undercover carpark, than his phone buzzed. 'Bugger... DI Mulligan.'

'My office, Detective Inspector, and bring with you all the information you have on the Gregory debacle, and you'd better have a good reason for turning over the property of an upstanding citizen.'

'Yes sir.' He looked down at his lunch and made the decision to eat it there and then, in the car. He had only just pulled the ring pull on his Coke can when there was a tap on the window. He grinned and lowered it. 'Hey. Good to...' were the last words he ever uttered. He didn't see a hand reach in to remove his mobile phone from its holder and raise the window just high enough for the arm to extricate itself. Neither did he notice the cessation of his, once spurting, blood leaking from the silenced .22 bullet wound in the space just above the bridge of his nose, and he didn't know that his world had suddenly become silent.

The car park was deserted except for one person walking calmly to a vehicle before climbing in and driving carefully away.

***

The Minister for Police was drumming his fingers on his desk as he stared across at the Police Commissioner. 'Is this normal, Commissioner?'

'Sir?'

'Your officers keeping you waiting?'

'He might have been delayed, Minister. These things happen.'

'Not when I demand his presence. I want him here within fifteen minutes.' He looked at his watch. 'I have an important function to attend, and I will not be late.'

The Police Commissioner's phone buzzed. He stood and excused himself. 'Sorry Minister, police business stops for no one and I have a plane to catch, so I'll put out a call. Someone will know where he is.' He left the room and spoke into his mobile phone… 'What do you mean he isn't answering his phone?'

'We've sent a car to track its location. It seems to be traveling east along Great Eastern Highway.'

'Why would he be doing that when he knows the minister wants to speak with him?'

'I can't answer that, sir… maybe?'

'Maybe what?'

The phone went silent for a long pause. 'Maybe he doesn't want to speak to the minister.'

'Find him and bring him in. I don't care if you need to drag him here in chains.'

'Sir.'

The Commissioner ended the call and returned to the minister's desk. 'We're looking for him sir. It might take a while.'

'Meanwhile, I understand some equipment was removed from

Mr Gregory's house.'

'There was a search warrant, sir. It was routine.'

'What has happened to this equipment?'

'That I can't say sir. DI Mulligan should be able to answer that question. When we find him, we can ask him.'

'Very well, call me the minute you have him under your control.'

'Yes Minister. May I…?' he indicated he should perhaps leave.

'Yes, go to your very expensive conference and let's hope that, while you're there some leadership rubs off on you to make it worthwhile. Make sure I'm informed when you have him.'

The commissioner turned and left the room. As he walked to his car, he made another call on his mobile.

***

'Shit that's all I need,' Bill Parker slowed his truck and searched for a safe place to pull over. The vehicle with the flashing lights remained in the proximity of his rear end and he was already close to loosing his licence. He at last he saw a truck stop area, rolled into it and stopped to wait for the inevitable.

An officer walked to his cab and called up. 'Routine check, sir. Have you picked up any hitch hikers?'

Bill answered truthfully. 'No, why do you ask?'

'Step down from your cab sir. Bring your papers with you.'

Weird, Bill thought, but he had no reason to not be compliant and the last thing he wanted to do was aggravate the cop. He grabbed his clipboard with his manifest, his licence, and his tacho details.

The officer took the papers and said, 'Thank you sir. While my colleague checks these out can you open up your truck so that we may check its contents?'

'Sorry, I don't have permission to break the seals.'

'No worries, sir. This warrant gives us that.' He handed Bill a slip of paper.

The stress tested Bill Parker's temper. 'What am I supposed to have done?'

'Do you know Detective Inspector Mulligan?'

'Why would I?'

'Well according to our mobile phone tracking device, he is in your truck.'

'What the fuck… I've never heard of the man. Why would he be in my truck? I just hitched up these trailers at the depot. They are both sealed, and I am the only person in my cab, be my guest.' He clambered into his cab and gestured for the officer to follow.'

While Bill was waiting for their next move it came with a muffled bang. He didn't hear it though.

***

Angela Carter finished serving dinner for herself and her son. It was his favourite, sausage and mash, how that had happened she'd never know. 'Got much homework?'

Oliver shook his head before stabbing his fork into a juicy snag.

She turned the TV on to catch the day's news and almost fell over backwards with the shock of the first item. A senior police officer had been found dead in his car in a nearby carpark. There had been no witnesses, and no weapon had been found. Details were sparse and his name was not released.

A second item referred to a truck driver being found shot dead in his vehicle after routine police stop on Great Eastern Highway just east of Merredin. Apparently, the officers who found him believed he might have picked up a hitch hiker who might be a person of interest in relation to the carpark murder. The police had issued a warning to local people to be on the lookout for an undescribed armed man. A do-not-approach warning was also issued.

Angela texted James:

Did you hear the news?

Mulligan. Keep it to yourself.

His prompt answer was an even bigger shock than the news announcement. 'Mulligan?' she said as soon as he answered his phone. 'I thought he was in-crowd.'

'So did I. Where does this find us? Since this investigation began, related murders are apparently becoming two-a-penny, and worse. There are already several killings and attempts that could be directly sheeted to the traffickers, including your friend Jackie who only survived with the help of Mandy Stephenson.'

'Would it be naïve to think that someone is attempting to eliminate all potential witnesses to the goings on around George Gregory?'

'No, and that puts you, me, and our families in the potential firing line. The trouble is that each target is a potential witness against Gregory and the activities of his, so far, unknown cronies.' James paused for a moment before speaking again. 'I think we need to beat Gregory at his own game, and I might make a house call on him. Wanna come?'

'As someone once said, "What have I got to lose but my life?".'

James mentioned the text he'd received from The Deputy Commissioner, Arthur Bertram.

'If I can drop Oli around to yours, then I'll definitely come.'

Chapter 51

Mandy's fingers danced on the keyboard as she entered what, to most people would be a string of meaningless characters. 'Let's see where this takes us.'

A video began playing. It was similar to those they'd seen earlier but in much higher resolution.

'That's defo Rebecca, and that room. It's being recorded in a domestic bedroom.'

The profile of a man's face appeared briefly, and they both sucked in air.

'That's Clitheroe.' Mickey said.

Mandy checked the date of the media. 'One week before Rebecca Connolly was murdered.'

A few seconds later Clitheroe mounted the sleeping Rebecca, and a voice in the background could be heard cheering him on.

'Interesting.' Mickey said.

'But Clitheroe is dead.'

'Maybe the owner of that voice isn't, at least not yet.'

'You have some free time, Mick?' Mandy picked up the bloodied paper. 'This might not be the best place to be studying this stuff.'

'Where then?'

'My place. I'll clear it with, Jean, my partner.' It was well past Mandy's knock off time when she called Jean, who didn't sound too enamoured about having visitors. She pressed loud speaking mode.

'He's a colleague and we need to review some sensitive evidence that will be hard to do at the office.'

'This about that case that nearly got you blown up?'

Mickey's face wrinkled with a frown. 'Look, Mandy, I don't want to be in the way. I'm kipping at a motel. If you give me a copy and access to a laptop, I can…' He didn't get the chance to finish.

'Is that Mickey Krakauer? I'd recognise that voice anywhere. Why didn't you say. Mick and I go back a long way. How's things Mate? You still seeing Jackie?'

'Up and down, you know, Jeannie.'

'Look old mate, take no notice of what I said earlier. Stay for dinner, there's almost always enough for more than two. That's if you don't mind eating an old dyke Mummy-to-be's cooking.' There was a chuckle in her voice and the matter ended when the line went silent.

'Well, you're a dark horse Mickey Krakauer.'

'Jackie Morton and Jeannie were mates when I met them. Jackie was the only one available of the two, and somehow, we hit it off. Thanks for saving her life, by the way. I guess that means we owe you?'

Mandy gathered up the files and handed them to Mickey while she picked up her laptop and a black box gizmo that Mickey didn't recognise. He raised his eyebrows.

Mandy smiled, 'We're gonna be looking at some terrible stuff Mick and that will keep our meanderings on the dark web private.'

***

James parked a hundred metres up the road from the Gregory mansion and said, 'We'll go on foot from here.' I'll use my police creds to gain entry, and you can slip in when he opens the gate.'

'What then?'

James shrugged. 'I'll say I want to ask him some questions. Hopefully he won't know you are there and, given he has no video surveillance, you might like to potter about to see if there is anything else interesting.'

'But your blokes and his cronies have been through the place with a fine-toothed comb. What else is to find?'

James shrugged, opened his car door, walked confidently to the mansion gate, and pressed the bell push on the intercom.

'Who is it?'

'Police, Mr Gregory, I have a few more questions for you, if you wouldn't mind.'

'This is outright harassment. I will be speaking to the Commissioner at the earliest opportunity.'

'No problem, Sir. I am acting on the instructions of Deputy Commissioner Arthur Bertram. As you no doubt know, your friend, the Commissioner, is on his way to the USA for the International Senior Police Officers Leadership Conference.'

The gate slid open and James walked in while Angela shadowed him, before disappearing into the shrubbery that followed the road around to Gregory's entrance statement.

Gregory's attitude was sullen when he opened the large, glazed door to face James.

'Interesting device, Mr Gregory. I'm guessing that only you have access to the door opener.'

'And my cleaner. Now what is it you wish to ask? I'm a very busy man and it better not take up too much of my time.' He pointed to a small room to the right of the entrance and followed James in. 'Take a seat Sergeant.'

James sat on the proffered white leather seat of a small sofa. 'What is it that you do, that keeps you so busy, Mr Gregory?'

'I work the stock exchange. There is nothing illegal about that.'

'What about the mid-teen girls that were found drugged in rooms in the cellar of your premises?'

'I've already answered that question to the satisfaction of the police commissioner.'

'But not to my satisfaction, sir. Perhaps you can tell me what you said to the commissioner that would so easily satisfy his curiosity.'

'Not without my solicitor's presence.'

James made a note in his book and spoke the words aloud so that Gregory could see what he was writing. *Mr Gregory claims he answered the question of the drugged girls to the Police Commissioner.* 'When was this sir?'

'Less than thirty minutes ago'

Between the hours of nine thirty am and eleven am. 'Thank you sir. So, you won't mind repeating his answer to your question?'

'My conversations with the commissioner are confidential.'

'If this matter ever comes to court, and if the Commissioner is called as a witness it might better to clear the air before that happens.'

A beep sounded from one of Gregory's pockets. He removed a mobile phone and looked at its screen. 'Seems you were followed, sergeant.' He pressed the door open button, and a man dragged Angela by the hair, into the room. 'Ha, this must be the other half of the musical act known as "The Carters".

Angela shot a pained, "I'm sorry" face at James.

He noticed that her wrists were secured with security grade zipper clips and said 'I'll only ask you once. Remove those ties or I will arrest you for unlawful detention.'

Both men laughed.

It was at that moment he recognised the thug. His gold teeth and a Death-to-Cops tattoo on his forearm gave it away. 'So, you're out at last, Jesse.'

A look of recognition spread over the big man's visage. He reached behind his back and drew a pistol from his belt.

When he pointed it at James, he said, 'I wouldn't think about it Jesse. If you go inside again, you can kiss goodbye to the rest of your life.'

Jesse grinned turned the gun towards Angela's head. 'Never shot a lawyer. I wonder what it feels like… Nah, Cops taste better.' He returned his aim to James and before he could apply enough pressure on the trigger to fire, he was looking at the business end of his own gun.

This time the safety was off. 'Don't have traditional safeties on Glocks and this is a Colt 45 ACP.' James remembered the Dirty Harry movie and almost said "Make my day, punk." Instead, he ordered the man to undo Angela's ties, which he did. 'Now turn around. I am arresting you for unlawful restraint.' He removed a set of cuffs from his back pocket and continued with the man's rights, as he snapped them shut. 'One down you to go.' He glared at Gregory.

Gregory said, 'You'll regret this.'

James shrugged and pushed the bikie in the direction of the large entrance doors. 'Open Sesame.' He pressed Gregory's remote, and the doors swung open. 'Ha! It worked.' As soon as they were clear of the mansion James called in back up to take his prisoner to the lock up and, while he waited, said, 'Did he do any more than just tie you up?'

Angela replied, 'If I said he groped me…'

'That'd be Jesse. How are you holding up?'

Angela handed him a thumb drive, 'I Found it near the entrance to the garage lift. I heard something drop the last time I was here, but I couldn't see what it was.'

'How did you get into his garage?'

'There's a button next to the door. I guess he assumes the gate is enough protection and, as you know, he has no CCTV. The thumb drive is a one terabyte *Arcanite*, so…'

Before he could respond a car arrived to collect the prisoner and after a brief exchange of words, he agreed to follow them back to the station.

Chapter 52

The autopsy shows that the bullet in the truck driver's head came from a Colt 45, more to come on that. Mulligan was killed with a .22LR at close range. There are only fragments of that bullet, which will make it a bit harder to track down the perpetrator. However, there are several registered users who have weapons of this calibre and perhaps we'll find one with a grudge against DI Mulligan.'

'So, Commissioner, how soon do you think the perpetrators of these crimes will be brought to justice? Before or after you return from your expensive Junket in the USA?'

'We have our best working on it as I speak.'

'That wasn't my question.'

'As you know, Minister, these things take time. We have a few suspects, and they will be interrogated at the earliest opportunity.'

'Then I will expect you to keep me posted, Commissioner.'

'Of course, sir.' The Commissioner excused himself and ended the call.

The moment the line went silent the minister tapped in a new number.

A voice answered, 'Has he gone?'

The minister nodded unnecessarily and said, 'Yes. What now?'

'That remains to be seen but you must take steps to destroy any evidence however miniscule, that can be used against me or the government.'

'That might not be as easy as you think. A significant data set has gone missing, and it is possible the police are working in the cloud storage as we speak.'

'I thought you said the cloud was one-hundred percent safe.'

'In comparison to government data bases it is. The addresses are encrypted and the data behind the addresses is doubly encrypted. Defaults have been incorporated to ensure that if anyone attempts access without permission, the system will immediately corrupt all accessible data that has been changed since the last backup.'

'I hope you're right, Mr Gregory. I've put my neck on the block for you, and you may be interested to know that I have built in my own safety measures which will ensure severe repercussions should you fail me.' The minister dropped his handset on to its rest and reached into his second drawer for the bottle that had become his crutch in recent times.

***

What the hell is a one terabyte *Arcanite*?'

'Maybe we should ask your friend Mandy.'

'That's what I'm planning to do when we get back. Thanks for everything, by the way. I doubt we'd have got this far without your involvement.'

'We lawyers have *some* uses then?'

James gently nudged his sister's shoulder with his fist and concentrated on the traffic. As soon as they arrived, he led her to Mandy's section and found her chair empty. 'Anyone seen Mandy Stephenson?'

A voice piped from somewhere in the room, 'She left early with that country cop. Said she wouldn't be back until morning.'

James wasn't sure the tone of the voice contained a chuckle, but he ignored it.

***

Jeremy Clydesdale spent the next hour deleting emails, pictures and other potential evidence from his laptop computer. He'd ensured he couldn't be tracked, by finding a collaborative expert to set up a VPN and was confident that any external connections were invisible to the world. At least his expert had assured him that this was the case and Clydesdale had used the excuse that he worked in government, so everything needed to be secure.

In the process of deleting the things he didn't want to be seen, he accidentally deleted several items he needed to keep. In his desperation, he spent another hour parrying away his Chief of Staff who, for some reason best known only to him, needed to speak with him urgently.

Everything is urgent with the COS. Time he used his initiative.

The process of recovering his lost data brought back things he'd just tried so hard to get rid of. Clydesdale desperately needed the help of someone with a better computer knowledge than himself, but he knew that might create even bigger problems. He needed to cross the Swan River to reach his home and perhaps a slip up might be the best way to deal with his problem. He could then claim the computer was stolen from his car when he forgot to lock it. A good dunking in grubby water would surely render it useless.

But Clydesdale knew he'd need to perform his computer's disappearing trick without witnesses and there was the rub.

***

'Something wrong?'

Someone threw a brick through our window in the early hours. We're both shaken but Jean has taken it particularly hard.'

'Angela found this.' He handed her the Arcanite thumb drive. 'Thought it might contain something of interest.'

She half-heartedly turned it over with her fingers and said, 'One terabyte? That's big.'

'Can you take a squiz?'

'I'll give it a go, but I must warn you the stuff on the cloud is going to be more difficult than I first thought. Our friend has built in a number of traps.'

'Booby traps?'

'One false move and you're metaphorically dead, Jim.'

'Have you been able to find anything?'

Mandy pointed to a file. 'There is a list of accessible files in there. All the others are under a military grade encryption.'

'Will you be able to crack it?'

Mandy shrugged. 'What we have found is a clear shot of DCI Clitheroe as he was about to mount Rebecca Connolly. That vision was mostly dubbed out on the web version.'

'So, Clitheroe was definitely into this, on or before the time when Tom Gregory was on trial?'

'Looks that way but it won't help us, given the prime suspect is dead.'

'Maybe we need a new tack. Perhaps we should try to discover why he was so suddenly taken out, and why several other potential people of interest have been murdered or had attempts on their life, since I took up the reigns of this *unofficial* investigation.'

'Well, I'm confident I know one person who is involved with the attempt to kill Jackie and Angela.'

'How can you be so certain?'

Mandy rolled up her sleeve to expose a tiny tattoo. 'It's the only one I have. George Gregory has one similar. That photo you saw on my desk. The man was a trusted friend and colleague. He didn't make it out alive, and there is only one other person who survived our tour. The three of us got tats to mark the occasion. I refused to have a huge sleeve installation of the kind they both wanted, so I insisted on the tiny bomb image. It was to be a remembrance not an art gallery.'

'Do you know where I can find him?'

'He's a senior member of the government.'

'Shit.'

Mandy shrugged. 'The bigger they are the harder they fall.'

'Are you saying that a senior government figure is behind the bombing of my house and that of my brother?'

'The pack on Jackie's chest and the trip wires were his MO to a tee. I can't speak for your door. I haven't seen that.'

'This senior government person?'

Mandy pulled up a picture on her screen. 'Recognise him? I do.'

'Jeremy Clydesdale.'

Mandy nodded. 'Back in the day we were part of a small covert team who gave back the Taliban what they tried on us. Clydesdale was as creepy as all hell and distributed most of his time between chasing young female soldiers and brown-nosing senior officers.'

'Can I take it you didn't like him?'

'That photograph. It's the only thing I have left of Greg. That was his name, by the way. Greg knew that Clydesdale was trying it on with me. You know why that wouldn't work but he wouldn't take no for an answer. Greg stepped up and put him in his place. He died two days later.'

'Clydesdale murdered him?' James said.

'As good as. He was sent on a job and never came back. The investigation came up with nothing other than Greg's incompetence leading to his own demise.'

'But you found otherwise?' Angela said.

'Greg was to sneak into a Taliban encampment under cover of darkness and place an IED while they were sleeping, the idea being to unnerve them. The device had been made by Clydesdale and was almost identical to the one used on Jackie. Except, in the case of Greg, he didn't make it to the encampment and in the wash up, I found parts of a timing device that would have ensured it blew before taking any Taliban.' She paused. 'Naturally the whole incident was hidden in the fog of war. Such a stupid term isn't it.'

'Were there any timing bits in Jackie's parcel?' James asked.

'Nope. Not from what I could see in the collected evidence.'

'You think the minister planted the explosives at my house?'

'Unlikely. Clydesdale was never one to get his hands dirty, he just made the devices, and we delivered them to the selected clients.'

'I thought you were in bomb disposal.' James said.

'According to all the records I was, and I did, on the occasions it was necessary, disable an IED or two. There is nothing on record about our covert practices and that little tattoo is all I have to remember it by.'

'So, when you lifted that device off Jackie's chest, it could have been booby trapped?' Angela's face had paled with the thought.

'Nah, Clydesdale's stuff wasn't that sophisticated all it had in it were movement detectors and they were slugged to stop tiny movements from causing a detonation. She would have needed to sit up to set it off. Her bomb and the tripwire explosives were designed to kill her and your entire family, leaving no witnesses. Jackie wouldn't have known that, and it must have taken a lot of courage to lie there as still as she did, for as long as she did.'

'We owe you.' Angela said.

'No, you don't, but if it's a debt that makes you feel better and helps you drive yourself to stop these bastards…'

Chapter 53

Making an approach to the Minister for Police will be nigh on as difficult as getting an impromptu karaoke date with the king of England. However, given what we now know, the king might be an easier target, James thought as they left Mandy to continue her work and made their way to the car.

Angela broke into his thoughts. 'When they said top dog, they meant it. He's your ultimate boss and you'll need something strong to flick him off his pedestal.'

'Like finding the lackey who planted the explosives. Once we get him and put him on a spot, I'll bet he'll be hard pressed to keep his mouth shut.'

'I think we might need more than that, Jim. There must be a reason why a man reaches Clydesdale's position, and then contemplates the actions we've witnessed.'

'Let's hope Mandy's work on that thumb drive you found, helps. Maybe there's something in there to unlock the Cloud encryption.' When they reached his car, he made a call to home. 'On my way and Angela will be with us for lunch. If that's okay?'

Angela interrupted him. 'There's no need I'll collect Oliver and take him home. I'd like some alone-time with him.'

'Forget Angela.' He tapped the loud speaking button.

'No,' Stacey responded. 'Tell her I've already made enough for us all and I need to thank her for what she's done.'

James looked at Angela and shrugged.

She lowered her eyes, in a way grateful for the company they'd provide. 'Thanks, Stacey!' She called to James' phone.

He pressed end, smiled, and said, 'That's it then, Ange. We're officially a family again.'

***

Minister Clydesdale opened his diary and found a clear date. He'd need to be quick as most of the time they filled up without his knowing. He focussed on the date and picked up his phone. 'Keep next Tuesday free I have a private engagement.'

'Yes sir. I'd already pencilled in the premier for a meeting, but I think he's reasonably flexible.'

'Make sure he is and lock that date out of any engagements.' Clydesdale ended the call and made another on a private mobile. 'I have another job for you this one you had better not stuff up.'

'Then you had better make sure the cash you already owe me, and the price of this job is up front this time. Usual place or you might be the recipient of my services.' The speaker ended the call.

There were only two living people who knew of his past. One, because of his connections, might present a major problem to control but Clydesdale had quid pro quo evidence in that respect. The other was a cop who'd already screwed up his plans and this time the elimination must be complete.

He made another call.

'Jeremy, how nice to hear from you. It's been too long.'

'I need your help.'

'Anything, old chap.'

'Those images…'

There was a long pause.

'The ones that featured… you know…'

Another long pause.

'For fuck's sake speak to me.'

'No need to be like that, old chap.'

'Well, you know what I mean.'

'I know very well what you mean, Minister, and I have given you plenty of time to reign in your underlings. If you wish to remain in government, you must protect me and my friends from your unruly police force. My home has been raided and searched twice and there is still not a single charge against me.'

'I am limited in what I can be seen to be doing, you must understand that.'

'I understand that you had what seemed to be a very pleasant time with a variety of young ladies at my parties. I'm not sure they enjoyed it as much as you, but that's by and by. The last few days have cost me greatly, Jeremy, in both financial terms and in credibility with my clients. It will take some time to repair the damage, and you need to ask yourself, what are you going to do? Not ask me what I am going to do.'

'I have already begun taking steps to eliminate potential witnesses and that, in itself, could end up in a shemozzle that could bring us all down. I understand the lawyer who defended your son is back on his case, and if it ever comes out that it was you who killed his teacher, I wouldn't be able to protect you.'

'You believe I killed her?'

'Didn't you?'

'If I did, I certainly would not be admitting it to the chief cop. Sort yourself out Jeremy and when you have something worth offering, contact me. Until then, you're on notice.'

The call ended.

Clydesdale listened to the silent phone for what seemed like several minutes before he realised, he was officially in the doldrums. He made his decision and advised his secretary he would be unavailable for the remainder of the day. Then he keyed a page of text into his laptop.

A few moments later he had rearranged his finances via an encrypted dark web banking site and had purchased hotel accommodation and airline tickets for his family. At least his wife would be glad of the holiday she would only learn of within the next hour.

***

Mandy Stephenson closed down her laptop and slipped it into its case. She then called Jean to say she would be home early and had some work she could only do at home. She almost opened a visitor's car, similar colour, and model, before remembering her usual spot had been taken when she arrived. She found her car several slots down and gestured, my mistake, to the slot stealing visitor, before slipping into her car to slide her key into the ignition. Moments later, Mandy's vision was overwhelmed a bright flash, but she heard nothing.

Mickey Krakauer was one of the first officers on the scene. The vehicle was in fragments and there was little left to identify its occupant. Several adjacent cars were badly damaged and only one was occupied. He wrenched open the distorted door and retched as he saw the condition of the driver. Possibly female, and in uniform, she was covered in blood and had numerous shrapnel wounds to her face and arms. She was barely alive as he dragged her as far away as he could, in the knowledge that he might be doing her even more damage in the process.

He then felt the blast of the car's fuel tank erupting as he began CPR. It singed the back of his head, and he smelled the stench of burning hair as several others gathered to help them both to relative safety. Sirens followed and the loose spray from fire hoses wet his shirt and chilled his skin.

'Who is she?' Someone yelled.

'I think it might be Mandy Stephenson,' Mickey replied, 'but she's so messed up, I…'

A pair of Ambos arrived with a stretcher and lifted the limp and bloody body onto it. Within seconds the skirling of sirens followed the ambulance from the car park.

Mickey attempted to wipe the blood from his uniform. 'Second time in a fuckin week,' he muttered. Before he could process the situation further, he was surrounded by officers of various ranks the most senior being Deputy Commissioner Arthur Bertram.

Mickey felt an arm curl around his shoulder.

'You did well Mick… Give this man some space.'

The crowd moved away.

Bertram ended a call on his mobile. 'Another ambulance is on its way, mate. You'll need to be checked out.'

Mickey shook his head. 'No sir, I'm okay, but I know someone who does need to be checked out, in more ways than one.' Despite the knowledge that he was being given direct orders by the Deputy Commissioner, Mickey ran from the car park and hailed a passing taxi before anyone could stop him.

'Cut yourself shaving,' the driver said.

Mickey replied, 'Shut the fuck up,' and yelled an address.

Chapter 54

Clydesdale's wife was surprised when her husband arrived home early, his face red and sweaty, and his demeanour touchy at the least. 'What's happened this time. Tough question in the house?'

'I've resigned. I've had enough and I don't think I've been very fair to you and the kids. I've booked us a surprise holiday, and as luck would have it my parliamentary pension matured two weeks ago.' He smiled and drew her into an unwanted hug.

Madelaine Clydesdale had long since ended her marriage in the biblical sense and his touch had begun to repel her almost as much as his bossy attitude. 'Holiday? Together? Where?'

'I can't tell you right now, but I think you'll like it. Are the kids home from school?'

Madelaine nodded. 'What should we pack?'

'We can travel light and buy new clothes when we get to our destination. Just pack enough for a couple of days.'

Madelaine shrugged and left him to his own devices. Just as his phone beeped with a text:

> Job Done. Where's the money?
> You have one hour to pay your dues or, well, I don't
> need to tell you what comes next. Do I Jeremy?

Clydesdale read the message and smirked. *First you have to catch me.* He unlocked a drawer in his desk and extracted his family's travel papers, shoved them into the inside pocket of his suit and shouted, 'Do hurry Madelaine or we'll be cutting it fine at the airport.' He slumped into a chair and began chewing his fingernails. Even the best plans could fall apart at the last minute.

***

Mickey Krakauer almost sprang over the wall and landed comfortably on his feet in recently turned soil behind some bushes. He could see the front door of the house, but he now knew the weaknesses of the security and he headed for the garage.

No one saw him press the *open* button for the garage, and no one saw him slip easily inside to slide the tool rack and expose the lift. He pressed the up button and the moment it arrived he stepped out into the hallway of George Gregory's mansion.

Everything was quiet. *Damn*, he thought, and found himself a place where he could hang around in comfort until his target arrived on the scene. Mickey hadn't a clue how long his wait might be, so he fixed himself a bite of lunch and pulled a can of ginger beer from the fridge in the extensive kitchen.

Mickey had silenced his phone to avoid an unnecessary disturbance, but he felt it vibrate in his pocket.

He'd received a voicemail from a number he didn't recognise. He put the phone to his ear and as he listened to Jackie's voice, he felt his cheeks warm and a smile break on his lips. The news changed nothing, but he felt much better for hearing it. He sent a text to acknowledge:

> Great news, Jack. Give her my best wishes. Love ya babe.

He picked up the TV remote and sat back to watch the tail end of an old movie. He might be a cop, but he was off grid with his boss's permission, and he was going to make every second count. A news bulletin followed the ads, and it was led with a breaking announcement:

'Less than three hours after The Minister for Police Mr Jeremy Clydesdale handed in his resignation to the to the Premier, his bullet-riddled private vehicle has been found abandoned on an industrial estate in Welshpool.

'Police are treating the matter as suspicious and there have been no subsequent sightings of him or his family. We'll keep you posted with any breaking news as it comes to hand.'

Mickey texted James:

Heard the news?

Yup. I think there's more to this than meets they eye. Where are you?

Can't say right now. I'll be in touch.

Mickey watched the bulletin to the end and offed the TV when he heard the front door motors whir softly to indicate someone had arrived. He stayed where he was and grinned as George Gregory almost departed his skin when he saw him.

'Get out of my house!'

'Not until we've had a deep and meaningful conversation Mr Gregory.'

'You're covered in blood.'

'I'm glad you noticed. It means if you happen to bleed during our conversation the DNA might be too contaminated to use as evidence.'

Gregory's face paled. He was happy to dish out punishment to helpless kids but the thought of being a recipient was something else. He pulled his buzzing phone from his pocket and put it to his ear. 'What do you mean he's resigned?'

…

'Bullet ridden? By whom?' his face paled, even further,

emphasised by the dark skin of the man in his presence. He swallowed hard and ended the call. 'Who are you?'

'PC Mickey Krakauer, at your service. Now you have learned of the departure of your minder. You might like to answer some questions.' Mickey pressed record on his phone and went through the standard preamble for a police interview.

Gregory said nothing. 'I will not speak without presence of my solicitor.'

'No worries, mate.' Mickey split in half an a4 pad he'd found while he was waiting for him to arrive. He handed him a pen and said, 'You can write it down instead. I've got all the time in the world.' He placed the other half on his lap and wrote "interview with Mr George Gregory" along with the date and time. 'Ready when you are, sir.'

Gregory smirked.

Mickey stood. Killed record on his phone and delivered an uppercut.

Blood spurted from Gregory's mouth as he bit into his tongue.

'Should get that looked at by a doctor, mate.'

'I'll see you in jail before I speak to you,' he spluttered.

'Nah. Because by the time I've finished with you, you'll need help going to the dunny.' Mickey stood again and drew back his arm.

'What do you want me to tell you?'

'The truth might be a good starting point.'

***

Mandy Stephenson's injuries were serious and would have been on the verge of being life threatening, had she not received the rapid treatment on arrival at the hospital. While officers were assigned to guard her and speak with her at the first opportunity, they were all warned that it might be several days before she would be strong enough to answer questions.

Her partner, Jean was given permission to be by her bedside for as long as required and she was sitting in civilian clothes, glumly holding Mandy's hand when James Carter arrived.

'I'm so sorry, Jean,' he said.

'She knew she was taking a big risk. I tried to talk her out of it, but she's as stubborn as a mule.'

James handed her the flowers he'd brought with him. 'I hope she gets to see them before…' he stopped himself. 'Before they shrivel up. They don't seem to last long these days.'

'It's the thought, Jim. I sometimes think Mandy can read minds, so she'll know you're here.'

'It could have been a lot worse. She didn't park in her usual spot. The bomber placed his charge on the wrong car, and he was picked up on CCTV. He's known to the department, and we reckon we'll have him in our tender loving care within a few hours.'

'What then?'

'I reckon he'll talk like a well-trained cockatoo and there'll be a few people quaking in their boots.'

'How high does it go?'

James shrugged. 'Jeremy Clydesdale has resigned. Apparently, his car was later found shot up in an industrial area. He wasn't there and his family have gone too. The official line is that he's been suffering from ill health for some time and, given an election is looming, his departure will give the government time to find someone to fill his shoes.'

'You said his car was found shot up?'

'That's all there is. A car, *belonging* to him, was found riddled with bullet holes, but no shots were heard and there was not a trace of blood.'

'So what do you think happened to him?'

James shrugged again. 'Arty Bertram's running the show while the commissioner is in the USA. Arty and I go back a few years we were in the same intake at the academy, and I know he's dinkum. If there is anything to be found out, he'll be on to it like a terrier.' His phone buzzed with a silent message. 'Excuse me.'

> Immigration suspect that The Minister and fam caught a plane to the PRC earlier today. Looks like false docs but we can't be certain yet.

'That was Arty. He reckons the minister skipped the country on false docs earlier today. That's between you and me. Don't breathe a word to anyone.' He raised his eyebrows.

'Sounds a bit sneaky though, doesn't it?'

'We are heading into tricky waters, Jean. There have been a number of murders and attempted murders, and they all seem related. Do you have your service weapon?'

She shook her head.

'Then I believe you ought to go home and get into uniform complete with your weapons. I don't think they have finished with Mandy yet and she might need all the help she can get.'

'But...'

'I'll stay with her. Go!'

James sat in the seat Jean vacated and took hold of Mandy's hand. 'She won't be long, I promise.'

Mandy said nothing.

***

'You'd better be prepared for some fall-out when you return Commissioner.' The Premier had summoned every ounce of gravitas, but he wasn't sure if it worked. He'd always been nervous of the power invested in the Police Commissioner, and no one was squeaky clean.'

'Is there a problem, Sir?'

'The Minister for Police has done what *you* might call a moonlight flit.'

'With respect, sir. How can that be a problem for me?'

'I'll speak to you about it on your return. Meanwhile do as I have requested and check there are no dirty little secrets that might suddenly pop out of the woodwork.' The Premier ended the call.

***

Arthur Bertram had just taken a sip from his first coffee of the day, when his silenced mobile phone began buzzing across his desk. He picked it up and looked at the screen. It was an overseas call, and he guessed who. The moment he pressed the accept button his thoughts were confirmed.

'What the hell is going on with Clydesdale?'

'Your guess is as good as mine, sir. I'd have suggested you ask him yourself but…'

'This anything to do with the Gregory affair?'

'What makes you ask that?'

'Um… Nothing. We can talk about that privately on my return.'

'No probs, sir, I hope it's all going well in the home of the brave.'

'Don't be facetious, Arthur.'

Arty Bertram grinned and pressed end. He'd been fast tracked, but he'd also spent time on the beat. He'd been aware for a while that something was crook and now, it seemed, the chooks were coming home to the roost, *and I think there might be a fox waiting for them.* He tapped James Carter's number on his phone.

'Sir.'

'Time to pull the pin, Jim. I want Gregory arrested for human trafficking and, while he's languishing in our splendid accommodation, I want you to take his place apart again, this time no limits, piece by piece if necessary. The warrants will be in your hands shortly.'

'We've been there done that, sir. The only thing we found was the antidote to the drug they were using but those in the earlier raid managed to *lose* all the useful records, like cameras and data. That should tell us something. Mandy Stephenson was working in the dark web cloud but she's now in hospital and barely alive.'

'This time it will be different. I believe we will shortly have the bomber in our hands, and I fully expect him to squeal like a stuck pig.'

'If we could only get some of the older girls to talk, they might throw some hints our way. Unfortunately, because of the drug they have no recall.'

'Meanwhile, arrest Gregory, grill him, and literally leave no stone unturned when you do his place over. He's a crim with connections, Jim. I'm convinced of that, and the chances are, he'll have got a bit cocksure over time.'

Chapter 55

Can I hook up Jackie Morton as a paid consultant? She has special skills, and she found the antidote when no one else could come up with anything.'

'She's a convicted criminal on parole, Jim. I'm not sure I can sanction that.'

'She is also intending to appeal her conviction and there are many of us who will support her, one hundred percent. We all know she was framed by Clitheroe and look where that got him.'

'Okay, as it's you, doing the asking and Jackie is an old friend, but it can't be official, and the payment might need to come from a special fund. You can leave that part with me for now. Arrest the bugger, Jim. Put the squeeze on him and rip his place apart.'

'Consider it done. I'll also need authority to question the initial search team?'

'That I can do. I'll get onto internal investigations and start an enquiry into the loss of evidential material. As of now, you are wasting time on the phone, Detective Sergeant.'

James grinned as he put down the phone. He immediately called Mickey Krakauer and told him the news. '…I only want trusted people Mick. Also, Jackie will be on the team as an unofficial paid consultant for the search. Can you let her know?'

'Yer on, Sarge.'

'This will be an intensive search so we might need special

equipment. Get what you think you'll need and use Arthur Bertram's name on any requisitions.' The call was ended by Mickey and James called Angela. 'Is there anyone in your chambers who would take on an appeal against Jackie Morton's conviction?'

'I'll ask around, but she'll need some good evidence. I've already started a pro bono appeal for Tom Gregory so that might stretch things a little. I'll call you back as soon as I know something.'

James' phone tooted with a text:

> Team of ten arriving soon and ready to search every nook and cranny.

> Okay, Mick. See you there in twenty minutes.

A thumbs up icon responded, and James made his way to his car.

A line of parked police vehicles stood outside the Gregory dwelling when James arrived. He saw Mickey's team waiting and gave them the nod to proceed.

A man with a cutting wheel, and clad in black police overalls, had stepped forwards to begin cutting the gate in half. When it opened and Mickey appeared, to lead them in.

The team opened the garage and had begun checking the walls, ceiling, and floor with gadgets.

A shout went up when someone discovered a cleverly disguised trapdoor in the ceiling. Half the team headed down in the lift while Mickey and Jackie followed James to Gregory's front door.

'No one home, Mick?'

'He's in, boss.' Mickey went back to the garage and returned with a grinning ape of a man. 'This is Bob Hawkins, Sarge. Tell him Bob.'

'You want that door open with minimum damage, boss?'

James nodded.

Bob Hawkins checked the door over, moved to the right-hand edge and slipped in a thin device he'd removed from his equipment belt. 'Now stand back while the magic happens.' He pressed a button on what looked like a car remote, and the door slid open on cue.

'That was easier than I expected.'

Bob tapped the side of his nose and turned to Mickey. 'Anything else Mick?'

'Nah, get back to the garage. We'll be okay from here.' Mickey raised his hand. 'Wait. Weren't you on the initial raid that found the girls?'

Bob's face turned red. 'Not a Kocher raid that one, Mick. I got the impression we weren't supposed to find anything, and anything we did find was dumped in a skip to be taken away for disposal.'

'Do you know where they took it?'

Bob shook his head. 'DI Mulligan was in charge of that. The last time I heard he was laying in wait at the morgue.'

'Okay, we now know there was some jiggery-pokery, but we have to find something to pin Gregory down. He's been given a get-out-of-jail-card by someone once, but it's about to be invalidated.'

Before James could say anything more, a group of men in suits arrived, while Gregory was ranting about the illegal entry to his property.

James showed his ID and handed him the search warrant. He then pulled a set of cuffs from his belt, turned Gregory around, and slipped them on his wrists. 'You can do the honours Mick.'

Mickey Krakauer shrugged aside the protests of Gregory's lawyers and began dictating his rights as he led him from his house leaving James to face the barrage of legalise from the bevy of suits.

'Your client has been arrested on charges of human trafficking. He will be charged with attempted murder and using an illegal substance to stupefy a person, or persons held in illegal confinement. On top of that he is suspected of having intercourse with underage persons without their consent. In other words, pretty much anything we can throw at him. You might as well go back to where you came from and await his call.'

The leader of the group seemed the calmest. 'Detective Sergeant Carter, isn't it?'

James lifted his ID. 'That's what it says here.'

The man made a note. 'I hope you've been looking after your superannuation, Sergeant.' He turned and led the group from Gregory's house.

'Interesting reaction,' Jackie said, speaking for the first time. 'Thanks for the job, Jim. I need all the help I can get.'

'I've asked Angela to look into an appeal. She's going to check with her colleagues.'

'I have no money. I can't afford an appeal.'

'Maybe money won't be important and when we garner enough evidence to prove you were improperly convicted, the lawyers will be falling over themselves to help.'

Jackie smiled, and then she frowned. Wetness filled her eyes, and she shook her head. 'Right now, we have a more important job to do.' She dabbed away her tears and strode from the room.

***

While her chambers had a policy of supporting special pro bono cases, there hadn't been an example for at least ten years. Her work on Tom Gregory's case had all been done in her own time. She had even recorded leave for the days she attended him in prison.

Angela Carter was suffering from an antagonistic conscience that had prevented her from getting on with a normal life. She had no choice but to do what she could for Tom Gregory who she firmly believed was innocent of murder. Whether the practice would have the same view of an ex-police officer found guilty of perverting the course of justice might present a whole new challenge.

She took a deep breath and knocked on the door of the Senior Partner.

'Come.' His muffled voice sounded through the thick oaken door.

He smiled when he saw who it was. 'Angela, so nice to see you. It seems like ages since you attended any of our social functions.'

Angela returned his smile and said, 'Nine-year-olds don't leave much time for socialising.'

Locke nodded. 'So how are you doing. I understand you've been ill.'

'I'm okay now sir but I need some advice.'

'This about that Tom Gregory case you've been dealing with in your private time?'

Angela felt chilled to the bone by his response, *you know about that*, she continued. 'No, sir. But I understand we have a policy of providing pro bono services to worthy cases.'

'That's certainly true. Are you asking for this Gregory chap to be looked after by us?'

'No, sir. This is something completely different.'

'Go on.'

About ten years ago a police officer was caught up in a raid on a bikie gang's attempted import of ice and although she was acting on the orders of a senior officer, she was convicted of perverting the course of justice. She has served most of her sentence and is out on parole. The general opinion of officers at the time is that she was set up.'

'Can they prove that?'

'That is something we'd need to determine.'

'The name of this officer?'

'Jackie Morton.'

'Aboriginal?'

Angela nodded.

Locke rolled his eyes. 'Leave it with me. If you intend running with this Gregory case, do you realise you might be entirely on your own?'

'Yes, sir. Thank you, sir.' She had turned away to leave his office when he spoke again.

'You are a much-valued junior partner, Ms Carter. We wouldn't want to lose you.'

'Thank you, sir.' She pulled the door shut and the heavily veiled threat caused hackles to rise on her neck. *He started with Angela and finished with Ms Carter.* She returned to her desk and called her brother, to tell him of the response.

His phone went to message bank.

'Call me when you get a minute. Thanks.'

Chapter 56

George Gregory seemed determined to name every billionaire in the country and even the Minister for Police was dragged into his rant. 'When *they* see what is happening to an upright citizen of this country, you will wish you had never set eyes on me.'

Mickey grinned as he handed him over to the dungeon keepers. 'Make sure he's comfortable, Bernie. We wouldn't want anything untoward to happen to him.'

'Where are you off to, now Mick?'

'Back to the grind, Bernie. It's gonna be a few long days.' When Mickey arrived at the crime scene, it was a hive of activity. He found James in a close conflab with Jackie who was grinning from ear to ear. 'Hey you two. Is there sommat goin on here that I should know about?'

'We found something Mick, well, Jackie did.'

Jackie was still wearing her nitrile gloves, and she grabbed his hand. 'Look.' She pointed to a cupboard beneath the polished black stonework top in Gregory's fancy, but barely used kitchen.

'It's a cupboard. We went through them all.'

Jackie opened the door and pointed inside. 'That's a false panel.' She squatted and reached inside to remove the panel. 'See?'

'Bloody hell, Jack.'

'Exactly,' James said. 'We have some forensics blokes coming over to give the contents the once over before we remove everything.'

'Think that is the stuff they used to immobilise the kids?' Mickey replied.

'Until it's tested, we won't know for certain, but I'd stake my pension on it.'

'So we'll have evidence that Gregory handled the drugs?'

'I hope so.'

***

'Aye up,' a voice called from behind them. 'Sergeant Williams. You got something you want me to check out?'

James pointed to the cupboard. 'We could have cleared it out, but I wanted to be sure we missed nothing.'

'No probs, Jim.' Sergeant Williams knelt at the open door and opened an aluminium case he'd been carrying. He set up a work light and peered closely at the packages and bottles that were stored on shelves in the narrow space. 'Okay. Clear the building and call the bomb squad. See that?' he pointed to a glinting hair thin wire that was stretched across the front of one of the shelves. 'Looks like a trip wire to me.' He encouraged everyone to leave the room and followed them shutting the door to close off the space.

'Good job we called you, Sarge,' Jackie said. 'I was about to pull everything out until DS Carter stopped me.'

'I've only seen one of these before, but we were lucky no one crossed the line then. There is probably a decent charge tucked away somewhere and certainly big enough to cause your demise, Ms?'

'Jackie Morton.'

Sergeant Williams nodded. 'Let's get this place cleared of people. There is a good chance the device can be remotely detonated or disabled for access.'

'We'd all better hope not. This is the first real evidence we've found.' James turned to Mickey, 'Did he have a mobile phone on him?'

'Sure did. It's secured with his personal possessions.'

'We need to check that phone. If he has an app and his lawyers wangle him out…'

Everyone moved several metres away from the cupboard.

Sergeant Williams said, 'This whole house should be cleared of personnel, immediately. Get that phone pulled now.'

Mickey tapped his screen with his finger. When the phone answered he yelled, 'Gregory's phone. Where is it?'

…

'Shit!'

'What's up Mick?'

'He's been released, fuckin habeas corpus, apparently his lawyers got to a judge.'

'Now what do we do?' Jackie asked.

'He won't know we've discovered his little stash so let him come back and we'll introduce him to it. Somehow, I don't think Mr Gregory will have the stomach to blow himself to bits.'

'What if he does?' Jackie slumped dejectedly against the wall beside the gate.

James replied, 'He'll be given the good old witch treatment. We tell him to empty the stash. If he's guilty he'll hold back, if he's innocent, he'll blow himself up and we'll know someone else is pulling the strings. Problem solved.'

***

Mandy Stephenson opened her eyes and looked around. The last thing she remembered was sitting in her car and about to head for home. 'What the…?'

Jean heard her voice and awakened from the nap she'd fallen into. 'Hey, they said it might be awhile before you could speak.'

Mandy turned to face her. 'What happened?'

Someone planted a bomb in a car. They believe it was intended for you, but he picked the wrongun.'

'The other car? Who?'

'Visitor. Must have parked in your place and the bomber thought her car was yours. They have him on video. They reckon he'll be in custody soon.'

'I feel like crap.'

'Well, I won't rush to get you a mirror then.' Jean leaned over, lightly kissed her on the lips and said, 'They reckon they got to you quickly, so scarring should be a minor problem.'

'Scarring?' Mandy raised her hands to touch the dressings covering her face. She looked at her hand and then the other.

'The blast shattered all the windows in all the nearby cars. It could have been so much worse.'

'I need my computer and the files that were in my car.'

'I'll ask, but…'

'But what?'

Jean shook her head. 'The firies did their best… so…'

'Shit. I'll need a new computer. Where are the things I came in with?'

'I'll ask?' Jean stood to leave.

'I had a one terabyte Arcanite thumb drive in the pocket of my pants. Get it for me. Then get me a computer. I was on the verge of solving this bloody shit… shit-shit-shit.'

'I'll do my best, but you need to get some rest.'

'If they find out we know where their stuff is they'll shred it as quick as looking at it. Hurry. Where's my phone?'

Jean opened the drawer on the bedside cabinet. 'Here. It's not my fault you know,' she said, almost throwing the device at her lover.

Mandy felt tears fill her eyes, and she reached out. She was too late the door had closed, and she was alone. As luck would have it, her phone had lost its charge, so she was no further along. She tried to reach the hospital landline but couldn't. She pressed the nurse call button and waited.

***

'While we're waiting, Jim.' She handed him a thumb drive. 'Here is all the stuff Mick, and I recorded on the way from Warakurna. Don't know how much help it will be and there'll be a few of Mickey's farts thrown in for good measure... some of the crap that bloke eats...'

'You were the one who scoffed all the cold stuff and the chocolate bars.' Mickey laughed.

Jackie grinned. 'I've missed you.' She gave him a squeeze.

'Nice to know someone is getting some intimacy in their lives.' Williams snarked.

'Your only jealous, sarge.' Mickey replied as a black saloon pulled up to where they were standing.

A man in a suit opened the rear passenger door and George Gregory climbed out. 'Well-well,' he said. 'My lawyers have lodged a nice batch of complaints against you Sergeant Carter.' He turned to Mickey. 'And the day George Gregory is taken into custody by a blackfella cop it will mean the end of his career. Got that, cuz?' Gregory walked to his door puffed out his chest, pressed his remote and opened his door.

He seemed surprised when the group of police officers followed him in, despite the protests from the suits accompanying him. 'Get them out of my house.'

James said, 'We are still executing a warrant, Mr Gregory. One more thing and we'll happily leave you alone.'

Gregory's face whipped around to face him.

'We found something, and we'd like you to confirm that it's yours or not, as the case may be.'

Gregory turned to his lawyers.

As one they shrugged and the tallest in the group said, 'If it's not yours you have nothing to fear.'

Gregory scowled and indicated that his lawyers should lead on.

'No Mr Gregory. They can wait here. I'll take you to it.' Despite James' look of resistance, Jackie Morton waved him to follow and led him to the kitchen.

When they arrived, Gregory frowned.

Jackie pointed to the cupboard. 'What do you keep in there, Mr Gregory?'

'How would I know? I don't use the kitchen. You'd better ask my cook.'

'Would you please give the cook a call and ask him or her to join us?'

'No. I will not.'

'Very well, you leave me with no choice.'

Before he had any chance to object Jackie had his arm up his back and him on his knees before the cupboard. 'The commissioner will be hearing from me,' he gasped.

'Maybe, maybe not.' Jackie reached in and pulled the false front away exposing the stash.

Gregory pulled back forcefully.

Jackie reached in to grab a bottle.

'N-n-n-no!' Gregory spluttered.

'Oh dear. Is there something we should know about?'

Gregory reached into his pocket and retrieved his phone.

Jackie was too quick. She snatched it and yelled, 'I have his phone, Jim!'

Chapter 57

It seemed like an eternity before anyone answered her call and her frustration grew with every minute that passed. At last, a young nurse poked her head around the door.

'Sorry, everything happened at once and… well, here I am.'

'The clothes I was wearing when I came in. Where are they?'

The nurse dropped on one knee to the bedside locker. 'They should be in here.' She lifted a bundle of clothes and placed them on the bed. 'Sorry. They were in such a state, your friend took them home and washed them for you.'

Mandy fiddled until she found her pants and reached into a pocket. Frustrated she tried the opposite one. There was nothing. Not even a second-hand washed-out tissue. 'Where are my things?'

The nurse frowned, 'I don't know. Perhaps if you describe them to me…'

'My phone is here but there was also a thumb drive that contains vital information…'

The nurse shook her head. 'I'll ask around.'

'You'd better do better than that. That thumb drive contains the evidence to lay charges in a major human trafficking investigation.' She held out her phone. 'Anywhere I can get this charged?'

The nurse examined the phone. 'It's an iPhone. Most of the chargers in here only work on Androids.'

Mandy pointed to the landline phone, and the nurse handed it to her.

'Thanks,' she said. 'Sorry to be such a grumpy bum.'

'Trust me,' the nurse said. 'I'd be worse if it were me.' She smiled, 'Anything else?'

Mandy shook her head, almost imperceptibly, and dialled a number. She waited for a while, until it rang out, and she left a message:

> It's me, James. Mandy Stephenson. I'm using the hospital landline. Sorry to be such a bother, but do you know if anyone found a thumb drive in one of my pockets?'

A few minutes later James responded to her call. 'How are you feeling?'

'Okay but I'll be better when I know what happened to the thumb drive. It was the big one Angela found in Gregory's garage. Plus, someone needs to get to my desk and salvage anything they can, before...'

'We're all bogged down with a search, Mandy.'

'Well, don't say I didn't warn you.' She slammed the handset on the rest and called Jean. There was no response.

***

'Give us the coordinates to make that stash safe or unlock your phone and we'll do it ourselves.'

Gregory smirked. 'You have nothing on me so go ahead.' He unlocked his phone and handed it to James.

James checked out the various apps but could find nothing applicable to a device that might be capable of triggering an explosion. He found the phone's settings changed it to unlocked and handed it to one of the other officers. 'Take this to the cyber division, tell them I need to disable a bomb, urgently, and this phone might have the coordinates.'

A few seconds later a siren could be heard as the man raced back to the station.

'Right, you.' He grabbed Gregory, hoisted him onto a chair and taped him to it with several metres of crime scene tape. Then he dragged him in front of the cupboard with his back to the explosives. 'Now we wait. You'd better hope our team can work out your little trick before you no longer care.' James waved everyone away from the area and instructed them to take cover, while he sat in the doorway and watched Gregory squirm.

'You'll go down for this, mark my words.' Sweat began drizzling down Gregory's face, even though the room was relatively cool. 'This would be considered torture by any court.'

'Only if there are witnesses.'

Gregory began to shake almost as though he was fitting.

'You are probably experiencing what your little captives might have felt. Good init.'

'Fuck you!'

'No sweat. Oh, except for you of course.'

'There's nothing on that phone.'

'So how do we disable the booby trap?'

'There's another phone. It's not here. I make a call and they disable it for five minutes.'

James held out his phone.

Gregory shook his head.

'Shit!'

Gregory grinned.

***

Mandy tried her partner's phone a second time. This time she answered, 'What!'

'I'm sorry.'

There was a long silence.

'I mean it.'

'What do you want?'

'They said you took my clothes to wash them.'

'Lucky you, huh?'

'Yep. Did you find anything in my pockets?'

'I don't even remember checking them but…'

'Can you try? There might have been a thumb drive…'

'Oh that.'

Mandy felt a surge of adrenalin. 'And?'

'I chucked it in a drawer in the study desk. They said you wouldn't be working for a while, so.'

'Can you find it for me?'

'I'll take a look. If I do, what then?'

'Just bring it to me and, if poss, get me a work laptop too. Please…'

There was another long silence.

Mandy listened intently. 'Hello?'

'Sorry I've just been going through a bout of big-footed kicking.'

'Hey, don't worry about the thumb drive I'll find another way.' She put down the phone, dressed in her street clothes and walked from the hospital. Ten minutes later she was at the door of their apartment and facing her stunned lover, 'I think we are going to need each other for a while. I'll look after you if you look after me.' She fended off a hug. 'Sorry too painful.'

'Cuppa?'

'Yes please.'

***

It had been several days since Angela had communicated with Tom Gregory and so much had happened. The recent events connected with his father made her feel even more convinced he was innocent, and she called the prison to arrange a legal visit. It was to be a date two days ahead. She knew he would be advised of her arrival and she felt relieved she was back on his case.

Her phone tooted with a text message notification. She thought it might be the prison confirming her appointment. It wasn't. It was Stacey Carter, her brother's wife.

Can we meet for lunch and a chat?'

Tomorrow? Where and when?

I'll get back to you.

Angela didn't wish to get involved in her brother's personal affairs but maybe it was a chance to close the gap. There had always been a tension between them for reasons she couldn't even explain to herself.

She pulled up Tom Gregory's file and called Jackie Morton.

Jackie's phone went to the message bank, so she left her a brief response. 'It's time to talk about Tom Gregory's conviction. Please call me when you get a minute.' She'd barely finished speaking when a text message arrived complete with an attachment:

Sorry operational, I can't talk right now. Check out this audio it might help.

Angela loaded the attachment and listened through her headphones. It was mostly general conversation, and she wondered how it could be considered relevant. She was almost ready to give up when Jackie's voice said:

'Hey, do you remember that day when Clitheroe had you transferred to the country?'

Mickey responded, 'Yeah. Didn't even get a chance to say goodbye.'

'The bastard told me he would be holding me responsible for you sticking him with the screwdriver.'

'Well, we all know about Slippery's tactics.'

'He said later that there was a big hustle in the offing and if I said anything about the fight you had, he'd make sure I went down for it.'

'The Feral's drug bust?'

'What else. He was suspended the following day. He lied about my talking being the trigger and, in his statement, he listed me as the go-to person for the heist.'

'Were you?'

'Don't be stupid Mick, you know what it was like back then. We didn't need suspicion of guilt to tarnish us.'

The voices remained silent for a while and Angela almost nodded off. She left her desk, made herself a cup of strong coffee and returned to continue listening to the audio. A few minutes in, she'd had enough and decided to use the practice's voice to text app. She set it up and imported the audio. There were hours of recording of which most was chit chat and the rustling of snack packs.

'Tomorrow, I'll print you out and work through you with a highlighter.' She looked at her watch. It was almost time to collect Oliver from school. So much had disrupted his life in the last few days he needed the stability of a return to normality. Her phone tooted. It was a text from Stacey with a venue. She tapped in a quick response, sent it, and headed for her car.

Chapter 58

George Gregory continued to sweat as he squirmed in the ties. James knew it wouldn't be long before he'd loosen them enough to break free and he needed to speed up the chain of events. He called the officer who had taken the phone. The response was negative. There were hundreds of contacts to wade through and many of them were considered, top ten percent and upright citizens. They could hardly ring each of them to ask who might happen to have the code needed to disable a booby trap.

He needed to make a decision, and he called Jackie over.

'Jim?'

'We need to make him talk and fast.'

'How. He can't disable it.'

'No, but we can detonate it.'

'Then we'll lose all the evidence.'

'Maybe not. Are the bomb squad still here?'

'I think so.'

'Do they have one of those robot thingoes?'

'I'll check.'

While he was waiting, he called Angela. 'Hi, still good after your brush with the Antidote.'

'I think so. I'm converting Jackie and Mick's audio to text. Hopefully it will be ready for a preliminary read-through tomorrow.'

'Great.'

'I'm having lunch with Stacey tomorrow. She texted me. Might be a chance to make friends properly.'

'Stacey?'

'Your wife, duh.'

'I know who she is, Ange, but she's taken the kids down south for a few days with her mum and dad.'

'So why would…?'

'Do you have a venue?'

'I'll text it. It was definitely from her. Her name came up on my phone.'

'Okay this is what I want you to do…' He'd finished his instruction when Jackie returned with a bomb squad officer who was driving a robotic device ahead of him.

'See that bloke over there. The one with his back to the cupboard?'

The man nodded.

'Can you detonate the charge with him sitting there?'

'You mean…'

'Yep. Blow the shit out of him if necessary.'

The robot driver's face paled. 'Kill him?'

James was deliberately speaking loud enough to enable Gregory to hear. But he couldn't see the handwritten note that James was holding towards the robot controller.

'Yeah, easy as. He pressed a few buttons on his console and a long device like a fishing rod poked out from the robot's superstructure. He spoke in a louder voice, 'I'll just drive it over there and twitch the trip wire, but first, I'll get the blokes to bring up sandbags so we can protect ourselves from the blast.' He looked up and around. 'Hope this place will survive it.' He reached for his phone and issued instructions. Meanwhile he drove the robot and aimed the spigot towards the rear of the kitchen cupboard.

Gregory's stress levels seemed to have peaked, and he'd begun thrashing around in the chair when he saw the sandbags arrive. 'You can't do this it'll be premeditated murder.' He yelled.

'Yeah, but it'll be satisfying.' James responded. He signalled to the driver to commence, and he drove his device towards the space at the rear of Gregory's chair.

A wail went up from the chair 'Wait…'

James raised his hand.

The robot stopped moving.

'There are two people I can call. Minister Clydesdale and…' The second name was mumbled and unrecognisable.

'The second name on the list. Repeat it clearly,' James replied.

'Tom Gregory, my son.'

'Tom. He's in jail and has no access to a phone, you'll need to come up with something better than that.' James signalled to the man with the robot.

'There is no app. There is just a mobile phone number. Once it accepts a call, the caller has thirty seconds to enter a code to disarm the bomb. You then have 15 minutes before it re-arms and if the trip wires aren't set by then…'

'Problem solved. Give us the phone number and the codes.'

'I don't know them.'

'Your son?'

'He doesn't know what they mean, they are in a letter I sent to him.'

'Which is where?'

'You'll have to ask him that.'

'Clydesdale, anyone know where he is?'

'According to the premier, he's done a moonlight flit,' Jackie answered.

'Well then, we are in a quandary,' James said. He paused. 'I have an idea.'

Gregory perked.

'We'll simply let the robot do its work and sit back.'

'There's a locked drawer in my desk.' Gregory had begun nodding furiously in the direction of his study.

'Mick? See what you can find and bring it here.'

'Boss.'

A few minutes later he returned with a brown leather satchel and held it up so Gregory could see it.

'That's the one.'

Mick handed it to James who opened it and spread a year's work, on paper, over the desk. 'What am I looking for George?'

'An exercise book, red if I remember.'

James found the document and flipped through the pages. 'What am I looking for?'

'Your sister's telephone number.'

James found a page with Angela's name on it. Beneath the name was a standard landline number and a date. 'How do I know if this is correct?'

'Call your sister. See if she answers.'

James found his mobile and rang the number on the page. A few seconds later Angela's voice answered.

'Hello James, I wasn't expecting another call from you so soon.'

'So this is your landline number?'

'Has been for a few years now. I don't use it much I'm mainly mobile these days.'

James turned to Gregory. 'It's her number, so?'

Gregory grinned. 'Work it out, Mr Policeman. You want to keep your evidence and I want to keep my life. Providing you get it right you'll have all the evidence you need. Screw up and you've got nothing.' He seemed to relax as though what was to happen would happen.

He handed the book to Jackie. 'What do you reckon?'

She took it and sat cross-legged on the floor with her back to the wall. It wasn't long before she had an answer. 'The triggering device needs to be a mobile phone, and a six-figure code is needed to disable it. If we phone without the code, we'll blow everything to kingdom come within five minutes.'

'So what do you suggest?'

'Your sister's landline number is a mobile device number in reverse. But it is missing two digits, 04. If we dial the number in reverse with 04 at the start, I reckon you'll hear that cupboard buzzing.'

'What about the six-figure code?'

'The date as written has six figures 010889. How old is Angela?'

'Thirty-five.'

'1989+35= 2024. I reckon they've used her number and her age as a code. Who in their wildest imaginings would consider something like that if they didn't have a starting point. Your call Jim, but I reckon you dial the number and as soon as it answers key in 010889. If it blows, Gregory gets the kind of rough justice he deserves. If not, we get the evidence we need to drag him through the courts.'

James instructed the crew to clear the room. When it was empty except for robot and Gregory, he dialled the number. A mobile phone vibration buzzed from the cupboard. He waited until it answered, then punched in the code and he listened to the message:

'You have a total of fifteen minutes to disconnect the trip wire and access the store. Ensure the trip wire is reconnected within that time. End.'

James signalled to the robot controller.

He moved his machine into position and everyone held their breath as he used the probe to unhook the trip wire.

Nothing happened.

Gregory gasped.

James dragged the chair aside and reached into the cupboard.

Within a short time, he had cleared the contents which included numerous plastic bottles with Russian labels, and a number of files and notebooks. He called to the robot controller. 'You can reconnect the trip wire.'

The probe hooked the loop back over its nail and ran through a flood of Gregory's piss as it backed away.

'Should have asked for a potty before we started, George.'

Gregory scowled at Jackie's barb, and she couldn't help her smirk.

Chapter 59

James saw Jackie and Mick deep in conversation and he gave instructions to the bomb squad to disable the device in the cupboard. Then with their swag of booty loaded into the cars, they headed back to the office where it could be examined in detail.

En route, he called Arty to tell him of their success and was stunned by his response.

'We are down a DI Jim. Mulligan's demise has left a hole in our management team. As of now you're the Acting DI in his place. You've walked all the preliminary exams and stuff, so there is no reason why you shouldn't be ready to move up. Well done, on the op at Gregory's, and now let us get this stinking business knocked on the head.'

'Thank you, sir, but...'

'No buts, Acting DI Carter. I'll leave you to inform your team and the documentation will be on your desk, in your new office, when you arrive.'

'Shit.' Just when I thought my life should be getting easier, I have to start all over again. He turned to his passenger. 'You heard that, Jack?'

She was grinning from ear to ear. 'You fucking deserve it, Jim, and I've got some news too.' She held her left hand for him to see the small diamond ring on her third finger. 'He said what with all that has been happening he hasn't had the time to shop around. It's not quite the Kohinoor diamond, but it's the thought that counts and I'm not that choosy. Anyway, he's promised to upgrade it at the first opportunity.'

'What are your plans from here?'

Jackie frowned. 'I dunno Jim. I'm on parole and I'm trying to get an appeal started. Until that's all sorted out, Mick's a cop and I'm not sure how that part of our relationship can work.'

'He's also the son of your parole officer.'

'That too.' She looked down at her lap. 'I wish…'

'Angela is talking to her people about your appeal.'

Jackie nodded. 'Why does it have to be so fucking difficult?'

James turned into the station yard and parked the car.

Mick was already there waiting for Jackie and from the look on her face, it was obvious to everyone, there was something wrong. 'Hey Jack, what's up?' he said.

'Nothing,' she replied as she joined the general melee heading into the building.

***

James headed to Mulligan's office and scowled at the mess. Sitting on top of the desk pile was the letter from the Assistant commissioner. He pulled out the top draw of his predecessor's desk and dumped it into the wastebasket, before dropping Arty's unopened letter in the drawer and slamming it shut. Next, he picked up the desk phone and called Mick. 'I'm in Mulligan's office, Mick. Can we talk, please?'

'Yeah boss.'

Mick arrived a few minutes later. Gone was the smugness of success, now he seemed angry. He pulled out a chair and slumped on to it.

'I spoke with Jackie on the way back and I hear congratulations are in order.'

'Not the way she sees it.'

'Mick, we've known each other long enough to know when things are right. You two are a perfect match, except…'

'Yeah except…'

'Talk to your mum. She'll be chuffed to bits. She really likes Jackie, and she knows she was badly treated. I reckon she'll have it all sorted in a trice.'

'Got the big promo then?'

James half shrugged half nodded. 'I'd like you on my team if you're interested.'

Mick shrugged. 'That all depends on Jack's appeal. If she wins a pardon… If not, I don't see how I can continue as a cop with a convicted criminal as my wife. She *will* be my wife, Jim, as soon as we can get that part of it together.'

'Meanwhile your "convicted criminal" fiancé is a paid-up consultant to the WA Police and Angela is putting together appeal documents. She will do everything she can. I promise.'

'I wish I had your confidence.' He stood. 'All done, sir?'

'Yes, so let's finish what we started.'

***

Angela slept badly, but she knew that it was crucial that she go along with her meeting with Stacey. She texted James, who said his team was in place and that she was to follow his instructions to the letter. She parked her car a distance from the venue and attempted to walk confidently towards her lunch date.

She didn't make it to the café before a squad of armed police moved in and dragged a newly disarmed man from amid its busy throng of diners. Angela froze and looked about. *What next?* She nearly leapt from her skin when she felt a tap on her shoulder and turned to see her brother.

'All sorted. He even had written instructions in his pocket. Stacey sends her regards and suggests you meet for a proper lunch when she gets back.'

Angela's face paled and James caught her before knees gave way.

He caught her, half carried her to a slatted bench and helped her sit. 'Breath deeply. We're nearly done.'

'If I hadn't called you, what would have happened?'

'My guess, he would have pulled out his gun and probably shot you.

He would then have panicked and probably shot several others.'

'That all?'

'Can I ask you a question?'

'Is that what a knight in shining armour usually says when he's rescued his damsel?'

James shrugged off the frivolity and said, 'Mickey Krakauer has asked Jackie Morton to marry him. They are now worried about the look of a crim and a cop as husband and wife.'

'Tell him to resign and the "look" goes away.'

'I don't want to lose him. What do you reckon the chances of your mob getting an appeal started?'

'Zip. I was going to call you later. They reckon if I'm running an appeal for Tom Gregory, it's too close to home. And it looks like I'm on my own there too.'

'I'll let them know then.'

'Sorry.'

***

James walked Angela back to her car and continued to his new office. When he arrived, he found his desk had been cleared of all the detritus of Mulligan. Someone had given it a polish and right in the middle was a post it note that said:

> Taken Jackie back to Merredin. Mum is concerned
> about her parole conditions. I'll call.

There wasn't much he could do, so he set the wheels in motion with forensics to examine the cupboard contents, and tomorrow would be another day of interviews with Gregory. *That should be fun.*

Chapter 60

Mickey and Jackie said little during their drive to his mother's home. When they arrived, she was waiting with a meal on the table and a generous supply of hugs for her daughter-in-law to be.

At first the conversation was stilted, but Imelda's ways helped to release the tension. Soon after they relaxed, she dropped the bombshell that neither her son nor his future wife was expecting. 'The ALS have agreed to run with an appeal. They want to start as soon as possible.' She handed Jackie a card. 'He's a good bloke. Lots of experience in the field and he's keen to help.' She paused for a moment or two to let them take in the announcement. Then she said, 'I'll no longer be your parole officer, Jackie. I've asked a friend to take over and she'll be in touch soon.'

'So, we can forget about Locke and Keyes?'

'Seems that way.'

'I'd better let Angela Carter know we don't need her anymore.' He tapped Angela's number on his phone, and she answered immediately.

'Mickey, how's things?'

'I thought you ought to know. The ALS are considering an appeal for Jackie. So, you can save yourself the hassles with your mob.'

'Well, that is good news, Mick, and I'm happy to help if I can. I've already done a fair bit of research and I've transcribed much of your in-car conversations with Jack. There is also some good stuff there for my Tom Gregory appeal, so it's a win-win situation. 'I'll still need affidavits from you and Jack when you're back in Perth.'

'No probs, Angela. Jack will be staying with my Mum, for a while but I'll be heading down in the next coupla days. I'll call when I'm back.' He pressed end and saw his mother's puzzled face alongside Jackie's. 'Summat, I said?'

Imelda Krakauer shrugged. 'You might have warned me.'

'And me,' Jackie said.

'Sorry, I thought...?'

'I'll get your room ready. She can have that after you leave.' The kettle had boiled, and the two women left him to head into the kitchen.

***

Angela's relief was palpable when the call from Mickey ended. She could now concentrate her entire effort on Tom Gregory. They'd still not agreed to her running his appeal pro bono, and it would have been a real stretch doing two, even if they had. While the printer spat out a large quantity of pages, she called James again.

As she bound them into a volume, she hoped they could both use, James answered his phone. 'Hi Ange.'

'Good news, the ALS are taking on Jackie's appeal so I can concentrate my time on Tom. Can we talk at some time to set up a strategy?'

'It might need to wait a few days until we get George Gregory secured, and it looks like some of the stuff we found in his hidey-hole is dynamite. Providing we can collate it in time, there will be a few red faces around the town. We found several exercise books containing lists of contacts. Alongside each name is a code and we'll need to crack it, but my best guess it references their "preferences".

'I hope you'll keep me posted in case there is anyone in there I should know about.'

'They are now booked as evidence and as you will expect, that might be difficult.'

'Thanks' bro.'

'Out of my hands now, given the nature of the finds, I expect a big noise will be coming in to take over the investigation soon.'

'You said you'd help with my appeal.'

'I'm still with you on that, but if it clashes with the findings on George Gregory's activities, I'll be stranded. You'd better get your act together quickly before it all hits the fan.'

Angela ended the call and knew exactly what she needed to do. Whether it would all work in her favour was something else. She remembered something she'd forgotten and rang James' number again. There was only a voice mail option. 'Sorry Jim, I forgot to ask you how Stacey and the kids are.'

*****

Mandy Stephenson inserted the thumb drive into her borrowed computer and began trawling through code named directories that seemed to contain mostly video files. There were two that had a range of file types. She emailed them to herself and copied the email to James Carter.

Her partner, Jean, placed a mug of coffee on the table and said, 'Hate to tell you this, but I think we are about to become parents.'

'Shit! What's happening?'

'It's all happening.' She winced. 'I think we'll need to make a dash soon.'

Mandy saved the contents of the drive to a cloud storage area, ejected it, and slipped it into her pocket before closing the computer. 'Ready when you are.'

Jean's timely announcement ensured they were at the maternity department in good time and while she was undergoing an examination, Mandy pulled up a docx file from one of the directories. There was no attempt at encryption and the contents, a letter in poor English, appeared to be a manifest for a specific cargo. The cargo in this instance wasn't washing machines, it was for ten mannikins, and it outlined the procedure for the export and receival of the goods at a port in Eastern Europe. Each mannikin, numbered serially, was described by skin colour and their presented age. In this instance, the age ranged from twelve to fourteen years old.

She pulled up another file. It was similar to the previous one, its date two years later. She was about to open it when a woman in scrubs entered the room.

She smiled and nodded to the birth suite. 'You do want to be there, don't you?'

Mandy nodded, turned off her phone, and joined her partner. 'About time, hey?'

'You bloody bet.'

***

His computer pinged to tell him he had a mail message flagged as important. He opened it and saw that it was the Police Commissioner. The message ordered him to release George Gregory, return his property and cease the investigation forthwith. James forwarded it to Arthur Bertram and followed it up with a phone call.

'What do I do, sir?'

'I'm not sure what to tell you, Jim. I've just received a similar notice advising me that I'm suspended at the Governor's pleasure. It's moved up a notch, mate, and we'll need to be very careful where we go from here.'

James re read the email. 'This *is* total bollocks.'

'You're right, and it tells me that the rot at the top of our society is much more entrenched than we might have thought. We will need someone smart enough to work behind the scenes and get them to fall on their swords.'

'Who?'

'That sister of yours she's a lawyer, isn't she?'

'Yeah but…'

'A little bird tells me she's about to start an appeal against the wrongful conviction and imprisonment of George Gregory's son.'

'You think…?'

'Can you think of any other way?'

'I'll ask her.' He reached for his mobile phone and noticed there was a voice mail from Angela. 'You rang,' he said when she answered.

'Sorry, Jim. I forgot to ask about Stacey. All the goings on of the last couple of days have, well, you know.'

'I can't answer that question. Stacey's incommunicado, down south with the kids. They're probably having a wonderful time with the grandies, but I do have a question for you. Can we meet? It's too sensitive for phones.'

'You know where I live. I'm about to leave the office and I can get a takeaway if you like?'

'Sounds like a good idea to me.' He gathered the files from his desk and locked them in the filing cabinet. He didn't think it was going to help him, but it might slow down the opposition. A quick check of the emails on his phone showed one with attachments from Mandy. He decided it could wait.

Chapter 61

She was feeling happy for the first time since she could remember. Jackie Morton had found her long-lost fella and discovered his feelings for her had grown with time. He didn't seem to mind her jail time, and when they were together, it was as though they'd never been apart. She had little in the way of things, but what she did have, she deposited in the drawer he'd cleared for her.

At last, she was feeling like she had a home and she'd known Imelda for years, long before she'd met Mickey and long before her incarceration. She'd always seemed to be the epitome of kindness, and Jackie wondered about her next parole officer, but she could only hope for the best.

Tomorrow the ALS lawyers would arrive to interview her and then, hopefully, her appeal could begin. The last thing she wanted was for Mickey to give up his career for her, even though he had said he would resign after their wedding. She was deep in those thoughts when James called.

'Tell Mickey to keep his head down. Maybe even head back to a Warakurna.'

'Why don't you call him?'

'Phone records. Things are happening, and he needs to keep a low profile. No one other than his mates at Warakurna know he's here, remember?'

'I think he's heading back to Perth, Jim. He's been gone an hour.'

'Call him and tell him what I just said.'

'Okay, if he can get a signal, I'll be lucky.'

'Just try. It's important. I might be needing a friend on the inside soon.'

'That bad?'

'Maybe worse than bad.'

The call ended. She rang Mickey's mobile and heard it ringing in the lounge room. 'Bugger.'

'Hello?'

'Imelda, it's me I'm trying to contact Mickey. It's urgent and the damn silly bugger's left his phone.'

'He'll be halfway to Perth by now.'

'Can we stop him?'

'Why?'

'Jim Carter just called. Stuff is happening, and he needs him out of the way for his own good.'

'Leave it with me.' The call ended.

When Jackie joined Imelda in the lounge, she was deep in conversation with someone. Eventually, she ended the call. 'Got a mate who lives down the highway. Given the time he left and the distance he would have travelled, she reckons she can get out ahead of him and flash him down.'

Jackie crossed her fingers.

Imelda followed suit and hugged her son's fiancé as though she were her long-lost daughter.

***

Mickey Krakauer's dilapidated ute was noisy, but with Yothu Yindi at full blast on the CD player, he could have been driving a top end Rolls Royce. He loved the loud music and the open road, even if it was only a dirt track. It was at times like this that he was free of all restrictions except those imposed by his employer, so he held his speed to the regulation limit. Years of driving had told him that you don't get there much quicker, but you'll certainly get there richer.

Mick was pondering all the weirdos he'd come across over the years, when he looked in his rearview mirror and saw a Hyundai closing on him with its headlights flashing. He pulled off the road to let the driver pass, but the car stopped just in front of him. He didn't recognise the driver, and he reached into the glove compartment for his Glock.

The driver climbed out and ran towards his vehicle.

He raised his hands in a "What's happening" shrug.

She knocked on his window.

He tightened his grip on the Glock's stock and then wound his window down.

'Are you Mickey Krakauer?' she said.

'Who wants to know?'

'Imelda's your mum, isn't she? She called me.' The girl, who couldn't be much more than eighteen, handed him her phone. 'Speak to your mum. She says it's urgent.'

Mickey reached for his own phone and rolled his eyes. It wasn't there. He took the phone from the girl who had already made the call and heard his mother's tinny voice emanating from the silenced speaker. He put it to his ear. 'What's the problem, mum?'

'Jimmy Carter rang. He didn't say too much, but some shit's about to happen. He says you should head back to Warakurna and keep your head down.'

'What about Jackie?'

'She'll be okay with me. She isn't a cop.'

Mickey ended the call, thanked the girl, handed back her phone and decided he'd drop in on his mum on the way past. He made a U-turn and determined he had enough fuel to get back. Then he turned up his radio and with AC/DC at the stops, the Rolls Royce took over from the ute and the girl in the Hyundai turned to follow him.

***

After ten years of agonising Angela Carter was at last feeling a degree of confidence that her first ever murder conviction might have a chance of reversal. She picked up her files, took a deep breath and started her car. The last few days had been traumatic for everyone. She knew George Gregory's arrest had set a large cat among an even larger flock of pigeons, and she was on a kill list.

Thankfully James had picked up on the first attempt, but she felt it wouldn't be the last, and now that Jim had been pulled off the Gregory case, yet again, she had lost her protection.

Her car started first go, there was no blinding flash and the memory of Mandy Stephenson's wounds sent a shiver down her spine.

The journey to the prison went without interruption, and she cast around the car park for people she would prefer not to see. It was all clear, and she made her way to the entrance with her heart thumping in her chest.

It was a relief to pass through the security and see him behind a table in the visiting lawyer's room. 'How are you, Tom?'

'Fine, miss. I wasn't expecting to see you again so soon.'

'Well, the reason I'm here is that I have some good news for you.' His eyebrows twitched. 'My chambers have agreed in principle to allow me to submit an appeal against your conviction with a focus on a full pardon and compensation for your lost years.'

'Is this related to my dad's arrest?'

'Not quite, although some of the information might help us prepare our submission.'

Tom Gregory's face remained placid.

'I hoped you'd be glad and at least a little excited by the prospect of being free.'

'I've lost everything that was meaningful to me. What would I do on the outside? I've missed out on my big chance and that can never be replaced by any kind of compensation.'

Angela's own doubts began to swirl around in her head. She steeled herself. 'It will be the principle, my friend. The correct evidence must be revealed, and you should be freed.'

Tom Gregory shrugged. 'Okay, let's give it a go, but what happens if we lose?'

'We might be able to get a significant reduction in your sentence.'

'And the appeal judges might increase it. Then where will I be.'

'I understand there is evidence that you were framed for the murder of Rebecca Connolly, by one of two suspects. If we can get that accepted by the appeal court, they'll have no option but to return a verdict of not guilty and you will then be pardoned for the crime you didn't commit. We need to work together on this, Tom...'

The door to the room opened. 'Time's up Ms Carter.'

'Are you with me?'

Tom Gregory nodded.

'As soon as I have something in place, I will come and see you again.' Angela stood. 'Chin up.'

The door closed behind Tom as he was led back to his accommodation, and Angela's brain went into overdrive. *There is something wrong here. He should be over the moon, and it seems like a real struggle to generate enthusiasm.* She transited the security area and found her way to her car.

Her mind had gone from overdrive to turmoil, and she didn't notice the ancient and battered BMW follow her from the carpark. She drove for a while and pulled off the road to make a phone call.

'Hi, Ange. All good?'

'I've just had a meeting with Tom Gregory. He's very down, and I'm nervous about getting into this appeal without my hands on the evidence.'

'I think my suspension might be lifted soon. George Gregory's cupboard was crammed with damning things about so many people in the upper echelon of the state.'

'Do you still have access to it?'

'No, But Mandy Stephenson does. The hard copies were in the cupboard, but the digital versions are stored on an encrypted dark website.'

'What about the rules of evidence?'

'We'll be bypassing those.'

'How?'

'You will have to read tomorrow's paper. I'll drop around on the way home. Stacey's still down south so I'll return the compliment and bring some grub and a bottle of wine.'

They ended the call and the thought of seeing her brother so soon, filled her with a sense of relief. With him around she felt safer, and Angela continued her journey via Oliver's school, to wait until the kids were turned loose. 'Good day?' she said after Oliver clambered into the car.

'Spose,' he said and clipped his seatbelt.

'Uncle Jim's coming around with a takeaway.'

Oliver shrugged.

'She wondered if one day he'd have a different answer and as she drove into her driveway, a battered BMW blocked her exit. She clambered out of her car and shouted, 'Excuse me. You can't park there.'

The driver grinned and aimed a pistol at her. 'Bye-bye, lawyer bitch.'

She panicked when Oliver ran towards him, shouting, 'You leave my mum alone!'

He maintained his aim, and she saw his finger tighten on the trigger and knew it would be first her and then Oli. Darkness took over from light and she didn't feel the hard concrete as she fell.

Chapter 62

Mickey stopped outside his mum's house to be greeted by Jackie with a big smile on her face.

'Forgot ya phone, ya mug.'

He hugged her, gave a kiss on the lips, and said, 'What's up?'

'I'll let your mum tell you.' She led him into the house and pointed to a chair.

A moment later Imelda arrived with a tray loaded with tea and home-made pastries. 'What have you got yourself into now?'

'I don't know. I didn't have my phone, remember.'

'Jimmy Carter has been suspended again. This time the deputy commissioner is off the rails too. He said you should get yourself back to Warakurna before they know you're missing.'

Mickey nodded. 'Yeah nah. I've got a better idea.'

'You gonna tell me what it is?'

'Nah.' He picked up his phone and removed the sim. 'Stick this in a drawer and I'll call you when I've got myself a burner. Don't you worry about me, mum, but take care of her for me.' He looked at Jackie. 'We're not the only ones who knows what's goin on. Keep your heads down.' Mickey left the house, dropped into his car and disappeared around the corner at the end of the road.'

***

The acrid sting of the smelling salts snapped her awake. She looked up and saw James and a tearful Oliver, grinning back at her. Angela felt over her body with her hands and rose to her knees. 'What the hell happened?'

James pointed to his car. 'That happened.'

A few moments later a paramedic found his way through the flashing lights and gathering melee. 'He reckons you fainted.' The man pointed to her brother before checking them both out.

She glared at James. 'The man with the gun. He was…'

'Was, is the operative word. I have a dash cam. It's all on that.'

'But he was pulling the trigger.'

'That was before he became a bonnet ornament. How are you feeling?'

'Shaky.' She looked at her son whose face was still pale from the shock of the event.

James held up a bag of takeaway food and a bottle of wine. 'We have a date remember.' He held out his hand, hauled her to her feet and ushered them both to the door.

The paramedic nodded to James. 'All good, mate. They'll both live.'

They shook hands, and he left to return to the melee, while James and his sister pulled the door shut on another crappy day.

Angela composed herself, while Oliver found a noisy video game and began playing it. James had earlier removed the SanDisk from his dash cam and began copying its entire contents to Angela's computer. When he finished, he made a further copy to her cloud storage, and then he found plates in her kitchen cupboard and set the table.

'What the hell is happening, Jim?'

'Let's eat. Then we can talk about where we go from here.'

Oliver filled his plate with a selection and returned to his game.

Angela picked at bits and pieces while James scoffed. 'You're missing Stacey?'

'How did you guess?'

She shrugged. 'Okay. Where *do* we go from here?'

A knock at the door made her turn. A look of horror crossing her face.

'It's okay, I've invited some guests.'

'Angela looked around at her messy kitchen and said, 'Well, thank you very much, brother.'

James opened the door and welcomed Athur Bertram and Mandy Stephenson. 'This is Angela, my sister. Without Angela's involvement we might not be where we are, investigation wise.'

Arthur Bertram introduced himself as Arty, and Mandy exchanged hugs with Angela.

'Nice to meet you both but…'

Arthur cut her short. 'But we have a major problem, Ms Carter. We have a case that deeply involves the top echelon of our society. They now know what we have at our disposal, and they are responding with their devious power in order to make it difficult for us to proceed.' Arty stopped for a breath and continued. 'Your brother and PC Stephenson have uncovered masses of evidence that will rock society and we have been effectively kneecapped.'

'We've sent snippets to the West Aus and a few nationals. If they decide not to run with them, we'll probably be doomed.' James took Angela's hand. 'If all else fails Tom Gregory might be the key, and you're the only one who has his ear.'

'I'm not sure I do. He seemed quite upset that I was close to putting in a submission for an appeal.'

'He was jailed as a kid, it's been a long time, and he probably thinks of the place as home, but I'm sure he'll come around,' James said.

'I wish I had your confidence, Jim.' She filled a large filter pot of coffee and pulled some fresh cups from her cupboard. 'It was almost as though he didn't want any further involvement even if it meant his freedom.'

'Let me show you something,' Mandy said. She lay her laptop on the table and opened it. A few seconds later a series of directories filled the screen. 'Most of these contain pornographic videos that feature senior bureaucrats, politicians, and celebrities. The celebrities are easy to deal with. They'll huff and puff and threaten us with legal action but at the end of the day what's there is there. It's the others that will make our job difficult. The state's bureaucrats and politicians have surrounded themselves with a wall of protection like you couldn't imagine.'

'You think releasing information piecemeal to the press will change that?' Angela said.

Mandy opened a file and pointed to the list of names.

'You are kidding me.'

'See that underlined red text incorporated in each name?'

'Some kind of link?'

'Exactly. Those links will only work if my computer is connected to the dark web via a router. May I?'

Angela activated her phone and found her Wi-Fi password. 'Try this.'

Mandy connected and pointed to the screen. 'Who would you like to see in action?'

'Okay, give Clydesdale a go.'

Mandy clicked on the link and almost a second later ten thumbnails appeared. 'Which one?'

Angela pointed to a picture of the ex-Minister of Police at a function. Mandy clicked on the picture and a video began to play.

The video featured several other members of parliament, but in the main, it seemed to follow the movements of Clydesdale.

'Well, that isn't too incriminating, is it?'

'Keep watching.'

About five minutes into the video Clydesdale was seen climbing an ornate staircase with a pretty, young woman, clinging to his arm.

The video ended and Angela said, 'Again, seedy but hardly incriminating.'

Mandy clicked on the thumbnail next to the first one that she played. This time there was no doubt about Clydesdale's intentions. They had moved into a bedroom where the girl suddenly seemed to become drowsy, and she flopped fully clothed on to the bed. What came next, made Angela gasp.

'Turn it off I don't need to see any more.'

Mandy obliged. 'That girl is listed in the Melbourne Police missing persons files. She was last seen one week before the dates on the videos you have just watched. She was fourteen going on fifteen-years-old.'

'Do you think she's been killed?'

'Worse, trafficked to another country for a life in prostitution.'

'The kids on the train and at Gregory's house?'

'We or, strictly speaking, you, saved their bacon. They are now in recovery, before being returned to their families.'

'The others?'

Mandy said, 'We may never find them but thankfully there is some information contained in the other files, about the supply routes used by the traffickers. That may give us a clue as to where they ended up. This is why we need the help of people like yourself, who are not directly under the command of the top end suspects.'

James patted his sister's arm and said, 'We might need to probe Tom Gregory's subconscious memory and see if he can tell us any more than we already know.'

'I'll try for another meeting with him but don't hold your breath on the outcome.'

Chapter 63

While they were finishing their coffee, Angela's son, Oliver, appeared.

'How did your game go?'

'Internet slowed right down, so I gave up. I didn't know we were expecting visitors.'

'Neither did I, but they're here now.'

He shrugged and left.

A few seconds later she heard the TV start up and called, 'Don't forget your homework.' There was no response.

'Sorry about his game,' Mandy said. 'Some of those dark web links can drag a lot of bandwidth.'

'My appeal against Tom Gregory's conviction is on the grounds that he was framed by a senior police officer. You all know who that was and what happened to him soon after this investigation began. An attempt was made on my life earlier today. My son was with me, and he could easily have become another innocent victim.'

They all nodded.

'So how the hell can I extract the further evidence I need to ensure the success of our appeal.' Angela put her head in her hands. 'How many people have mysteriously died since we started this, Jim?'

James nodded. 'I reckon they might be attempting to clear the decks before the real battle commences.'

'So, who's next? You, or the Deputy Commissioner, for Christ's sake? They've already tried to kidnap your kids and some moron, claiming to be your wife, invited me to lunch. You've both been deactivated by their system, Jim. Mandy's supposed to be on sick leave after an incompetent wannabe assassin chose the wrong car. Mickey Krakauer? Where is he? And Jackie Morton's appeal crosses similar lines. Will she suddenly disappear?'

***

Mickey Krakauer pointed his car in the general direction of Perth, though he wouldn't be taking the easy route. He'd be taking the long route using the back doubles as far as he could and then he'd lose his car and go off grid.

Mickey couldn't wait to break free of convention and return to his roots. His dad had taken him deep into the bush as a kid. Back then everyone used the term walkabout, though now it would be frowned upon. To Mickey, it was exactly what he would be doing but in the city.

Jimmy Carter and he had been mates from the day they joined the force. Now Jim was an acting DI, but that made no change to their relationship. *I've found my girl and on the day we marry, I'll become a civilian.* He had nothing to lose by going feral and he had ways of operating that the higherups wouldn't understand if they hit them in the face. He fired up Yothu Yindy, opened his windows and let it rip.

He stopped for a bite in Beverley and then headed to Canning Vale. He had a mate there who owed him. He'd turn up unannounced to prove the debt still had credence and from then on, he'd be on his own and trawling the underbelly of Perth. AC/DC carried him onwards until he found the unpretentious home that was owned by Bill Bloxham.

He parked a little up the road and locked his car. Despite the recent goings on, he was still a cop, and his demeanour would be recognised by some who might take umbrage. Bill was a retired cop who knew stuff, and the last thing Mickey wanted was to draw undue attention to him.

He noticed curtains move next door as he knocked softly. A few moments later the door opened to expose the face of a much older man than Mickey expected.

The man frowned and tipped his head to one side, 'Mickey? Mickey Krakauer?'

'G'day, Bill. Got a few minutes?'

'Gotta fucking lifetime, mate, what's left of it. Come in. Rosie! Put the kettle on, we have a visitor.'

Mickey followed Bill through to his small kitchen and sat in the proffered chair.

'So, what gives? Didn't expect to see you again.'

'It's a bit of a shaggy dog story, Bill.'

Bill Bloxham laughed. He'd been famous for his longwinded jokes with silly endings. 'You remember those.'

'Who could forget? Anyway…' Mickey stopped talking as Bill's wife arrived to make some tea.

'I knew he wouldn't be able to keep away from it for long. What's happening now?'

'Hello, Rosie. It's Mickey, remember?'

She plonked some teabags into a pair of mugs and poured boiling water over them. 'I'll be out the back if you need me,' she said before flouncing away.

'I take it Rosie still doesn't like cops?'

'She's okay. It's taken us a long time to get settled in and have the neighbours trust us.'

'Okay. I won't keep you long.' Mickey took a sip of his tea. 'Remember Jimmy Carter?'

Bill nodded.

'He's just been made DI. And already he's suspended.'

'Shit that didn't take long.'

'Deputy commish has gone down with him.'

'Arthur Bertram? I thought he was next in line.'

'Jimmy got unofficially involved with an investigation into human trafficking. It scratches the top of the tree if you get my drift.'

Bill nodded sagely. 'So, what's new there?'

'So, I need a bed for a night, and then I'll be on my way.'

Bill grinned. 'Goin walkabout, Mick? You'd better take care, times have changed.'

'I'll call it groundwork. The plutocracy can't operate without minions, and I've never known a happy minion.'

'Big words for a black fella.'

Mickey smirked.

'I've heard word of a big operation that exports kids and young girls. You know my views on that kind of shit, Mick.'

'The name Gregory mean anything?'

'The kid Clitheroe locked up or his dad?'

'His dad.'

'Rumour had it, his dad was into porn, and Clitheroe had some connection.'

'The porn has grown into an enterprise. The girls are used and then shipped. Most are underage by as much as three or four years.'

'I hear Mulligan bought it. Connected, you reckon?'

Mickey shrugged.

'If the deputy commish has been dumped, so there must be some crazy power shit happening.'

'I only need a bed for the night, mate. I don't want you inveigled into something you don't need.'

'Rosie!'

'Yeah?'

'Can you make up the spare room for Mickey, just for one night?'

Rosie rolled her eyes and disappeared.

'Not a word to Rosie. Okay?' He looked at his watch. 'Beer?'

Mickey nodded.

***

'Because we're officially out of the action, we must find a way that won't see us all landing in jail. It wouldn't surprise me if there wasn't a special needs squad looking for ways to shut us down completely.' Arthur turned his face towards Mandy. 'You are the only officer involved who is still active, even though you're on sick leave.'

Mandy pointed to the laptop and waggled the thumb drive at him. 'This contains everything you need to collapse the government and its high-level support group.' She pulled up a list of names. 'Everyone on this list features in the videos at one level or another. Everyone. Doesn't that tell you something?'

'They're all male.' Angela said more as a circuit breaker than a serious statement.

'Not so.' Mandy opened a directory and clicked on a video. 'Recognise her? The problem we have is that it's become an ingrained activity, and they are all back pedalling, as fast as they can, to avoid stigma.'

'What do you propose?'

'Weed out the minimalist offenders, put the frighteners on them and get them to come to the party with a promise of destroying the evidence against them.'

'It could work.' Arthur Bertram rubbed his chin. 'Bit worried about destroying evidence though.'

'I said "promise" we don't necessarily have to delete it. It can be locked in a Dark Web vault forever if necessary. These people don't deserve to be freed of their guilt, but the kids who have been damaged by them, need justice. We also need to track down those who were shipped offshore. Don't you think their parents deserve that.'

'Shit, Mandy it's a big ask.' Arthur Bertram shook his head. 'Who will decide who gets the chop and who gets to survive?'

'I can write an algorithm that will shave of the top forty per cent in terms of seriousness. We'll then do another run and build in a stupidity quotient. There will be some who accidentally got caught up in something regrettable.'

'We need the drivers, the ones who kept the ball rolling and freed the red tape from the paperwork. The kids shipped overseas had passports and visas in new identities that can't, as yet, be traced. The movers and shakers who achieved that must be a priority.'

'The last batch. Those we found at Gregory's place. What happened to their paperwork?' Arthur Bertram said.

'Sadly, sir,' James said. 'That all went missing in the first raid and DI Mulligan is no longer around to answer questions.'

'Any of his people available for interview?'

'By whom, sir, neither of us can action an order to pull them in.'

'Mandy?'

'I'm only a PC, sir.'

Chapter 64

'Find this bloke, Mick.' Bill Bloxham handed Mickey a dogeared post-it note. 'He's a complete arsehole who'll shoot you as quick as look at you. Worse still, he hates black fellas. Lucky for you he hates child molesters *even* more, hey?'

'Great, so I have to find this Clarke Shipton, and hope he doesn't shoot me before I tell him my story?'

'I'll let him know to be on the lookout for you.'

'Great, so he can be there waiting with the gun loaded and ready.'

Bill grinned. 'Best I can offer mate, but you'll be right. Trust me.'

Mickey finished his beer and said, 'I'd better get a good night's sleep then. It might be my last.'

'Better have another beer if that's the case.' Bill handed him an ice cold stubby.'

Mickey leaned back, cracked the top and put it to his lips. 'You're takin the piss?'

'Who me?' Bloxham downed the remains of his stubby and cracked another. 'Haven't had this much fun since… I dunno.'

They killed off several more of the cold brown soldiers before Bill burped, loudly. 'Time for beddie-byes, mate. If I'm not around when you leave. Make me proud of ya.' He tossed his stubbie into the empty carton and lurched towards his bedroom, from where Rosie could be heard snoring loudly.

Mickey turned in, but lay awake for the next three hours pondering what he would do when he met Clarke, his soon to be new bestie.

*****

'I need to be at home with my partner. She's gonna need some help with our bub. No worries, I can do some work on the algorithms there.' Mandy picked up the computer and headed for the door.

James followed her and said, 'If you need anything just holler.'

'Don't worry. This really is just a math problem.'

He watched as her rental car turned at the end of the street and vanished from view.

While he had confidence in Mandy's ability time was of the essence and he knew the word was about. No one could keep that kind of secret long. First it would be a comment after a beer or two in the pub, later names might even be mentioned. James knew the shredders were about to see overtime, of the likes of WA inc.

He called Jackie.

'The lad's gone and I'm all on my lonesome, well except for my mum-in-law to be. What can I do you for Jim?'

'Angela's run a print of your car-speak statements and other guff that predates your trial. I'll need you to go through it all and pick out the bones.'

'You want me down there?'

'Is Imelda up for it?'

'No worries, Jimmy,' Imelda called from the other side of the room.

'Thank god for privacy,' James called back.

Imelda's distant voice sounded again, 'She has the ALS coming today, but I'll make it right, Jimmy. I'll SMS you.'

Before the call ended, he heard enthusiastic voices but couldn't make out the context.

With Jackie's statements, if tied with some of the dubious

evidence put forward by Clitheroe, she might have a good chance of a positive response. James was confident that Clitheroe's interference in several trials had probably led to many wrongful convictions or worse, wrongful dismissals.

He called his sister for a progress report.

'All done, Jim. I've made copies so we can get more eyes on them. Do you want to drop by and pick one up, I'm at my office.'

'Can we meet in the carpark?'

'Yeah, okay.'

'Two copies please. I have Jackie coming to town to go through and confirm her comments. I'll be there in ten.'

***

It was nearing dusk when Mickey Krakauer arrived in Newcastle Street and sniffed the early evening air. It would be a warm night, and he remembered the dubious smells of his early days as a cop. The stink of big inefficient petrol engines, stale beer, even staler perfume with a side whiff of cannabis. That was a long time ago, and little had changed. Except this time, he was a cop off the leash and heading for a confrontation with a man he would normally be seeking to arrest.

He'd been given an address in Beaufort Street, and as he walked in that direction, loud music interrupted his thoughts, but he couldn't make out the tune.

'You've been away too long, Mickey Krakauer.'

He turned towards the voice and frowned. 'Bin busy. Yourself?'

'Oh, you know, bit a this an bit a that.'

'Still doin the…?'

'Nah, moved on to the more mature clients.' She smiled that smile that almost sucked him the first time, as a young cop.

He shuddered when he realised, she'd almost succeeded for a second time. 'I've moved on Kell.'

'Hardly anyone's called me that in years.' Kelly Coulson reached

352

out and touched his arm. 'I've missed our little get-togethers, Hon.'

'I'm on business, Kell, and you might not believe this but I'm getting married to my old partner.'

'The one who got sent down by Slippery Clitheroe, Jackie something.'

'Jackie Morton. She's working on an appeal.'

'Anything that asshole did should be appealed. Shame its only the top end of town who can fight back.' Kelly looked deeply into his brown eyes and said, 'You say you're on business. You no longer a cop?'

Mickey's senses were telling him how this relationship could only be bad news. He responded, 'Special project, I can't discuss it. Sorry.'

Kelly's face cracked into that smile again. She lifted a hand as though about to wave and raised one finger.

Mickey felt the grip of strong hands crushing his arms. Then everything went from dusk to night, and he was propelled into a side street. He'd deliberately left his service weapon at home, and he wasn't seeking confrontation with anyone.

He felt himself dragged for several metres and would have been happier to make it easier for his captors by walking. Then they turned into a doorway with a staircase, and he felt his toes clonking on the steps as they dragged him up to the first floor.

Next, he was pushed into a softly cushioned chair, and he remembered the Monty Python "Spanish inquisition" sketch, *Oh no, not the comfy chair*. Darkness became light when the black bag was removed from his head and he looked around to see Kelly Coulson, alongside a man who was sitting behind an ornate desk.

'Krakauer, they tell me?'

'You are?'

'You'll find out soon enough. Kelly? Is this the bloke you were goin on about?'

Kelly nodded.

'Just a precaution, Bill Bloxam called. You know him?'

Mickey nodded.

'About this trafficking business?'

Mickey nodded. 'Underage kids being shipped overseas.'

The man waved the two heavies away and turned to Kelly. 'Do you trust him? He shafted you.'

'We were kids, Clarkie.' She smiled at Mickey. 'He's grown into a fine figure of a cop, hasn't he?'

'Hey, hang on you two…'

'What can we do to help, Mickey?' the man he now knew as Clarke Shipton, relaxed and waved a ring cluttered hand in the air.'

'What's your poison. Mick?' Kelly said.

'Light beer'll be fine.'

'Good. While she's getting our beverages, I'll tell you what I think I know, and, let me tell you, it will cause such a stink when it gets out. First, the kingpin is Jeremy Clydesdale. He skipped the country at the first whiff of a scandal. Before you go looking too far into it, George Gregory didn't kill Rebecca Connolly…'

'We aren't sure about that at this stage.'

'Let me finish. DCI Clitheroe and George were using Rohypnol to let them have their way with a variety of young females and Rebecca Connolly was one of them. George and Slippery were drugging, and porking, her on a regular basis, and George had a side hustle of web porno.'

Mickey already knew this part of the case. He nodded.

Shipton opened a drawer.

Mickey flinched.

Shipton smirked. 'Don't worry. If I was going to kill you, you wouldn't see it coming.' He produced two photographs and lay one on the desk in front of Mickey. It was a picture of an attractive young woman who looked like she might be in her late teens - early twenties. 'My daughter. She'd be turning sixteen soon. She's been missing almost three years.'

'She looks a lot older than fourteen in this,' Mickey said.

Shipton nodded his head rocking motion and said, 'She always was ahead of her time.' He dropped a second picture of a sweet and innocent looking girl dressed in the uniform of a well-known private girls' college. This was taken exactly a week before her thirteenth birthday night out, with friends.' He tapped the first picture.

'Shit.'

'I tried the cops, but I got nowhere. The investigation started okay. They turned up, all full of piss and importance, and just as quickly walked away.' He scowled. 'Now Mickey Krakauer, a bloody black fella, has turned up to find her for me. That right, Mickey. Is that the best they can do?'

Chapter 65

Mickey swallowed hard. It wasn't the racist barb that hurt it was the fact that he might be considered somewhat less of an officer because of his skin colour. 'Well fuck you, Mr Shipton. I'll look elsewhere for help in finding the kids who've gone missing of which, by the way, your daughter is just one.'

Shipton flinched as though he'd never been spoken to in that way by anyone. His face froze, and he stuttered. 'Fuck. I am so sorry Mickey.'

This time it was Mickey's turn to be stunned and he couldn't help his sneer. 'Really?'

Shipton stood just as Kelly returned with their drinks. 'See Mr Krakauer is booked in to the, you know,' he tipped his head in a conspiratorial way, 'at my personal expense.'

Kelly turned to check on Mickey's expression. He looked nervous.

'When we've finished here, you can drive him around there.'

Kelly's eyebrows rose as she placed their drinks on the desk.

'Leave us, Kell.' The moment the door closed Shipton's mood changed. 'Can you forgive me? You don't deserve that kind of treatment from anyone least of all me. I know you're out on a limb, Mickey, the word has it that half the force has been stood down and a DCI from the east has been brought in to take over where the locals left off.'

'Not quite half, Mr Shipton. I can't say anything about this new DCI, but I happen to be the only one in this "unofficial" investigation that hasn't been suspended, and that's only because they think I'm still out in woop woop black fella country.'

'Call me Clarkie all my mates do.'

Mickey nodded. 'Mine call me Mick. Where am I sleeping?'

'Top place, Mick. I know when I'm wrong.'

'Bill Bloxam said you might be able to help me. So can we start talking turkey, or am I wasting my time?'

Shipton stood and left the room. He returned soon afterwards, holding a thick lever arch file. 'This is everything I have to-date.' He lay it on the desk. 'Take your time, Mick. Anything you need, there's this button.' He pointed to a place just above the drawer that held the photos. 'Kelly will be waiting to be at your service.' Shipton walked from the room again and this time he pulled the door shut.

***

When Mandy Stephenson arrived home, she was greeted by the screeching of a frustrated infant. 'Jean, is everything okay?'

'No everything is not okay.' Jean was red faced and her eyes teary. 'I've tried everything I can think of, but I can't get him to feed.'

Mandy wrapped her arms around the distressed woman and their baby. 'I've heard there are some techniques available. I'll check it out.'

'I'm sorry, I haven't been able to fix anything for dinner.'

Mandy held up her phone. 'Waddya fancy babe?' She phoned through the request, googled "difficult breast feeders" and printed several results that might be helpful. 'Here we go.' She read out several potential problems and when Jean responded, she called up the method. Within a few minutes, peace reigned, only to be shattered by the doorbell and their dinner.

With the hunger of both partner and bub sated, she was able to focus on her main concern. The list was long, but she soon worked out how to break it down into primaries and secondaries with tertiaries and quaternaries in separate buckets of their own. Then she ran the program and her jaw dropped when she saw the preliminary result. She saved the first report made a minor change and ran it again.

The key people were there in each case. She now had a list of the worst offenders, and they represented a major nightmare. It wasn't just a few unknowns who had briefly transgressed. It was top end businesspeople and politicians from all parties. In some cases, they appeared together. Further examination led to a linking of social gatherings that went from one extreme to the other.

Mandy knew she was entering a difficult territory, but she never anticipated these extremes. She tapped her iPhone and waited for James to respond. The first call went to a message bank. She tried again and his voice answered.

'Yeah?'

'Sir. It's Mandy Stephenson.'

'Who?'

She heard shuffling and a cough.

'Mandy. Sorry, I was in a deep sleep. What time is it?'

Mandy saw the time on her phone and gasped. 'Oh, golly, sir. It's three am. I didn't realise the time.'

'Well, I'm awake now, so what's the problem?'

'I've just run my first report and it makes scary reading.'

'Will it wait…'

'Yes… Of course, it will. I'll come around in the morning with the results. I'd rather not send them via the airwaves. Good night, Jim. Sorry, I mean, sir.'

***

Mickey's journey through the documents was deepening his own trauma. He'd seen the damage caused by Gregory and some of the pointless "evidence" illegally gathered by Clarkie's people read like a horror movie script. He was beginning to understand why the decent cops who'd tried to break through were stymied at every turn. The names mentioned, read like a Who's Who of the local plutocracy. People had enjoyed their little flings and then cast aside the poor wretches who had provided their ephemeral pleasures.

He snapped a few pics of relevant pages with his phone and walked around the desk to press the button.

A moment later Kelly opened the door. 'Everything okay, Mick?'

'Yeah, but I think I need some sleep.'

'No worries.' She held up a set of car keys.

Mickey picked up the file.

'You can't take that away, Mick. Strict instructions.'

Mickey nodded, handed her the file, and followed her to the lift. They arrived soon afterwards in the underground carpark of a hotel, the name of which Mickey hadn't noticed.

Kelly handed him a hotel room key. 'It's all fixed just let yourself in and hit the sack...' She smiled and blinked her eyes. 'It *has* been a long time, Mickey Krakauer.' She leaned in to kiss him on the cheek, perhaps she was a little too enthusiastic and hoping for something more.

Mickey pushed her away gently. 'I'm fixed up, otherwise...'

'Suit yourself. I wasn't expecting your hand in fucking marriage.'

Mickey pressed up on the lift call button and when it opened, he realised the level of esteem that Clarkie now held him in. He smiled inwardly, *not bad for a Woop-Woop black fella, hey, Mickey.*

***

Angela Carter welcomed Jackie Morton to her room and offered her a coffee.

'Thanks, I'd love one.'

'How did it go with the ALS?'

'They say they might be able to get a case together, but *I* mustn't get too excited.'

Angela nodded. 'They'll have a lot of work to do before they can commit.'

Jackie nodded and raised her eyebrows.

Angela escorted her to a meeting room, handed her the printed copy of her mumbled recording, and said, 'Take your time. It's all here and I just need you to go through and pick out the parts you think may be most relevant to your appeal. Once that's done, I can send it to your new lawyer. In return, I'd also like you to define passages that might have relevance to the Tom Gregory case, can you do that?' She handed Jackie three high-lighter pens.

'What's the third pen for?'

'Anywhere you think there may be a cross over.'

Jackie nodded, and a clerk placed a large cup of coffee on the table.

Chapter 66

A knock on the door disturbed his sleep. He opened his eyes and looked around at the room he'd barely noticed when he arrived. The view was of a plushness he'd never before experienced, and the clock was telling him it was eight am. 'Who is it?'

'Kelly, Mick. I'll meet you down in the lobby lounge for breakfast.'

Mickey took a quick shower and selected a t-shirt, jeans, and thongs from his travel kit. *Bit down market but, hey.* He found Kelly at a table for two and flip-flopped his way across the room. She looked different. Bare of makeup and wearing a simple business suit and silk blouse ensemble that probably cost more than he earned in six months of cop's wages.

'You lookin real good this morning, Kell.'

She smiled. 'I'm glad you noticed.' She pointed to the buffet and then led him via the coffee and tea station back to their table. 'Clarkie has taken a real liking to you. No one is more surprised than me. He's usually such a racist bastard.'

'I have something he needs.'

'Desperately.' Kelly nodded and filled a bowl with muesli.

Mickey went the whole hog, on the full English.

'I'll never understand what blokes see in that crap,' Kelly said.

Mickey pinched his taut gut and said, 'See any flab?'

Kelly rolled her eyes. 'You always were a fit bastard.' Her head turned towards a couple who were about to take a seat nearby. She saw them glare at Mickey and frown. 'You gotta problem?' she said.

The man scowled and ushered his partner away.

Mickey smirked, 'You always did have a way with words, Kell.'

'This girl of yours?'

'Jackie?'

'I remember her. I recall she didn't like me too much.'

'She was a cop. You and I were…'

'Happy days, hey?'

Mickey nodded and showed her the document images from his phone. 'Jordan Castile, and Arial Kronsky?'

Kelly nodded.

'Plus, several back benchers, and at least two cabinet ministers so far, an I've still got some readin to do.'

Kelly nodded.

'All effectively untouchable, under the present regime.'

'Castile and Kronsky own most of the land mass of WA. You will find diary entries that show small groups of politicians meeting with them at various times in discrete locations. Usually this occurs just before major decisions are made.'

'Proves nothing. Were the diary entries obtained under warrant?'

Kelly laughed. 'Clarkie's background has prevented him from doing anything that might bring the law down on him even harder than it already is.'

'So not evidence then?'

'That's exactly what Clarkie's lawyers said.'

'This new DCI from over east?'

'Clarkie reckons he's been brought in to find insufficient evidence to continue with a police enquiry.'

'That'd be right. so where do we go from here?'

'We were hoping you'd tell us, Mick.'

Mickey slurped the remains of his coffee and pushed away his empty plate. 'Good feed. Thank Clarkie for the room and tell him there isn't much more I can do.'

***

Seeing her words in print, filled Jackie with amazement. She began by flipping through the whole document to see if anything jumped out at her. *Bloody better grammar than I can manage.*

The door opened and Angela's face popped around. 'All good?'

'This aint my stuff it's too neat, and the grammar is…'

'I ran it through a grammar and spell checker so it would be easier to read. Feel free to make any changes if you find anything wrong contextually.'

'I wish Mickey were here. He's much better than me with this sort of thing.'

'Only one person knows how to contact him and that's my brother. Jim believes we need to go into a deep cover mode, because as soon as they know we're on to them they'll shrink into the wood pile.'

Jackie nodded. She'd already high-lit several passages and stopped at a section when Mickey was talking. He'd said how difficult it was to get to a certain point in some investigations. It seemed there would be an inherent block on certain individuals. She saw her edited reply and realised it wasn't exactly what she had said. She read it over and over before picking up her empty coffee cup and going on a walk to find Angela.

'Promising?' she asked.'

'Have you the original of this?' She showed her the edited print out.

Angela nodded. 'If it helps. More coffee?'

Jackie nodded, and a few moments later a clerk arrived with a ream of paper and a fresh drink. Jackie flicked through to the section she was looking for and saw the passages that had been inadvertently edited out. She grinned. 'Gotya!'

She remembered Mickey's cold sausages and chips and the newspaper he had laid out on the centre console to keep them from wandering all over the car. They'd both commented briefly on the two high-profile names on the front page. And she remembered recalling how Clitheroe had made a big thing of his connections with those same names, but that wasn't what triggered her mind.

It was the DNA results that could have equally designated Rebecca Conolly's child as either Tom Gregory's or his father's. She recalled how any suggestion was pooh-poohed but nothing further was done. It was believed that George Gregory also had connections with the names on the paper's front page. Jordan Castile and Arial Kronsky.

Their legitimate business interests were well and truly trumped by their connections to the Ferals bikie gang and their business model. She recalled having a conversation with Jim Carter about the girls they employed, but at the time, he was too involved in the drug importation links.

Jackie Morton picked up the desk phone and dialled James' number.

He answered, 'Ange?'

'Jackie. I'm calling from her offices.' She heard him say, "Shit!" before the line went dead.

***

There would be no point turning up with her findings at the station, so Mandy Stephenson headed directly for James' home. He looked flustered when he opened his door.

'Come in.' He grabbed her arm and almost wrestled her through to his home office. 'Sorry. I've just had a call from Jackie Morton…'

'And?'

'It was from Angela's office. On their land line. They have a policy of recording all calls.'

'So?'

'So, if this blow-in, who's been assigned to take over the investigation. You know that "unofficial" thingo we've been engaged in…'

'Ah…'

'It was brief but might trigger an alarm somewhere.'

'What now?'

'What have you got?'

Mandy plugged in a thumb drive and pulled up a tailored list of folders on his screen. 'Pick what you like from that.'

James selected the first folder labelled "Castile". A series of files appeared, some documents, some videos. He clicked on the first document. His *Excel* program loaded, and a multi-sheet table appeared. It seemed to be some form of ledger that included dates, times, sums of money with obvious fake names like M Mouse and D Duck, and links to other files. He clicked a link, but it went nowhere.

Mandy explained that the links were corrupted, but the files were accessible via the folder lists.

He backed out and clicked a file with the same name as the link. 'Well, well, Mr Castile, you've been a busy boy.'

'Do you recognise her?'

James shook his head.

'Check the date of the file.'

He did. 'That's almost two years old.'

'There are some going back ten years, the video quality isn't as good but, now click this one.' She pointed to a file created only days earlier.

'Shit. That could be one of the girls we found in Gregory's place. She can't be much more than fourteen years old.'

'She's also out cold and Castile is…'

James touched her arm. 'I can see what he's doing.'

'So, where do we go from here?'

'I'll need to contact Mickey.'

'He's off grid, isn't he?'

James tapped a number on his burner.

'Imelda.'

'Jimmy Carter, howya bin.'

'Where's Mick?'

If a phone could shrug his would have. 'He said he'd be playin in the dark for a while.' There was a pause followed by an exclamation. 'Wait, Bill bloody Bloxam. Give im a call. Can't say it'll help but Mick and he were pretty thick back in the day. You never know.'

'Do you have a number for him?'

'Sorry, mate, but Jackie's a bit happier since she spoke to the ALS. She's at your sister's place goin through some stuff for her appeal.'

'Okay thanks anyway, Imelda.' James felt a little mean cutting her off but there was no time to lose. He did a search for Bloxam with a B. Nothing. Bloxam with a W. There was only one in the state. He tapped in the number.

The number seemed to ring for ever, then a gruff voice answered. 'Who want's im?'

'Bill, Bill Bloxam.'

'E's out.'

'I'm after Mickey Krakauer. Can you tell him to call Jimmy Carter when he gets back?'

'Fuckin, Jimmy Carter. I might have known.'

'It's urgent Bill.'

'Shit… try Clarkie Shipton?'

'Jesus Christ.'

'Not quite but he likes to think he is.'

'Thanks.'

'You didn't hear it from me.'

James turned to Mandy, 'You're a still a cop with creds?'

She nodded.

'Grab your laptop, we're going visiting. We'll take your car.'

Mandy followed James' directions to a run-down building in Northbridge. When they arrived, she said, 'Do you need me?'

'Yup.' He opened the door and marched directly to a pair of shabby doors that might have once been green. He pushed them open and almost ran up the stairs to the plush offices that occupied the first floor. He could see a familiar face at a desk beyond the glazing. 'Kelly Coulson. Long time no see,' he said, as he pushed in to be greeted by two heavies who appeared like magic from a side door.

Kelly raised her hand to slow their progress and said, 'Friend, I think?'

'Where is he?'

'Who.'

'Mickey.'

'Not with me, more's the pity.' She pointed to a closed door. 'Clarkie might know.'

The door opened and Clarke Shipton appeared with a semi-automatic pistol at the ready.

Mandy put one hand on her Glock and flashed her police creds with the other. She spoke clearly over the cricket commentary on a TV screen to the side of Shipton's desk 'We come in peace, Mr Shipton.'

Shipton looked confused.

'Mickey Krakauer?' James said.

'He couldn't help. Just like the rest of you fucking wankers.'

James nodded to Mandy. She set her computer on Shipton's desk and called up the oldest file. 'Know this man?'

Clarke Shipton almost passed out when he saw the video. He steadied himself and said, 'Jordan Castile.' Then he slumped into his chair.

'The girl?'

'My daughter.' He pulled out a handkerchief and blew his nose. 'Is she dead?'

'We don't know.'

'Mickey said he couldn't be of much more help.'

Chapter 67

The timing could not have been better. The cricket was overwritten by "BREAKING NEWS" in large red letters.

A young reporter, pictured outside a corporate office building in St Georges Terrace, began speaking as soon as the vision appeared.

'Mr Jordan Castile has today made a statement that there is no connection between him and certain missing children. This was following the receipt of evidence by this station that claims he has not only had carnal relations with underage girls but has also encouraged others to participate.

'We understand that, despite our initial and private discussions with Mr Castile, he will be initiating court proceedings against our station. You heard it here first.'

The cricket resumed.

Shipton burst into tears.

The sight of the state's best-known villain and toe-cutter in such a state of distress caused those present to shiver with the tension of the moment.

'Mickey Krakauer, you little fucking beauty,' Shipton said, suddenly drying his eyes.

'Still not evidence,' James said. 'What we have is technically stolen.'

'No, it isn't, sir,' Mandy said. 'The thumb drive, that the text and videos came from, was collected during a warranted search of

George Gregory's home. It's all available online, if you know where to go on the dark web.'

Clarke Shipton's chest puffed out. He smiled and reached out to shake James' hand just as Mickey Krakauer pushed in through the door.

'I gave it my best shot, boss. I had nothing more to play with.' Both James and Shipton turned to acknowledge his statement.

Kelly's arms reached around his waist and hugged him tightly.

He gently unwound them. 'Sorry Kell. Maybe in another life.'

***

The next few days saw the girding of the legal loins of the big chambers as they angled for a chunk of what would be a major action involving a billionaire and a TV Station.

Both would be up to the challenge and neither side could know how deep it might cut.

Angela Carter's company, Locke and Keyes, swung into action not fully understanding that she was about to embark on a pro bono appeal that might blur the lines and limit their flexibility.

She called the prison and made an appointment to speak with her client. Two days later she waited patiently for him to appear.

He was late, and the guards said he was no longer interested in proceeding. After some to-ing and fro-ing, she succeeded in getting her meeting.

He was sullen when he arrived, and he crashed onto the chair in what seemed like a tantrum.

'There is strong evidence that the DNA used to convict you might have been incorrect. It is highly possible that your father was the parent of Rebecca's baby.'

'They said it was mine. They said the evidence did not lie. The court accepted the words of their experts, and I was convicted.'

'Wouldn't you like to be free again?'

'Why? My life ended when I couldn't take up the scholarship. I have no skills that will enable me to earn a living, and I get three meals a day in here. I can't even see Rebecca to tell her I'm sorry I mucked up her life.'

'I've set the wheels in motion now and an appeal will take place if only in principle, and I'd like your cooperation.'

Tom Gregory shrugged, 'Okay, what comes next?'

Angela explained what had happened with his father and the upheaval that would surely follow. 'Meanwhile under the cover of the big news we'll be working diligently to set you free. Do you understand?'

'They were assholes both of them.'

'Who?'

'My dad and Clitheroe.'

Angela nodded. 'You owe them nothing. Remember that.' She stood to leave and sucked in a deep and satisfying breath. 'I might have failed you the first time, Tom, but I intend to succeed second time around.' She shook his limp hand and said, 'You will be hearing soon. Be ready.'

***

Mandy Stephenson kept her powder dry and remained on sick leave away from the machinations of the blow-in DCI. She used her time to put together a strong case that would defeat the big money on truth alone, but she knew the next months would be difficult. Her wounds would soon heal and her ability to work in the dark would become increasingly difficult.

Angela Carter kept her up to date with Tom Gregory's appeal which seemed to go unreported in the media. As more names and information were released so grew the lawyers' feast.

Using their own devices, the media IT wizards found their way to the dark web, made even more discoveries, and Arial Kronsky was sucked into the overwhelming mire that had the potential to bring the state to a standstill.

***

Eventually Tom's appeal reached the courts, and the trial proceeded along its predictable course, with the judges reserving their response to a date six months into the future.

Tom didn't seem to mind the delay in his verdict. He had waited ten years and was now well and truly under the influence of a Stockholm-like syndrome. He'd made more friends than he'd ever had at school, and he got along well with the guards.

Angela remained frustrated by the delays, but she knew from experience that this could happen. She was becoming even more concerned with the delays to Jackie's appeal against her conviction, but she could do little as it was in the hands of the ALS.

The most positive outcome was the relationship with her brother and his family. Mickey had successfully applied for a compassionate transfer to the city, and that meant he and Jackie had become de facto aunt and uncle to their kids.

The stream of resignations that followed took almost everyone by surprise, but also took the heat out of the system. No one wanted the state to collapse for the want of a degree of clemency, and it was rumoured that, in order to protect themselves from prosecution, low end players would be granted the option to vanish into obscurity, subject to the provision of information, before records of their inadvertent slips were destroyed.

Missing children files were reviewed, nationwide and those of the accused, who could cast light on their possible location, were drawn into complex plea arrangements.

It promised to be a dirty business and a number of legal practices opted out of being tagged as potentially compliant with the defence of paedophiles and human traffickers.

However, Locke and Keyes jumped in with both feet on the side of the defence, in the belief that the lion's share of the business would be theirs and, even if they lost a percentage of the cases, they would still be well ahead financially.

Angela Carter was promoted to senior partner and the raise in her retainer, though appreciated, increased her feeling of being sullied. When she put out feelers, she found herself rejected by others in the profession and put that down to her initial loss in the Tom Gregory case. *No one want's a loser.*

As the cases edged excruciatingly to trial, her frustrations began to grow and then the bombshell hit with the judgement of Tom's appeal. He had won and was immediately released from prison with the promise of a pardon.

Next her role would be ensuring the justice system followed through, and that he was compensated for what might have been a massively monetised career in the American basketball system.

All the aggravation of the previous years, suddenly dissolved into a period of extreme euphoria on Angela's behalf and she set to work to ensure Tom received the best possible deal. Each morning, she would awaken and prepare breakfast for herself and Oliver, before delivering him to his new private school, which promised a high level of student security.

Oliver settled down and made new friends quickly. Regular visits with her brother and Stacey became the norm and the family traumas of earlier years were lost in a new bonhomie.

Once Oliver was ensconced, she would head to her office and continue with Tom's proceedings while working towards the defence of people she found utterly repulsive. Feelers into the profession still reflected a reluctance to accept her, even though she had won the appeal. It was almost as if she had become a pariah, and her mental health began to suffer.

At last, the hearing to set Tom's compensation was listed. A month, to go through everything, and have further discussions with Tom. She called him.

'Hello, miss,' he said.

'One month to the compensation hearing. We'll need to talk, first thing, to make sure nothing goes awry.'

'Yes, miss.'

Today was Wednesday, 'Friday, 10am okay for you?'

'Spose.'

'It's important, mate.'

'Spose. See yas Friday.'

Angela ended the call while shaking her head. *There're millions at stake here and all he can say is "Spose".*

Chapter 68

Diplomatic missions around the world suddenly found they had a renewed purpose. The information recovered from the dark web and provided by those hoping for a reduced sentence enabled several of the missing, once children, to be retrieved and returned home. Sadly, many were now adults and worse, hardened addicts who's addled brains could barely remember their earlier lives. At least there was hope.

Angela Carter stared down at the printout of the judgement relating to Tom Gregory's compensation and pardon.

It was a little less than expected but still a significant sum that would enable him to resurrect his life and hopefully move forward to a more fruitful future. She decided to visit his accommodation, rather than use the phone to advise him of the news. On the way she picked up a chilled bottle of champagne. *Surely it will be worth a small celebration at least.*

Angela could smell the heady fragrance of cannabis before she reached his door. She knocked.

'Hey, miss. Just chillin. Come on in and meet my pals.'

Angela handed him the champagne. 'Sorry I didn't think there would be others.'

'No worries, they'll be okay.'

She followed him through the unkempt hall to a filthy kitchen with dirty pots in the sink and takeaway packaging littered around the floor.

He pointed to a table and swept some debris from a chair. 'This is Pauly.'

The man he'd called Pauly nodded, grunted, and sucked on what looked like a defunct meth pipe.

'This is Sally.'

Sally was out of it and didn't respond.

'And this is the love of my life, Becky.'

Becky was also in cloud cuckoo land, with her head resting on her arm that was resting on the table.

'So, lawyer lady. What's new?'

Angela handed him her card and said, 'I need to see you in my office first thing tomorrow morning.'

'Ooh, good news then?'

'I'll tell you tomorrow.' She turned and walked from the house, shook herself, and sucked in a deep breath of fresh air. She'd bust her gut for this man, and he seemed hell bent on rewarding her with failure. She opened the door of her car and was about to step in when she heard his plaintive voice.

'Sorry, miss.' The house door slammed shut at the same time as the door of her car.

She started her engine and drove home via Oliver's school. At least he was pleased to see her but when he slumped into the car, she noticed his black eye. 'What happened to you?'

'Aussie rules.' He looked away.

'What would you like for dinner tonight?'

Oliver shrugged. 'Whatever.'

She'd no sooner opened her front door when her phone rang. She ignored it, 'I'm on Oliver time now. Whoever you are, you can wait until the morning.'

***

Mickey Krakauer grinned when he saw the note from Arty Bertram. He'd been assigned a role in a suburban station as acting sergeant. He immediately tapped Jackie's name on his phone and she answered almost immediately.

'Hey big fella, guess what? The ALS got my appeal goin. They reckon in six months I might be an innocent person.'

'I hope not that innocent.' He heard her giggle.

'What time you be home?'

'Might take an early mark. You not the only one with good news.' Mickey ended the call and leaned back in his chair. *Fuck you Clitheroe.* He looked at his two stripe epaulettes and imagined the third leaping into place. 'Thank you, Deputy Commissioner. Thank you.' The next call he made was to James Carter.

'He rang me. I told him if he made that blackfella a sergeant, I'm outa here.'

'So, when are ya leavin, sir?'

'Any minute. Fancy a beer?'

'I promised Jack an early mark.'

'Well, I'll grab a six-pack and see you at yours.'

'Yer on, boss.'

The radio in James' car erupted into sound the moment he turned the ignition key. A song by Taylor Swift led into the news that began with the announcer saying "There has been a major shake up in the WA Police force. The current police commissioner has resigned with six months of his contract still to run. Deputy Commissioner Arthur Bertram will take over his role in the interim."

James raised his eyebrows but didn't listen to much else. 'Good onya Arty.' He stopped at a bottle shop and grabbed a sixpack. *Something else to celebrate.* He'd called Stacey to tell her he'd be a little late, and she'd groaned.

'Call me when you're leaving. What I've made for dinner can't be over cooked.'

Life wasn't meant to be this complicated, he thought, but he made a mental note to get away quickly. He arrived before Mickey, and Jackie was in an unusually bubbly mood.

'It's on Jim. We'll be in court soon.'

James gave her a hug just as Mickey's wheels stopped on the driveway. 'Ah sorry, Sergeant. I didn't know this lady was yours.'

'Sergeant?' Jackie's face lit up like a thousand suns.

'And Arty Bertram is the new commissioner.'

Jackie led them through the house to the patio and James ripped the pulls on three cans. 'I can't stay too long. I've been told there's something special on for dinner.' He drew back a swig and relaxed. 'What a year!'

'Tom Gregory's a free man. Next it will be me. And then…' Jackie gulped on her stubby.

'And then we can get on with livin.' Mickey said, clunking his stubby against each of the others.

James finished his drink and had stood to leave when his phone tooted. It was the station. 'DI Carter?'

…

'When?'

…

'I'm on my way.' He turned to face his friends and felt the blood drain from his face. 'Ambos answered a 000 and found a body.' He called Stacey to tell her he'd be late.

She groaned. 'The kids'll be hungry if I don't start.'

'Sorry, I don't have a choice, I'll be as quick as I can.' He pressed end and called Angela. 'Bad news, sis?'

'What, Arty being made commish?'

'No. Theres a body. I can't say for certain yet, but it might be Tom Gregory…' He heard the gasp at the other end. 'You, okay?'

There was no answer.

'I'm on the way over there now and I'll try to keep you posted.'

He heard the line go quiet. She'd ended the call. He knew the strain had taken a huge toll on his sister, but his duty was to the dead man first. He sent her a text:

I'll drop in on my way back to the station.

There was no response.

Two squad cars with flashing lights greeted him as he arrived at Tom Gregory's home, and he saw officers escorting three heavily intoxicated people from the building. He identified himself.

'Forensics are in there now, sir.'

He nodded, and as he pushed through the tape, he saw Angela's car draw to a halt. He waited for her to approach and said, 'You can't go in there. Not until everything's been thoroughly checked.' He nodded to the officer guarding the entrance, pointed to Angela, and said, 'No one to enter until I give the word.'

Angela scowled and began strutting back and forth. She called her office and spoke to her clerk. 'Papers in on Tom Gregory's compo yet?'

'On my desk. Would you like me to open the package?'

'No. wait until you hear from me.'

***

James physically cringed when he saw what was waiting for him. The body of a man was hanging from a thin wire that stretched through roughly punched holes on either side of a ceiling joist. His feet were almost touching the floor and, although the face was badly distorted, there could be no doubt that it was Tom Gregory. The thin piano wire had cut through his neck allowing blood to spurt from the wound.

'Seen enough, Jim?' the man leading the forensics team said.

James nodded, and they cut the wire to lower the body to the floor.

'You know him?'

'Tom Gregory. He's the son of the bloke who is being done for trafficking underage girls among other things.'

'Shit! From what I can tell so far, it looks like a straight-out suicide. The people with him were at the point of overdose and couldn't possibly have been involved.'

'Any note?'

'Haven't been through his pockets yet but there was nothing immediately apparent.'

'Can you check now?'

Nitrile gloves flew in and out of pockets returning only a scrunched-up tissue, a few coins, and a broken ball-point pen. 'Sorry.'

James acknowledged as his sister's shrill voice became louder from the outside. He headed towards the sound and saw her anguished face staring into her mobile phone. He reached out, took it from her, and turned it around to read the text on the screen:

> So sorry lovely lawyer lady. You did everything you could, but you couldn't make my guilt go away.
>
> I killed Rebecca Connolly because she was having sex with my father and DCI Clitheroe. She knew I loved her, and she tried to deny it, but I knew. I knew it had been going on for a long time.
>
> There is a biscuit tin in the roof of our old house. Find it. Everything you need to confirm my words is in that.
>
> Thank you, miss.

He reached out to hug his sister, but she pulled away and strutted to her car without saying another word.

James Carter called Arthur Bertram. 'Something's come up, and I'll need a warrant to search a property that is no longer owned by the Gregory's.'

'Fix it Jim. I'll back you if there are any problems.'

James called Stacey. 'I'm on my way. Hope dinner isn't too ruined.'

***

On the way to her home Angela passed the High School that Tom Gregory had attended. The memories it stirred made her shiver but what made it worse was the vision of an attractive young woman wearing a teacher's lanyard. She was showing a tall young man some paperwork, and he was growing more excited by the minute. She checked her phone. The time was almost three thirty.

The youth was nonchalantly bouncing a basketball while the teacher was speaking to him.

Angela stopped her car and wound her window down, in the hope of catching a snippet of their conversation. She heard the word "grades" but was too late for anything more. The woman returned to the confines of the school and the young man punched the air as he rode off on his bike.

A few minutes later, a slightly overweight middle-aged man walked to a car on the school grounds. He looked at his watch and waited patiently. It was as if he had all the time in the world.

The teacher exited the building, pulled her lanyard over her head, and tossed it onto the back seat. She then handed him the keys to her car, and said in a loud voice, 'You drive Uncle John. It's been a really long day.'

Angela felt inclined to follow them but decided. 'It's none of my business.' She pointed her car in the direction of Oliver's school and when he clambered into the car, she grabbed him and caused him to wriggle as she smothered him with wet motherly kisses. 'Pizza?'

'Without the slop?'

She kissed him again and felt her entire life hadn't been totally wasted. She now had Oliver, and a repaired relationship with her brother. 'Would you like to have Jack and Andria stay for the weekend?'

He shrugged. 'S'pose.'

THE END

About the Author

Dan Cotton spent the first fifteen years of his working life travelling the world with the Grey Funnel Line (Royal Navy). He then joined the world of commerce and pretty much carried on travelling as before. In the eighties, he started a business that eventually listed on the Stock Exchange and delisted in 1989 after the crash of 1987. He didn't make much money, but he learned the hard way, about the underbelly of high-end business operations and decided there were better ways to earn a crust.

Twelve years in the IT world kept him going until he decided to do his own thing and start an art gallery with a picture framing service. In the event that he doesn't make squillions from his writing, he'll still be framing, painting and writing until he carks it.

*

Who is Dan Cotton? Sometimes, even he's not sure. He's one of those folks who, no matter where they are in the world, will always be mistaken for someone else:

*

Having written nothing more than business proposals and letters, he started on his first manuscript and soon realised he badly needed help. That's when he joined the Katharine Susannah Prichard Writing Centre (WA) and, with encouragement and critique from KSP's Thursday Night Group, he has been able to complete two trilogies comprising, "Triptych", "Toxic Trade" and "Terrorist". This novel "End

Game" is the second novel of a second trilogy featuring a character, Syrah Barberra, who first appeared in Toxic Trade.

*

He has written a number of short stories, poems, and drabbles. These are published in various anthologies. In addition, he has completed another full-length work, "The Second Meridian," in the speculative fiction genre.

*

For fifteen years, He's been a member of a team who compete annually in the *Open Section* of "Write A Book In A Day" [www.writeabookinaday.com]. *This is a national competition* aimed at improving child literacy while raising funds for children's cancer research. Several of the team's entries have been winners, or highly commended, and have since been privately published. Not only is it a hard day's slog it's one of the best ways of testing one's writing, and Dan wouldn't miss it for quids.

Also, by Dan Cotton

The Second Meridian

Global warming has reached a tipping point and The President of the United States believes the world will be a better place if split, north and south, by an imaginary border that protects the wealth of his powerful friends from a resource hungry world. Imported goods will have massive tariffs, technology exports overpriced, and all immigration will be banned.

The imaginary border, known as The Second Meridian, is only one part of his plan. Another is to send hundreds of handpicked elites into space to orbit, in pods, for the duration of the impending nuclear war, before returning to rebuild.

One pod escapes orbit, and with nowhere to go, the crew, five males and five females, must ponder their fate as they are drawn closer to the sun.

End Game

It's 2055 and Western Australia has long since seceded from the Commonwealth to become an independent republic.

It seemed like a good idea back then, but with changes to the constitution, following a rigged referendum, a one-party state has emerged. Now, only those with corporate or political citizenships have rights, and all challengers are financially destroyed by a corrupted judiciary.

Syrah Barberra wanted nothing more than a quiet life until they killed her family. Now twenty years later, technology has advanced, and her time has come to fight back and restore the status quo. Supported by a mysterious reincarnation of, Magnus, her long-dead husband, she calls on the help of some old friends.

Full Circle

Syrah Barberra returns to Perth, Western Australia, with expectations of joining the legal practice of an old friend and becoming a proper mother to her first child. The friend has a different understanding and when offered a specialist position by the Police Commissioner, Evan Watkins, she's reluctant.

Pregnant with her second child, she knows she will be available for only two or three months, but Evan is undeterred. He knows her skills and needs an outsider, a cleanskin, to clear up a corrupt mess on his patch.

She takes the job, on the understanding that she will have a free hand, and that when her time draws close, she will be released from her obligations.

What follows takes her back to her childhood and opens her eyes to the true nature of those she reveres the most.

Acknowledgements

Thanks to my friends at the **Thursday Night Group** (attached to the Katherine Susannah Prichard Writing Centre WA) who are my major source of ongoing encouragement and inspiration. Without them, I might have given it all away (Some might say I probably should have). Thanks to Tim Nelson for quietly easing me through any matters relating to law and plot, Barry Morley's inciteful attention to filler words, also Gillian Clark, Victoria Mizen, Ilene Aveling, Sue Carameli, and Kath Evans, for listening and providing their varied, fearless, and much appreciated female views on my blokey style. TNG is the one place where I know I can get that much needed, wider audience viewpoint, delivered raw, unselfconsciously, and with sometimes hilarious results.

*

My greatest thanks are for my staunchest ally, Deborah. For being my life and business partner and managing to suffer through my angst and frustrations over the last 44 years without poisoning my coffee.

*

Last, but not least our Border Collies, Echo and Tika, and all the departed dogs who have faithfully warmed my feet during the loneliness of the writing hours and who now lay at rest on our property.

Chapter 1

Papers cluttered his desk, except for a small area that was almost a shrine displaying the last known photograph of his daughter. She was pictured sweet and innocent, like any other thirteen-year-old kid in her school uniform. Almost three years had passed since Kaitlin disappeared, and though he could not shake the feeling of her being still alive, he'd learned there would be no going back.

Each day that passed gave him hope that she might one-day be returned to him. She was all that was left of his ten-year marriage to Virginia, a woman who seemed to love him despite his myriad of faults. There was no photograph of *her* on his desk. He could no longer bear the memories. She was caught in the crossfire of a stupid gang fight that had nothing to do with her. She'd only been there to remind him it was Kaitlin's birthday, and he should try to be home early for her.

He recalled laughing and brushing off her comments. 'Of course, lovey. I wouldn't miss it for the world,' were the last words she heard before the bullet meant for him struck her in the heart. The killer escaped, and Clarke Shipton had not forgotten. One day he'd get his revenge and then it would, as they say, be served chilled.

The door to his office opened slightly.

'Boss?'

'Come in Kell,' he said.

Kelly Coulson moved cautiously towards his desk and rocked her head in a questioning manner.

'Any news?'

Kelly smiled, then nodded. 'There're two guys outside. They reckon they've found someone who could be her.'

'Where?'

'Bosnia.'

Clark Shipton put his head in his hands and, without looking up, said, 'Brothel?'

Kelly showed no reaction. 'It might not be as bad as it seems.'

He looked up at her, his face creasing with an angry frown, as he snapped, 'How could there be anything worse than that?'

Kell shrugged. 'The Embassy is looking into it. They say if there's proof it's Kaitlin, they'll have her home within a week.'

'Drugs?'

'Serious addiction likely.' Kelly dropped a printout of an email on his desk. 'This has the location and the name she is working under. They say her papers appear genuine for her new surname, and that might stall the embassy effort.' She dropped another piece of paper onto his desk. 'They also sent this.'

Shipton's expression froze. He looked across at the framed photograph of Kaitlin when she was thirteen. In the picture Kelly had just handed him, her once clear bright blue eyes were blackened around the rims, the dimples on her cheeks replaced by sunken hollows. 'It's her. It's definitely her.' He instinctively pressed the new photo against his heart. 'Any ideas?'

Kelly dropped a manilla folder on his desk. 'They're outside. Two of them, ex special forces and they specialise in what they call "recoverance".'

'What are you waiting for?'

'Pricey, boss, so before you commit, you should meet them and make a value judgement.'

'How long will that take?'

'How long have you got?' Kelly stepped back and pulled the door open to allow entry to a pair of dishevelled strangers with three-day-old beards. 'I give you Bib and Bub.'

'What!'

Bib took a pace forwards and dropped into a visitor's chair. Despite his appearance, the man spoke with a cultured British accent and said, 'We don't do things by halves, Mr Shipton, sir, and we have the credentials to prove our success ratio.' He signalled to Bub, who took the seat alongside his colleague. 'He's a bit rough around the edges, I'll give you that, but we make an excellent team.'

Shipton turned towards Kelly and mouthed, 'What the fuck?'

'Like I said, boss, they don't come cheap, and you'll need to make your own value judgement.' She left him in the company of Bib and Bub and pulled the door shut behind her.

'Now we're alone, Mr Shipton. Let me introduce the team. Major David Ashton-O'Sullivan, SAS and MI6 retired,' he pointed to himself. 'Yours truly. We needn't go into the reasons for my early retirement, and this is Staff Sergeant Bob Clayton, Ex Australian SAS, and before I go any further. We approached your people, not the other way around. We also know of your history, and your somewhat dubious relationship with the constabulary.'

Bib handed Shipton a proforma account. The top line said, "Bib and Bub Recoverance Services Inc".

'Fuck!'

'Take it or leave it.' Bib said.

They stood as one and were about to leave when Shipton stopped them. 'This is a hell of a lot of money for just a deposit.'

'She's your daughter and, from what we're hearing, it might be a pittance in the longer term.'

Bub spoke, 'My daughter is in a private rehab facility. I wasn't there for her as a father, and she fell into the wrong company. It's costing the proverbial arm and leg, but I'm working on it and she's worth every cent to me.'

Shipton turned to Bib and said, 'If I give you the go ahead for this excursion, what will I get?'

Bub spoke with a wry smile. 'You think of it as an excursion?'

Shipton squirmed. 'I didn't mean that exactly…'

'You'll get back your daughter back in one piece. How we achieve that will remain our business, in confidence. The day you take her in your arms, Mr Shipton, you will pay the balance plus any contingencies.' Bub pointed to the total sum at the bottom of the page.

Bib smiled. 'Despite his appearance, he really is an old softy, you know.'

'Bib and Bub?'

Bib shrugged. 'Who'd employ a pair of ugly nutters who call themselves Bib and Bub?'

The more he fronted these men, the more he began to realise they had more going for them than a pair of stupid names. Clark Shipton etched his signature at the bottom of the proforma and reached for his cheque book.

'Sorry, sir. Cash only and we understand that cash will be difficult to obtain at short notice, but you are the one in a hurry. We have all the time in the world.'

'I'll have the deposit by close of business today.'

Bib and Bub stood as one, and Bib extended his hand. 'Pleasure doing business with you, old chap.'

A moment after they left, Kelly burst into the room. 'You've signed them up?'

Shipton's face turned red. 'I've promised them a 50% deposit, up front, by COB today.'

'Shit. The gum nut babies. I hope you know what you are doing, boss.'

Shipton shrugged.

***

Mickey Krakauer stretched out on his settee with his head resting on Jackie Morton's lap. 'Coupla days and we can make proper plans, hey? Jack.'

'I never thought this would ever happen, Mick.' She tousled his black hair and leaned down to kiss him on the lips. 'Who'd a thought it?'

'We're a weird bunch, aren't we? Five of us signed up to be cops on the same day. One is now the Commissioner of Police. One is a DI, another is dead, and there's me and my ex-cop jail bird lover.'

Jackie screwed his hair in a knot and slapped his cheek. 'Soon to be a fully pardoned ex-cop jailbird, mister. You'd better not forget that.'

Mickey's phone shattered their brief romantic interlude. 'Kell? What's up?'

…

'Shit, when?'

…

'Is he serious?'

…

'Should I come over?'

…

'Okay, okay, I'll see if I can get a bead on them in the system. I guess if they go under the names of Bib and Bub, it should be easy enough.' The line fell silent, and he rolled his eyes. 'That was Kelly Coulson. Clarkie Shipton has just signed up a couple of reputed ex SAS types to recover his daughter from a brothel in Bosnia.'

'So, what has that got to do with us?'

'There are still a lot of kids missing. If they're successful and the word gets around, there'll be all kinds of incompetent wannabes signing folk up.'

'How do you know the mob Clarkie's signed up are incompetent?'

Mickey shook his head. 'I don't think they are. I heard something a while ago, about a couple of guns for hire. These guys were super clinical and left no forensics worth mentioning.'

'Bib and Bub?'

'Not sure.' He looked at his watch. 'I think I might pop over and have a chat with Clarkie. We've been sorta, "best of mates", ever since we closed down the Gregory mob.'

'Well, don't be late. I'm still all jittery about the pardon and I'll be needing a cuddle.'